Through the Fire

A Chronicle of Pergamum

i

HEARTBEARTS OF COURAGE

Volume One

Through the Fire
A Chronicle of Pergamum

By
David Phillips

Century One Chronicles
Toronto, Ontario, Canada

THROUGH THE FIRE: A CHRONICLE OF PERGAMUM –
HEARTBEATS OF COURAGE, BOOK 1

©2020 by David Kenneth Phillips
Published in the United States of America

Canadian Intellectual Property Office CIPO Registration Number:
1152513

ISBN 978-1-9994752-0-8

Century One Chronicles, P.O. Box 25013 Morningside Avenue,
255 Morningside Avenue, Toronto, Ontario, Canada M1E 0A7
(See page 432 for details.)

Front Cover: "Antipas and Miriam Arrive in Pergamum"
Illustrations and composition of front and back cover by Dusan Arsenic
Map of Pergamum by Anoosh Mubashar
Back cover photo by Sarah Grace Photography

From early readers:

The mixture of so many diverse elements— social/societal interaction, religious tension, human nature, history, politics, intrigue, ethics, Jewish culture and history, early Christian, Roman and Greek cultural elements, and the conflict of transitioning cultural norms—[*Through the Fire* puts] a face on many issues of twenty-first century family life while placing them in a first-century neighborhood context.

Lou Mulligan
Financial Consultant and Investment Officer

It is fascinating to "experience" the clash of beliefs and faiths: Greek mythology, Roman emperor cult, Judaism, and, in stark contrast, the new faith in Yeshua Messiah, who challenges the society simply by what followers do, let alone what they say. To some, this faith is attractive, drawing them in from far away, an unseen and gentle force (as with Marcos and Anthony), while others despise it as nonsense (Commander Cassius). [This] book is as much a Bible history and geography lesson—that is very important—but it is also very entertaining (sometimes I laugh out loud), and it is heart-warming, like the love stories.

Dr. Michael Thoss
Pharmaceutics and Small Molecules Marketing

Through the Fire...helped me understand the Greek context of early Christianity...[and] made the struggle of the Christian faith more real.

Robert Lumkes
Teacher

I have read this book and found it easy to read and engrossing. It certainly details how things were back then! And are the pressures much different today?

George Jakeway
Retired Medical Doctor

I love the book you have written. You are an excellent writer, and these books will capture the hearts of many.

Maggie Marissen
Author and Book Editor

...a powerful story, full of rich insights into the life of faith as well as into the world of those first-century believers in Asia. I loved Antipas wrestling with the Scriptures and journaling his struggle with accepting Anthony for Miriam. This is really an amazing project, and I pray the Lord will receive much honor through your labors on it.

George Bristow
Teacher and Author

For Cathie
My lifelong constant companion and friend
on the journey and toward the destination

For widows, orphans, and
those affected by slavery and people smuggling
and for people of compassion who
come alongside the brokenhearted.
For those who suffer persecution
through loss of family, criticism,
falsehoods, beatings, imprisonment,
loss of property,
or death.

Heartbeats of Courage

Book 1: Through the Fire: A Chronicle of Pergamum
AD 89–91

Book 2: Never Enough Gold: A Chronicle of Sardis
AD 91–92

Book 3: Purple Honors: A Chronicle of Thyatira
AD 92–93

Book 4: The Inn of the Open Door: A Chronicle of Philadelphia
AD 93–96

Book 5: Rich Me! A Chronicle of Laodicea
AD 96–97

Book 6: Fortress Shadows: A Chronicle of Smyrna
AD 97–111

Book 7: An Act of Grace: A Chronicle of Ephesus
AD 111

Book 8: The Songs of Miriam: A Collection of Miriam's Songs

A Chronicle of Pergamum

Characters

*Indicates historical figures
Major characters are shown in bold.

Emperors

Vespasian*, Emperor of the Roman Empire: AD 70–79, deceased

Titus*, First son of Vespasian and Emperor of the Roman Empire: AD 79–81, deceased

Domitian*, 38, Second son of Vespasian and Emperor of the Roman Empire: AD 81–96

Governors and Officials

King Decebalus*, 44, King of Dacia

Marcus Fluvius Gillo*, Governor of Asia, AD 89–90

Aristocratic Families

Quintus Rufus*, 46, Mayor of Pergamum and a priest of the imperial cult

Manes Tmolus, 57, and Clytemnestra Tmolus, 53, a family in Pergamum

Atydos Lydus, 55, and Apolliana Lydus, 51, a family in Pergamum

Atys Tantalus, 35, and Omphale Tantalus, 33, a family in Pergamum

Eumen Tantalus and Attalay Tantalus, 6, twin sons of Atys and Omphale Tantalus

Bernice, 31, Nursemaid for Eumen and Attalay Tantalus

Hermes, Former Head Librarian of Pergamum

Priests in the Temples and Their Families

Lydia-Naq Milon, 51, High priestess of the Altar of Zeus in Pergamum

Diotrephes Milon, 26, Lydia-Naq's son, a teacher in the gymnasium and high school

Zoticos-Naq Milon, 40, Lydia's brother, Head Librarian of

Pergamum
Damon, 37, High priest of the imperial cult of Caesar
Nestor, 45, High priest of the Altar of Zeus
Mehu, 40, High priest of the Egyptian temple

In the Roman Military
Cassius Flamininus Maro, 42, Commanding officer of the garrison of Pergamum
Anthony Suros, 33, Legionary from Legion XXI, the Predators since AD 74, now a reservist

Lawyer for the City Council
Marcos Aelius Pompeius, 35, Lawyer
Marcella, 36, Marcos's wife
Florbella, 8, Marcos and Marcella's daughter
Marcosanus, 22, Florbella's personal slave
Potitus Vinicius, 26, A young aspiring lawyer in Pergamum

At the Gymnasium
Diodorus Pasparos*, 37, Gymnasium headmaster, elementary and high school of Pergamum

People in Pergamum
Thorello, 42, Physician at the Asclepion, the hospital complex
Vincenzo, 21, Athlete, hero of the Games
Horacio, 41, Senior clerk in Custom House, responsible for supplies to Pergamum
Cratia, 41, Wife of Horacio and mother of Trifane
Trifane, 22, Horacio and Cratia's daughter, a student in the library

Rabbis and Council Members
Jaron Ben Pashhur, 40, Rabbi in the synagogue of Pergamum
Nadav, 38, An elder in the Council of the Synagogue, Adara, Nadav's son
Hanani, Elieonai, Nekoda, Parosh, and Zattu: Council elders in the synagogue of Pergamum

<u>The Ben Shelah Family and Household</u>
Eliab Ben Shelah, 89, and Ahava, his deceased wife, Jewish merchant born in Alexandria, Egypt
Their 12 children: Anna, Deborah, Amos, Antipas, Zibiah, Simon, Daniel, Joshua, Judah, Azubah, Samuel, and Jonathan
Antipas Ben Shelah*, 65, Jewish businessman in Pergamum; Ruth Bat Caleb, his deceased wife
Miriam Bat Johanan, 24, Antipas's granddaughter
Onias Ben Harim, 40, and Abijah, 42, Antipas's steward and his wife
Their children: Eliezar, Jarib, Aliza, Nessat, Talia
Antipas's servants: Urbanus, Philo, Philogulos, **Yorick**
Jewish widows in Antipas's village: Sheva, 56; Damaris, 43; Chavvah, 52
Non-Jewish widows in Antipas's village: Barbara, 24; Ilithyia, 24; Nikasa, 23
Ateas, 19, and **Arpoxa**, 18, Scythian slaves from Scythia, a region north of the Black Sea

<u>From Ephesus</u>
John the Elder*, 82, A follower of Yeshua Messiah, living in Ephesus
Demetrius*, 40, Messenger to the assemblies of believers in seven cities

<u>Roman Army Deserters and Rebels</u>
Flavius Memucan Parshandatha, also known as Mithrida
Sesba Bartacus Sheshbazzar, also known as Sexta
Claudius Carshena Datis, also known as Craga
Gergius Adaliah Rehum, also known as Taba

Prologue

The Kingdom of Pergamum was at one time the most powerful kingdom on the Aegean Sea in what is now the country of Turkey. The city of Pergamum boasted the second largest library in the world, and scholars flocked there to learn every branch of knowledge. After the kingdom passed into the hands of Rome, some families continued to yearn for a return to past glory. Others gloried in Rome's accomplishments. One day a stranger came to live in Pergamum and created a stir. His name was Antipas, and his way of life was contradictory to the norm in Pergamum. Why he became important is the basis for this chronicle, which is narrated as historical fiction.

"Fear not, for I have redeemed you, I have summoned you by name, you are mine. When you pass through the waters, I will be with you; and when you pass through the rivers, they will not sweep over you. When you walk through the fires, you will not be burned ... Do not be afraid, for I am with you." Isaiah 43:1–4

Bless those who persecute you; bless and do not curse. Rejoice with those who rejoice; mourn with those who mourn. Live in harmony with one another. Do not be proud, but be willing to associate with people of low position. Do not be conceited. Do not repay evil for evil. Be careful to do what is right in the eyes of everybody. If it is possible as far as it depends on you, live at peace with everyone. Do not take revenge, my friends, but leave room for God's wrath, for it is written, "It is mine to avenge; I will repay," says the Lord. On the contrary "If your enemy is hungry, feed him; if he is thirsty, give him something to drink. In doing this you will heap burning coals on his head." Do not be overcome by evil, but overcome evil with good. Romans 12:14–21

The Ben Shelah family

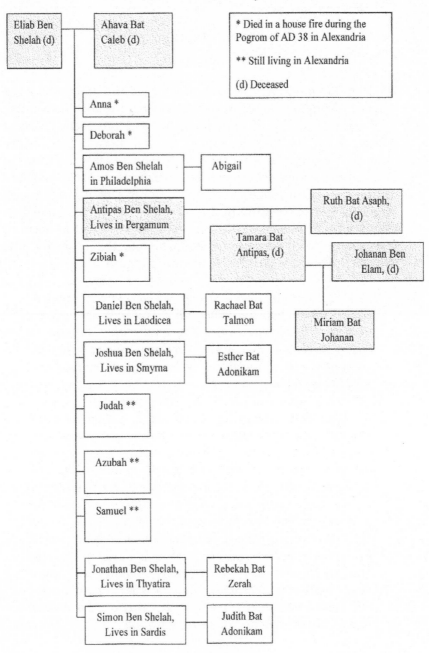

Eliab Ben Shelah (d)

Ahava Bat Caleb (d)

* Died in a house fire during the Pogrom of AD 38 in Alexandria

** Still living in Alexandria

(d) Deceased

Anna *

Deborah *

Amos Ben Shelah in Philadelphia — Abigail

Antipas Ben Shelah, Lives in Pergamum — Ruth Bat Asaph, (d)

Tamara Bat Antipas, (d)

Johanan Ben Elam, (d)

Zibiah *

Miriam Bat Johanan

Daniel Ben Shelah, Lives in Laodicea — Rachael Bat Talmon

Joshua Ben Shelah, Lives in Smyrna — Esther Bat Adonikam

Judah **

Azubah **

Samuel **

Jonathan Ben Shelah, Lives in Thyatira — Rebekah Bat Zerah

Simon Ben Shelah, Lives in Sardis — Judith Bat Adonikam

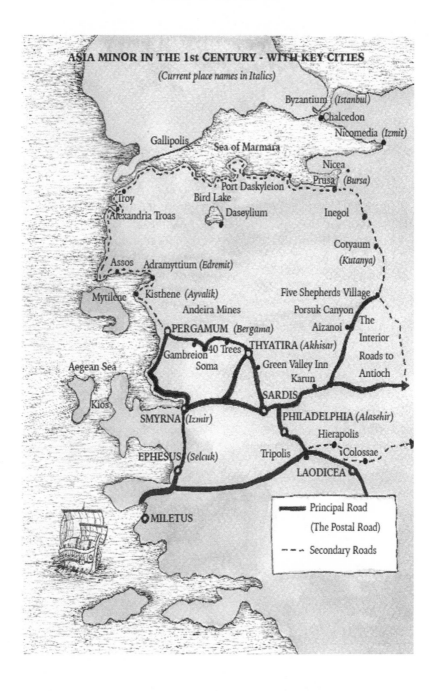

THE CITY OF PERGAMUM IN THE PROVINCE OF ASIA MINOR

1 Acropolis
2 Imperial Temple
3 Aristocratic Houses
4 Temple of Dionysius
5 Greek Theater
6 Library
7 Temple of Athena
8 Altar of Zeus
9 Upper Agora – Market
10 Odeon – City Council
11 Peristyle House
12 Temple of Hera
13 Temple of Demeter
14 Gymnasium – School
15 Running Track
16 Road up the Acropolis
17 City Gates
18 Lower Agora – Market
19 Foundations New Temple
20 Asclepius – Hospital
21 Insulae – Poor Homes
22 Roman Garrison
23 New Roman Houses
24 Roman Forum
25 Great Arch
26 Roman Theater
27 Stadium
28 Amphitheater
29 Selinos River
30 Antipas's Village
31 Trash Dump
32 Water Supply
33 Marsh

Through the Fire

Part 1
The White Dove

February
AD 89

Chapter 1
Antipas

ANTIPAS'S HOME, PERGAMUM

A recurring bad dream left Antipas Ben Shelah's heart pounding. Although the night was cold, the skin on his neck felt hot and sweaty. Antipas saw himself setting off to a wedding when, suddenly, red and yellow flames and smoke poured into the sky. "Anna! Give me your hand! I'll pull you out through the window! Your wedding is in three days!" he screamed.

But the blaze kept him out of his sister's reach. She was trapped behind a wall.

Flames kept leaping up, consuming their house. The smell of burning flesh caused him to gasp. He cried, and now he was running through the house but couldn't find his way from one room to another. He knew every room of their home in Alexandria, Egypt. A hand reached in through an open door. Another sister needed his help. "Deborah," he yelled, "why are you in Anna's wedding dress?"

Now a Jewish soldier was shouting, coming through the door, and bending down. The man fell on his hands and knees, examining the floor of their house. Beside the soldier, several bags were overflowing with dirt.

Antipas grabbed a shovel, the one he had used to dig a storeroom under their house. Beside the bags of dirt were others full of grain ready to be lowered into the hidden storeroom.

He woke up panting. As if to chase the nightmare away, he shook his head. Several things in it were obviously wrong. He had never been to a wedding in Jerusalem. Anna's glorious day was forever destroyed by the fire in Alexandria.

The hole in the floor of their house, where they hid food...why did his dream tonight take him back to Jerusalem?

It took several minutes before his heart was beating normally again.

After nineteen and a half years in this city, I feel less at home than when our family first arrived. I must sleep! Father will need my full attention!

But Antipas did not go to sleep, not for a long time. His mind went from one task to another. People in his village were busy making bricks, tending to animals, blowing small glass bottles, mixing oils and spices for perfumes, and selling them at both shops the family owned on the acropolis.

He turned over, trying to find a more comfortable position. Onias, his steward, would have to take on some of his responsibilities until after the funeral.

Blessed art thou, O God, Lord of the universe, for giving me Onias and his family. A faithful steward is hard to find. Bless him, his sons, and his daughters.

Prayers at night were Antipas's way of overcoming the fears created by his nightmares. His heart became quiet, and he fell into a deep sleep.

Antipas was no longer young. At sixty-five years old, he had trouble straightening up in the morning; it took several minutes before the blood flowed freely through his body. His presence was still commanding though. A sparkle in his eyes and a steady gaze hid his inner fears from his family and friends. He took a drink of water as if to wash away the aftertaste of fires, ashes, and the black smoke rising from his bad dream.

But he was not concerned about his own health this morning. It was his father, Eliab Ben Shelah, who demanded his constant attention. His father, now so frail, had brought his family to Pergamum from Alexandria, Egypt, via Jerusalem many years ago. Eliab was an old man now and had been gradually losing strength.

"Miriam," Antipas called softly to his granddaughter, "how is he?"

"He's not doing well, Grandpa. In the middle of the night, he started coughing and having strange breathing!"

"Did he cough for a long time?"

"For a while, but now he's just breathing very deeply and slowly. Grandpa, I'm afraid!"

"Go to bed, my child. You need to sleep. I will take over."

Antipas rubbed his broad forehead as if he were ordering his thoughts for the day. *I must awaken Onias and have him watch*

23

Father for a while. I'll have him send messages for my brothers to come to Pergamum. It will be our last farewell. Sleep, Father, while I go to the cemetery to collect my thoughts.

Pulling the blanket closer around old Eliab's neck, Antipas touched the purple veins on his father's hand. These hands had once been so strong, but now the bones were prominent, the veins soft under the skin. Antipas moved the oil lamp to a high shelf, pulling his cloak tighter against his lean body for the morning was cold and the wind starting to blow.

Eliab and Antipas had built this house on a slight slope going down to a river. Many years ago, this land, half a mile outside the city, had been a pasture. Now it had been transformed into a small village.

Antipas went out through the front door and walked over to Onias's house, close by on the village property. Onias Ben Harim, the estate manager, was already up and ready to take over watching Eliab. They both returned to the house as Antipas gave instructions on what to do if Eliab woke. Antipas would be at the cemetery.

As he walked off into the dark, Antipas prayed, a habit he had kept since his earliest days in Alexandria.

Show compassion, Lord! I wanted Miriam to be married before Father closes his eyes. He is dying, and I grow old myself. If Miriam has no husband... All my brothers have children and grandchildren, and I haven't found Miriam a husband among our people.

The warm smells of farm animals comforted him, and he took another deep breath. The cows would be milked soon in the area above the farm, where the green pasture sloped down to the river. The quiet calm of a cold winter morning was a welcome contrast to the tightness in his stomach.

After the dark night comes the light of day, he thought, *but for me, it's the opposite. At the synagogue,[1] the elders have cut me off from reading the scriptures. Father, you have maybe another week*

---

[1] The location of this ancient synagogue is unknown. Perhaps thirty-five percent of Pergamum during the Roman period has been excavated. Bergama, the modern city of more than fifty thousand people, covers over previous civilizations. Modern construction makes it unlikely that excavations on the rest will take place. The current grid pattern of Bergama's streets is probably the same as in antiquity.

to live. How will I live without your sensible guidance? Were you not the wisest businessman I've ever known?

On the acropolis above him, triumphs of architecture stood out against a dull yellow sky. Antipas went down the hill, past the homes of his workers, and arrived at the river. He turned right onto a long colonnaded street that led to the amphitheater. Perhaps it was because his father's death seemed so close at hand that he had decided to walk through that place where death was common.

The amphitheater was quiet and dark. Antipas looked around in awe, for its remarkable construction was a model of Roman engineering. He knew that fighters clashed and killed one another in the circular sports arena to the roars of approving spectators.

Antipas ran his fingers along the stone blocks of the massive eastern entrance. In the dim light, he could barely make out the names of the most famous athletes of Pergamum inscribed in Greek on the white marble. These names ensured that famous men would never be forgotten. He read a name: Vincenzo. Antipas had heard about the young man who was the most recent "overcomer," the first to win at wrestling for three successive years.

The place was immense. Now the morning light permitted him to see the dim outline of the theater's cascading white marble seats. They reached up on each side to the top of the two opposing concave hills. A low wall separated the spectators from contestants. He winced as he tried to imagine the pain of men who fell to that stone floor in battle. He knew why he had never come here. Sports and fights frequently drew men to the amphitheater to watch and gamble on the outcomes, and he would never be a witness to that.

Walking down the steps into the sports arena where the competitions took place, he imagined comparing himself to the gladiators but found the difference was too great. He was slight of build. They were thick-chested, tall, and strong.

Antipas gazed at the vast bowl shape of the amphitheater, contemplating the place of death as entertainment. He looked around at where twenty-five thousand spectators often went mad, shouting, demanding blood, and cheering for the victor. The weaker ones died, while the muscular and cunning triumphed.

After a while, he continued on his way to the cemetery to the gravesite of his family. His family's two graves were unremarkable for a natural death had been their lot. Deaths in the arena were unnatural and unnecessary.

He often thought about the mysteries of life and death. Lines he had written on a papyrus manuscript the previous evening came back to him.

February 10: Lord, I often ask questions, but today I am only in search of safety for my family. Another nightmare disturbed my rest. Once again, I was a witness to destruction brought against our family in Egypt and Judea. Leaving Jerusalem, I made a promise. If you gave me a peaceful life, I would find a way to let people know how majestic is your name in all the earth.[2] Yet I see little fulfillment of this purpose. My life is weighed down. My father may live only a few more days, and my granddaughter is still not married. I have no idea where I might find her a suitable husband.

JEWISH CEMETERY, PERGAMUM

Antipas arrived at their family plot in the cemetery as the sun broke over the horizon. Like the other Jewish graves in Pergamum, each headstone was marked with a menorah. God's light had overcome the chaos of darkness at creation.

Standing in the early morning, the light was getting brighter, and he could clearly see the outline of the two headstones—that of his mother, Ahava, dead these five years, and of Ruth, his wife. His father would soon be laid to rest here. Of all his family, only Miriam remained at home—his precious granddaughter, whose parents had perished in the fall of Jerusalem. He fell to his knees, saying his morning prayers as he held his hands high and swayed back and forth.

Oh, Lord, you saved us in Alexandria and again in Jerusalem. "Do not hide your face from your servant: answer me quickly, for I am in trouble. Come near and rescue me; redeem me because of my

---

[2] Psalm 8:1

foes."[3] *Lord, my granddaughter will soon be twenty-four years old. Nadav has refused to let his son, Adara, become betrothed to Miriam. Loving Father, please help me find a husband for her.*

Satisfied that he understood the time required to prepare the gravesite for his father's burial, he left the cemetery. As he walked back toward his village, a small girl passed him, followed by her young slave. The slave did not look happy.

A little girl leaving the city so early in the morning? Do her parents know?

ANTIPAS'S HOME, PERGAMUM

Following breakfast, Antipas met with his steward, Onias, in the great room of the house. "I want you to send each of my brothers a note by pigeon. Write, 'Father is dying. Come at once. Antipas.'"

Onias looked at his master. "Shall I send the same message to each of them?" The servant had just celebrated his fortieth birthday. Like his master, he had a trim black beard, and this morning he was wise enough to question the message without touching on sensitive family issues.

"Yes, write the same message for Amos in Philadelphia, Jonathan in Thyatira, Simon in Sardis, and Joshua in Smyrna." Antipas paused. "Oh, for Daniel in Laodicea, it should be 'Father has asked for you. He wants to see you again.' Yes, that sounds better for Daniel."

Daniel was the only brother who put business ahead of family relationships. All five of his brothers tried to accommodate him, but it was a strain on their relationships.

"Is there anything else for today?"

"Yes. How much money have we put aside for the redemption of another slave?"

"We have two hundred fifty denarii—half of what you need for another male slave. But if you want to buy a female who promises many children, the cost would be higher."

"Is the new house almost ready to receive a slave? The Festival of Zeus starts in mid-April. Will it be completed by then?"

"Yes, we don't need to buy much more material, master."

"Oh, remember that I will need enough food for my brothers

---

[3] Psalm 69: 17–18

for the required evening family feasts after the funeral. Now, about our business today: prepare new perfumes for the Upper Agora. I'll take them there myself. Also, for Thyatira, prepare a shipment of clay pots, perfumes, and blown-glass bottles. When the delivery cart returns, I want it to bring bronze and clay lamps from my brother Jonathan for our shops."

"Consider it done, master," said Onias. "Is that all?"

When Antipas frowned, two small lines formed between his eyes. "No, I'm very concerned about Yorick. I bought him at the slave market five years ago. Gloomy should be his middle name. Find out what is bothering him."

"Fixing Yorick will take longer than fixing drips from a roof on a wet winter's night. Have a good morning, Master Antipas."

Antipas watched his servant go and had an uneasy feeling that he was right.

Eliab Ben Shelah lay on his back, breathing heavily. When he was young, people in Alexandria knew him for his head of black hair, but he now was very gray and slightly bald. His forehead was wrinkled with the cares of the passing years.

Antipas rose from the table and went to his father's bedside. "Hail! Good morning, Father."

"Hail! Good morning, my son. May the light of God always shine on you!"

"And may the Lord give a long life to you, Father!"

"He has done so. The end of my path is in sight." The old man's voice was hard to hear. "I have lived a full life. I want to see my children before my days are over. I will bless my sons living here in Asia Minor."

"Yes, Father. I told Onias to release the pigeons kept for emergencies. Each one will carry its own message. They will all know of your wish today. We want to see you together, so I am contacting them all. And, yes, I also sent a pigeon to Daniel."

Eliab nodded slowly. "Good. I want to bless all of you. Please have Miriam come now to sing songs of Jerusalem. How my heart longs for our Holy City. My heart is heavy for her sons and daughters."

Antipas lifted his face in thought. *We shall mourn you for forty days, Father. You have been all that a father should be, even when fires of destruction burned in Alexandria and in Jerusalem. I will be*

28

lost without your practical advice.

"Is there anything else, Father?" he asked in a quiet voice.

The old man nodded again. "I will close my eyes. With Miriam singing beside me, I will walk through Jerusalem. That is the pilgrim city I love, if only in memory. Blessed be the name of the Holy One."

For the next hour, Miriam sat beside her great-grandfather and sang to him. Her warm hands clasped the old man's cold fingers. Looking down on him, her soft brown eyes became moist. Her forehead was smooth, set in an oval face with olive skin. Her lips often quivered, from either excitement, joy, or anticipation.

Today, in the cold air of an early morning, her expectation of a coming death brought out poetry and worship. Hers were songs sung by ancestors for countless generations.

Chapter 2
Eliab

ANTIPAS'S HOME, PERGAMUM

The next morning, Eliab awoke slowly in the dim room lit with only a small oil lamp on the wall. He was aware of someone in a chair beside his bed snoring softly.

Alone with his thoughts, Eliab began to think of his blessing for each son: Amos, Antipas, Daniel, Joshua, Jonathan, and Simon.

He remembered how his son Antipas was named after the great Jewish general who made treaties of friendship, forging ties between Jerusalem and the nations at war with the Jews.[4] That heroic figure made an alliance with Egypt and was the author of many victories.

Because of these exploits, he was made a citizen of Rome and won freedom for Jews from standard taxes. Eliab and Ahava had named their baby son for that hero because, as an army man, he was also known for piety, justice, and love for his country. Eliab's mind came back to the present, and he drifted off the sleep again.

THE CAVE, ANTIPAS'S VILLAGE

Antipas walked to the cave for the early Sunday morning Holy Meal gathering. The cave was a long shed against the rock cliff at the edge of the property. They had started using it for meetings after Antipas began to ransom slaves. His father had first broken bread there with only a few others, mostly widows. Now many people broke bread there together.

---

[4] Josephus wrote about Jewish General Antipater (also Antipas) in an extensive section on military, religious, and diplomatic developments during the time of Julius Caesar. He was known for courage, honesty, leadership, success in business, and ingenuity (Josephus 14.1.3.8–14.11.4.283). This reference is the source of my choice of the name. Eliab and Ahava, his parents, hoped their son, Antipas, would develop these same qualities.

How much I owe my father!

This morning something full of deep meaning, perhaps the impending death of his aged father, gave him an unusually close sense of understanding the death of the Messiah.

On Monday, the sky sparkled with soft yellow-silver rays breaking through the thin band of gray clouds in the east. After the homing pigeons had taken his messages, Antipas looked for his brothers to start arriving.

That afternoon Antipas welcomed the first two brothers, Jonathan from Thyatira and Joshua from Smyrna, the two cities closest to Pergamum. The three brothers gave long hugs, greeting each other with affection. They did not need to say much because words at this time meant less than shared silence. The last time they had been together was at the funeral of their mother, Ahava, five years before.

Antipas sat with his brothers, who had the same black beards and trimmed, short hair cropped close. Since the death of their mother, Antipas looked older, worried—and not just because Eliab was dying. The conflict at the synagogue was an increasing burden.

The old man lay on a single bed in the room, his head close to the wall. It was frigid inside Antipas's home, so thick blankets of black wool covered their father's body. But no matter how many sheets and blankets were laid on him, he still felt cold.

The next day, three more sons arrived from more distant cities: Simon from Sardis, Amos from Philadelphia, and Daniel from Laodicea.

Their father looked very weak, but he was fully awake and greeted each son as he entered the room. Eliab listened to what each had to say, taking in the details. At eighty-six, even dying, he still commanded his family. His sons knew from long experience how their father combined both effective business decisions and affection in all he did. He had built up his business across the Eastern Mediterranean by being cautious, inventive, and honest. Each word was insightful and compelling.

Eliab looked deep into the eyes of his six sons. "Your warmth springs from your love for the Eternal One of Israel. The Almighty has chosen not to give us answers to our many questions, so we will never know why our Holy City was devastated or why

Romans rule us. He gave me one more day with you. In this, my soul is glad."

Late in the afternoon, all the brothers gathered around Eliab's bed for his final blessing.

Turning to Antipas first, he said, "My son, you are like a victorious lion, hunting for the truth. You are strong, but you have the heart of a gentle lamb. Because you are strong, you do not cry out. When you become weak like a lamb, your enemy will be ashamed. Often you have walked through fires of affliction. Your strength is faithfulness. It will keep you from the traps of your enemy. You will look the enemy in the face, and you will be an overcomer."

He closed his eyes and lay still for a few moments. Although it took all of his remaining strength, gradually, over the next hour, Eliab gave five more personal blessings to each of his sons. Each blessing amazed, bewildered, angered, encouraged, or prodded with remarkable insight into their beliefs and intentions.

Finally, the old man closed his eyes, and using all his remaining strength, spoke in a soft voice: "All...are included in...my will." He lay back, exhausted by his efforts. The sons looked at each other in the soft light of the flickering lamps.

After many minutes of silence, Eliab's eyes opened wide. Both Amos and Antipas, sitting nearest his head, put their hands under his frail, cold shoulders. He tried to sit up and fell back on his pillow. "So that all..." he gasped, "will know that the Lord is God... Yes, you will be my people...and I will be...your God."

His voice trailed off, but he gathered his strength for his final thought. "I will sing of the Lord's great love forever...with my mouth I will make...your faithfulness known...through all... generations."[5] With that, he closed his eyes and breathed no more.

His family sat stunned. Eliab had chosen the first lines of a psalm written after Nebuchadnezzar had attacked the city and destroyed Jerusalem. The psalm dared to question the Almighty's commitment to the covenant. Like that writer of old, Eliab's last moments were both a confession of pain and of purpose for his sons. As death was taking him, he found the strength to echo Ethan, the Ezrahite, the author who struggled with doubts

---

[5] Psalm 89:1

brought on by the destruction of the Eternal City. After fifty generations, the House of Ben Shelah still spoke of the Lord's great love and faithfulness.

His greatest sadness, Eliab's worst moments, had been lived during the siege of Jerusalem. He made no room for revenge as he breathed his last. Instead, his final confession was a declaration of faith in the everlasting God of Abraham, Isaac, and Jacob. In his final moments, Eliab's last words were a recognition of the covenant.

Chapter 3
Jaron's Plan

HOMES CLOSE TO THE NEW FORUM

Rabbi Jaron Ben Pashar, the chief elder of the Synagogue of Pergamum, was up early. He brushed his long beard and reached for his prayer shawl. Deep-set eyes gleamed as he wrapped the blue and white cloth around his shoulders. His wife was still asleep when he pulled the front door shut behind him and locked it.

Jaron's house was built next to Nadav's, the scribe who took care of so many things: correspondence, keeping track of money given through tithes and offerings, and protecting the sacred scrolls.

The night before, Jaron and Nadav had been discussing a problem they perceived as a threat to their Jewish flock. At first, they thought that Antipas's actions were the result of Jews following Egyptian ways, but now they knew differently. His beliefs regarding the carpenter Messiah clearly were a danger to all the families under the care of the elders at the synagogue.

These two friends met frequently. Their purpose in sharing thoughts with one another was to preserve the spiritual purity of their community, which consisted of about fifty families. They had resolved to spend the early morning hours together for two weeks. Through conversations and prayer to Adonai at the synagogue, they intended to determine what course of action against Antipas they would recommend to the other elders.

Nadav, who was a head shorter than Jaron, drew his cloak around himself and scowled. "Antipas is not a true Jew; he is a Grecian Jew, one of the Diaspora from Egypt. He gives a bad name to those of us who came as true immigrants."

Jaron nodded in agreement. "He believes erroneous ideas

about the covenant. Why did he ever begin to meet with non-Jews, gathering them around him as if they are his flock? And did you hear the latest? He is planning to purchase another man at the slave market."

"Those people are not a flock, and he is not a shepherd!"

"I fear for anyone who pursues his own interpretation of the covenant."

Nadav asked, "What would be the best way to stop him from teaching about the Nazarene?"

Jaron agreed that this was the most serious issue. "We demanded that he stop! We warned him! He intentionally ignores our covenant! The time has come for more than just words! We must use discipline...force him to respond."

They drew their prayer shawls over their heads to ask the Almighty for wisdom. Nadav clasped his hands together before praying and sighed. "And to think that I ever considered that my son, Adara, could be betrothed to Miriam! That will never happen."

Nadav talked about the accounts and recalled donations from Antipas and Eliab. "It must be done carefully. We do not want to lose him from the congregation. After all, these two men have been generous contributors to the synagogue coffers."

The next day Jaron and Nadav called aside a friend. "Hanani, we would like your advice."

Hanani always felt comfortable nibbling another morsel. No surprise, then, that he needed an extra-long belt. He inclined his head with interest, and Jaron continued. "Antipas is ever more out of control! He has bought many slaves and set them free. They know nothing about the covenant. He accepts people who don't believe in the covenant. They are moving him further away from us, and I fear he is drawing others to himself instead of to Adonai."

Jaron had been considering drastic action to force change on Antipas, patiently awaiting the right time to explain his plan. "What if we declared him a non-Jew if he does not comply with our demands? What if he were to be faced with expulsion? Would that force him to agree?"

The others nodded in agreement, and Jaron's lips formed a half-smile. Antipas would have no choice but to comply. He had brought Hanani and Nadav in at the beginning of the process so that no one in the congregation could accuse him for initiating this decision. He was the last of the three to leave the synagogue, and he walked home with long, eager strides.

Chapter 4
Arpoxa

TANAIS, BOSPORAN KINGDOM (ROSTOV-ON-DON, RUSSIA)

Shivering from the cold, two men in Tanais, more than five hundred miles north of Pergamum, pulled their cloaks tightly around themselves. Even in the dead of winter, these two deserters from the Roman army were fearful that their presence might become known.

Winds buffeting the Bosporan Kingdom blew fiercely, gusting at times and slashing their faces like a knife before dawn on this early February morning.

Flavius, the older of the two men, got down from his horse, keeping his voice low. When he spoke, he had a raspy sound to his words. "Good thing you heard Menus complaining about his debts, Sesba. Said he had a sister named Arpoxa. T'was brilliant what you said to him. Money in exchange for his sister."

Sesba was a man of medium build. Like Flavius, he had five days' growth on his chin. "After he left, I asked around the tavern, 'Anyone seen that girl?' A drunkard commented, 'I heard she's slow on her feet. She doesn't leave the cottage.' Another said, 'I went to Menus's place. She's eighteen. As beautiful a creature as you'll ever see.' Oh, Flavius, I'm looking forward to this!"

"Arpoxa! You don't know it, but you are about to bring us riches." Flavius laughed with a self-satisfied optimism. "The money we will earn at the port today will clear up our debts!"

Flavius and Sesba had watched their debts grow faster than clouds announcing a coming blizzard. For the last few days, they had been cleaning the local tavern in return for sleeping on two narrow beds. Their dirty room was home to bed bugs as well. Since they had arrived the previous summer at Tanais, the most northerly port on the Black Sea, neither man had found decent pay, only odd jobs.

They walked their horses along Lake Maeotis, near the

commercial city of Tanais.[6] Flavius, the older of the two, bent down, leaning against a stone wall and looking at the dark shape of the cottage they were about to enter.

Flavius was shivering from cold as well as keen anticipation. "Hope this works. We can't live like this any longer; we're running out of money. Have to do something. The army must not catch us. Execution for desertion...that's not our path."

"The last six months have been difficult. I hate running from place to place, always judged as being vagrants. Will this character or that one turn us in to the army? Well, this morning our luck is turning," Sesba whispered.

Winter winds cut through their fur cloaks after sweeping across hundreds of miles of flat, fertile land. They treaded quietly along the snow-covered path to the door. They approached under a full moon, ready to enter noiselessly. Daylight would come soon. Thank the winter gods of frost and snow for a cloudless sky. Tomorrow the sun would warm them a little.

Flavius's teeth were chattering. "Her brother, Menus, said he would leave the door latch open. Push the door. He left a small lamp burning. Rush in and grab her. Beware! She will yell, scream. I'll grab her arms while you stuff this rag in her mouth and then wrap this blanket around her. Can't have her dying from cold, can we?"

Before pushing the door open, Flavius explained, "Menus needs money. Unfortunate dog, can't stop himself. Borrowed too much watching horses race last summer. Tomorrow two thugs as big as black bears are coming to squeeze money out of him. So we are helping him by trading his sister for the payment of his debts."

Flavius pushed the door open, and it squeaked. Menus slept close to the door, and Arpoxa was sleeping against the wall away from the door. The cottage smelled of stale beer, dirty clothing, and rotting vegetables.

"Menus," Flavius said in a loud whisper, "we're here. Come to give you money."

---

[6] Lake Maeotis, between Ukraine and Russia, is known today as the Sea of Azov. Tanais, an ancient city that began about 500 BC as a Greek settlement for trading furs, timber, and slaves, gave entrance from the Sea of Azov to the Don River. The Tanais ruins are to the west of Rostov-on-Don on the north side of the Don River.

Arpoxa was already under a blanket in bed, so Flavius quickly dropped his own blanket on top of her, and Sesba helped roll her up tightly as she struggled to get free.

Arpoxa screamed and twisted her head to bite Sesba's hand.

"Who are you?" she screamed. "Let me go! Menus, my brother, help me! Menus, who are these men? My brother, why don't you help me?"

Sesba stuffed the rag in the woman's mouth.

Flavius held her tightly in the blanket as Sesba coiled a rope around her, binding her from her shoulders to her legs.

"Here's the money," growled Flavius, pleasure growing with every word. "You wanted the full price for a female slave, but we asked around. You only need seventy denarii. We need and want things too. Well, what you want, you won't get, but we will give you what you need. Here, this will pay off your gambling debts. Take it."

Menus raised his voice, ending in a scream. "You can't do this to me! As a slave, she'll have many children. She'll make her owner happy. The girl is only eighteen! She can give birth to twelve children during her life, maybe more." He lashed out like a mad man. "She's my sister! Flavius! Think of the riches she will bring to her new master!"

Flavius laughed raucously as he threw the leather purse at Menus's feet. It contained the last of the money they had been hoarding to see them through the winter. Selling Arpoxa would more than make up the loss. "Work for a change! Get a job!"

Sesba snarled. "It's all you get! This will pay off your debts!"

"But I won't have any left! Flavius! I need the money! I wanted more than this! What will I have to live on?"

Sesba flung Arpoxa over his shoulder. She was bent over, head down. He struggled to hold her as he walked out the door. Flavius mounted his horse, and Sesba tied the struggling girl behind his friend.

Menus screamed obscenities after them in the dark. "You dirty crooks! I know who you are! You're deserters from the army! I'm going to learn which legion you served in. And your rank. You will pay for this!"

Flavius yelled back at Menus, "Make sure that you also tell them that you sold your sister to us to pay off your gambling debts. I'm sure they'll be interested in that too."

Even a long way off, Flavius could still hear Menus calling down every god and evil spirit he knew in hateful words.

TANAIS HARBOR, BOSPORAN KINGDOM (ROSTOV-ON-DON, RUSSIA)

Flavius and Sesba rode down the hill to Port Tanais. They had arranged with a slave master to take the young woman to a ship. The previous day, he had told them, "Several days from now, weather permitting, my vessel will sail across Lake Maeotis. Port Phanagoria is the main point for gathering slaves from Scythia and the Bosporan Kingdom."

The two arrived at the dock in Tanais shortly after dawn. "Here. As promised, a young woman. She will be a good slave," Flavius began. In the early morning light, he was all smiles. He knew the value of words spoken as smooth as olive oil.

"Let me see her!" The slave trader's gruff command took Flavius aback. The trader often bought men and women and was alert to tricks of many kinds.

Flavius demanded, "Pay me first. At a slave market, her new master will pay five hundred denarii. I want only half that much."

"Only after you let me see how good-looking she is. I'll be the judge of what she's worth."

Flavius went to his horse and lifted her down. He set Arpoxa on her feet, but as soon as he withdrew his arm, Arpoxa fell down.

In the early light of day, he could see Arpoxa's hair was long, the color of wheat at harvest time. Her eyes were bluer than the sky above them. Soft groans came through narrow lips. Her dirty tunic showed a mature woman, tantalizingly beautiful. Her hand was wrapped around her deformed toes, trying to warm them up.

Flavius gasped at the woman sprawled out on cold paving stones. "What in the name of Mithra! Menus didn't tell me this!" When he was angry, overjoyed, or simply bewildered, he swore in the name of his Persian god.

The slave master stood tall. He approached the two men and growled. "Idiots! You brought a woman who can't stand up. Look at her! She's worth nothing! Nothing! Both feet turned inward! You ask for two hundred fifty denarii! Well, I won't give you fifty! She's barely sellable! Come to think of it, I don't think I could even give her away!"

Flavius's shoulders dropped. He had commanded eight

hundred soldiers in Legion XXI, but at this moment, he had no authority. His gruff voice was reduced to a whine. "She'll give birth! Sell them. Each son will get you five hundred. Girl children will be slaves too, worth many times more. Give me two hundred fifty. Keep her for yourself. Be the father of her children!"

"Shut your mouth! Only forty denarii, that's all, Flavius. I advise you to take it before I report you to the authorities! I would make more money by turning you in."

Being caught as a deserter was an automatic death sentence. "Take her then. I'll accept the forty denarii!"

As they slowly left the harbor area, Sesba moaned in disbelief, "We lost money! That crook Menus didn't tell us his sister had clubbed feet."

For a long time, Flavius said nothing, riding back to the city with his head down and muttering to himself. Suddenly, he looked at Sesba and said, "Let's get to the tavern, have a mug of beer, and talk about an idea I just had."

As they sat in a dark corner, Flavius became animated as he laid out his thoughts. "Do you realize how much that slave master makes? We lost money on that woman, but I think Mithra, our god, is showing us the way to riches. We were high-ranking soldiers, and we have the knowledge to build an organization that can make us very wealthy. Losing thirty denarii may be the best thing that ever happened to us."

Chapter 5
Eliab's Will

ANTIPAS'S HOME, PERGAMUM

All the families on the Ben Shelah property were expecting this moment. They heard Miriam crying and knew what it meant. People came running, and soon all thirty-five households were sharing in their loss. Widows played mournful funeral flutes long into the night.

The next day in the cemetery, they were all faced with the fragility of life. The terrible words of finality were uttered: dust to dust, from *aphar* and *epher* in their Hebrew language.

Antipas felt numb from grief. As his father's body was laid in the ground on Monday morning, wrapped in a white linen shroud, he looked up at the sky.

I know that I will see you again, Father, when the trumpets sound. I know you will live again. What I don't know is how well I will survive without your guidance.

Eliab slept with his fathers.

Later that afternoon, Amos removed the will from a particular niche in the library. As the eldest son, it fell to him to read it aloud. "Our father's will...let me open the scroll. Hmm, it says that the property in Pergamum and his estate in Egypt will be divided into ten portions.

"Father has...sorry, I meant to say he *had* nine surviving children. Six of us are here, three back in Egypt. It says that as the oldest son, I will receive two of the ten portions. Twenty percent goes to my household."

He looked up and said, "That's acceptable to everyone I hope." Then he unrolled the scroll farther. "Here is how the rest of his inheritance is to be divided. Eighty percent for the other eight brothers and sisters. Each household will receive ten percent."

"A fair distribution," said Antipas, glancing around at his

brothers.

A dark color formed on Daniel's cheeks. Memories long laid to rest came alive, and Antipas knew there was a new controversy brewing in addition to the one with Jaron and his friends at the synagogue. His brother Daniel wore a frown, and he knew what that meant.

Daniel left the room, confident his brothers would think he was in mourning, but once out of the room, he gave way to his feelings. He was the best dressed of the six brothers. He wore a gold necklace with a small gold key attached. His hair was thick and black, whereas his brothers' hair was sprinkled with gray and shades of white. He was full chested, and beneath his tunic, his well-shaped legs implied an athletic past.

His face carried the lines of many worries, and he muttered, "Father! You willed only a tenth of the value of this property to me. Yet Antipas built his village on the property that now belongs to all of the brothers. Thirty-five dwellings plus his home and that of Onias—thirty-seven houses plus the other buildings, and none of these improvements are part of your will! A family squabble is sure to erupt over this!

"Does Antipas get to keep all this for himself? What about all these developments? The workshops and houses? They are worth so much! How can we sell the land and get our share of the inheritance while Antipas has his buildings occupying every available space?

"What were you thinking of when you wrote your will, Father? Didn't you know the considerable problem this would create for us all? Are my brothers as disappointed as I am?"

Miriam's concerns had nothing to do with the will or Eliab's estate. She could never describe in her own words what Eliab meant to her. Great-grandfather Eliab and Antipas, her grandfather, were the two men closest to her. She longed to have her own home, but Grandfather Antipas had still not found a suitable match for her.

That evening she wept, grateful that in the darkness, no one could see the constant flowing of tears down her cheeks. No one heard her soft-spoken words as she tossed and turned on her bed.

"Grandfather Antipas is an old man too. What will happen if

he dies before he finds a match for me? He says he is looking for a suitable husband, someone he can fully trust, someone who knows our Jewish traditions and worships our Messiah. But it is hard to wait. What if I never have my own family? I feel so alone...panicked...every time I start to think these thoughts. Please, God Almighty, let me sing again. Since the funeral today, I can't find words to sing but only feel small and alone, afraid and scared. Who will love me after my grandfather dies?"

Many mourners had come to Antipas's home. One after another, families from the synagogue expressed their love for the old man, crying with profound grief. Flutes played, and people wept. For a week, the home overflowed with mourners from mid-morning until the sun's rays began to lose their strength.

Most of the guests from the synagogue spent hours visiting with them, and each family brought food at least once. Eliab had made such a contribution to their welfare. He had been very generous during his life, and the Jewish community found in him a man who loved the Lord more than wealth and prestige.

Antipas noted that each of the men from the council in the synagogue came to pay respects, but Jaron, the ruler of the synagogue, and Nadav, the scribe, were absent. They, more than anyone else from the congregation, should have been there.

Antipas had hoped that Nadav's son, Adara, would come.

I think this is a sign that Nadav would never agree to Adara being married to Miriam.

The next day, the eighth day after Eliab's death, the brothers said their farewells and left the village to return to their homes. Each would later send a note by pigeon saying that they had arrived safely. The brothers had been together for seven days of mourning, and Antipas felt things getting back to normal after his brothers left for their homes.

Talking with his employees in a workshop, Antipas sensed that Yorick, one of the blenders of perfumes, was continuing in doing poorly at his job.

"Please come to my house this evening," Antipas said, inviting Yorick to speak in a quiet place. When he finally arrived after sundown, the young man said little, refusing to look Antipas in the eye. He sat in a chair, slouched over, looking sad.

"Yorick, what's the problem? I've noticed that during the last year, you have become sullen, and you hardly talk to either Onias or to me."

"I'm not sullen!" Yorick would only look at his own feet.

"Well, you don't seem satisfied. Are you unhappy living in this little village?"

"No, I am happy here." He didn't sound convincing.

"So there's something else, is there?"

"I need more money."

"I told you before that when the quality of your work picks up, I'll have Onias pay you more."

A thought passed through Antipas's mind. "Perhaps you are looking forward to getting married. Is that it?"

"Yes, someday I want to get married, but I don't have anything to give as a dowry to a woman's father."

"Well, be honest with yourself. You often arrive late to work. Sometimes you don't mix the perfumes in the right way. At other times, you haven't filled the bottles to the right level. Several times you've been absentminded, letting perfume spill on the workbench. If you improve, then I will make sure that you get a much better wage at the end of each day."

The conversation was not going any further, so Antipas put his hand on Yorick's shoulder, blessed him, and led him to the front door.

Yorick strolled down the road, head down, looking dejected and discouraged. He was the most complicated of all the personalities Antipas had redeemed from the slave market. Antipas knew he wanted more money, enough perhaps to move away from the village and start a family. Antipas shook his head regretfully. The young man seemed to believe he should be able to enjoy the things of life without working for them.

Chapter 6
Ateas

TANAIS HARBOR, BOSPORAN KINGDOM (ROSTOV-ON-DON)

Arpoxa screamed and shouted as a man picked her up. He had one hand around her stomach, the other around her chest. A slap across her face brought tears, and she whimpered. The slave master ordered two men to lower her into the hold of a ship where several other slaves were wrapped in cloaks against the cold.

The slaver shivered as a northerly wind blew the last clouds away. He looked down and shouted, "You'll be fed and kept here out of the cold. In a week, this ship sails south." Turning around, he muttered, "Why did those halfwits bring me a lame woman?"

Arpoxa took a breath and, overcome by the stench, panicked. *I'm going to vomit.* She tasted bile and swallowed the acid. She crawled into a corner away from the other captives and shivered from the cold. Voices in the dark called out in desperation. Arpoxa wept for hours, but no help came.

"You're just like the rest of us" came a man's voice in the ship's gloomy hold. "You were snatched away from your family."

She realized that various Scythian languages were represented. "My brother hates me, but I want to be home, not here! My mother and father died, and my uncle..." She started to weep again.

She hit her hand against her forehead as if she intended to pound something into her memory. *Flavius! That's his name. I heard my brother screaming it. I'll remember him—what an evil man! I'll never forget him and never forgive him. I will get even with both of them one day.*

Six days after she was placed in the hold, the ship docked at Phanagoria, the main port of the Bosporan Kingdom. After an hour, the overhead hatch was opened, and two more slaves were lowered. One man held onto two crutches as he was pushed in against his will.

Arpoxa could understand his words, even though he came from a city where they spoke a slightly different dialect.

"Don't do this to me!" he yelled to the men closing the thick wooden door. "My father and uncles will pay you to release me! Tell anyone from Bilsk[7] that Ateas needs help!" but the hatch slammed shut.

In that cold and miserable space, Arpoxa realized there was no one to extend concern or mercy.

The young man, who had struggled against being lowered into the dark hold of the ship, cried out, "Help me! I'm not supposed to be here! Please! Notify my uncles! I'm from a powerful family!"

Laughter rang out. "Did you get that? A lame man from a powerful family!"

Arpoxa heard terror in the newcomer's voice. "Who can help me get out of this place?"

"What's your story, stranger?" someone asked. "What do you mean that you're from a powerful family? You look pretty powerless now."

"My uncles are traders on the Silk Road. I used to ride with their caravans as a guard until my leg was broken in an accident. We had no doctor, and it was set wrong. My name is Ateas, and in Bilsk, I'm an important person." He stopped speaking.

---

[7] Bilsk today is a small village in the District of Poltava, Central Ukraine. Archaeological research shows it was a large city. At forty square kilometers, it was one of the largest in the world during the height of its influence, seventh to sixth centuries BC. Its ramparts, constructed as earth walls up to fifty feet in height (16 m) extended twenty-one miles (33 km) and enclosed the city. Bilsk was erected beside the Vorskla River, enabling trade from Europe to reach into the steppes of Asia. Herodotus (*Inquiries* Book 4 'The Geography of Scythia') described its inhabitants: "The Budini, for their part, being a large and numerous nation, are all mightily blue-eyed and ruddy. And a city among them has been built, a wooden city, and the name of the city is Gelonus. Of its wall then in size each side is of thirty stades (18,000 ft long = 5.5 km), and high and all wooden. And their homes are wooden and their shrines. For indeed there are in the very place Greek gods' shrines adorned in the Greek way with statues, altars and wooden shrines and for triennial festivals in honor of Dionysus."

"Tell us more," came a woman's voice in the dark.

"I could shoot arrows and hit the mark when my horse was galloping at full speed! But last summer I broke my leg when I was helping a neighbor dig a well. Unexpectedly, a boulder fell out of the wall, halfway to the surface. It landed on my leg. My people didn't have a doctor, so the leg wasn't set right, and I can't walk properly."

"You've been captured by thugs. You are now just a slave...like us...going to be sold," said the same woman.

"But I know important people, wealthy men, who can do something."

When raucous laughter met his statement, the young man pulled back against the thick wooden hull. Arpoxa spoke in a hushed voice. "When you were lowered, I saw you are crippled like me. I'm crippled too but worse than you," she whispered.

He spoke softly. "Crippled too? Why are you in this miserable place?"

"My brother had debts, and he was threatened for not paying. He arranged to have me kidnapped. I was born with club feet." Hesitantly, she asked the stranger, "What's your name?"

"Ateas."

"Do you always use crutches?"

"Now I do. I used to ride horses as a caravan guard, and I was good at it," he bragged. "What is your name?"

"Arpoxa."

"Really? Arpoxa? Like our great Scythian queen? Well, my name was meant to inspire trust—Ateas, our greatest king.[8] He died a long time ago." The grim humor of their situation brought a bleak laugh. "Imagine! In the dark hold of a ship, headed for the slave market. You carry the name of a queen, and I..." He didn't finish his sentence.

He reached out his hand toward her, and she drew her hand back. "I didn't mean to make you even more afraid. I won't hurt you," he whispered to her.

"I can't trust anyone!" she hissed. She was shivering, more

---

[8] Ateas is named for King Ateas (429–339 BC), one of Scythia's most famous and powerful monarchs. He unified many of Scythia's tribes. He was killed in battle at the age of ninety while fighting the Macedonian king, Philip II; after his death, the Scythian empire fell apart.

from fear than the cold.

"Here, you can trust me," said Ateas. "I brought something with me from Bilsk. I hid this silk scarf inside my tunic. It was part of my payment last year for guarding the caravans. I am going to give it to you. Maybe they will search me, so it will be safer with you."

Reaching out her hand toward the stranger, she fingered the softest material she had ever felt. "Does anyone else know about this?" she asked.

"No, only you," he answered. "I'm giving it to you."

"Then I am going to trust you," she said. She wanted Ateas to see her smile, but the darkness hid everything.

The next day the hatch opened again, and beside the slave trader stood three guards. "Get out, slowly, one by one. You are coming to a building where you will be kept until ships start sailing to the south. Then you will be taken to Chalcedon. From there, it's either to Pergamum or Athens to be sold as slaves."

CHALCEDON, PROVINCE OF BITHYNIA AND PONTUS (KADIKOY, ISTANBUL, TURKEY)

The weather delayed Ateas and Arpoxa's ship for a few days. It sailed down along the eastern shores of the Black Sea, picking up a few more slaves, and after many stops, it arrived at Chalcedon, a port in Bithynia.

"Welcome to Chalcedon! You are all going ashore now!" the slave master bellowed. "Tomorrow, we sail. The strongest men and most beautiful women will bring the best prices!"

The short man rubbed his hands gleefully. "For the next several days, you'll get good food. I want you to look strong and healthy when you stand on a slave platform!" Greed oozed from every word as he continued to rub his hands together.

In the weeks since Ateas had met Arpoxa, a strong friendship had developed. They were almost the same age. Ateas was taller than most of the other men being taken to be sold. However, his injury caused him to bend slightly when walking, so he looked older than his nineteen years. His arms were muscular, useful when digging wells. His beard shone almost a golden yellow in the bright Chalcedon sun. Arpoxa was a year younger.

Ateas and Arpoxa were the last two slaves off the ship. The

other slaves, bound together two by two with iron chains, were already off the pier and heading to the baths by the time Ateas helped Arpoxa onto the dock. He had to help her with every step she took. Soon they were far behind the others.

Earlier in the day, the rain had cleansed the streets. The air was calm. A gentle wind wafted across the small bay, and flowering trees spread a sweet scent of spring. Seagulls soared and circled, searching for food. Cobblestones glistened in the late afternoon sun. Men lounged in small clusters, and fishermen prepared their nets for the next day.

"Hurry up, you two! You're slowing everyone down!" yelled the slave master. "For someone who can't run away, you surely bring a lot of inconvenience to me."

Arpoxa held onto Ateas's arm and whimpered, "Will anyone want me as a crippled slave?"

As they followed the other captives to the public baths and a hot meal, Ateas saw a cluster of people gathered at the small Temple of Dionysius. Festivities were taking place, with singers and dancers preparing to welcome the new moon. This evening would bring dancing, wine, and much joy.

They were hobbling past the temple when Ateas suddenly stopped and took Arpoxa's hand. "I want to be with you always," he said urgently. "Will you marry me, Arpoxa?"

"But Ateas! Won't this be dangerous? I'm worried..."

"Stay here with me for just a moment. I'll tie that silk scarf around our necks like we do in Bilsk. Will you let me ask this priest to pronounce us as husband and wife?"

"Yes, I want to marry you. No one else has ever been as kind to me. I love you, but I've only known you for six weeks! And..."

"This is our perfect chance, Arpoxa! The slave master has gone on ahead. He'll be busy watching the others go through the bathhouse. We'll never have another opportunity like this!"

"But..."

"But what?"

"I'm afraid that I'll be separated from you. I couldn't stand to be married and then to be taken away. What would I..."

"But you want to, don't you? You want to spend your life with me?"

"Yes, but if we are sold to different masters..."

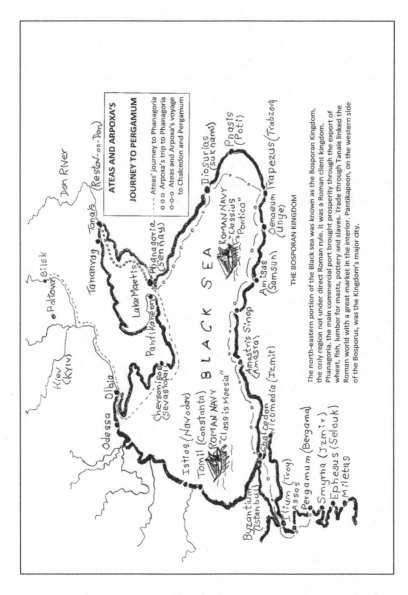

Close by was a priest of Dionysus instructing the dancers for the event later on in the evening.

Ateas called to the priest. "Can you pronounce us husband

and wife?"

The priest, a heavy-set man, did not understand Ateas at first, and he waddled over to them looking very puzzled. Using several hand signs that he had learned on the Silk Road, Ateas finally made his request understood. The priest smiled, delighted with this spontaneous entreaty.

Arpoxa reached deep into the one pocket of her tunic, pulled out the silk scarf, and wrapped it around both their necks. She smiled and balanced against Ateas as he bent over and kissed her.

"I pronounce you husband and wife!" the priest said. "Come and dance with us tonight!" After a few seconds, he realized what he had said and blurted out, "Or perhaps you can just watch."

A rough hand reached around them just as she was about to remove the scarf.

"What are you two doing?" bellowed the slave master. "I leave you for a moment, and you're pretending to get married!" Arpoxa tried to hide her present, but he sneered, "Ah! I'll take that!"

He wound the soft silk scarf around his hand and pulled it slowly over his wrist. "Very nice quality... Where did you steal this? Oh, this is lovely," he said, fingering the scarf. "I have a lady-friend who will like it."

Before Ateas could answer, the slave master gave them a shove toward the group heading to the baths. "I have been talking to the other slavers. Defective slaves don't sell well to the perfection-minded Greeks. I'll have to hope that someone in Pergamum will want you. Now catch up to the others!"

He returned to the baths with Ateas and Arpoxa. The others were starting their cleansing. At the evening meal, he talked with other slave traders. "I have two lame slaves in my ship," he said. "They might make good house slaves. Neither of them can walk well, so they can't run away. Unfortunately, neither of them can do much in the way of hard work. I'm not sure I'll make any money on those two, but I'm taking them to Pergamum for the Festival of Zeus slave market."

Chapter 7
The Slave Market

THE SLAVE MARKET, THE NEW FORUM, PERGAMUM

Both the wealthy and the poor had gathered at the New Forum market area. The first major event of the spring was underway. There was plenty of space here for people to buy and sell their wares, and today slaves would be purchased.

Animals, spices, food, carpets, jewelry, perfumes, clothing, select woods for carpenters, precious metals, cups, and pots— everything could be bought and sold in the New Forum. Bright-colored awnings covered sidewalks close to the colonnaded porch along four sides of the market. Animals for sale filled the designated areas where they were tethered. Children played everywhere and were shooed continuously away by merchants. Commotion, excitement, and merriment sounded.

Sellers of cures displayed their wares on white cloths spread over the white marble pavement.

"I have powerful medicine!" yelled one man. "These dried crocodile livers cure all ailments: stomach, lung, heart, kidney, and digestive problems." He crouched over his brown and black imported dried parts of African animals.

The New Forum had become the social and administrative center of the city. Its officials acted like spoiled princes. Their task of overseeing the civilian life in Pergamum made them powerful because of favors they could give or refuse. Here, not only goods and slaves were sold but ideas were shared, people learned from one another, and gossip abounded.

Antipas stood under the *stoa*, the long, colonnaded porch running the length of the New Forum. Today, Miriam stood close by him. She had asked to spend her twenty-fifth birthday with him. He knew it was an unusual request. She usually kept away from auctions where slaves were sold.

"Onias," Antipas said quietly, "I want you to carry out the transactions with the auctioneer. Learn what you can about the men and women being sold then come and talk to me."

Antipas always stood away from the auction platform. His first time here, his eyes blazed with emotion as he watched a ten-year-old girl forcibly taken from her mother. Two slave owners walked away, and a family was forever divided. That mother's screaming and the girl's sobbing still came back to him nineteen years later. He rested his back against a corner of the colonnade, watching the preparations for the slave auction.

One ship brought slaves from Africa. Another vessel came from the Black Sea. In a few moments, the slaves would be on the viewing platform. The wooden stage was as high as a man's waist. Several poles were set into the marble pavement, and awnings stretched between the poles to provide shade.

Now twenty-four slaves were being led into the market area. Each slave was bound at the wrists except for the two lame slaves tied to each other's leg by a length of rope. All the slaves, men and women alike, walked naked onto the platform. Antipas's stomach churned as he counted them. Men and women were on display to people who occupied themselves gazing upon human flesh: arms and legs, genitals, and breasts.

The few clothes with which they had come were piled at the base of the platform. Some had to be dragged onto the platform against their will, receiving whippings for their rebellion.

From his place under the colonnade, Antipas watched wealthy men noisily gathering. Those who could afford slaves crowded close to take it all in. Professional purchasers counted coins. Personal bidders stretched their necks, evaluating today's merchandise.

Antipas was curious about the others who would be bidding at the auction. He watched Zoticos, who had a high position in the library. The outgoing, handsome man had made his name by purchasing scholarly materials from across the Greco-Roman world. The librarian stood with his Scythian slave under the protection of the *stoa* as the sun's rays filled the marketplace. Antipas recalled the slave market auction six years ago, when Zoticos had taken the Scythian slave to his house on the acropolis.

On the other side of the auction area, Antipas spotted Marcos, the city's chief counsel. He came with his slave, a young man.

Standing beside Marcos was the gymnasium headmaster, Diodorus Pasparos, talking with a friend.

This slave master was in Pergamum for the first time.

"Stand up!" he barked. "Walk around! Turn around!" He pushed the lame woman with a stick, yelling, "Walk faster!" She almost fell over. A young man standing beside her caught her, and tears flowed down her cheeks. Humiliated, exposed, and naked, the captives stared in fear. Terror was expressed in their eyes.

Antipas wondered which of the slaves he would take home today. They were from places across the empire. He knew that slaves from Persia were usually compliant, with prices varying according to estimates of health. Men from Africa brought prices related to their perceived physical strength. From their appearance, most were Scythians, beyond the Black Sea region. These slaves brought the highest prices, especially if they were literate in Greek and possessed good looks.

"Can anyone understand these foreigners?" shouted the slave master. Antipas knew that people from the Black Sea spoke strange languages.

Zoticos's slave volunteered himself and was taken onto the platform to translate. He talked with three men and a woman then turned to the audience, providing a brief description of each of the unfortunate people. People laughed at his broken sentences, and while he had never learned to speak Greek well, they still followed his awkward descriptions.

In his poor Greek, he introduced the slaves to the buyers. "The woman is dancer. Eighteen-year-old. That old man love horse. This man farmer. This one from Scythia, and he strong, thirty-five-year-old. This woman had four small children in house, twenty-seven-year-old. She is sad today. Sad every day after house burn down."

He made funny faces, imitating their misfortunes. The crowd roared its approval, appreciating the impromptu show and the humiliation of the slaves. The tiny bits of information made the crowd curious to know more about their individual misfortunes.

After talking to the last two slaves, Zoticos's slave explained, "This man sad. Stone fell on his leg in well. Has broken foot. Now crippled. Walk with crutches. Nineteen-year-old."

He pointed to the last slave and described her, a Scythian with hair the color of straw. People saw a beautiful face and a perfect body but two deformed feet.

Zoticos's slave continued his commentary, "This woman born this way. She walks twisted feet. Eighteen years old. In my country, we say cursed. Clubfeet from mother, she cursed."

A gasp was heard. The slave master held up her long blond hair, letting it fall slowly through his fingers. A collective murmur was heard from the crowd. Antipas wondered how people could believe that as a punishment for adultery, a mother would give birth to a daughter with a clubbed foot. He shook his head in disbelief. How could people think that the gods would take revenge against an unborn child?

The slave master made a snide comment. "She's unusually beautiful from the waist up. From her knees down, she has nothing, but when she is on her back, waiting to entertain the next soldier, who will see her twisted feet?" He squeezed the shoulder of the beautiful young woman, and she turned away from him.

The slave master took her hand and let it fall. "What a waste!" The woman looked up at the lame man standing beside her. He was leaning heavily on crutches. He looked down at her and spoke in her ear, and she blinked several times.

Onias came back from the auction platform and described the physical characteristics of each slave.

Antipas was ready to work out his strategy. A moment like this always stirred great compassion within him. He put aside the physical descriptions of the slaves. Something was binding the two lame ones together, something other than that short rope. They might be a brother and sister. The memory of the young daughter being ripped from her mother came back, and Antipas made his decision.

He looked up and saw Zoticos's slave bounding from side to side across the platform. He made a face and wiped mock tears from his eyes. People in the crowd laughed at this. Encouraged, he imitated the woman who was bound by one clubbed foot to the young man's broken leg. One slave making fun of others in the slave market brought further laughs.

The previous night, Antipas had read a passage precious to him because of his own journey from Egypt. It was a passage he included during every Passover celebration for the people under his spiritual care. It told of his own trials when he had left Jerusalem, when his daughter Tamara, Miriam's mother, had slipped away forever, entering eternity.

The passage from Isaiah reminded him of Jerusalem and the death of his only child. The arrow that had killed her had come from one of his own people, a Judean soldier standing high on the walls of Jerusalem. The wound became infected, and in Antioch, a year later, she died, never having regained her health.

Isaiah's words stirred deep emotions within him, and he echoed the words again. "He gives strength to the tired and weary and increases the power of the weak. Even youths grow tired and weary, and young men stumble and fall; but those who wait on the Lord will renew their strength. They will soar on wings like eagles; they will run and not grow weary; they will walk and not faint."[9]

When he had given the scroll back to the attendant in the cave, a feeling of great compassion had swept over him. He finished the meeting by saying, "I want to walk along God's pathway until the day I die, and my prayer for each one of you is the same: Be faithful until the end. Now the slave market is coming, and I want to find the right person for our village. Please pray with me about that. Leaving Jerusalem, I prayed, 'If you give me a safe place to live, I will thank you each year by giving freedom to one slave.' May God lead me to the right person tomorrow."

Everyone in his community was making guesses about the next redeemed slave. They knew this kindness was part of Antipas's vow to God years ago when he came to Pergamum, and they were always excited by someone new coming to join their little village.

Now he contemplated the scene before him because twenty-four slaves would be sold before noon.

The crippled slave who could not stand on his right foot was young, perhaps not more than twenty. Beside him, now sitting on the platform, was the young naked woman about the same age. No one would buy those two people in this market, and he winced at the thought. They would be shipped along to the international

---

[9] Isaiah 40:29–31

slave market.

That slave with the broken leg...he knows the woman who is attached to him by a rope, but does the slave master know something about them, a clue that he hasn't told to the crowd? Men examine women slaves for their bodies. I see something else but do not yet understand.

Antipas gave instructions to his steward Onias and then stood under the roof of the *stoa* behind one of the pillars to observe the proceedings.

The master of the slave market shouted loudly as he began the auction. "Slaves for sale! I am selling five from Africa today and nineteen who came from Phanagoria, known to be the source of the best slaves!"

Healthy slaves cost the equivalent of three donkeys. Noisy, raucous, and vulgar, the auction caused spectators to shiver with both disgust and excitement.

Now only three slaves were left. The finest of them was a strong young man with blond hair and bulging muscles. He was sold to the highest bidder, Atys Tantalus, for five hundred denarii.

People cheered loudly as the auctioneer yelled, "Sold!"

Finally, the last two came for up for sale. The auctioneer hadn't even begun to ask for bids. He looked at the two weak and crippled slaves and pointed at them. Many had decided to bid on the woman, but no one wanted the crippled male slave. Antipas wondered if he could read their thoughts: Why would anyone want a slave who had to use crutches and could not do manual labor?

Antipas's opportunity had come. As instructed, Onias shouted, "I'll take the crippled man and the crippled woman if you sell them together. I'll pay the same price that you got for that strong male, five hundred denarii."

His loud voice brought an instant reaction. People gathered in small groups. Obviously, the buyers were surprised at the unusual offer. A buzzing sound swept the New Forum, and Antipas wondered if a slave master would receive a counter-offer. Then silence descended on the marketplace.

Antipas watched the slave master speak to his helper, and broad smiles spread across the strangers' faces. The auctioneer raised his hands high and roared, his voice echoing in the New Forum: "Going once, going twice!"

A man from Kisthene, the summer resort city north of Pergamum, was dressed in an expensive white toga. He began to raise his hand, and Antipas saw a broad gold band covering half his right arm. The stranger lowered it quickly.

Antipas wondered if the auctioneer had spotted the gesture, and he held his breath, waiting and praying.

"Sold to the man with the short beard!" shouted the auctioneer.

Gasps of surprise sounded, and the well-dressed man from Kisthene waved his gold arm band in the air. "Hey, mister, you didn't tell us they would be sold together! Who would buy a lame man? This isn't what we expected!"

The lame young slave collapsed to his knees. Antipas could see tears spilling down the young woman's face.

"Done!" screamed the slave master.

As instructed, Onias reached into the bag and counted out the coins to purchase the man and the young woman. Antipas knew from previous experience how long it would take to fill out the required paperwork. Once the additional coins were paid for the tax to Rome, the injured man and lame woman were his.

The slave auction was over.

Later Antipas would write their papers, legal documents stating that the full price had been paid for their freedom.

With the contract between Antipas and the slave master signed and paid for, Onias jumped onto the platform and removed the cord binding the two together. Leaning down to give them back their tattered clothing, he helped the young man to his feet. Antipas stayed in his place, watching and waiting.

Balancing himself, the slave with the broken leg pulled his tunic over his head and held out his hand to help the young woman get up. She balanced awkwardly on her deformed feet. She pulled her grimy slave's tunic over her head as quickly as she could, obviously relieved to be clothed in the public square. Onias helped them both down the steps from the platform.

People who stayed until the end scoffed, knowing that Antipas had instructed his steward to buy slaves. Previously, they had only sneered at Antipas for his generosity, but today they jeered loudly.

The Egyptian priest yelled, "Look! He buys slaves only to set them free! This foreign Jew is an outsider. He comes to purchase worthless slaves with twisted feet and broken legs!"

Loud laughs and vulgar taunts flowed. Someone yelled, "He bought a beautiful young woman. Will he even notice her feet?"

Antipas had studied the look of pain in the young man's eyes. He wondered what was going through the mind of the crippled woman. He could see that this crippled man felt genuine tenderness for this woman.

Most buyers of slaves do not care about the expressions on the faces of slaves because they do not see them as real people.

Antipas called Miriam, who had been sitting out of sight. She helped the crippled woman as she shuffled away from the auction. The man and woman looked at each other and spoke words that Antipas could not understand.

The crowd watched silently as the small group—Antipas, Miriam, Onias, and the two slaves—moved slowly through the market. Antipas walked slowly as the crippled man helped the young woman. She moved with obvious pain.

Antipas led them to the wagon at the edge of the New Forum. "Onias, please go to my store and bring two new tunics. The one for the woman will be smaller. The man needs our largest size."

When Onias returned, Antipas, Miriam, and Onias formed a small circle around the two slaves. At the same time, Ateas and Arpoxa took off their old, smelly clothing and put on beautiful linen garments.

While they were changing, Antipas thought, *The redemption price is paid. They will have a transformed life. Gone are the clothes that told everyone they were slaves. Instead, the new clothing speaks of belonging to a family.*

Antipas wanted to take their shame away, so their old clothing was thrown into the cart to be burned. Unable to speak to them, he motioned with his hands to indicate that they would be leaving together. Onias and Miriam helped them onto the back of the cart, and Onias drove away from the city. The wide avenue followed the curve of the river.

When the horse turned into his little village, Antipas turned around. "Miriam, for two weeks, you have been helping to furnish this new house with three small rooms. I had Onias put a stone bench against the front wall. It's where they will wait for conversations. Our community will receive them and embrace them. Now, will you walk beside the young woman and help her into her new home?"

Antipas knew he would be criticized by some in the synagogue for spending his time in the slave market before one of the holy days of his Jewish calendar. He thought about that probable conflict and laughed out loud. Joy bubbled within him.

Isn't that what the Exodus was all about—slaves being freed from bondage?

Antipas watched the young couple take their first steps of freedom, and his heart soared with joy. It was now clear to everyone. The man and the woman belonged together. They were a husband and wife.

The rest of the city celebrated the Festival of Zeus each year, but Antipas celebrated a different occasion.

He called going to the first slave auction of the year his Festival of Freedom.

The wagon pulled up beside a new house. After much gesturing and calm words that they didn't understand from their new owners, it became clear to Arpoxa that this was where they were to live. In a new house. No one had ever lived there! Ateas leaped down onto the ground, balancing on his one good foot.

Arpoxa needed help to get down from the wagon. When she understood that Ateas was saying they were going to have their own house, her mouth gaped in disbelief. She stared at him, and instantly a flood of tears flowed. If she had normal feet, she would have jumped into his arms, but the young woman could only stand awkwardly on her two twisted feet. She hugged him, leaning on his shoulder, not willing to let him go.

"Ateas, what is happening to us? This is so unbelievable!"

"I don't know. Why did the old man give us new clothes?"

"Maybe he is going to hurt us!"

"No, these people have been kind and have not said one harsh word."

Ateas started to say something and laughed loudly. He put his hand on the back of her head, pulling her close, touching the tips of their noses, and she cried tears of joy. "We're going to stay together! We have a house!"

Arpoxa sat on the stone bench and sobbed. "Ateas, my husband. A master who is kinder than anything we could ever have expected has bought us. We are going to be his slaves!"

Chapter 8
Marcos and Florbella

PERGAMUM, PROVINCE OF ASIA MINOR (SOUTHWESTERN TURKEY)

The day after the slave market, the lawyer, Marcos lay on his back, staring at the dark ceiling. He didn't need the light of day to see it all happen again.

It began one sunny day when he wanted to be alone with his wife. "Marcella, let's climb the hill behind our villa. I'd love to have a few moments alone."

"Me too, Marcos. Let's celebrate! Honestly, I'm exhausted. So many meals served to your relatives all month long!"

Half an hour later, having climbed the steep hill beside the Sea of Marmara, he placed his arm around her shoulder. "Look across the bay. Oh, how I love the glimmer of light playing on the water! Look at the water from this angle."

"There's Nicomedia! The sun is blazing on our city!"

"Yes, I was born and bred in Bithynia's provincial capital. Come here. Look at the red roof on our summer villa, built as a copy of the most elegant summer homes near Rome."

Underneath his feet, the earth rumbled. Part of the hill gave way in a landslide. "Marcella! Deep underground, Hades is grinding his teeth!"

A moment later, he screamed, "Oh no! My four brothers and all the family members are inside! They are preparing a special meal for you. How will they know..."

She screamed, "Lucius, Onesime, Alypos, Antipastos!"

"How can I warn my brothers?" He was shouting, screaming. "Get out! Run for safety!"

"They can't hear! We're too far away."

"Marcella! Look! The villa is sinking. They didn't get out in time! The sea is swallowing everything!"

He was on his knees, weeping. "Marcella! Hades has swallowed them! Everything...everyone...my brothers—all gone!"

Marcos turned over in bed. Sweat covered him. *Why can't I put this behind me? It eats at my mind when I need to be alert at the council meetings. I don't want to look like I'm daydreaming. City counselors are always alert to lawyers not paying attention to details.*

He wanted to scream. *But I've never yelled at Hades. And anyway, that would wake Marcella. She shouldn't be burdened with how often the memory of that terrible event three and a half years ago still keeps me awake.*

Trying not to wake Marcella, he turned onto his side. He fought against these visions, but they wouldn't stop coming. For two years, he hadn't spoken of them, ever since he had won the coveted position of Senior Counsel of the District of Pergamum. He had moved his family from Nicomedia, hoping it would stop the dreams from coming.

Hades. His spell was on Florbella, his daughter. *What can I do to take away this wretched curse? Hades, Bringer of Death, there must be a higher power than yours to bring her health. We are grateful you didn't swallow our precious daughter. Now she's all we have left.*

A rooster behind his house crowed, announcing a new day. Marcos got out of bed, shuddering with each step because of the cold floor. The freezing floor tiles swiftly brought him back to the present. *I must have Marcella buy some new rush mats for our cold floors.*

At age thirty-five, he was the youngest man to ever relish the title of Chief Counsel of the District of Pergamum. Two years before, a committee of the city council had interviewed him as a candidate for the position. Officials were impressed by this lawyer. They saw in his face and heard in his words the characteristics they most prized: knowledge, persistence, loyalty, and dedication to work.

A subject during the questioning dealt with inheritance laws. At that, they witnessed a sparkle light up his eyes. Nothing held their attention as much as his descriptions of family conflicts. He didn't go into his personal loss from the earthquake.

He gave them examples of how well-to-do men in Rome

successfully passed on their wealth. After cleverly giving this free advice to the committee members, he was sure the prestigious job was his. But now he was worn out. The bad dreams wouldn't go away.

Marcos and Marcella's home was richly furnished. Just as they were moving to Pergamum, the villa had come up for sale on the west side of the city. The window of their bedroom on the second floor faced the New Forum, the city's recently completed market and administrative area.

He walked to the window, filling his lungs with winter air. With the shutters partially open, he gazed at the pink-tinged sky, wondering again what to do about the curse Florbella lived with.

In an hour, the streets below would be full. He made a promise. *Before the Festival of Zeus returns, I will persuade the gods to provide a cure for Florbella. My sleep must return so I can concentrate on work for the city council...and I must stop Marcella's tears.*

The rooster also awakened Marcosanus, the young slave Marcos had bought the year before to watch over Florbella. He yawned, stretched, slowly got out of bed shivering, and put on his day-wear tunic. He trudged down to the little girl's room carrying a small watch-lamp in the dark of the house. She had instructed him to wake her early and take her to watch the birds near the marsh.

Entering the room, Marcosanus whispered, "Wake up, Florbella! The rooster has crowed, and the sky is clear...a good day to watch the birds. Must we go today?" whispered the slave, who was twenty-two years old. "It's too cold outside! Your father is already awake I think. Don't you want to stay inside today?"

Marcosanus didn't mind Florbella watching birds along the river's edge. Still, the young man hated having to awaken so early every day. Also, he didn't like the cold winds of February.

Florbella put a finger across her lips as if to indicate she didn't want any noise to wake her mother. She shook her head, the quiet way to say, "No!" and laced up her sandals.

A chilly morning to walk outside. Maybe today I will understand what keeps birds in the sky while flying. And Marcosanus must obey!

The child was eight years old, but she moved quickly,

gathering the warm clothes and blankets she would need.

KAIKOS RIVER BASIN

Florbella walked down the small hill to the New Forum and turned west, heading to the marshland. Her father had agreed that she could leave the house when guarded by Marcosanus.

She paused to watch a line of twenty slaves plodding slowly along the road, starting their two-day march from Pergamum to the mines in the rocky hills just east of Adramyttium.[10] She watched soldiers riding horses at the head and the tail of the miserable troop, ensuring that defiant men who had been disobedient to their masters would not escape a second time. She didn't need anyone to tell her that it was a solemn warning for other slaves tempted to rebel.

The other day, she had heard her father warn her slave, "Men sent to the mines rarely came back alive. So, Marcosanus, don't get any crazy ideas about running away."

Having found a spot near the water's edge in the marsh, Florbella looked down. She couldn't see all the reflected details of her face, because the sun wasn't fully up yet, but she often spent time looking at herself.

As always, her long, pitch-black hair was done up in two braids, the way her mother, Marcella, wanted it. Her small ears stuck out from her head a little. Strangers first noted an intelligent gleam in her dark brown, almost coal-black, eyes. The delicate features of her face added to the impression of a natural intellect.

She waited quietly. Sometimes she stayed this way in silence for hours, hardly moving. All around her were the sounds of the birds in the marshland. She pulled her bright-colored little blanket around her tightly.

During the winter, white-tailed eagles, little grebe, black-necked grebe, and cormorants filled the long, thin river basin of the Kaikos River where it drained into the Aegean Sea. Farther up the river, close to her home, gadwalls, pochards, and coots nested.

---

[10] Adramyttium, located five miles (9 km) south of Edremit, Turkey, was a port city of considerable importance in the northwest area of the Kingdom of Lydia. St. Paul's journey in Acts 27 involved a ship from this port.

Florbella had spotted a black-necked grebe, and for the moment, it was her favorite. The bird dove into the water and returned with its feathers shining and a small fish in its beak. A pair had built a nest that floated in the water, attached to some reeds. Florbella focused on the lovely birds as she sat on her blanket beside a bush that sheltered her from the wind.

Her neck bent back as she followed the flocks of birds from the far north of Europe spending their winter months in the marshlands of Pergamum. They sheltered many other birds, the collared pratincole, the small bird with the light brown feathers on its back and the thin black collar around its white chin.

Now the spur-winged plovers with their long, pointed wings scurried about on the bank of the marsh and made her twist and turn in her hiding place as she followed their movements.

She loved watching them run and pause as they hunted for food around the tiny bay. She longed to touch the feathers covering their bodies, heads, necks, and tails. Their brown wings lifted them so quickly from the marsh, and they asked the same question, over and over: "Did-he-do-it?"

From somewhere at the edge of the marsh, someone threw a stone at a tree. Florbella looked up then relaxed. It was only Marcosanus, her slave, who was always doing things like this.

It was his way of communicating to her that they should go home. He didn't like waiting when she went to watch birds, so he tried to interrupt her. He was restless and didn't understand why the daughter of his master, an important man, spent so much time looking at birds.

She tried to keep each bird in her mind so she could go to sleep that night thinking of them. In her mind, the night was colored by the vibrant nesting, squawking, singing, soaring creatures all around her.

Her slave complained aloud. "I'm freezing. Let's go home!"

She ignored him. Clouds turned to white as the morning sun rose higher, and still she asked the same question: *What keeps birds in the sky? If only I could hold one, then maybe I would know the answer.*

Marcosanus threw another small pebble at one of the birds. His aim was getting better. Occasionally, he hit one. She wished she could hold one. But he was so noisy!

Why doesn't he stop? Why is he such a nuisance?

Chapter 9
Gifts of Perfume

UPPER AGORA AND ASCLEPIUS HOSPITAL

Marcella was standing beside the niche on a wall in their house, and she called her husband.

"Marcos, I want an expensive perfume. Today please!"

"What for, my dear?"

"As an offering to Hera." She held a small statue in her hand.

"Why? I'm happy to get some, but why the urgency?"

"Perhaps our goddess will favor us with a miracle. I'm feeling desperate! I need Hera to help, so I need an expensive perfume."

"I thought of something else to do for Florbella. Let's take her to the physician, Doctor Thorello, at the Asclepius Hospital."

"Oh, Marcos, why not go to the Altar of Zeus too? Inquire about an appropriate sacrifice for Florbella. We have to do something!"

Marcos waited until Florbella came back from the marsh, and then he walked to the Upper Agora with his daughter. It was a long walk and took almost an hour as they passed many buildings. Everywhere, it seemed, people had something to sell. Smells of all kinds flooded the air.

"Look, Florbella! Small booths everywhere, side by side."

The girl's head twisted and turned like one of the birds at the swamp, taking in everything. People need only a tiny niche to sell grain, onions, and other produce from their farms.

He walked up the crowded path, past the Odeon, the central building where the city council gathered and where he worked.

He was short of breath when he reached the Upper Agora. *Last year, a walk like this didn't bother me at all, but now... Age must be catching up to me.*

"Let's go into this shop, my little one."

He stepped into a shop just as an old man was leaving. He had a trim black beard. "Good morning."

"Good morning to you too, sir."

He found the sales lady. "Who is that man?"

"Oh," she said, folding up a tunic, "he is Antipas Ben Shelah, the owner of this shop, a Jew from Alexandria. That village over there across the river, where he has about thirty little houses, that's where he lives."

Marcos nodded then turned his attention to his current task. "I'm here to buy perfume. People say it's the best there is in Pergamum. Can you show me your highest quality?"

Florbella held his hand tightly. Marcos knew she was frightened by so many people.

They went to the shelves where the perfumes were kept to select one for an offering to the little goddess in their living room. He picked up one of the sample perfume bottles and sniffed at it tentatively.

Marcella wants a bottle of perfume. Then I need a second one for Doctor Thorello, and I might need a third as a gift at the Altar of Zeus.... I love these times with my daughter, and I want her to get used to the city's daily activities.

"Florbella, do you like the smell of this perfume? What about this one? Which one do you think the goddess would like best?"

She examined the delicate colors of the glass bottles, pale yellows, greens, and blues. The young girl pointed to a small glass bottle, recently blown at Antipas's workshop in his village. Florbella rubbed the smooth, round glass bottle around her hand softly then rubbed it against her soft cheek and closed her eyes.

Her father opened the sample bottle and let her sniff the fragrance. She nodded her head and smiled.

Marcos blinked repeatedly after he learned the price.

"I see you are taken aback! Well, they are the best in the marketplace! Of course! Our master, Antipas, uses a secret recipe to keep the fragrance long after it is put on.

"Here, little girl. Put some on your wrist or under your chin. Now take a deep breath! This oil will bring you close to the deep mysteries of Egypt. Some people say it's the kind of oil used to preserve the ancient kings there. It's sure to bring health to anyone! There, did you like the smell of it?"

Florbella nodded her head vigorously in agreement.

Chavvah, the sales lady, spoke with a distinct accent in the

Greek language. Marcos identified her as a Jewish immigrant from Egypt.

After haggling to a lower price, he agreed to take the three bottles and patted his daughter's shoulders as they left the shop. She smiled up at him.

With Florbella holding his hand, Marcos strolled back to the lower part of the city. They walked from the acropolis to the New Forum then along the Sacred Way to the Asclepius Hospital.

Halfway along, at the Western Gate of the Roman Theater, the child stopped to look at the massive stones wedged together at the top of the enormous archway twenty-five feet above her.

They arrived at the entry room of the Asclepius Hospital and were met by an attendant. "Good morning. I hope Doctor Thorello is here."

"Unfortunately, he is away for three weeks. Anyway, he never comes to the gate himself," said the attendant, helping a blind man to a chair. "He is far too busy. I will find another doctor who can talk with you."

"No, please tell Doctor Thorello that Marcos Pompeius, the lawyer serving on behalf of the city council, came to request time with him after his return."

The attendant shook his head as if in doubt and left to find someone with higher authority to speak with him.

Marcos watched Florbella, who had wandered out of the room. She walked up to a man who was bent over and touched the arm of a sick man. She smiled at another and laid her hand on the arm of a man whose leg was swollen. She felt his sore, swollen leg and smiled at him.

Marcos brought her back into the entry room.

Another attendant finally came, one who was obviously more solicitous and aware of Marcos's status. "How may we help you, Honorable Marcos Pompeius?"

"I've come to see about my daughter. She is eight years old, yet some evil has not allowed her to speak; otherwise, she has perfect health. Please tell Doctor Thorello that I must see him."

"When he returns from Sardis, I will tell him right away, and we will inform you."

Marcos took a bottle of perfume from his bag and gave it to the attendant. "The perfume is for the doctor, and this sestertius

70

coin is for you," he said.

He knew the power of a quarter-day's wage. It would make sure that the famous doctor would contact him when he returned from Sardis. Bribes, even small ones, were remembered and kept doors open.

Arriving home, Marcos gave a bottle to Marcella. She walked to the niche in the wall and deliberately poured two drops onto the tiny head of the statue.

"Thank you, my dear husband. I will do this every evening as a libation to Hera. Surely the goddess of home and hearth will hear us. Her powers will be awakened by such a sacrifice."

"We have been praying every day for a miracle. How many months? Marcella, you keep track of the time better than I do."

"Almost three years. Expensive perfume poured out as a libation is what we need. It's more likely to bring results to our prayers. That's what a woman at the marketplace told me."

"You mentioned earlier about going to the Altar of Zeus. I asked around and people told me to see the famous high priestess at the Altar of Zeus. They say she knows powerful words. I'll go to the top of the acropolis to give her the third bottle of perfume. I hope her incantations will help Florbella."

KAIKOS RIVER BASIN

Days later, holding her finger to her lips, Florbella signaled to Marcosanus. *You must not move or make noise and definitely not throw stones this morning!*

The weather had changed. Some birds were starting their flight back to their lands in the far north. She settled into her little hideout, watching the birds fly over the marsh.

Suddenly one bird caught her attention.

It flew into the sky but suddenly fell back to the earth. She felt so angry. Marcosanus had hit a plover with one of his stones, injuring it!

Why does he always have to throw stones at birds?

"Did-he-do-it?" the bird called to her as it left the marsh, flying in short attempts toward the mountain.

"Did-he-do-what?" she wanted to say.

"Did-he-do-it?" called the wounded bird again.

Yes, Marcosanus did it! I'm so sorry! I'll find you and bring you

71

back to my house and make you well. Wait! Let me catch up with you!

Wanting to help the bird, she started following it. Its body was almost black, easy to see when it was flying but hard to find on the ground. She saw its dark brown wings fluttering when it fell to the earth again.

The bird was slightly hurt but still attempting to fly. It kept accusing her slave with its call as it flew in spurts and starts. At one point, she almost caught up to it, but it made another attempt to escape.

The bird was obviously disoriented, and it flew toward the mountain with Florbella following. The bird flew over a small group of people gathered on the Sacred Way, going toward the hospital.

They all look so sick. How can these people get out into the marsh to watch birds or spend time looking at the colors and shapes of clouds unless they get better?

She moved past sick people, crossing the long avenue and trying to keep her eyes open for the wounded bird. Passing an arch on the roadway, she looked up.

How do stones stay up in the sky? Birds fly but stones don't, and yet those massive blocks stay way up there. I wish every bird would remain in the air like the ones that stretch their wings out and seem to float silently through the air.

She followed it up the hill into a meadow. It was unable to fly long distances now. She kept up with it more quickly in the fields where cows and sheep grazed above the city on the foothill of the mountain.

Suddenly, it shifted direction. It turned east and flew short distances toward the acropolis. Now it was easy for her to keep up, but both the bird and the girl were getting tired.

Florbella looked down on the city and delighted in the new view. To her right was the Asclepius Hospital. She had never been to this place before. The hospital had always been on her left before when she was in the city.

Below, she looked down into the Roman Theater, the amphitheater, and the Roman Stadium. The city of Pergamum opened up before her in the valley below.

I must come here again! All these colors! Greens and browns. Oh, the glow of the sun coming through the smoke rising from the houses!

Florbella lost sight of her bird again. Because it had been flying in that direction, she wandered a little more to the east, looking for it. Climbing over a fence, she found herself high above a small village. A shudder passed through her at a memory.

This looks like where I lived near Nicomedia. That was before the earthquake and that horrible day.

She was far from home, but she didn't feel afraid; she was trying to help a wounded bird. She would find it, take it in her hands, and then take it to her home to bring it back to health.

When I get it in my hands, I'll examine its wings to learn what kept it floating in the sky.

She looked around. Marcosanus was still following her carefully. He would never risk being responsible if something terrible were to happen to her.

There! In front of her! The most beautiful thing she had ever seen!

Cages full of birds were piled one on top of another. Each pen had several birds in it. She saw the names beside each box, carefully written in small Greek letters: Smyrna, Thyatira, Sardis, Philadelphia, and Laodicea.

She had no idea what these names meant. She only saw many birds. The pens up higher had pigeons in them, and below them were others with smaller birds: doves. She opened the door of a cage, reached in, and held a white bird in her hands.

Her heart beat furiously. She forgot about the wounded bird she had been chasing as she put her hand over a white dove. She took it tenderly.

Never before have I held a bird! The dove is so warm, its little snowy feathers so soft. The moment was precious. She had watched birds for so long in the marsh, and now she had one in her hands!

Florbella touched its head and watched it turn from one side to the other. Then she froze. Someone was standing behind her.

Miriam looked at the little girl who had come to the birds, who had reached in to take a dove to hold. She came just at feeding time for the birds this morning.

"Hail! Hello, little girl," Miriam said slowly.

Silence! Apparently the child was fearful.

73

Miriam examined the beautiful linen tunic she wore. She probably hadn't come here to steal. From her clothing, she came from a wealthy home. Perhaps she was lost.

"My name is Miriam. Do you like birds?"

The child beamed, putting her cheek to the head of the dove. Her loving action was her response. She obviously felt elated, enthralled to be able to hold a dove this close.

"Do you like birds?" Miriam asked again.

Florbella didn't raise her eyes.

Maybe she is a child who wandered away from the city.

"Come with me to our house. Bring the bird with you. Do you want something to eat?"

Holding her treasure to her chest, Florbella followed Miriam into the little village.

Miriam took Florbella to her house, and the child sat on one of the couches. Miriam served fresh milk, hot bread, goat cheese, and honey. Florbella simply looked at the bird and stroked it lovingly.

Miriam didn't know what to say, so she watched the child eat. After a while, some young people from some of the thirty-six houses in Antipas's village came to practice their music.

Music flowed from flutes, tambourines, and cymbals. An older boy played a small drum. It was thin, with a big, round, flat surface, and made a loud sound. Miriam looked at Florbella. The smiling girl's tears fell on the little bird's head.

Florbella wiped the tears off as something stirred inside of her, something she had not felt for a long time. She felt peace and a warmth that she hadn't felt since...since that awful day at the seashore.

She went to Miriam, putting the dove into the hands of the young woman. They went to the bird cages, and Miriam carefully placed the bird inside a pen. Then they returned to the group of lively young people. Florbella listened to them for a long time.

Suddenly Florbella thought of her mother. She wanted to stay longer, but the sun was high in the sky, and she should have been home many hours ago! She looked at Miriam's face and knew that she could love this young woman.

Miriam is her name! She's so beautiful. Could I be her little sister?

She would remember that name and the birds. She knew she would come back. She liked the sound of the woman's name.

Miriam, you will be my new friend. I love the way you sing songs.

"Come back to us again," said Miriam, taking hold of Florbella's hand. "We sing every Wednesday at this time. Come again and hold the little bird in your hands if you want.

"Count four more days, and then it will be Sunday, and you can come then also. Every Sunday, we meet very early in the morning, just before the sun comes over the hills. Do you want to hold a dove again? Do you want to hear the songs again? Can you help us to sing them?"

Each question was answered with an affirmative nod.

It had been a long time since Florbella had felt such a sense of safety among strangers. Music did that. Yes, it was music and the little bird, safe in her hands.

Marcosanus was waiting for her at the gate. He expressed annoyance, wanting to know why she had stayed in a strange house all morning. He had waited a long time for her, and he was famished.

He had to show her the way to start back to their home, but Florbella wasn't lost for long. She walked down the hill, following the river road to the New Forum.

Not far away, she saw the hill where she lived. She was almost home, and her heart was beating very fast. Her parents did not know about the wounded bird or the music created by Miriam's friends.

ASCLEPIUS HOSPITAL

Doctor Thorello returned to Pergamum and sent a messenger saying that they could come to the hospital the following morning.

"Come, Florbella. We are going to see the doctor today."

They waited in the library until the doctor was ready for them. The room was full of light, and a white pillar stood in the center. Around the pillar, two snakes faced each other.

An assistant had explained, "Just as snakes shed their skins and are 'reborn,' patients who come here shed their illnesses. Thankfully, they all regain their health. To remind them of this, this symbol is prominently displayed in several places around the hospital grounds."

They were finally taken to a small examination room where the physician met Marcos. "I am sorry that you had to wait for my return. I thank you for your patience and for your confidence in my abilities."

"You are welcome. I love my daughter very much. She can no longer speak. My wife and I want to know if you can heal her."

Doctor Thorello looked into Florbella's ears. He said, "Can you hear me? Nod if you can hear me please."

She nodded, looking him straight in the eyes.

"She will wait in the library while I show you around the Asclepius," instructed the famous physician. "Now, tell me more about what happened to her. Was there some event that caused her to stop speaking? She appears to be very healthy."

"When an earthquake happened three years ago near Nicomedia, she was trapped under some rubble behind our house. Since then, she hasn't spoken but seems to be very healthy. She only wants to look at birds or examine small things with different colors."

"I assume that as a lawyer, you can pay for her treatment here," said the doctor, entering the outdoor treatment area.

How much will that be? Marcos wondered.

"Some people can't pay," the doctor went on. "A patient may not want to pay for their healing! So that person sits in this pit. We gradually fill it until the level of the water reaches their chin. Then they hear a voice from the mountain, a voice of the gods, demanding, 'Pay for your healing!' If people want to get well, of course they decide to pay. They always agree!"

Marcos looked around. He had heard of the not-so-subtle way that the Asclepius forced sick people to pay for their treatments, and he saw the hole in the wall of the pit where the "voice" would come out.

It's a trick. How could a voice come out of the side of the hill? They have one of their people somewhere at the end of a tube coming to the pit!

The doctor led Marcos to treatment areas scattered around the hospital grounds. "We have several kinds of therapy to help people. Plays are held here. This theater accommodates three thousand people, and by attending the plays, they learn to think new thoughts and imitate the characters in both dramas and comedies."

"And theater productions lead to healing?"

"Yes, they do. Friends and family members come as a way of encouraging them to heal. Some disturbed people respond to baths. Massages and mud treatments are always well received. Some patients tend to the beautifully maintained flower gardens and find it very comforting. Music, too, is therapeutic; some people sing in choirs during the day and in the theater in the evening."

The doctor dropped a denarius on the stage while Marcos sat on the top level. The acoustics sounded perfect. Even with the doctor speaking quietly, he could hear everything from the back row.

They went back along a colonnaded passage. Flowering plants along the sides were being cared for by patients. "We call this passageway the doorway to heaven. You're a lawyer. Do you see beauty such as this in a courtroom?"

They chuckled at the differences in their places of work.

Next they entered a long underground tunnel. Water trickled from a spring originating within the mountain and flowed down one side of the steps at the tunnel entrance, creating a running brook.

Spread out along the roof of the long tunnel, six small windows along the ceiling let in narrow shafts of sunlight. Dust particles danced in columns of light, giving an aura of mystery to the long, dark hallway.

"There is something in the sound of the water here that helps many people. Here, your daughter may be freed from whatever evil is preventing her from speaking. This is where many patients love to spend the day, especially during the hot summer weather.

"The cares of the world flee away in the presence of a gentle light blending with the magic of trickling water. As patients cool themselves, water ripples down the steps. Sitting outside the openings in the roof above, men with deep, majestic voices read the ancient poems of Greece. From the sky, as it were, comes great inspiration through the voices of the gods."

All the therapies at the hospital offered healing, but Marcos was concerned about the dark tunnel; it unnerved him. He knew that Florbella would be terrified by it.

The famous doctor led him to another section of the hospital. "This large, round room is where our most seriously ill patients come. Spices and herbs are sprinkled into small fires around the room.

"When the smoke is inhaled, the patients often see healing visions. Resonant voices speak from above, sounding like the gods. Patients call it the 'Room of Visions.' By the way, thank you for the bottle of perfume that you left. My wife will treasure it."

Marcos knew that these deep, dark caverns in the earth would only make Florbella worse. It would remind her of being trapped after the earthquake. Why should she live through all that again?

Returning to the library, he thanked the doctor for the tour and told him that he would talk to his wife about the treatments.

He led Florbella home to Marcella.

Marcella sat across from him that evening after Florbella had gone to bed. "Did it go well, my dear? Will Doctor Thorello help us?"

"I don't know how to tell you this, but I will not let her enter the Asclepius Hospital. No matter how skilled the doctor might be, I will not permit her into those dark places. The door of the Asclepius Hospital, famous for those emblems of snakes winding around the pillar, speaks of darkness. There is a tunnel with pleasing sounds, the rhythm of running water, but it might make Florbella worse. She doesn't need any of the therapies offered there."

"Is there another way?"

He mused. "I have that third bottle of perfume. Tomorrow I'll take Florbella to the Altar of Zeus. On second thought, I've seen the stone statues around the base. The images of Zeus fighting all the beasts from the underworld might frighten her.

"No, I won't take her with me. I'll go alone. I'll wait until everyone else has left—no one needs to know of our family tragedy. I'll talk to Lydia-Naq, the high priestess. I'll give her the third bottle of perfume. What more will she require to bring health to Florbella?"

Chapter 10
Lydia-Naq and Diotrephes

LYDIA-NAQ'S HOUSE, LIBRARY OF PERGAMUM, ACROPOLIS

Lydia-Naq Milon, high priestess of the Altar of Zeus, was being prepared to look perfect, as always. Today was one of the most auspicious days in the whole year. Individual sacrifices offered today would give exceptional powers to a person providing the animal; spring was here at last. No longer would people have to endure cold nights.

Her personal slave was making comments about her as she prepared her mistress for the day.

"Lydia-Naq, your eyes immediately command attention. You usually have black lines painted around them, but today your eyelids will be tinted with a bluish color."

Another slave shaped her long black hair. "High priestess, I'm combing it out and brushing it until it shines. Sprigs of fresh green leaves will be woven into your hair. I know how much you love to reflect eternal fertility. The festival is your opportunity to talk about the never-ending potential of rejuvenation."

The first slave asked, "What is the most beautiful thing about Lydia-Naq? Is it the lines of her face, her expressive lips, her luxurious hair, or the womanly silhouette of her figure?"

Lydia-Naq encouraged such speculation. She enjoyed the admiration it brought her.

During Lydia-Naq's morning preparations, another slave brought her a written message from the home of Hermes, the chief librarian, concerning his failing health.

She rushed to share this news with her brother. The distance from her house to the library was far enough to work out fully what she wanted to say to him.

She entered the Library of Pergamum through the entrance hall. It was narrow, with a very high ceiling.

Thank the gods for the circulation of air in this building. It keeps the rooms cooler during the hot summer days that are soon to come.

The priestess walked up the steps to her left to an enormous reading room, the largest of the four spaces on the upper floor. Students stood at stone podiums built into the white marble walls, their scrolls open for reading and research.

She went into the next room, where her brother was checking off lists of manuscripts ordered against those already delivered.[11]

Walking with a firm step into her brother's office, she greeted him. "Good morning, Zoticos, my brother."

She was beautiful today, dressed in a white linen tunic with multiple narrow rows of embroidery across her bosom, crossing in the middle and attached to the opposite hip. These cords outlined her gentle, feminine form.

No one would believe that she had just celebrated her fifty-first birthday or that Diotrephes, her son, was twenty-five years old.

"Well, good morning, sister," Zoticos replied, fulfilling the social requirements of the younger brother.

She saw him motion with his head, looking at the door beyond Lydia.

His lips formed the words "Don't come in now!" The young woman who was about to enter Zoticos's office wore the tunic usually associated with the Guild of the Carpenters.

Lydia-Naq turned to look as a young woman hurried away, clearly anxious not to be seen. *No, Zoticos! Another affair? And with one of the ordinary people, a girl from one of the guilds. Why don't you find a wife from a worthy family?*

"My brother, I have important news! Hermes, the chief librarian, is unable to move the right side of his body, and his speech is difficult to understand. Special sacrifices will be made on his behalf in all six acropolis temples today."

Zoticos looked at her with his mouth gaping open for a few seconds. "Well, I am very sorry to hear that. Hermes has worked for decades to restock our collection. May the gods heal him! The library is almost as large as when Marcus Antonius packed up our

---

[11] Details on this and other buildings come from the German Archaeological Society. Detailed descriptions of the library emerged during excavations. Hermes is fictional, but his role is based on archaeological evidence.

scrolls and sent them away."

Lydia-Naq closed her eyes at her brother's words. Scenes sometimes came upon her. She swayed and stood with her hands on both sides of the door to keep from falling. Dropping into a momentary trance, she saw King Attalos III of Pergamum writing a scroll, bequeathing his capital to the Romans in his will.[12] She saw fear on his face and recognized the loneliness that came from power devoid of trust.

He couldn't trust anyone in the kingdom to keep it together!

In her spell, she saw General Marcus Antonius with red feathers on his helmet and a flowing red cape. He was seated beside Queen Cleopatra, squeezing her hand. Half a dozen slaves waved ostrich feathers to cool the air around the Egyptian queen, and the scent of perfumes filled the room. The last of Pergamum's two hundred thousand books were being taken out of the building by hundreds of slaves and carried to ships close by. Many vessels had already sailed to Alexandria.

Startled by the vision she had just witnessed, she commented aloud, "They were piled in boxes and sent on ships to Egypt. For decades, the library was empty. Scholars lost their livelihood."[13]

"What did you say, my sister? Is something bothering you?" Zoticos asked, cleaning a space on his desk.

"No, I'm thinking about how the library's scrolls were given away. Such an injustice! But Hermes was appointed chief librarian, and he made it the purpose of his life to replenish the shelves. Newly copied scrolls have been collected from Greece, Italia, and other distant places, and you have been in charge of redeveloping this part of the city's resources."

"Yes," he added, "the aristocratic and merchant families of the city generously donated to pay for rare books. We are rebuilding the library. Pergamum will be famous once again, as it was in the past."

"I came to tell you that Hermes is gravely ill. I hate to give you this short notice, but I want you to be with me at all the sacrifices for him today. The officials must see you in the procession from temple to temple. My brother, we'll be going the usual route:

---

[12] When Attalos III died in 133 BC, the Kingdom of Pergamum passed into Roman hands.
[13] Marcus Antonius donated the library to Cleopatra about 30 BC.

starting at the Imperial Temple then to the Temple of Athena. From there, down through the Greek theater to the Temple of Dionysius.

"Afterward," she continued, "we descend to the Temple of Demeter, then across the road to the Sacred Square of Hera, and, finally, back up the hill for our evening sacrifice at the Altar of Zeus."

Zoticos had stopped what he was doing, listening intently because the news came as a complete shock. "Hermes is the person who has done more than anyone else to improve Pergamum's status. Fifty years ago, Pergamum began losing ground to Ephesus. Then the council appointed him as Chief Librarian, and he influenced your promotion as high priestess."[14]

Lydia-Naq nodded her agreement. "Yes, my brother. We are slowly moving back to where Pergamum should be in its importance. We will move it further soon.

"Now I must go to the Imperial Temple for the morning sacrifice to the emperor, and it will include petitions for health to return to Hermes. Today is considered auspicious for the healing of physical diseases."

She stepped out of the library and hurried to the Imperial Temple. Devotion was expressed to Domitian and had been to previous emperors since Augustus Caesar. For her and everyone else, every day began and ended with the words "Caesar is lord and god."

As she moved toward the temple, she found herself looking across the valley to the other side of the river, wrestling with an irritation.

Antipas's small but growing establishment rested on that hill, sloping down to the little road beside the river. Every year there was a new house and another building too. Smoke rose from several of the buildings.

She had heard that Antipas set a slave free each year and built a new house for them. No one else did this. Could this newcomer to Pergamum be a potential threat to their city?

---

[14] Professional assignments varied from one city to another. The length of time that a high priest or a high priestess could serve was for one year in some cities. In other cities, it was for life. For the purposes of this novel, Lydia-Naq and others serve for life.

Why am I concerned about a man I don't know? The building closest to the road must be where they make glass bottles, that one is where pottery is made, and there, charcoal for his kilns from villages up in the mountains. Sand for the glass comes from the creek flowing into the seashore village of Atarneus, halfway to the summer villas in Kisthene.[15] How many buildings will spread across that hill?

Zeus is telling me something about Antipas. I listen carefully because on this day of sacrifice for physical healings and fresh images of the past, I sense danger.

She had just been warned about the Jew, Antipas, and she would have to think about that some more.

When the morning worship of the emperors was finished, priests and priestesses reassembled for the sacrifice procession, petitioning the gods on behalf of Hermes. Zoticos was waiting, and Lydia-Naq pulled him into the parade to walk beside her.

"Zoticos, I truly love and respect Hermes. He is an old man and has labored with great dedication."

"Well, I'm always amazed at his breadth of knowledge. He asked me to buy so many scrolls! He knows ancient authors, men who wrote about magic, religion, the dark arts, and the mysteries of life."

"I don't want to see Hermes die. I need him to continue to be a mentor for you. Zoticos, think for a minute! Who else is qualified to become the next chief librarian? Hermes must get better...for a while at least."

THE ALTAR OF ZEUS, THE ACROPOLIS

That afternoon, Marcos watched the procession arriving at the long base of the Altar of Zeus. Many people stood around him, waiting for the opportunity to speak with the high priestess.

Two weeks had passed since his discouraging meeting with Dr. Thorello.

I'm feeling desperate. The most promising possibility for

---

[15] Kisthene (Ayvalik, Turkey) has long been a site for the summer holidays. Archaeological findings indicate the presence of dwellings for at least 2,300 years. Its name means 'City of Quince,' for the abundant fruit trees in the region.

83

healing my daughter is to invoke the power of the high priestess.

It was his first time to witness the entire event, so he stood and observed. Before the sacrifice ceremony began, the virgin priestesses gathered in lines on the broad steps of the impressive structure, ready to welcome the high priest and his attendants.

A cry went up from the waiting crowd, indicating that the bull being sacrificed had given up its life. Blood spurting out of the dying animal's neck was collected in a bowl. Then the high priest sprinkled it on the horns of the altar.

Lydia-Naq stood at the top of the steps while flames consumed the dedicated portions of meat. Some of the sizzling meat would be given to the priests and priestesses. The high priestess looked around, surprised at how many people had come to the sacrifice for Hermes.

The offering today will have a good effect on Hermes. May he live a little longer. Oh, surely nothing like this altar has ever been constructed before.

"Zeus is so perfect in every way." Lydia-Naq loved repeating the same simple phrase she had first heard when she was six years old. Those words had made her want to dedicate her life to this place. Those words, describing the frieze of Zeus, were repeated to all new priestesses in training.

Lydia-Naq turned from the people on the steps of the altar and walked to the edge of the cliff. She inhaled deeply and then slowly let out the air. It had been a perfect day to appeal to the father of the gods for healing Hermes!

Zeus! The flowering shrubs covering the whole hill are glorious!

As she looked over the cliff, Marcos came up to her, bowed slightly, and introduced himself. The day had passed quickly, and the sun was approaching the western horizon.

"Hail, Priestess! May I talk with you?" he asked.

She could tell he admired her bronze complexion, her intense gaze, and her dominating, beautifully formed face.

Just thinking this way, she felt more powerful. "Yes, you can always come here, especially today," she answered warmly. "I have seen you at civic events and know you are a newcomer to Pergamum helping to build up the city. I'm told you are brilliant and have a delightful sense of humor lacking in most lawyers."

"You are most gracious, Priestess. I need a miracle. Some evil spirit from beneath the earth has caused my daughter to stop speaking. In January, she turned eight. Would an offering to Zeus restore her health? You see, she was speaking until three years ago. She is intelligent, but..."

His unfinished story was enough for her to grasp the pain he felt for his little girl. "Of course. Come with me, and I shall show you the miracles and the power of Zeus."

She decided it would be best to show him the supremacy of Zeus by explaining the successive scenes of battle in the long frieze on three sides of the altar. The many scenes depicting the victories of Zeus were the pride of her life. By healing his daughter, she hoped the city lawyer would come under the Nestor's influence. She felt a thrill as she anticipated an increase in her influence.

"Honorable Marcos, have you ever heard the whole story of Zeus? Each panel tells another important part about his life story. Zeus fought giants in the underworld, but since they were too strong for him, he enlisted Athena's help, the great goddess of the Greek world.

"These stories come to us from Greece, and our Lydian heritage still shines through the craftsmanship we see in the sculptures around the altar.

"Come with me, and I'll explain the stories to you. Is that all right? Good! Here is Athena with a helmet on her head and a shield in her left hand. She is wearing a breastplate made of snakeskin, and she is seizing the hair of a young, naked winged giant. Beside Athena stands Gaia, the mother of all the giants of the earth, pleading to spare them.

"The snake on Athena's breastplate has come to life and has already poisoned a young giant. See how Nike, the goddess of victory, is pictured? She will forever fly to crown Athena with a laurel. Power and glory flow through the figures of polished and painted marble.

"The next frieze illustrates another fight. Leto, the mother of Artemis and Apollo, is holding a torch in her hands, burning the wings of a giant called Tityos. This ugly giant is a man with bird feet. Defeated, he has fallen on his back, forever immobilized."

For half an hour, Lydia-Naq explained the friezes, the prized sculptures of Pergamum.

"If you bring a suitable animal as a sacrifice, then Zeus will remove the power of the evil spirit."

"What kind of sacrifice will Zeus demand? Oh, and I thought that you might accept a bottle of perfume."

"Certainly! I'll accept your perfume as a gift. Where did you buy it? What kind is it? How valuable is it?"

"I purchased the most expensive perfume I could find. It comes from the shop close by, the one owned by the Alexandrian Jew, Antipas Ben Shelah."

A cloud passed over Lydia-Naq's face as she led him back to the entrance stairs of the altar. There, other gods commemorated the defeat of the giants.

"This is the most splendid Altar of Zeus in the world!" Words could not express Lydia-Naq's admiration. "Zeus is tender; he will certainly heal your daughter. Bring a young lamb. It must be perfect in every way. No blemishes. Only a real sacrifice will heal your daughter."

"I will bring it right away."

Marcos gave her the perfume and walked away in deep thought, speaking to himself. "Marcella will approve. A lamb will bring Florbella healing."

Early the next morning, Marcos went to the agora and spent an hour finding a suitable yearling lamb to purchase for the sacrifice. He took it to the Altar of Zeus, explaining to the priest that Lydia-Naq had prescribed the sacrifice to heal his daughter's affliction.

Afterward, he sauntered down the acropolis and considered what he had just done.

I am a practical Roman, trained in legal matters. This sacrifice to Zeus is like a contract. A lamb, purchased in the marketplace and offered to Zeus, was prescribed to deliver Florbella from her affliction. Zeus is more powerful than the spirit that robbed her of her ability to speak.

The impressive altar made that clear.

Chapter 11
Zoticos

ZOTICOS'S HOUSE, THE ACROPOLIS

The next day, Zoticos-Naq Milon held a black olive between his fingers. He was hosting his sister, Lydia-Naq, for breakfast at his house. Zoticos wore a new white linen tunic. His hair was ruffled, his forehead showing signs of distress as he complained about his scrolls.

In speaking about Zoticos or addressing him, people often used the word "Naq." Translated from the Lydian language, it meant "honored" and was a title of respect to be used outside the home. Because his sister was the high priestess, the title of honor was always used at the Altar of Zeus.

Zoticos was thrilled when she joined him for a special meal early in the morning. Zeus gave him delicacies—tasty olives! The olive tree meant everything: food for people at almost every meal and oil for cooking, lamps, soap, and medicines.

They were in one of the elaborately built houses at the top of the acropolis as Lydia-Naq Milon reclined on the couch, enjoying the meal he set before her.

"Have you finished your work at the library?" she asked.

"Well, I'm not quite through cataloging the new scrolls," he answered, now rolling a green olive around between his fingers. "Some scrolls that we ordered a year ago did not arrive on the last ships in October. Egyptians from Alexandria, the ones working on the building of the new temple, claim they have the greatest collection of knowledge. Yet these men know nothing about how most of the scrolls in Egypt were taken from Pergamum. Our scrolls taken away—that still makes my blood boil!"

A slave rushed in, "Master, there's a problem in the kitchen again!" Zoticos left the room to silence two slaves who were quarreling.

A slave brought water to Lydia-Naq. Looking out of the window of Zoticos's house, Lydia-Naq contemplated the city of Pergamum far below. Smoke rose from thousands of dirty, poorly constructed two- and three-story wooden buildings. For a moment, she set aside her position as the high priestess of Zeus. For years, her determination had been to re-establish the glory and greatness of Lydian culture. Rome was subtly destroying their heritage and memories.

Another trance fell on her, and she saw people speaking her ancient Lydian language. Awakening from the spell, she spoke to herself. *As the high priestess, I have the power to stop what Rome is doing to my people. The Library—the logical starting point for my plan. Pergamum to rise again!*

Zoticos returned, and Lydia-Naq placed her hand on his shoulder. An intense sensation rose in her heart as she suddenly visualized a scheme to achieve that goal. Her younger brother was politically in a position to carry out many of her wishes for the city's future.

"Zoticos, I have been thinking about some critical outcomes for the future of our city. This has occupied me for a long time! You and I can change the future and return our city to the roots of the Lydian language."

Her eyes shone with the excitement of passion. "Remember our family history! Only a few families stood up against King Attalos III, who stupidly donated our city to Rome. His action caused public dismay, and then the riots started. The Roman Army intervened. People died, but many families, including ours, never accepted his written will.

"The empire may have stamped out the people of Bithynia and conquered them, but we know, deep in our hearts, that we Lydians are superior to Rome. They build roads, buildings, and aqueducts but crush the customs of our fathers."

Zoticos looked at his sister with a face showing some bewilderment. She realized he was not relating to her concern.

Why can't my brother see it's not about accumulating more scrolls? Can't he understand the connection between what he does as a librarian and how he could help restore Lydian pride within the Roman world?

Zoticos went to his couch and reclined. He nibbled a brown, dried fig. "Well, what do you suggest?"

Lydia-Naq knew she could lead him to a destiny far more significant than anything he could achieve himself. He was perfectly positioned to restore the Lydian language to the people, to move Rome aside slightly, and to inspire appreciation of the strength of their past. Her younger brother was ideally situated for the task—except for his two weak points: his love of scholarship for its own sake and his attraction to beautiful young women.

"This province has become too Roman. As a librarian, you have a task!" She paused and drew a deep breath. "A more nationalistic spirit is needed. We will not do anything illegal and will not risk the wrath of Emperor Domitian. That would only bring us disaster. We must not be seen as trying to oppose Rome at all. Look how Domitian has elevated the importance of Ephesus with the new Imperial Temple to be dedicated there!"

Domitian increasingly takes powers into his hands. The Senate in Rome doesn't agree with his actions. Many senators are complaining about their loss of influence. Despite this, the emperor demands everything his way—the games, public spectacles, and the size of his new palace.

She picked up another dried fig. "How can you use your present position? Administrator of New Acquisitions means you are the ideal person to become the chief librarian. Hermes is about to retire. Many others want his job, but I have the power to see that you are the one selected. We must cause people to thirst for their roots again, to revive their love of Greek tragedies, Greek thought, and Lydian superiority."

Her words were a command. Zoticos sat up straight, and a new light appeared in his eyes.

She knew he understood. General Marcus Antonius had donated Pergamum's library as a gift to Cleopatra many decades before. Lydia-Naq wanted a library full of scrolls again; she also longed to hear their mother's language spoken more often.

Greek and Latin had pushed the lesser-known languages aside until only a few could speak the ancient words handed down from the Lydian people of long ago.

"Zoticos, I'm planning special events for the Festival of Zeus in April."

I see that I have your full attention. Good. Enough for today. Firstly, you will develop a new group of students. They will be able to teach the Lydian language and history to others, spreading our influence far and wide. Our culture must not die out. Men and women trained by you will teach our language to a younger generation. Secondly, find a beautiful young woman, and begin your own family. You are a butterfly, flitting from one flower to another. May Zeus help you!

Lydia had several tasks before her: to help her brother and her son to extend their family traditions over this city and other places.

For her son Diotrephes, she wanted to lead him to the best position possible.

And for her brother Zoticos, she prayed for a wife.

I can then lead both Diotrephes and Zoticos to restore the pride of the Lydian people in this province.

LYDIA-NAQ'S HOME, THE ACROPOLIS

Later that same morning, Lydia-Naq stood on her small balcony, dwelling on her inner thoughts. Far below, the city was alive as people filled the streets. The city throbbed as thousands of people went about their day's work.

On either side of the main avenues were two- and three-story apartment buildings called *insulae*, or "islands," of the poor. A family would usually rent one of the crowded, dirty *cenaculi*, or apartments, for shelter in the city. Steps on the outside took people up to the second and third stories. There were no toilets inside and no running water. Garbage littered the streets.

Many people there were day workers, free citizens with no guarantee of a job. Insulae owners rented out cenaculi at exorbitant prices. They demanded prompt payment and threw people onto the street ruthlessly if they missed paying their rent. A family would even go into debt to not be evicted since empty apartments were difficult to find.

Lydia-Naq took in the scene below her, feeling genuine pity for the people. Few remembered the language of her ancestors, the beautiful, poetic expressions of the Lydian Kingdom. She was going to do something about it, and today she had brought her brother, Zoticos, into her plan.

Our culture has been forgotten. I will work to restore our language and our customs!

THE GYMNASIUM, THE ACROPOLIS (ELEMENTARY AND HIGH SCHOOL)

The sun had been up for an hour the next day when Lydia-

Naq prepared to leave her house high on the acropolis. She tucked her *stola* around her, securing her long outer garment with a metal clasp at the shoulder. She held a dozen freshly picked white, red, and yellow flowers in her left hand. Her face glowed. Gold and silver threads had been laced through her abundant black hair. Satisfied that her slave had done her hair perfectly this morning, Lydia-Naq opened the door and stepped into the warm morning.

This time of year, many shop owners brought extra gifts to the Altar of Zeus, and each day more sheep were offered to Zeus, the father of the gods. The early flowers around the city and across the valleys announced the beginning of spring.

Lydia-Naq climbed the path leading to the altar. She looked past the Greek Theater, observing the three most prominent homes built along the cliff. Lydia-Naq shared a deep friendship with the three aristocratic families living there. They gave her much support and confidence. Like each of them, she longed to restore the city to its rightful position in the world.

Those three families are the true Lydians! But so much is changing! Why is Rome sucking out their life? Our people no longer know their history because it is not being taught to the children. I must be cautious. That will require confronting Rome without risking my position—or my son's life.

Atys Tantalus and his outspoken wife, Omphale, lived in one of the houses. They were known as one of the most powerful families in the city. Still young and building up wealth by using their fortune and fame, they lived in the house closest to the little cliff. Below a steep embankment was the impressive Greek Theater. Omphale, a large-chested woman with rounded shoulders, always had a smile on her face. She was happy for her rambunctious five-year-old twins, Eumen and Attalay.

Atydos Lydus and his wife, Apolliana, the second family, were parents of a small clan, and she enjoyed spending time with their children, who were now grown. Apolliana, now the grandmother of fifteen busy grandchildren, complained of constant aches and pains in her hands and feet.

Manes Tmolus, the patriarch of the third family, was clearly the accepted leader of the city council, where crucial decisions were made. His wife, the slim, beautiful Clytemnestra, like Manes, was a descendent of one of the three original families of

Pergamum

These three families represent an unbroken Lydian tradition, going back over eight hundred years to kings who ruled in the region before the Lydian Kingdom had become a reality.

She looked below at the huge Greek Theater. It filled the gentle curve around the cliff at the top of the acropolis. It was the steepest theater ever built, and its design left her breathless. She admired the engineers who had shaped that section of the cliff on the west side of the acropolis. Often she stood watching all ten thousand seats fill before well-known actors performed famous plays.

Together with the other symbols of power and tradition, this place of entertainment is the pride of ancient Pergamum.

Lydia-Naq Milon picked up her pace toward the Altar of Zeus as a small crowd of people pressed on her, each imploring her with their individual needs. Escaping from the mass of people, she quickly climbed the twenty-seven massive, broad steps to the top of the altar. Her many prayers to Zeus were uttered earnestly because of so many sad situations. Many people had suffered illnesses during the long, cold winter.

Hear my plea, Zeus, the god of gods. I urge you to open your heart to these people. I am Lydia-Naq, the neck on which the head of the Altar of Zeus turns.

She smiled, remembering the first time she had heard subtle compliments from younger priestesses. Those comments hinted at her ability to make the high priest of Zeus bend to her will.

After Lydia-Naq completed her morning prayers, she returned to the front steps of the altar, where she found Nestor, the high priest, just arriving. She carefully and slowly explained to him that "they" needed to plan an even greater festival this year. He immediately approved the idea since it would bring more people—and sacrifices—to the temple. He suggested that she take care of the details and that he would approve them.

Nestor was old now; he was becoming physically weaker and less interested in taking care of the stressful day-to-day decisions. He relied more and more on the skills of the high priestess.

Her son, Diotrephes Milon, lectured at the gymnasium, and she had arranged to drop in and see him this morning. He was waiting for her at the central doorway.

Seeing him here, where he worked, she stopped in mid-stride. He was the most handsome young man! His body was like that of Zeus for his broad shoulders narrowed down to a slender waist. His loved to show off his stomach muscles, and his legs were those of an athlete. But it was his face that she prized.

When he was a baby and she was nursing him, she loved looking down into his dark brown eyes. When he spoke he captivated all his listeners.

"How are the students in philosophy and Greek?" she asked.

"Oh, you know how students are, Mother! They complain when memorizing long speeches; afterward, they are proud of having done it." His eyes shone with pride.

Looking around to ensure that no one else could hear them, she said, "I need to talk with you about something important, my son."

"What is it, Mother?" he asked, giving her his full attention.

"I will make a special sacrifice for you at the beginning of the Festival of Zeus on April 15. I will pour an oblation of fine wine to the goddess of fortune. You are important to my plans for the future of our city."

"What plans? I thought teaching was what you wanted me to do."

"Your teaching position works very nicely into the first part of our plan."

"I care very much for my people. Ours is one of the few ancient families left here. How many other families are pure and completely connected to the past? Our family witnessed the Golden Age of the Kingdom of Sardis and later, the rise of the Kingdom of Pergamum. We witnessed the defeat of the Galatian Tolisgot tribe and then the Tektosages tribe. Both times the odds were completely against our much smaller army.[16] In Sardis, many men in our family died in the last battle against the great Syrian king, Antiochus Hierx. But what do those ancient victories have to do with me now?"

"For the sake of our people, the old ways must come back, and we are to be part of making it happen. I dream of the rebirth of

---

[16] Attalos I (ruled from 241–197 BC) was the first great king of Pergamum. He defeated three armies of Galatian tribes in Anatolia (today's Turkey) and was given the name Soter, or "Savior."

the Lydian language. I see you as a teacher to help organize the reestablishment of our Lydian heritage. I want you to be one of those who will be remembered with honor for this achievement."

"Mother, new ways are coming, and they will crowd out the past. I was buying a tunic in the lower agora. I noticed people around here from everywhere—from the lands far to the north, from Syria in the east, and from Egypt in the south. People are still talking about that old man, the Jew, from Alexandria. He's the one who recently died.

"How does anyone live to the age of eighty-six if not through the pleasure of the gods? Yet the old man didn't sacrifice to Zeus or pour out oblations! They say he worshiped the God of the Jews and was hardly sick a day in his life. He survived the fires of Alexandria and the destruction of Jerusalem. He came here to extend his family enterprise."

She tossed off his opinions. "Oh, these little groups! They pose no problem to us. You'll see; their gods complement ours. They have different names but almost the same concept. Egyptians are helping to construct the New Temple at the base of the acropolis. There, gods and goddesses of all the lands will be exalted.

"They originally wanted their gods to be in a separate area of the temple, but that would not work well. Of course, the greatest place of worship is the Altar of Zeus. Our own King Eumenes II built it![17] Now, Diotrephes, Zeus, whose being lives within your name, requires something from you for which he will return great honors to you."

---

[17] Eumenes II (ruled from 197–159 BC) supported poets, artists, historians, and philosophers. Mathematics, literature, astronomy, mechanics, shipbuilding, and architecture reached their golden age during these years. Attalos II (ruled from 159–138 BC) constructed important buildings of Pergamum during his forty-three-year rule, including the library. He brought artists, musicians, scientists, philosophers, sculptors, and writers to the city.

Chapter12
Diodorus

DIODORUS PASPAROS'S HOME, THE ACROPOLIS

Diodorus Pasparos had finished his classes at the gymnasium and was about to leave for his noon meal and then the hot baths. The Pasparos's home was one of the largest on the acropolis, gradually enlarged by each succeeding generation.

For decades the Pasparos family influenced the education of boys in the ways of both Greece and Rome. The first director of the gymnasium possessed an ability to teach and had built a modest home, occupying a small flat area. It was immediately below the Odeon building, where the city council convened.

Over the next four generations, the family had purchased adjacent dwellings. The mansion was noted for its ornate floor mosaics and its expensive furniture. The walls were composed of colorful inlaid marble of many colors.[18]

For Lydia-Naq's plans to save Pergamum from completely submitting to Roman cultural domination to succeed, she needed the help of several others. The headmaster of the gymnasium would be the most difficult person to get onto her side. She frowned because he had previously expressed strong opinions against bringing back old languages.

Spring was now officially here, and Lydia-Naq inhaled deeply as she walked quickly down the steep steps of the acropolis toward Diodorus's home just above the gymnasium. Oleander bushes bloomed in blazing hues of bright pink, light red, dark red, and white.

Diodorus was on his way out when she arrived. Lydia-Naq bent her head back and smiled up at him. Ordinary people enjoyed describing him: "He's the tallest man in the city, and he has the lowest voice." His deep voice had a rumble that both set students at ease when he was happy and petrified them when he was irritated.

---

[18] A bust of Diodorus Pasparos is on display in the Museum of Pergamum. The fourth-generation headmaster in this story is fictional, and Diodorus owning this house on the Acropolis is conjecture.

Lydia-Naq knew of his unending love of literature and law. After all, he was usually the one on stage to introduce a new play or to sing when a Greek chorus needed a deep male voice.

He ushered Lydia-Naq into the highly decorated room and let her remain standing. "I am already on my way out."

She looked down at the mosaic floor. The mosaics on the floor, like everything else in his house, met the standard of perfection.

"I won't keep you long. I want to know if next October you can add the Lydian language to your curriculum."

However, Diodorus Pasparos would not support her ideas. "Rome united the whole world under its shadow," he declared tartly. "Will a Roman province ever be allowed to return to its own unique traditions? Do you want special privileges only for Pergamum and ancient Lydian culture? No! The present glory of the world is found in the City of Seven Hills. We teach the young men who will then teach the next generation."

"But, Diodorus, don't you demand perfection in everything? Could you not add another language as a class and thus perfect the students' knowledge of our past?"

"My instruction follows the philosophy of Cicero. Among the great writers of Rome, he stands head and shoulders above everyone. Look at how the empire offers impressive advantages to the world in health, agriculture, and navigation; exports and imports; the construction of buildings, roads, and aqueducts; and irrigation and mining.

"Emperors unite the world, but you want to revive a minor kingdom! Forget about that tiny kingdom, the civilization of the Lydians! Listen to the wisdom of Cicero, who wrote, 'True glory is to be found in the development of the affections, in confidence and admiration. True glory is the unspoiled character of an honest man.' This is what I teach and..."

"So you don't want your students to know about our past?"

"If you come to my classes for the sixteen-year-old boys, you will hear us teaching. Cicero's duties of public office include maintaining the rights of property, abstaining from excessive taxation, ensuring everyone the abundance of the necessities of life, and being above the suspicion of greed. But most of all, tolerate no corruption!

"My purpose, motivating everything that I do, is to prepare

my students to be the best citizens possible in Asia Minor. By following the teaching of our most influential thinkers, I try to raise a generation of young men who will return Pergamum to her position as 'Queen of the Aegean Sea.'

"I want them to be the most perfect young men in Asia Minor. This is my purpose, and it reflects my values. Now, forgive me, but I must go to my noon meal and the hot baths. I am already late."

She clenched her jaw for he had cut her off before she had adequately expressed her vision. But Lydia-Naq would not be defeated even by Diodorus quoting Cicero. "I thank you for the time you have given to me in your home, Diodorus."

Debating ideas that pitted her against Diodorus's pro-Roman thoughts would not be useful. Lydia-Naq would not argue with him, because she needed him on her side.

As she prepared to leave his house, she noticed the many mosaics on the floor of his great room. One of the sixteen figures, in particular, caught her attention. It was a grotesque mask worn by actors on the stage.

Antipas, that mysterious African Jew... What if Antipas is like an actor on stage? Could he be wearing a mask? Has he come to our city for a secret evil purpose? If so, I will discover that evil and exploit it against him. Diodorus introduces Greek tragedies in the theater. Tragic plays reveal the secret lives of even the strongest men. O mighty Zeus, thank you for again showing me the path forward. The visit to this house has given me a plan.

Climbing the acropolis back to her house, she considered that now her only plan to begin teaching the Lydian language was through Zoticos and the library. Officially teaching through the gymnasium would have been much more efficient, yet on her other important concern, she was confident that she would find a way to bring Diodorus to agree with her on a common enemy: Antipas.

Chapter 13
Antipas's Perfumes

ANTIPAS'S VILLAGE, PERGAMUM

Antipas read slowly to the small group of four scribes who were writing out a passage from Hosea. He was having new copies prepared for his workers situated in several new stores along the Aegean Sea. Reading each phrase and carefully repeating four or five words at a time, the younger men wrote on new scrolls. They copied each phrase onto the long scrolls of papyrus.

"After she had weaned Lo-Ruhamah...Gomer had another son. Then the Lord said...'Call him "Lo-Ammi"...for you are not my people...and I am not your God.'"[19]

One of the young scribes put down his quill and stopped writing. "Could you explain this story, Antipas? Why did Hosea marry a prostitute? Why would God say that this story is like that of his people?"

Antipas paused. This happened so often. He would be dictating and then have to begin teaching. "Hosea took his unfaithful wife back," he began, "to teach the great lesson of God's loving-kindness. Although the Israelites had prostituted themselves to other gods, God predicted that they would multiply and prosper. One name, 'Not my people,' would be transformed into another name, 'You are my people, and I will be your God.'"

He knew he would get many more questions. This was a moment for teaching, and there would be no more copying of the text. "Let me explain what mercy is," he began.

Later Antipas stood beside the birdcages deep in thought. He was used to building a new house in the village each year, and the latest one was occupied by the two cripples. He knew their names

---

[19] Hosea 1:8–9

now: Ateas and Arpoxa.

After placing grain in the pigeon cages, he stooped to the lower level to open the dove cages. The shadows of the late afternoon were lengthening. The day was almost over. A little hand was there beside his, and he looked over and saw a little girl who seemed to be unafraid.

"Hello, little girl," he said. "What's your name?"

Something about the way the girl held her head reminded him of Tamara, his daughter, when she was about the same age. Like Tamara, she obviously loved birds.

She gave no answer, but the young girl reached into the cage, taking a white dove in her hands. Antipas waited, not sure what to do. Florbella looked up into his face. She held the dove close to her chest, smiling at him, obviously feeling safe and confident with this old man.

Antipas remembered Miriam speaking about a little girl coming to the birdcages. She came two or three times a week and didn't say a word but enjoyed the music rehearsals in their house.

Miriam told Antipas that the little girl had a slave who was looking out for her. He looked around. Sure enough, a young man watched from the entrance gate. The little girl showed no intention of putting the bird back.

Should I ask her to put it back or not?

Antipas had completed what he came to do, and it was time to leave. "My family and I will be going down to a gathering of the people. There will be singing and music. Do you want to come with us?"

The little girl looked at the sky for a few seconds, judging the time of day before enthusiastically nodding yes.

The day was ending, and it was time to go to the cave. Antipas checked his pouch, feeling the notes of what he wanted to say while leading the Erev Pesach celebration, the eve of the annual Festival of Passover.

He walked down the hill with Florbella following close behind, gently clutching the white dove. People were already gathering at the elongated room built against the side of the rock cliff with the lower eastern end facing the river.

Although it was a shed, it was long, dark, and narrow and looked like a cave once inside. Opposite the cliffside was a wall built of red-colored bricks with a door where people quietly came in. Open windows let in the remaining light of the afternoon and provided ventilation.

The cave served two purposes. People frequently gathered for services and to talk with one another during the week.

Before it was enlarged, it was only used for drying bricks and pottery. Slow, even drying was needed for pottery before being fired in the kilns. At the lower end, several pieces of pottery lined the shelves, airdrying after coming from the potters' wheels. Steps followed the incline of the hill and connected the cave to the potters' house slightly below it. The potters' house was large and typically had seven men forming pots, bowls, drinking cups, and other vessels. Today, the potters' wheels were silent.

Some of the people present lived in the city; the rest had homes in his little village. Antipas and Miriam lived in the large central house. Onias, his servant; Onias's wife, Abijah; and their children, Eliezar, Jarib, Aliza, Nessat, and Talia, lived right beside them.

Jews lived in fourteen of the village houses, and Gentiles occupied the other twenty-three. Seven non-Jewish families had come to work as free citizens. Usually, free citizens could not count on a guaranteed income, so they were all pleased to have a house and a job and to be working for a man like Antipas.

The thirty-eighth house in the village, the one just completed, already had the two new Scythian residents. They didn't speak much and generally stayed in their home.

Today was the eve of Passover, leading into the seven days of the Feast of Unleavened Bread. Antipas walked to the front and waited while people came in.

Carpets covered the ground so no one had to sit on the dirt. These were shaken out and rolled up for storage after each service.

Onias glanced at his wife, Abijah, and three daughters on the women's side. They had lived close to Jerusalem before those terrible days of destruction.

Abijah and her three daughters also sat with Miriam.

Nessat, the older daughter, was fifteen years old. Her name meant "miracle" because she was born prematurely, and her parents considered it a miracle that she had survived. Aliza was the most talkative. Talia was two years younger. Her name meant "dew."

100

Florbella sat next to Miriam holding the white dove. The cave was crowded this evening. Men sat to Antipas's left with women on the right, and a few Jewish men sat together at the back wearing skullcaps.

Antipas and the other Jews would celebrate their own unique event after midnight. Still, for this earlier service, all the persons in his village were invited. Many brought friends from the city.

Everyone stood for the prayers and readings.

Antipas lifted his prayer shawl and uttered the words precious to his people for countless generations: "Hear, O Israel! The Lord our God, the Lord is one. Love the Lord your God with all your heart and with all your soul and with all your strength."[20] He never tired of the ageless revelation of the covenant.

A young man came to the front and chanted a psalm. Two young people in the front row played a small cymbal and a tambourine. Others played a harp and a drum. Florbella waved to the musicians who had been in Miriam's house. People stood to sing, and Florbella beamed, swaying to the music.

A large scroll was taken from the back and reverently brought to the front. Two men held the scroll while Antipas stood between them to read from the book of Exodus. The passage recalled the ten plagues and safety as the Jews left Egypt. When he finished reading the selection in Hebrew, he gave a translation of the reading in Greek. He suggested that the freeing of slaves from Egypt should be retold in each household, with each father teaching his children.

Antipas talked of sheep, the meat served at the Passover meal, and about special unleavened bread.

Florbella didn't understand many things but felt safe so close to Miriam. Another lady sat next to them, and Florbella felt warm and secure between the two adults. Antipas completed his message and led another song. Florbella heard one word repeatedly: Yeshua. She could see by the dimming sunlight at the window that it was time to return home. Handing the dove back to Miriam, she gave her a hug and ran out. Her slave had been waiting anxiously, not too far from the door. Fear kept him from entering the cave.

---

[20] Deuteronomy 6:4

ANTIPAS'S VILLAGE, PERGAMUM

Of all the people living in Antipas's village, three Greek widows and three Jewish widows took the most time and care. Rising early, as was his custom, Antipas had left his home and climbed the hill behind his house.

Standing near the birdcages where he kept the pigeons and doves, he raised his hands toward the heavens, praying for each of the widows one by one. Today his intercession had been mostly for the three Jewish women.

He then put out feed and water for the birds and returned home to pick up a delivery to take to the city. Antipas carried the small sack with great care. Inside were his most expensive perfumes, and they would be sold in the Upper Agora shop. His less costly perfumes were delivered to the Lower Agora. Each delicate, individually crafted glass bottle was wrapped with wet leaves from the vineyards, kept moist to protect the glass during transport.

This set of forty-three new bottles was green-gray in color. Each bottle was made with a carefully fitted sealing stopper held in place with a linen cord secured with sealing wax pressed with the Ben Shelah mark. This prevented leakage and assured the buyer that the bottle had not been tampered with.

This was a weekly event. In addition to stocking the shelves, Antipas needed to talk to the three Jewish widows, Sheva, Damaris, and Chavvah, who tended the Upper Agora store. He always gave them wages on time, and his presence greatly encouraged them.

Sheva, one of the first two widows living on his property, was forty-five years old, and she was an excellent promoter of Antipas's products. She became a widow in Jerusalem during the siege. Her husband had been one of the priests pleading for surrender, but other priests had refused to talk with the Romans. He died after a brief illness.

Their five children, weak from hunger before they came to the city, died from starvation. She left Jerusalem with Antipas when his family fled, their hearts beating fast, panic in their eyes, and reduced to skin and bones. Later they arrived in Antioch together. When Antipas and his family left for Pergamum, Sheva stayed in Antioch but became lonely and depressed. A year passed before Antipas invited her to join the Ben Shelah family in Pergamum.

Damaris, forty-three years old, was short and slightly plump. Her rare memory for names impressed customers at Antipas's shop. She had been a widow for twenty-three years. Her husband had been an innocent bystander, killed during one of the first attacks on the Roman garrison in Caesarea by the Jewish Zealots.[21]

Ethnic antagonism grew, especially after Jews who were building a synagogue accidentally constructed on land owned by a Greek. He refused to sell the property to the synagogue leaders, even though they offered to overpay its value several times.

The conflict turned malicious when another Greek man, in an offensive jest, offered a bird as a pretend sacrifice, placing it on an upside-down earthen vessel next to the Caesarea synagogue. It was taken as an insult as Jews that had been healed of leprosy would often bring a bird as a sacrifice after healing took place. The congregation was enraged, understanding the action to have been a racial insult.

"Are they saying that we are lepers?" one man yelled.

The bird-sacrifice insult drew the anger of the younger Jews, and riots broke out. Zealots had helped to stoke the explosive atmosphere, and at the first sign of trouble, they were ready to attack. They assaulted the Roman guards that had gone to the synagogue to stop the rioting. Damaris's husband, hearing the confusion, ran to the building, and a Roman soldier, mistaking him for one of the Zealots, killed him close to the front door.

The Zealots, believing God was going to give them an instant victory, attacked the city garrison. Commander Florus immediately took extreme measures and ordered the soldiers to attack without restraint, demanding that all Zealots be rounded up. Innocent Jews were taken into custody, some dragged out of their homes and most denying their participation in the rebellion promoted by the Zealots. Florus indiscriminately punished people without a trial, and over 3,600 died that day.

Damaris was pregnant at the time of her husband's death; she lost the baby when she was thrown to the floor as soldiers searched her home. She had never held a child of her own to her

---

[21] This incident occurred in AD 66.

breast, but she enjoyed helping young mothers in Antipas's village. Sheva and Damaris came together by ship from Antioch the year after Antipas arrived. Their arrival prompted Antipas to start building houses; their home was the first built in his village. Now they sold items in his shop; he paid them a regular wage, which included housing and a community where they were accepted.

Chavvah, the most talkative of the three Jewish widows, worked a few days each week in the shop, and the other days she kept the home for the other two women. Antipas had added a room in their house at the village, so now each woman had her own bedroom. Chavvah, who was fifty-two, was only one year old when the first anti-Jewish riots occurred in Alexandria. Her profound grief came from losing her husband and six children during riots in the second pogrom. People often came to Antipas's shop just to talk with Chavvah during business hours. She loved to chat with women as a kindly grandmother and give advice.

The road into the city was crowded with people going about their work while camels, horses, and donkeys jostled for space.

Antipas crossed the newly completed bridge over the Selinos River. The river ran through the middle of the land donated by the city council for the new temple. Constructing a large temple here required a stroke of engineering genius. Useless, swampy areas on both sides of the river had been filled in, and a massive bridge had been built that would last for centuries.[22] The foundations of the temple's outer walls were being laid on top of the bridge. The foundations extended over sixty-seven Roman paces to the east and the west of the river.[23] Consequently, the ancient, small Temple of Artemis was being replaced by a vast temple where other gods and goddesses would also be recognized.

Five Egyptian men approached him, crossing the space where

---

[22] The bridge remains intact, a classic feat of engineering, so much so that few realize that the river passes below the streets and shops in Pergamum (Bergama). The Red Temple, or New Temple, was completed in the second century AD. The 200-yard-wide bridge over the Selinos River, part of the Red Temple, is still intact after 1,900 years. I placed the construction of the foundation in AD 91 and the temple completion about AD 160.

[23] Sixty-seven Roman paces were equivalent to 108 yards or 100 meters.

the foundation stones for a mammoth temple were being installed.

"Look!" called one Egyptian immigrant. "It's the man from Egypt who shames us by saying, 'The gods of Egypt are no gods at all!'"

Shouting and loud voices on the streets were a common occurrence. Still, the intensity of this outburst caught the attention of everyone around.

Fear was like a knife suddenly stabbed into his back. Antipas stopped.

What is happening here? If they attack, will my perfume bottles be broken?

Chapter 14
Anthony

PHILIPPI, PROVINCE OF MACEDONIA, GREECE

On a small farm near Philippi, a large city across the Aegean Sea from Pergamum, Anthony Suros ran his hand across his forehead and down the long red scar on the right side of his face. He looked older than his thirty-three years.

Anthony had joined thousands of soldiers that called Philippi home following years spent on battlefields. Three small documents lay before him, side by side, on a square wooden table.

Dated October 30 in the eighth year of Domitian, the first one registered the farm in his name for "significant contributions to the empire during his service in Legion XXI, the Predators."[24]

The second parchment noted a change in his army status: "January 14: Army Reservist: Assigned as instructor for recruits until the completion of twenty-five years in the army."[25]

Anthony reread the third document before placing it beside the other two. Only ten days before, he had received a new commission. It read, "February 1 in the eighth year of Domitian: Assigned to Pergamum, Province of Asia, as an instructor of scouts. Report to the commanding officer at the Garrison of Pergamum on March 15."

He opened the door of his small wooden house and looked at Philippi, two miles away.

Domitian has decided to fight King Decebalus. Again! He wants experienced legionaries to train young recruits. Scouts! But when I am instructing young men, I will not tell them my full story. Betrayal isn't supposed to happen in the army!

Dreams of revenge often returned since Anthony was attacked under that bridge. Now some of the details of the event at the long wooden bridge over the Neckar River in Upper

---

[24] The date on the first document is October 30, AD 88.
[25] The date on the second document is January 14, AD 89.

Germanica came flooding back.

He wanted to stop dwelling on revenge. He wished to spend his energy finalizing the rental of his farm while he was gone. Atticus would rent the land, and Anthony could come back next year to see how the arrangement was working out.

ROMAN HILL OF VICTORY, PHILIPPI

Later that afternoon, Anthony Suros stood on top of the historic Roman Hill of Victory, a mile to the northwest of Philippi. His horse tossed its head beside him. The rocky acropolis, a mile away to the east, stood guard high over Philippi. From this small hill, his farm to the west was easy to spot on the plain. His house was between the two tall trees.

For sixteen years, he had served as a legionary in the distant Roman province of Upper Germanica. Anthony had been severely wounded, suffered, and almost died. Few thought he would survive. "Special circumstances" was the phrase used in Rome regarding his injuries.

When the inquiries were over, he had been awarded his farm in Philippi. He slowly recovered to the point that he requested to serve as an instructor for scouts and was accepted. Now Anthony would rent the land out while he trained young recruits in Asia. If a minimum required rent for his property was returned to the garrison office, he could return when officially retired and reclaim his farm.

A mist of memories clouded his eyes. He squinted as if to push away the thoughts. In the open air, he talked to himself. "Too painful... Ever since this treachery from soldiers—of my own legion! — I can't trust anyone. I wake up in the night to that sword coming down, slicing open my face, then blackness. Two faces, I can almost remember them...but not the third person.

"I want to scream for revenge, but words don't come. A legionary does not take revenge against soldiers."

He closed his eyes, alone with his thoughts.

My sword stabbing his leg...then falling to the ground. Everything goes black. Will these memories follow me forever? Maybe my new assignment will help me to forget.

The need for revenge, to hit back at the one who had tried to kill him, grew stronger each day.

THE AGORA, PHILIPPI

Anthony walked into the room where there was a group of noisy retired soldiers at the Philippi Inn. He had come to know them well during the winter days when it was better to be inside than outside. Games occupied their hours while they ordered cheap wine and talked of war. He watched them, moody and downcast.

These retirees...twenty-five years on the front lines in Upper Germanica. Some faced fierce warriors in Britain or skirmishes with Persians. We love hearing each other's stories of war and glory. Yet I can't really enjoy them now. My mind continually returns to that attack as I try to put all the pieces back together. What was happening before I was attacked?

At the beginning of December, Anthony and Atticus had met for the first time and had talked together several times since. Atticus had been an auxiliary stationed in North Africa. He had injured his back while fixing the axle on a broken wagon. Because he could no longer work in the army, he had been discharged with a small stipend. It was not enough and would not last more than a couple of years. His wife was much younger, and they looked forward to raising a family.

Atticus had once commented, "I'm thinking of settling in Philippi. Do you know anyone who has a property I could rent? It would have to offer me something in return. I'll need to raise crops to sell." At that time, Anthony did not know he would be looking for a renter. Now that he had received orders to go to Pergamum, he hoped that Atticus was still interested.

He spotted Atticus seated alone at one of the tables in the back and wandered over to him through the crowd.

Anthony pulled out a chair at the small square table next to his friend and hailed an attendant to bring them some wine.

"Atticus, you had asked me earlier if I knew of a good farm to rent, and it turns out, I think we can help each other." Anthony explained that he now had a job as an army instructor, and he described the requirements for renting the farm. "Do you have enough money for a down payment?"

Atticus was receptive. "That is a reasonable amount, and I can afford the rest by growing crops and selling them."

Anthony was convinced the army would allow Atticus, as a retired auxiliary, to rent, but he would have to clear it with the garrison office.

The next day, Anthony received assurances from the commander that his proposal had been accepted. Atticus would deposit rent in the garrison office at the beginning of each year.

When Anthony officially retired, several years later, he could return to live on the farm. For the first time in days, the knot in his stomach unwound a little. He had just enough time to complete the rental arrangement with the army authorities before leaving for Pergamum.

MILITARY GARRISON, PERGAMUM

Anthony recorded the rental agreement for his farm, gathered his few belongings, and went to the port of Neapolis.

Hearing he was going to Pergamum, people said, "You have to attend the Greek Theater there!" He boarded a ship to cross the Aegean to Ephesus, where he registered at the Army Provincial Office before traveling by horse to Pergamum.

The Garrison of Pergamum was on a hill to the west of town. It was away from the bustling traffic of the various markets. The military occupied the area because it provided a view of the entire city. If a disturbance broke out at the acropolis, one of the temples, or any government building, guards would know right away.

Mountains to the north were covered with winter snow. To the east was the acropolis and the river valley to the south. The garrison bordered the property of the Asclepius Hospital. Its eastern boundary ran along the Sacred Avenue, which connected three essential areas of the city: the New Forum, the Roman Theater, and the hospital. On the south side, it faced the newly-built Roman villas.

As he approached the entrance gate of the garrison, he wrapped his fingers around his sword for confidence. Considering the severity of his wound, his recovery had been remarkable.

I'm an instructor. What will the young soldiers remember after my first day's lessons? Will their first impressions of the army be as clearly remembered as mine are?

He was seventeen when he joined the army, desirous of sharing in the glory of his father and his forefathers. All of them had been soldiers.

The voice of his instructor came back to him: "Scouts change the direction of a battle. They can often bring about extraordinary victories."

That first lesson was about a catastrophic event that happened decades earlier. During a battle, the Germanic tribe had gone after the general and killed him. When scouts didn't detect the Teutoburg Forest trap, three legions were annihilated in Lower Germanica. The army considered that defeat to have been Rome's greatest tragedy.

I will instruct my recruits, "Always go after the leader; the rest will fall by the wayside once the commander has been killed."

Confident in his ability to prepare scouts for battle in the distant forests of Europe, he called to the guard, "I am Anthony Suros reporting for duty." Anthony entered the large Garrison of Pergamum.

A permanent building on one side, the barracks, housed up to three hundred men. A smaller building, the training center, provided sleeping space for fifty army recruits. Between these two buildings were two others: One was the administrative building, and the second building housed the officers. All the structures were built with light-brown stones cut from a nearby mountain.

Beyond the training area, the land sloped down toward a creek, and this was used as a mock battlefield. Walls and defense towers, like those of an enemy city, lined the western part of the camp and were used for practice in offensive warfare.

Anthony was taken to the training center where he would stay while he was the instructor for the scouts. The guard said, "In half an hour, you'll be taken to the commander's office. Prepare yourself to meet Commander Cassius Flamininus Maro."

He unpacked his gear and settled into the sparsely furnished instructor's quarters with a single bed, a chair, a small square table, and a shelf above the bed.

He quickly washed off the dust from his trip, shook out his tunic, tied on his breastplate and greaves, and waxed his shield. It was oblong and convex, four feet high and two and a half feet wide, and made of lightweight wood covered with bull hide. Plates of brass covered the hide.

Over his shoulders, he wore the red sash that identified him as a scout. His short, two-edged sword hung from his waist. He didn't carry the *pilum*, the formidable javelin. Instead, he used the bow and arrows when scouting for the army.

A short time later, the guard took him to meet the commanding officer.

At the office door, a gruff voice from within bellowed, "Come in!"

The guard opened the door and gestured for Anthony to enter. He saw the commander sitting beside a table covered with maps.

'Soldier, this is your commanding officer."

The garrison commander stood up to receive his new instructor. Anthony saw a soldier who was born and bred in the East. He guessed that the bronze tan on Cassius's face spoke of endless days spent under the scorching Mesopotamian sun. His face, like others born in Zeugma, was dominated by a long nose. A streak of white hair topped a thin face. He was of medium height, but the way he stood on his feet and held himself straight upright spoke of a lifetime of disciplined military service.

"Sir, I am Anthony Suros, reporting for duty. I am the reservist ordered to train scouts for Legion XXI."

The commander looked Anthony over approvingly, but his eyes narrowed slightly at the soldier's scar. "Welcome to the garrison. Tell me your name again, soldier. Where are you from? What was your previous army term of duty?"

"My name is Anthony Suros, sir. I come from Philippi. Before that, I was deployed in the province of Upper Germanica. I carry an order to report here for the purpose of training scouts. Apparently, Domitian still wants to settle the score in Dacia."

"Looking at your face, you have seen more than your share of action. How did you get the scar?"

"It came from a wound received while on scouting duty along the Neckar River. We had word of advancing soldiers from a Germanic tribe."

Cassius spoke caustically. "You come to teach, to show young men how to be scouts. They will see your scar and will give you a nickname. They might call you 'Wounded Scout.' Probably just 'Scar.'"

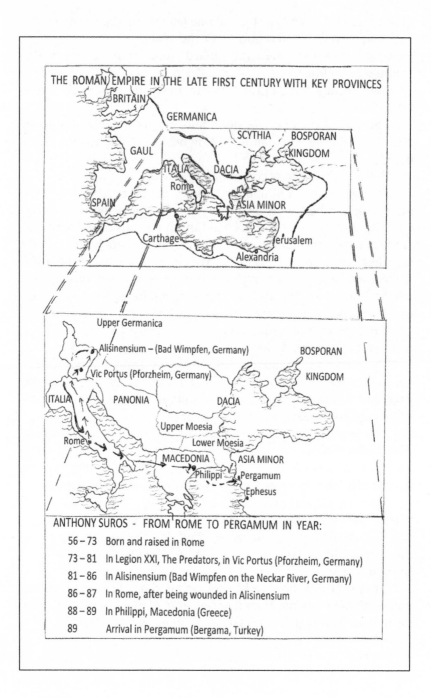

THE ROMAN EMPIRE IN THE LATE FIRST CENTURY WITH KEY PROVINCES

ANTHONY SUROS - FROM ROME TO PERGAMUM IN YEAR:

56 – 73   Born and raised in Rome

73 – 81   In Legion XXI, The Predators, in Vic Portus (Pforzheim, Germany)

81 – 86   In Alisinensium (Bad Wimpfen on the Neckar River, Germany)

86 – 87   In Rome, after being wounded in Alisinensium

88 – 89   In Philippi, Macedonia (Greece)

89   Arrival in Pergamum (Bergama, Turkey)

"The recruits may call me 'Scout with a Scar' or anything else, sir," replied Anthony quickly. "I came to train them as scouts for battle in the thick forests of Europe. I have the experience to do it well."

Anthony was dismissed without another word.

The next day, Commander Cassius assembled all the new recruits to give them his standard indoctrination speech as they started their six-month training. His voice had a cutting edge to it, and he was used to humbling new recruits.

"I am Cassius, commander of this garrison. I must see that you are turned into able soldiers of the Roman Army. You have come through the recent levy. Do you think you know how to wrestle and fight? Just wait. We will teach you much more through repetition every morning and every evening. You will practice every tactic needed for the battlefield, carrying out all the correct movements. You'll practice them endlessly until you do them automatically and in your sleep.

"You come from many little villages up the valley. You are sons of blacksmiths, millers, and farmers. Your fathers have strong arms, but we will make you stronger. You will relish the glory of traditions five hundred years old! You will learn to love discipline!

"You are being trained to subdue Dacia.[26] Tribute will eventually flow from Dacia to the empire after a grand triumphal march in Rome after we defeat King Decebalus!

"Now, that's glory! Nothing can compare to when you march past the emperor, dressed for battle. You will pull your humiliated Dacian slaves behind you. Domitian will certainly

---

[26] The war against Dacia is simplified here. Dacia occupied the area today known as Romania and Moldova and portions of Ukraine, Slovakia, Poland, Hungary, Serbia, and Bulgaria. Rome's struggle to dominate this area lasted from about AD 85 to 112. In AD 88, Commander Tettius defeated King Decebalus. A minor rebellion in the Roman military broke out, led by Lucius Antonius Saturninus on January 1, AD 89, necessitating the breakup of the combined forces under Tettius. King Decebalus used the cessation of hostilities in Dacia to regroup. Anthony's story is told bearing in mind the need for reinforcements to Legion XXI, the Predators, which Domitian sent against King Decebalus.

receive Decebalus's diadem."

Cassius's instructions were only slightly exaggerated. He intended to intimidate new recruits.

By the end of the first morning, the new soldiers were groaning with pain. They had thrown their *pila* a hundred times and drawn their wooden practice swords more times than they could count. Their arm muscles agonized at the constant exercise with the javelins.

On the second day, he shouted, "March and run, carry heavy burdens, and master offense and defense lines! The weak ones die while the strongest triumph. The only difference between our daily exercises for the next twenty years and a field of battle is blood spilled on the ground. Every day, in the rain and in the sunshine, in summer and in winter, you will practice each offensive and defensive movement. I intend to make you aware of every danger. Agility and strength, endurance and discipline— these will save your lives! Obey without question or complaint!"

The next day they marched for an hour out of the city toward the Aegean Sea and then back. One young man complained that he was almost too exhausted to continue. He learned that no excuse was permitted in the Roman army.

The garrison's commander finished the third day's instruction by telling them that they would receive thirty denarii at the end of the month. "Regular pay is yours. At the end of twenty-five years, you will receive your own land and join another Roman colony. Cowardice or disobedience will be rewarded with the severest punishment."

That evening the young men had such sore muscles that they could hardly stand.

Cassius knew how sore they would feel, so on the fourth day, he only lectured them.

"Today you will learn about the legions of Rome. You are joining Legion XXI, the Predators. Each legion is composed of ten cohorts."

He went on to describe the details of a legion, how it was organized, and how discipline was maintained. His lecture lasted the whole morning.

A week later, training became harder, much harder. Heavier-weighted training weapons were introduced into their exercises.

They engaged in long marches, groaning inwardly but refusing to complain outwardly.

RECRUIT TRAINING GROUNDS, GARRISON OF PERGAMUM

Commander Cassius had completed his lectures. Several days had passed, and Anthony was allowed to take his twenty new recruits aside. They were selected from all the recruits as experts in archery and had the skills needed to become scouts.

Anthony's wish was to instill the deepest values of the Roman army's loyalty and honor in the hearts of his new recruits.

"You will be fighting against one of the fiercest tribal groups in the north. They live in the forests. I know what I am talking about because I fought them for sixteen years. In my last year, I dropped my guard for a moment, and this scar was my reward. Now I am a reservist teaching you what I learned."

He showed them his face. The red scar touched his right eye and ended at his jaw.

"Your enemy is Decebalus, King of Dacia. You will face the fiercest barbarian fighters as well as rivers, forests, and swamps; it will not be easy to defeat him. Hills crowd you in, separating you from the other legions of Rome. You will hate those rivers: the Niester, the Tibiscus, and the Lower Danube. You will detest dark, impenetrable forests. Hate and revenge, excitement and fear—these are the emotions of war.

"I will teach you how to see things in the forests. What are the weakest points of your enemy? You will be the ears and eyes of Legion XXI. You will learn to trust your senses as never before. In battle, remember this: Eliminate their king, and you will have scattered the enemy.

"Your best arms will not be swords or arrows, although you will constantly depend on them. Your mind is your most important weapon. Protect your legion with the information you find. You will live on the front lines and may even have to give your life to save an entire fighting cohort or a regiment." He rubbed the red line on his face. "And if necessary, you will give your life under torture."

Anthony used his injury to lift the recruits' spirits, who now understood that glory included suffering a temporary defeat and coming back, ready to fight again. The scar that had brought a caustic comment from his commander had been turned to his advantage. The scouts trusted him because he knew the dangers of battle.

OFFICE OF THE GARRISON OF PERGAMUM

Marcos, the lawyer, waited for a soldier at the gate to relay his request to speak to the garrison commander. Looking at the angle of the sun, he realized he would be late for his Friday morning appointment with the city magistrate.

The soldier returned quickly and admitted him through the main gate. Cassius's office, located in the center of the complex, was a stark room. Cassius stood in front of a square desk of dark wood close to one wall.

Maps lay open on another table in front of a soldier who was talking with his commander. A long red scar marked the side of his face.

"I was told you have a request," said Cassius, addressing Marcos. "What is it?"

"Thank you for receiving me, sir. My name is Marcos Aelius Pompeius. I am Chief Counsel to the city council. Last night there was a disturbance in the city."

He looked at the maps and then continued. "Some soldiers were boisterous in the taverns. I've been requested to register a complaint. If it had been a festival night, we would understand their being so noisy, but last night was not a festival."

"We will look into this. Any disciplinary action that needs to be taken will be administered. I can tell you that those men were not regular soldiers. They are practicing warfare morning and night. The men who caused your problem are new recruits, and they had been granted a rest night at the end of their first month of training. Is there anything else?"

"No, that is all, sir," Marcos replied.

Cassius turned to the man at the map table. "Suros, see the lawyer out to the front gate."

Anthony led him out of the office building into the bright sunlight and across the military compound toward the front gate. Off to one side, young recruits faced each other in a training field. Each held a shield in his left hand and a short wooden sword in his right hand. They were not ready yet for real swords with sharp edges lest they hurt one another in their ineptitude.

The instructor was not happy with one new recruit. "Believe me when I tell you that you would be dead if you attacked like that, soldier! Stand forward on your toes, not back on your heels. You must stand on the ball of your foot. There, like that! It gives you better balance and quicker action! Now, repeat the drill again, all of you!"

"New troops in training," Anthony explained as they passed the sweaty recruits. "I came to Pergamum to teach our best men to become scouts. That instructor is right! If you're off balance, you can quickly lose your life in battle."

Marcos looked at the legionary beside him. Anthony stood out in any crowd. He was taller than average and well-built with strong shoulders. His curly black hair was a treasure that a sculptor would love to chisel in stone. However, that long red scar... Clearly this soldier had been fortunate to live after receiving that wound.

Anthony spoke again. "These men will eventually join some of the best troops in the empire in battle against Dacia. I came here from Legion XXI, the Predators. I am training legionaries since I cannot be on the front lines anymore. The scouts I train will face the greatest dangers in battle."

Marcos knew there was a long story behind this soldier's few words. Anthony took the silence as an invitation to continue. "I come from a military family of five generations. On my mother's side, we were one of the first tribes in Gaul to submit to Julius Caesar. My father's family came from Spain. Suros is our family name from Eslida, in the area of Castellon de la Plana.

"My namesake was the great commander, Marcus Antonius— no relation of course! He fought Cassius and Brutus but was defeated by his former friend, Caesar Augustus. Have you ever been to Philippi? I have land there, a small farm."

"I thought that only retired men received farms," Marcos said. As a lawyer, he had a natural curiosity about exceptions to rules.

"That is true. I was not supposed to live after I got this wound. I was removed from the Predators and given land as a wounded legionary because of special service to the empire."

"What happened?" Marcos asked.

Anthony could tell that the lawyer was becoming more interested in his story, and pride filled his voice. "Six years ago, many villages and tribes were pacified, but rebellion remained. There are two kinds of rebellion. One is that of the Upper Germanic tribes. They agree not to fight but then hide behind the trees, draw our army into wild places, and try to gain the upper hand. We have to secure the high ground and, where possible, cut down wide swaths of forest to protect ourselves."

He paused. "After I was attacked, they said I probably would not live, but I did. In Philippi, I recovered and asked to be an instructor. My land is now rented out, and here I am in Asia, training scouts."

Marcos walked back to the acropolis, wondering if he could continue the conversation another day, sensing that there was much more to learn from that soldier. "Two kinds of rebellion," Anthony had said, but he only talked about the rebellious Germanic tribes.

What is the other kind? There is more to this newcomer than appears on the surface. Is he wounded inside, just as he is outside? Pain shows in his eyes. It belies the easygoing nature he wants to project. Is Anthony talking about a political rebellion? Was he somehow connected to Celsus Ceriales, our governor, who was executed three months ago?

MILITARY TRAINING GROUNDS, THE GARRISON OF PERGAMUM

The next day Cassius walked with Anthony around the military training grounds. In the distance, the mountains at the head of the Kaikos River shone with a soft purple hue on the eastern horizon.

The military training camp had a panoramic view. The new legionaries trained a hundred times at going up and over the walls. Skills needed to burrow under walls to cause the collapse of an enemy's fortifications demanded specialized teams, men with massive muscles, thick necks, and stiff backs.

Below the garrison, to the west, a gently sloping hill was used for battle formation tactics. Recruits training to attack a city wall practiced running in a line up to a tower. As a group, they formed a "turtle," placing their shields over their heads while the men in the middle set up a battering ram. Used against a gate, this weapon could open the way into a walled city.

Cassius sat down on a large flat rock and gestured for Anthony to do the same. "Tell me more about yourself, soldier."

Anthony lifted his right hand to his scar before he remembered his determination to break the unconscious habit. He had started stroking his wound during the months when his life hung in the balance.

Soldiers loved to talk about their exploits, but Anthony would not talk about how he was almost killed. Not today and perhaps never. That betrayal would stay buried.

Betrayal... It awakened him—sometimes screaming—at night and could be dangerous if the whole story became known.

"You see this scar across my face? While scouting on the east side of the Neckar River, I was attacked. I don't remember some of the details of how it happened, but members of my scouting team found me later. That's why I'm here and not buried on the battlefield."

Anthony remembered the unusual discussion he had overheard. Three officers had been planning a rebellion.

An inner voice went over the conversation he had had dozens of times. "Two tribunes and...who else? The third one...I could never remember his name when giving my report in Rome. They were making comments about political matters, huddled over a table at the evening meal. I reported them to the general. And then...enemy soldiers were reported close to the bridge where the Neckar River flows past the village of Alisinensium.[27] I was assigned to investigate with a new team. I turned just in time to catch a glimpse of my attacker, poised to strike. A short sword—a Roman soldier, not a barbarian fighter. Twisted my head... My flesh cut... Falling... I struck at my attacker's leg with my sword, and everything went blank. My memory fails me. I cannot tell Cassius those details. Treachery within my ranks... I'll never see those officers again."

After a slight pause in the conversation, he observed, "Commander Cassius, my role is to prepare soldiers. They will fight in the forests of Europe where the battlefields and the enemies are very different than here."

"Warfare is different in Upper Germanica from that in the East?"

---

[27] Vic Portus, or Pforzheim, a town to the southwest, was taken two years before, and this victory led the army to open up the region as far as the Neckar River. The village of Alisinensium is known today as Bad Wimpfen and is on the Neckar River in southwest Germany. The Roman army constructed a bridge there about AD 83.

"I will tell you a few stories about fighting in forests when we have our next meal together, sir. We pacified Vic Portus and built a road to the new outpost of Alisinensium. The victory at Vic Portus, a hub for Germanic tribal power, was crucial. It opened a large section between the Rhine River and the Neckar River. Alisinensium has become an important village, one of the few places where a bridge crosses the Neckar."

Cassius was an expert in the wars against the Persians. Keeping fighters from the eastern region between the Tigris and the Euphrates Rivers was his area of expertise.

Anthony wondered: *What does my commander know of European forests? He has never seen one, much less fought in one. The soldiers being trained by Cassius to fight the Dacian king will face disaster unless they know how to confront enemies hidden in the dark forests instead of on an open plain.*

FORESTED TRAINING AREA, GARRISON OF PERGAMUM

Sunday evening was a different kind of celebration for the recruits assigned to Anthony. The elite group being trained as scouts sat in a circle around a fire. One man kicked a log farther into the flames, and scores of sparks rose quickly upward with a whooshing sound.

Anthony was preparing them to fight in forests. By working together as a team, they could offset the advantages the barbarians possessed by fighting on their home soil. A new kind of pride washed over them. They perceived how discipline and knowledge resulted in their being able to take on more challenging assignments.

The recruits talked among themselves. One said, "I would not have believed how our instructor's mind works. He asked, 'What do you see?' See? We had a whole city in front of us, and all that I saw were tall walls, parapets, and gates. But Scar Face asked, 'If you were here trying to fight against this city, what would you need to tell your commander to defeat the enemy?' That's when I realized how little I knew about war."

Another soldier commented, "He told me, 'Make a map of the city; find its weakest positions! Report to me! I am your commander waiting to attack!' But I couldn't! I couldn't find a single weak position! The acropolis is high and secure, and the armory at the top commands a view in every direction. You could never break into this city."

There was a moment of silence. "I felt really foolish," said another. "He told us, 'Target the water system.' Who could have known that the city's water comes from four springs up in the mountains? I didn't realize that high-pressure stone pipes bring water across the valley on the north side of the acropolis. 'Cut off their water supply!' he demanded. 'Cut the aqueduct, and the whole city will be affected.'"

Anthony had then shown them the sources of water for the city. He led them to the aqueduct, saying, "If this were an enemy city, you could wreck its water pipes at night. That would put fear into every soldier guarding this city. By destroying the water system, you would cause chaos."[28]

One young man scowled at the comment about Anthony's scar. "We should respect him, not make jokes about his face. He deserves to simply be called 'Instructor Suros.'"

"Fair enough," said the first recruit. "Let's call our instructor by his proper name."

The warmth of the fire and the animated conversation drew them together. Anthony was not only going to teach them to use their eyes and ears but also to depend on one another for their security. They were no longer individuals brought together from various villages; he was forming them into a close-knit squad. Confidence never known before was being born. Sparks from the flames sped upward as tiny lights in the black sky, the fire exploding once more.

Anthony was going to teach them to make a battleground reconnaissance map during the next week. They knew his advice: "To be a scout, you must be both an archer and an artist!" They joked about who was the worst sketcher. Later he had promised to show them how to protect themselves as they walked through the forests in the mountains.

---

[28] Water in Pergamum came from four springs in the Pindasos Mountain range, seven to ten miles (10 to 15 km) away. Two springs were tapped from Geikli Mountain and two from the Kozak range. High-pressure pipes brought the water to the top of the acropolis. Two other canals brought water from the eastern valley.

Chapter 15
The Fear of Confrontation

THE NEW FORUM

Marcos was on his way to his law office through the New Forum at the base of the acropolis. The city council, halfway up the acropolis, was meeting today, and important decisions were to be made regarding taxation. The construction of the bridge and the foundations of the New Temple were costing more than the estimates.

Marcos saw a small man with a short, square beard. He knew his name was Antipas and that he was a Jew. This was the same man he had seen leaving the Upper Agora, the man who owned the store where he had bought perfume.

The high priest of Dionysius was loudly addressing Antipas. He stood almost as wide as he was tall, a sure sign of much over-indulgence. "We, the people of Pergamum, are building this large temple! It will bring all the gods together: Cybele, Artemis, and the gods of Syria and Egypt."

Other voices rang out, and now Antipas was surrounded by five Egyptians dressed like priests. One of them, a priest by the name of Mehu, wagged his finger at Antipas. "I am told you have no statues of your god. If you cannot see him, then he doesn't exist! In Egypt, we know what all our gods look like."

Antipas spoke softly and without malice. "No man has ever seen God. He is above the heavens, so he cannot be seen."

"Then how can you worship him?" questioned another Egyptian priest. "How do you bring him sacrifices? Maybe your sacrifices are invisible too!" he added in jest.

Hundreds of people stood close together, some pushing and shoving, each vying for a better position. The crowd loved verbal sparring.

Marcos listened attentively to everything that was said during the debate. Something about the demeanor of the short man and his knowledge of distant lands impressed him. It turned out to be an impromptu debate between the Jew and the priests for which, to his lawyer's mind, Antipas was better prepared.

ANTIPAS'S HOME, PERGAMUM

Later that evening, when Antipas and Miriam sat down to their meal, silence reigned. Miriam was still pained by Eliab's death, and she wondered what her grandfather was thinking.

"Grandpa, are you silent because of your father's death...perhaps feeling the big hole he has left in our home?"

"No, something happened today. I learned that I am afraid of conflict. Something fearful came back to me, and a chill went down my spine."

"How is that? What happened?"

"I was walking to the Upper Agora when a local priest and five Egyptian priests stopped me. They're in the city to help direct the construction of the New Temple. They confronted me loudly over the existence of their Egyptian gods."

"Will the priests cause problems later?"

"I don't know. Those Egyptian priests weren't violent, but they did put a scare in me." He looked down at his hands, deep in thought.

Egyptians...our home ablaze in Alexandria. Fire, torture, and death... I was thirteen when I first became afraid of Egyptians in Alexandria. My job now is to protect Miriam, not to get Egyptians riled up. I didn't want a public dispute—not after the weeks of attending to the funeral and my family and neglecting the work of my shops. Today was to be dedicated to managing my store in the Upper Agora.

"The priests asked why I don't believe in their gods, and I said, 'I believe in the one true God, maker of the heavens and the earth.'"

"Did that make them angry, Grandfather?"

"Yes, very angry. Mehu is the high priest, their leader. He said, 'You are wrong! There are many gods, and in the New Temple, all the gods will be worshiped.' We talked for a long time, and a great crowd gathered to hear us debate.

"I said, 'I am a Jew, and we know about the many gods of Egypt. But we Jews are different. We believe there is only one God. He is the Creator of all, the sun and the moon, the stars, and everything in the world. All living beings take life from Him.' That caused a massive stir. It's the first time that I've been accosted in public like that."

Antipas put his head in his hands. "Miriam, at first I was afraid of what might happen, but the longer I talked, giving witness to what I believe, the more I felt my spirit being strengthened. It was strange. When I was telling them the truth in public, I felt stronger."

Miriam and her grandfather paused for prayer at the end of the day. Before supper each evening, Miriam spread a special cloth on the table and placed a candle on it. Before eating, Antipas prayed. "Blessed are You, O Lord our God, King of the Universe. You have supplied us with food, family, and community. We bless your name."

Miriam told him about the little girl who was coming to their meetings. "The child never talks, but she listens intently. I think she must be mute or possibly just timid. I have seen her many times now, but I still don't know her name."

Following their evening meal, while still reclining on the couch, Antipas prayed again. He mentioned the people who lived in his village, naming them one by one. Miriam prayed silently for the nameless little girl and whatever problems her family was going through.

Antipas finished praying and wiped tears from his eyes. He often did that now in the evening. Unresolved conflicts within his little community caused concern.

He reviewed the debate at the New Forum. The additional worry of a budding conflict with Egyptian priests brought beads of sweat out on his brow.

Chapter 16
Bernice, Eumen, and Attalay

ARISTOCRATIC HOMES, THE ACROPOLIS

Bernice, who was the slave assigned to the twin boys in the Atys Tantalus family, treasured her job, although she was exhausted at the end of each day. The family was one of the three ancient aristocratic families of Pergamum. Her parents had been well educated, and Bernice was named after the goddess Nike. Bere-Nike, her name, meant "Bearer of Victory."

In Cyprus, where she grew up, Bernice had lived in a house with delicate mosaics on the floors. Her lover gave her a marvelous life before he was shipwrecked. The shock came when she learned he had lived on borrowed money, always hoping to make a quick fortune from blown glass, perfumes, and spices.

When she was sold as a slave at age twenty-four, along with everything else to pay for her lover's debts, her world collapsed.

Today while the Atys Tantalus family went to the market, Bernice was careful. She kept the twins close by at all times because she knew from experience how much trouble they could get into if they were left alone.

Wealthy families spent hours comparing the qualities and defects of their slaves. Bernice's master, Atys, appreciated the way she went about her work. He especially approved of her teaching his children the myths of Greece.

"And our boys will be victorious, as befits children named after the ancient kings of Pergamum," the wealthy man boasted to his friends.

Bernice esteemed the family's symbol, the owl. It was woven into rugs, on the family crest, and carved into the stone lintel over the front doorway. The family called themselves wise, and she felt proud to be a slave in a great home.

This Friday morning was perfect for teaching the boys,

Eumen and Attalay. Their sixth birthday was coming in two weeks, at the end of the Festival of Zeus. She wanted them to be prepared for studying at the gymnasium next September. They would know more about the gods and goddesses of ancient Greece than any other boys.

She led the twins from the main room in their house to the terrace overlooking the valley below. At the bottom of the hill was the small village of that Jew from Egypt. "Look, boys, in the distance, beyond the Roman stadium and the amphitheater, you can see dozens of people. Each one is the size of an ant. They hardly move, waiting to be seen by a physician at the Asclepius Hospital."

Eumen and Attalay were more boisterous than usual this morning. "Sit down! Both of you!" she commanded in an urgent tone. "This is a special lesson about the gods. This story is very exciting, and you can act it out. But you must promise me never to act out this story here on the terrace. Promise me?"

The boys nodded and looked sheepishly at each other.

"Once upon a time, the king of Crete was called Minos. He had many cows and horses, many animals, but he didn't have a good bull. Poseidon—do you remember what he is the god of? Yes, that's the right answer, Eumen! He is the god of the sea, and he gave a bull to King Minos. He was supposed to sacrifice the animal, but King Minos didn't want to sacrifice the bull. It was far too beautiful an animal to kill.

"He didn't think that Poseidon would see him, just like you don't believe that your father will see you when you are misbehaving. Poseidon watched and saw that King Minos was keeping the bull for himself. Poseidon punished King Minos by making the king's wife, Pasiphae, fall in love with the beast.

"Later, Pasiphae had a child. It was a strange creature, with the body of a human and the head of a bull, a fearful thing! People on Crete called it a Mino-taur, 'Minos's bull.' It made loud, scary noises, and this animal had a terrible temper. Because it was so dangerous, it had to be shut inside a room carved inside a mountain. No one could find the Minotaur because it was trapped in a tunnel with many turns and false hallways to get lost in.

"The path to where the Minotaur lived was called a labyrinth. King Minos found out that he had two bad people from Sicily working for him, Daedalus and his son Icarus. So he had them shut up in the labyrinth, believing that the Minotaur would kill them.

"However, they were so intelligent that they managed to kill the Minotaur. As they entered the mountain, they unrolled a string so they could find their way back to safety. They followed the line back to the entrance, and that's how they got out alive.

"Now, how would they get back home across the sea? They didn't want King Minos to find them again, so they made wings of feathers stuck together with wax and put them on their arms to fly like birds.

"The daddy, Daedalus, was wise, and he flew close to the water and got back to Sicily quickly.

"But the boy, Icarus, was naughty, like lots of boys. He wanted to be better than his father. He flew higher and higher, enjoying the experience of flying like a bird. Finally, he flew close to the sun. The sun was so hot it melted the wax in his wings, and he fell down into the sea and died.

"Now, do you see why you have to obey your father when he tells you not to do something dangerous? You must learn to obey!"

As always, the boys loved her stories. Dreaming of dangerous adventures, they went off into the house, pretending to fly like birds.

Bernice genuinely enjoyed their enthusiasm. The two boys could never take the place of her two baby girls, sold in the slave market at the same time she was auctioned off, but she loved children and enjoyed these two boys.

Chapter 17
The Festival of Zeus

THE ALTAR OF ZEUS, THE ACROPOLIS

Friday dawned bright and clear. An ideal day in the middle of April was obviously a gift from the gods. Lydia-Naq sat longer than usual in her bedroom, attended by her slaves. Her makeup and hair had to be perfect. Her linen tunic brought from Egypt was finished to her specifications. A pearl dangled from each ear, and a large emerald hung on a gold chain around her neck.

As one slave combed her hair then plaited it into a braid, another servant held other necklaces and several matching bracelets for her to view. A third slave washed her feet and put on her sandals, wrapping the dark brown leather straps around and up her long, shapely legs. The green laurel in her hair was topped with a delicate crown of gold. No goddess could be more beautiful.

Satisfied that everything was complete, she left her home and started walking to the Upper Agora. She arrived shortly before the first procession of the festival was to begin and moved to the head of the column. Looking behind her, Lydia-Naq examined the dozen virgin priestesses and the new priestesses-in-training behind them.

Nestor, the high priest, dressed in a new bright red toga with yellow stripes, was about to begin the procession. The entire column formed within the limited space of the Upper Agora.

Lydia-Naq never tired of the powerful emotions she felt when the festival procession started each year. Sensations of pride washed over her as the cymbals, harps, drums, tambourines, flutes, and cheers grew louder and louder.

The high priest led the procession, and this year's festival was underway. Winter snows had melted, and crops had been planted. Wildflowers covered the hillsides. Zeus and the other gods would surely bring am abundant harvest.

Behind the priests came men who served Zeus, leading the

animal sacrifices. First, a white bull came with a cord tied through a ring in its nose. A wreath of flowers covered the bull's head, and children ran beside it, singing.

Other animals would also be offered today. Wildflowers cut fresh from the hillsides this morning lay strewn along the pathway. The parade path, made by children, was like a carpet of red, yellow, and white. Spring colors rejuvenated both young and old.

Lydia-Naq's twelve priestesses followed her up the short incline from the Upper Agora to the Altar of Zeus.[29] They stood on each side of the front of the altar, forming a diagonal line on the twenty-seven broad steps, eleven paces wide.[30] The platform of the altar was a pedestal eighteen and a half by nineteen Roman paces. Lydia-Naq wished she could wrap her arms around the architects who had created such a perfect monument to Zeus.

It was almost a square.[31] The entrance faced the west, and worshipers faced the east. The steps leading to the altar at the top were made of polished pure white marble. Looking down from the Altar of Athena or from the library, Lydia-Naq saw the horseshoe-shaped base of the altar formed with Ionic columns.

The outer sides were decorated with enormous, high relief friezes carved from white marble painted in brilliant life-like colors. The reliefs were the civic pride, the treasure, and the legacy of Pergamum.

Each carving memorialized a different victory of Zeus during his primordial fights against the many giants of the underworld. The stories of Zeus's exploits surrounded the massive pedestal, honoring victorious gods. The tales came from *The Iliad*, *The Odyssey*, and other sources. The entire frieze was about seventy paces long[32] and higher than a tall man could reach.

---

[29] The Altar of Zeus is now housed at the Museum of Pergamum in Berlin. Its purpose, as an altar and as a temple, continues to be debated. The date of its construction is not known. Which king actually built it is still debated. German archeologists continue this research through the German Archeology Institute.

[30] The steps are approximately 19 yards or 18 meters wide.

[31] The pedestal is approximately 31 yards by 32 yards or about 29 by 30 meters.

[32] The frieze around the base of the altar is about 120 yards long or about 111 meters.

The upper floor was surrounded by walls to the south, east, and north. While the lower walls outside explained the exploits of Zeus, the father of the gods, the inside friezes related the life of Telephos, the legendary founder of Pergamum.

Lydia-Naq continually trained new devotees. She examined the twelve young priestesses, each one radiant and joyful. Five priestesses would step down from service this year, having completed their duties. Their time of selfless sacrifice to Zeus brought life to their deity. She had been keeping her eyes open for the most beautiful young women every day for the past few months, anxious to impart Zeus to another five priestesses-in-training.

The festival has started. Everyone in Pergamum will be touched in some way during the next two weeks. They will be witnessing the gifts of the nine muses: epic tales, poetry, musical instruments, sacred verse, chorus, dance, tragedy, comedy, and astronomy!

She almost shuddered, overcome by a wave of joy.

There would be prizes for those who memorized *The Iliad* and *The Odyssey* through the sacrificing of bulls, goats, and sheep. Most people would receive a little bit of meat!

What was a festival without lots of music? The city buzzed as the beauty of the women and the spring's fragrance in the air flooded the senses. Triumphs of Zeus shaped countless conversations. Lydia-Naq's responsibility today was to keep the steps resplendent with beautiful women. She had instructed them about singing songs, waving flowers and ribbons, and dancing and moving gracefully. Age-old traditions came alive once more.

During the festival, only men were allowed to walk upon the upper altar platform. Therefore, the high priest and his attendants climbed the steps between the two lines of women, leading the white bull and other sacrificial animals. During the next thirteen days, until April 28, scores of animals would follow the same path. Some of the meat would be sold in the butcher shops in the marketplaces.

Nestor raised his voice to officially proclaim the beginning of the festival. "We acknowledge our emperor! Caesar is lord and god!"

The priestesses dedicated to Zeus radiated color and delight like wildflowers waving in the breeze. Each woman glowed, her long, shining black hair tied in an identical style. Their linen tunics outlined a glorious femininity, the quality Zeus admired in his relationships with the goddesses on the distant slopes of Mount Olympus.

With the invocation of Domitian's name, the music began anew. Songs and music would last for two weeks. Those who were judged to be the best musicians would receive a special prize on the last day.

All wanted the award.

The white stone with a new name written on it by the priests would hang around the victor's neck. Only the high priest and the judges knew the interpretation of the new name given to those who won the competition.

That precious stone would be treasured for a lifetime.

THE NEW FORUM

Marcos walked to the bottom of the acropolis and up to the New Forum. In ancient times, heavily armed soldiers guarded these entrances. Today people came and went happily, although soldiers still scrutinized the throngs that passed through in either direction.

The New Forum was planned differently from the other two marketplaces. It displayed the efficiency of Rome and used the ample flat space at the bottom of the acropolis. Its architecture allowed soldiers to control crowds easily. It was majestic! More importantly, it had adequate space for camels, donkeys, and horses. It regularly witnessed the arrival of new religions, and debates took place here.

Having stopped to listen to a public debate that seemed more like a loud argument, Marcos saw the short Alexandrian Jew standing at the center of a small group of priests. He was the same man who had paid far too much for two crippled slaves.

For the second time in a few days, the Egyptian priests surrounded Antipas, trying to drag him into another dialogue about religion. They were not satisfied with the results from their previous attempt to have a public debate.

"Antipas," said Mehu loudly, "today is a holiday, a time for public debate. Come and talk with us! We want to continue our previous discussion."

Antipas had apparently agreed to speak. He put his hands

behind his back, listening and waiting.

Marcos decided to take in the verbal contest. It seemed appropriate that close by were the foundations that marked the base of the New Temple of Pergamum.

Mehu stuck out his chin, declaring, "Our gods are known to us from ancient days. They speak to us and give us life. As priests of Egypt, we have come to give life to our gods here in Pergamum." Scores began to gather, forming a large circle as the voices of a debate rang out.

Antipas continued to stand with his hands behind his back. He was not so fearful as the first time they had accosted him.

He nodded his head and responded to Mehu's challenge. "Your artists paint the gods on the walls of temples and tombs. After your princes die, their servants seek eternal life for them. The dead are buried with magical embalming, and their bodies are preserved forever."

Passersby, sensing something exciting was happening, gathered quickly.

Antipas rocked back and forth on his feet. "Your gods die every night and then come back to life in the morning."

He continued at length, reminding them of the paintings over the bodies of embalmed kings. Eternal life for them was guaranteed by the pictures on the walls of their tombs and the great sacrifices made to honor their memories. Then he asked, "After so much attention, did any of your rulers ever come back to life?"

The direction of his question left them off balance for a moment.

While they were thinking of an answer, he added, "My people also believe in eternal life. But we believe it is for everyone, not just the rich and powerful. Unlike your gods, we worship a man who died, who was crucified by Roman authorities, but then came back to life. A grave could not hold him, even when sealed and guarded by Roman soldiers. His name is Yeshua, and he grew up in Nazareth. He partook of our pains, even death. I believe he was the perfect sacrifice, the one we Jews were waiting for."

Antipas knew the importance of sacrifices in all temples, so he kept on, ignoring their attempts to interrupt him.

"We say he was a perfect sacrifice to God, and because of that, he is declared worthy to forgive us for the transgressions we all commit. A miracle happened—he rose from the dead and came out from his tomb—alive! Witnesses saw nail scars in his hands and feet. A spear had pierced his side. Many people saw him after he rose. Soon after, the Messiah returned to where he came from—heaven—but he will come again."

Several people in the crowd muttered in disbelief, but others cheered for here was a new teaching, something they had never heard before! The noise brought others dashing to see what was happening in the New Forum.

The five Egyptians all spoke at once, trying to drown him out. Antipas raised his voice, but he could no longer be heard. He bowed politely and walked away.

Marcos turned to go. His mind was jumping from one scene to another. Over two weeks ago, listening to Lydia-Naq on the acropolis, he had heard stories set in stone. Masterful sculptures would recount the victories forever because stone would never decay. In marble, Zeus would forever be defeating giants.

He had offered a lamb to Zeus so that Florbella's speech would be restored, and he hoped Hades, the Destroyer, would soon lose his grip over her.

To his right, just east of the New Forum, a team of Egyptians was working with stonemasons to complete the foundation of the mighty temple to honor many gods. Unexpectedly, he had just heard a short man making his presence felt in the marketplace by merely explaining his beliefs.

His ideas sounded odd in a way that Marcos couldn't describe. There was a sense of peace in those words that he hadn't encountered before.

He kept up an inner conversation, planning what to say to Marcella. *The New Forum—a place for the exchange of new ideas. Strange that this Jew bought two lame slaves and took them to his home.*

Compassion is not typical in the marketplace. And here this man is again, talking more nonsense, confronting Egyptian priests with a story about a man rising from the dead. Imagine anyone coming back to life, with scars still in his hands!

The high priestess talks about gods, glory and success, prosperity, and fertility but not about deep hidden things within us, like shame and fear...and pain. Are those beyond her concerns?

Marcos walked home at a faster pace. He would have to tell Marcella about what he had witnessed this morning.

ANTIPAS'S SHOP, LOWER AGORA

Two days later, on Wednesday, Antipas was satisfied that he had not cowered before the Egyptian priests. Still, he was concerned that some in the crowd would not understand his explanations.

This store had been launched in the Lower Agora shortly after he came to Pergamum. It had given him good profits ever since. The three Greek widows running this shop were young, under the age of twenty-five. Barbara, the widow from Miletus, had no children. Ilithyia had met Antipas after her husband left her for another woman.

And then there was Nikasa. From the beginning, Antipas intended to include different kinds of people in his community. Nevertheless, his efforts were almost shipwrecked by his providing what some people called "too much generosity."

Antipas grimaced. Nikasa, the Samaritan refugee from Cyprus, was the most difficult and refused to get along well with others.

Practical considerations had led him to a temporary solution, which in the end worked well. The two Greek widows and the Samaritan woman were given separate rooms in one house at his village.

This young, head-strong Samaritan woman simply causes too much friction!

Such thoughts brought deep lines across his forehead.

LIBRARY OF PERGAMUM, THE ACROPOLIS

Lydia-Naq had been called to her brother's office, and she stepped as quickly as she could on her way there. There were only two days left in the festival.

After she arrived, Zoticos asked a young scholar studying in a corner to leave his office. "I need to talk to my sister alone. Please return in ten minutes."

When the scholar was out of the room, Zoticos turned to Lydia-Naq. "Well, my sister, I've been thinking about what you said. You have opened my eyes to new possibilities during the last several weeks. We will continue the work of Chief Librarian Hermes even though he is not expected to live much longer.

Prayers made on his behalf have not made a difference, and he lies at home unable to move. In fact, the paralysis has spread. His right leg is useless, and he seems increasingly frail.

"I am going to count on you, my sister, to have me confirmed by the Council of Ephesus as the new librarian to replace Hermes."

She listened with growing interest. Something new and creative, even enthusiastic, was stirring within her brother.

"Sister, we need a bold plan!"

"I agree with you, Zoticos. What do you have in mind?"

"Well, if I am appointed as the new librarian, I will initiate a course for twenty to twenty-four students, starting in the fall. I will include men and women, and the graduates will become future teachers.

"Will they be trained to restore Lydian thoughts, proverbs, and language?"

"Yes! We will train these teachers with the skills needed to train others. I will demand five days a week from each of them. The library will pay for their studies."

Lydia-Naq rocked back on her heels. "I am very confident I can have you appointed as Chief Librarian. We won't get any support from the headmaster of the gymnasium. Still, we will get agreement from the oldest men in the city, the aristocrats. And do you have a name for this program, my brother?"

"Yes, we will call it 'Restoring the Paths of Ancient Pergamum.' Will you please make a personal sacrifice at the altar on the day we begin to train our new students? I will want to start these classes in October, after the meeting of the Asiarchs."

Her happy smile was an open compliment of Zoticos's "grand plan." However, she smugly believed it was her careful coaxing that had influenced his decision.

Zeus will be proud, Lydia-Naq thought. *You will be promoted! Oh, Mighty Zeus, see to my brother's advancement. Aid me to influence the Ephesus Council to grant Zoticos this position!*

Once again, a strange mixture of emotions flowed within her, a combination of elation, wonder, fear, and majesty.

She would soon go to the Council of Ephesus to argue that Zoticos should be confirmed to replace Hermes.

Later, Lydia-Naq watched the dying golden rays of another day shining on the white marble of the acropolis. The finely dressed stones glowed with a warm orange color as they reflect the dazzling sunset.

She stopped in front of the altar and raised her eyes. She watched the gently rising black smoke from the evening sacrifice. Her thoughts and softly spoken words were her twilight prayer.

"I devoted my son to you in my youth, Zeus. I was a virgin priestess. After that, at age twenty-six, I married. Due to my prior training, I was selected for lifelong service to your altar.

"When I began intensive training to become a priestess, I promised you that my child would serve the heavens. Shortly afterward, my husband suffered a sudden illness. I dedicated my unborn child to you, partly as a prayer, partly as a promise if you would heal my husband. He died three days later. Even so, I kept my vow to raise my son as a devotee to you. Zeus, you nourished my child, and Diotrephes lived.

"Now you have given me a warning. I must find out what is happening in that little village at the base of the acropolis. I cannot go there, but Diotrephes could go in my place. He'll bring me the information I want. The time has come for my son to serve you."

She walked home with her head held high, thinking about her son. Her hand pressed against her stomach, thrilled with the power she felt when she had created his name. It was noble, containing a double meaning: "dedicated to Zeus" and "nourished by Zeus." She spoke his name out loud. "Diotrephes!"

Chapter 18
Unexpected Music

ANTIPAS'S HOME, PERGAMUM

Antipas had built his home directly opposite the marble buildings of the acropolis. Across the river, high above where Miriam stood, gentle wafts of smoke from temples gave witness to the many sacrifices being offered.

She breathed deeply and listened to the songs people were singing. Some were about the gods, others about love between men and women. Many talked about heroes of old. A thought came to her, and she rushed home to tell her grandfather.

"I want to compose a song that I could sing at a service."

"What would you sing about?"

"I want to paint word pictures the same way the people of this city describe daily life in their well-known melodies. I use the psalms for my meditation every day. How I love those ancient words! I've been saying them ever since I can remember...."

Since before my mother died. But why can't I bring back the memory of my mother's smiles? Those memories have vanished.

"For you to sing in a service, my child, would be a significant change from our standard ritual. Women have never been permitted to do what you want to do now."

"I know that, and I am willing to listen to your guidance. Some words are in my mind. I would sing with instruments. Maybe the words of my namesake, Miriam, would serve for the basis of a song."

"Hmm, yes, Miriam, the sister of Moses, as told in Exodus, led the hosts of Israel in jubilant songs. Well, one time only, and we'll discuss it afterward!"

Two days later, she ran through the words and melody of her first completed composition several times.

ARPOXA'S AND ATEAS'S HOUSE, ANTIPAS'S VILLAGE

Everyone was curious about the young couple from the slave market. For a month, the ex-slaves had been shy to talk to people in Antipas's little village. However, realizing now that they had a permanent place to stay, they wanted to tell their story.

Using sign language and minimal words, Miriam had learned that their names were Ateas and Arpoxa. She helped them learn enough elementary Greek to tell others about themselves at a village gathering.

Days before the gathering, the couple requested several kinds of cloth and two lambskins from Miriam. They said it was for clothing, but lambskin seemed to be an odd request. Miriam supplied what they needed from the village storeroom, and they started making the clothing. They stopped only when Miriam had time to drop in and work on their language training.

The village meeting with Ateas and Arpoxa was held late in the afternoon on a Sunday. Many of the families gathered around the open space in the middle of the village. A dozen men prepared the food for a community meal.

The couple emerged from their house and hobbled into the clearing's center. They wore strange clothing fashioned in a way that most of the villagers had never seen before. Onias placed a bench for Ateas and Arpoxa in the middle of the group. Some villagers brought rugs to sit on in the grass.

Miriam introduced the couple. "After only a short time in our village, we are ready to honor Ateas and Arpoxa. They used to live in the north. The weather is colder north of the Black Sea. These are the clothes they would wear during their long winters, but here in Pergamum, winter months are shorter."

Arpoxa had made a set of padded and quilted leather trousers for her husband. The pants were tucked into boots, and he wore an open tunic. On his head was a tall, pointed hat made from the sheepskin with white wool showing on the outside. He lifted the cap off and showed everyone that it had little patches over his blond hair and ears to keep him warm in the winter.

Arpoxa wore a woman's garment of woven wool. On either side of the neck, she had stitched the outline of an eagle flying. Its feathers, bent up at the tip, balanced on wafts of air as she remembered seeing on her farm.

Brightly colored appliqué work on the sleeves caught all the workers in the Ben Shelah village by surprise.

"How can a foreigner come up with these gifted skills?" asked one man. He was a potter and recognized quality craftsmanship.

Using her limited vocabulary, Arpoxa began her story of how they got here. "Old father has trees, new trees, new land, new place, and new house with lots horses." She struggled to remember the vocabulary Miriam taught her during the week. People cheered her on, wanting to know more.

Miriam helped out. "She is saying her grandfather settled in a new place. He cut down the trees and made a new farm. Then he used the trees to make their new house. They raised horses on their farm."

"New sheep and land and cakes and raisins and wine."

All of a sudden, Arpoxa bent over and cried. No one moved. Were these the tears of joy, or was she in grief because she had been removed from her people? It was hard to tell.

She refused to say anything else, but Miriam assisted. "Her family raised sheep and had lots of lambs. They had raisin cakes and wine. Probably that was part of their family diet or maybe part of their religion."

After the silence of a moment, Ateas stood up. People expressed intense interest as they watched the dramatic scenes of his life unfold. He told his story without words. First, he got down on his knees to indicate that he was small.

"Was this when you were a little boy?" someone yelled.

He rose up a bit and moved as if he were riding a horse. Someone else yelled, "You became a horse rider when you were a little bit older."

Ateas took a stool and sat on it. Then he pretended to ride, whipping his horse. He stopped, gave something to an imaginary person, took something back, and then turned around, riding back the way he had come.

All understood his actions as a horseman riding a long way to trade in a different place. He stood up, rested on his crutches, put his fingers on his eyes, and then pulled his eyes slightly, changing his face.

"I can't believe it," a perfume maker called. "Did he ride as far as the land where people have slanted eyes? Is Ateas talking about the Silk Road? Could he have ridden as a guard?"

After he sat back on the stool, Ateas took an imaginary bow

in his hand. He mimed placing an arrow in it then let the arrow sail, immediately raising his hands in jubilation for hitting the bull's eye. He did this over and over again. He changed his posture, and now he was riding the horse, but this time he used the bow and arrow while riding the horse.

He stopped, and everyone knew it was a change of scene. He bent to the ground then made as if he was digging. Each time he threw more dirt away, he went down farther and farther. At first, everyone laughed at his exaggerated actions. Then he fell over, indicating something falling on him. People gasped.

Miriam interpreted his actions. "He was digging a well! The ground must have given way, falling on him. Oh no! His right leg is broken!"

Ateas stood up and showed everyone his broken leg. People gasped again as they thought of the pain he must have endured.

The perfume maker remarked, "His leg has never been set correctly. How long was he trapped in the well? Who saved him?"

Ateas moved as if walking then beckoned for a child to come over to him. He put the child's hand around his wrist and showed that he had been taken as a slave.

Onias raised his eyebrows to add to Miriam's comments. "I think he has been saying he was trained as a horseman to trade with neighboring tribes and nations. He was an expert archer, protecting the people with the goods. He must have been riding a horse and shot arrows when the robbers came close!"

Miriam nodded in approval. "Keep talking, Onias."

"Here's the way I see it. He apparently traveled all the way to the East, where people have eyes like that. When he was digging a well, the side caved in, or maybe it was a stone, and his leg was broken. Perhaps he was unable to make a living and was then sold as a slave. We don't yet know how he became a slave, but I think that is his story."

Two sheep had been butchered, and the meat was cooking over an open fire. The children in Antipas's establishment ran and jumped, enjoying the unexpected event.

After Ateas and Arpoxa's stories, the evening meal was served with food from Antipas's personal storehouse. Everyone knew they were only beginning to get the story.

Miriam called out before the meal was served, "Once Ateas has learned Greek, he will tell us of far-off, fascinating places. We all have questions, such as how did he protect traders on the Silk Road?"

THE CAVE, ANTIPAS'S VILLAGE

That afternoon as dusk approached, Antipas walked downhill toward the cave with Onias for the evening services. The end of the Festival of Zeus meant the time had come to pay taxes to Rome.

As a Jew, Antipas did not have to pay the same levy other citizens paid. "Onias, I am still required to pay the old temple tax as well as the tax on my business operations. Exemption from additional fees is one blessing of being a Jew. Some things about being a Jew are an advantage in this society."

Miriam sat down on the carpet in the cave. She heard a scraping noise and looked up. The young Scythian man limped in slowly, holding the hand of his wife. It was the first time they had joined with the others at a meeting, and they sat on the floor at the back of the room, close to the shelves holding newly made pottery.

The cave was full this evening as Miriam went to the back to be with the couple. She took Arpoxa's hand, knowing the younger woman would understand little if anything of her explanations. She thought their expressions indicated they no longer felt as afraid as on their first day in her grandfather's village.

"Arpoxa and Ateas, look at the people here. It's our time to meet as a community. We refer to ourselves as friends. You are free now. That means you are no longer slaves. You are one of us!

"We call this gathering the Household of Faith. It was Eliab, my great-grandfather, who first used the expression.

"When we lived in Alexandria, our family employed some Egyptians who did not fear the God of Abraham. However, some became interested in the Jewish faith, and they would sit at the back of our worship gatherings.

"After the first pogrom, when our synagogue was burned, we met in a house until we later moved to Jerusalem. After we fled the Jerusalem siege, we were hosted by believers in Yeshua, the Messiah. Our family came to faith there through their teaching.

"When we moved to Pergamum as a family, great-grandfather Eliab wanted nonbelievers from the village to attend.

141

Eliab declared, 'Faith connects us with the men of old and our belief in Yeshua, the Messiah. The Household of Faith speaks of the continuing covenant. So this will be the new name for our meetings and our community.' My great-grandfather continued to hold worship gatherings in our home. You can come here because you are accepted by all of us."

Miriam smiled to see the couple beginning to investigate the activities of the community.

They will do well! She is learning Greek quickly. She'll have to do something that doesn't require a lot of moving around. The man is a craftsman; he shows interest in pottery.

A young man about Miriam's age, a stranger with black hair, sat at the back on the other side. He was handsome, and his clothing showed him as belonging to a wealthy family. Looking more closely, she saw he appeared uncomfortable with his surroundings.

He talked nervously to one of the men, and she overheard his conversation as he introduced himself.

"Hail! Good evening! My name is Diotrephes."

For some reason, Miriam shuddered as she heard him say his name. *Who would give a baby the name "nourished by Zeus"?*

She returned to her place at the front of the group and found that the little girl had come to sit with her again. The child acted more boldly now, although she still had not spoken. Miriam and Antipas had concluded that she was mute for unknown reasons. It was not an uncommon condition in the city.

The child looked around, smiled, paid attention to the speaking, and swayed in time to the music; she could hear, just not talk. Since that first visit, she had come to all the meetings early on Sunday mornings before the sun rose and each evening whenever Antipas led a meeting during the week.

What keeps her coming to the Household of Faith? Miriam wondered.

Each time the child came, she showed more confidence. She no longer went into the cave holding a bird close. The girl's young slave, her protector, her *paidagogos*, who accompanied her, never came in, although he had been invited several times. He was not interested in the music and the meeting, so he spent his time throwing rocks into the river.

142

Miriam looked down at the child.

What's going on in her little mind? She is intelligent behind those sparkling eyes.

Prayers were said, and hands reached upward in humility to the Ancient of Days. Antipas spoke, the scrolls were read, and now it was time for Miriam to sing her new song.

She was very nervous because it was not the way that they had traditionally chanted the psalms. She was about to do something very different. If continued, it would make music a significant part of the worship time.

Now, in front of the gathering, Miriam was ready to sing—not just the words from the psalms but using her own words to explain the truths she had heard all her life. Taking phrases from old scrolls and combining them in song with some supporting phrases from the new manuscripts, she had come up with two songs.

Smiling and trying to contain her exhilaration, she announced, "I wrote two songs. The first one is for the children, the second one for adults. Both are about the greatness of the Lord, the One who is greater than all gods."

She nodded to the three girls sitting on the floor, and they started to play the melody that they had practiced with Miriam on flutes. At the appropriate point in the tune, Miriam began to sing her first song. When she sang it a second time, Onias's three daughters, Aliza, Nessat, and Talia, joined in, singing it with her.

Then the same song was sung once again, and two boys joined in with a drum and cymbal. She could see that the people loved this rendering of the psalm. They sang it several more times, relishing this new and different song. By the end, all knew the words by heart.[33]

Great is your name, O Lord our God,
 Loved above every name!
Messiah's mercies deep and broad,
 Splendor, your rightful claim.

Hills, trees, and forests sing for joy,
 You judge the world in truth.

---

[33] Miriam based her song on Psalm 96.

God reigns! His praises we employ,
    Joyfully, from our youth.

Countless people see your majesty,
    In strength you made the earth;
You judge the world with equity,
    We shout your mighty worth.

As was the custom of the people, each line was sung twice. She introduced her second song with a brief explanation.

"For us truly to worship, we must know the One who receives our worship," Miriam said. "This song is called 'The Name.' Listen while we teach you the words."

He's here! Shepherd, Savior, and Comforter,
Mighty Lord, Eternal, Blessed Father!
The Holy One, Jacob's Portion, Master;
Righteous One, Creator, and the Most High;
God of Grace, King of Glory, now come nigh;

He's here! "Emmanuel," the angel sings!
Yeshua Messiah, salvation brings;
Prince of Peace, Lord of lords and King of kings!
Son of God, Son of Man, the Great I Am;
The First and Last, a Lion yet a Lamb!

The Spirit's here, sent in Yeshua's name.
Counselor, Comforter, helping the lame;
Redeeming, He delivers us from shame.
Sent from the Father, pointing us to Him;
Convicting us of lawlessness and sin.

As Miriam sang, Antipas walked over to where Florbella sat and placed his hand on her head. Miriam watched him, knowing he was worried about her. They had never heard the child use her voice. He stood for a moment, praying earnestly, imploring the Lord to restore her ability to speak.

While Miriam sang the song once more, Florbella made a small noise and said a word.

Miriam had sung the name Yeshua, but the little girl

pronounced it differently, saying "Jeshua" with a pronounced "J." The Jewish way of saying the name had a softer sound at the beginning.

Miriam returned to her place and put her arm around the little girl's thin shoulders. Florbella put her arms around Miriam's waist and squeezed tightly.

The girl whispered the name. "Jeshua," she said again, happily running away from the cave and motioning for Marcosanus to go home with her as quickly as possible.

MARCOS'S HOME

Florbella's slave could hardly keep up with his little charge as she ran home. The quiet little girl had never shown such energy! She burst through the door into the courtyard with a loud bang.

Marcella and Marcos, seated together on the couch by the fountain, both turned quickly to see what had caused the commotion. They were used to her going in and out, but she never ran in like this!

Florbella ran to her father, jumping onto his lap. "Jeshua!" she said in a loud voice, and then she started humming the song she had learned at the cave. With gaping mouths, her parents both looked up questioningly at Marcosanus as he stumbled in behind her.

The young slave told them where she had gone. "She has been spending time with people who sing. No, she was not in any danger. She has only ever been with other people."

Marcos tried to hide his excitement. When the earthquake destroyed their summer home near Nicomedia, his daughter was imprisoned for two days, unable to leave the hole in the ground.

He believed she wandered around the city as an expression of enjoying her freedom after being trapped in the ground. The suddenness of her now talking was a shocking miracle.

"What are you saying, my little one? What does the word 'Jeshua' mean?" he gasped.

Marcos gave her a big hug and stood her up on the floor. Emotions overwhelmed him. The muscles on his face were tense, strained. He was afraid to even be so hopeful.

"You're speaking! Florbella! You said something! But what on earth does it mean? What is 'Jeshua'? What are you talking about?"

All the while, Marcella had stopped her embroidery work and

stared with wide eyes and open mouth at her child. She stood up, her eyes began to water, and the embroidery she was working on fell to the floor of the courtyard. She hugged their daughter, falling to her knees on the colorful mosaic floor. Tears flowed down her cheeks.

"What's happened to our precious daughter? You have started to talk again! Oh, our prayers to Hera are answered!" She was overwhelmed and turned to the statue of Hera, the goddess of their home, standing guard near the door. The goddess received her prayers a dozen times each day.

Unable to grasp what had happened, she burst out, "Finally, my daughter is starting to speak again. After praying to the gods for this... 'Jeshua' must mean something about her healing, but what?"

Chapter 19
Highs and Lows

ARPOXA'S HOME, ANTIPAS'S VILLAGE

When Arpoxa first had arrived at the village, she couldn't say a word to Antipas or Miriam, not even "thank you," in Greek or Latin. Miriam's conversations with Arpoxa became more interesting as the young Scythian woman increasingly learned the words for things in the Greek language.

One day Arpoxa hobbled awkwardly to the workshop with Miriam where tunics lay folded, ready to be sold in Antipas's shops.

"Tunic...plain is," said Arpoxa.

"Do you mean 'The tunic is plain'?" asked Miriam.

"Yes, the tunic is plain," the younger woman replied, accepting the correction.

"How could the tunic be better?" Miriam asked.

"Tunic is better than plain, now is better with color," Arpoxa said, struggling with grammar.

"The tunic can be better if it is not plain. Would it be better with colored embroidery?" suggested Miriam.

"Lots more not plain, in Greek, I mean" came back the quick reply followed by a grin and a question. "I fix?"

Miriam took several of the cotton, wool, and linen tunics to Arpoxa's home. The newcomer began embroidering them with small birds on the collar and various colored patterns around the hem.

Over the next few weeks, these decorated tunics were in high demand at their Agora shops. Arpoxa was made a paid worker at the village workshop.

They truly enjoyed being together: Miriam because of Arpoxa's sincerity and quaint expressions; Arpoxa because she was proud of her expanding knowledge of the Greek language. Because they now shared everyday experiences, they found they could often laugh together.

147

Arpoxa's smile spread across her face. She was accepted here. She wanted to say, "If you could understand my language, I would tell you that all of you dress without imagination. We love bright colors; you have such ordinary colors!"

The next week, confident that they were accepted in the village, they again dressed up in their Scythian clothing for a Sunday afternoon gathering in the village. Arpoxa hobbled over to her husband.

Holding her right hand around his waist, she slowly spread her left hand in a circle. Looking at everyone individually, she bowed her head. Her hand was closed over her heart, expressing a wordless thank you that everyone understood. They wanted to be accepted, and they were. This was their new place, their new home.

"This day was happy day for us," Ateas said to Miriam later that evening, referring to the moment when clapping and affirmation had followed their wordless gesture. Joy had exploded from the circle. Everyone in the village knew what it was to be a stranger. Hadn't each one been taken in during a time of personal crisis or pain? Now they were included in the small community.

Recalling the emotions of the evening together gave Miriam the means to help them improve their language skills, and she felt the thrill of growing friendship. She had not only helped them to tell their story but she was helping them to be part of a community.

OMPHALE'S HOME, THE ACROPOLIS

Bernice prepared to tell the twins another story. Today she would explain more about Helen of Troy. During the last months, she had made sure they knew the names of many gods and goddesses they would hear about. Daily life was punctuated by expressions and proverbs that made sense against the background of Greek values and traditions. Already Eumen and Attalay were familiar with the broad outlines of many stories of Greek gods. Helen of Troy was Bernice's favorite.

She had just finished asking the boys questions about the Minotaur on Crete and King Minos. A labyrinth was made for the creature. Daedalus and his son Icarus had been put into the maze to be killed by the wild beast. But they killed it instead and then

148

escaped to fly back to Sicily on feathered wings held together with wax.

Bernice moved her chair close to the doors opening onto the terrace. The morning was warm. Spring's celebration had been perfect. The festival was over, and she was so proud of her charges, her master's two boys. People looked at them and said what an incredible gift of the gods it was for them to have twins.

"They will be like the two brothers of old who made Pergamum great!" people boasted. "Those brothers were kings and had a city named after them, Philadelphia, the City of Brothers Who Love Each Other. These two boys will also be great men!" When Omphale heard comments like these, she drew her boys close to her ample bosom and smiled into their eyes.

However, her master's wife was in a bad mood today. "Come here, Bernice!" yelled Omphale. "I want you to do my hair. Why did my other slave have to get sick today? She always does my hair. Now I will have to do it myself."

"I can't come. You told me to never leave the twins alone," replied Bernice.

"I want you! Put my hair in braids! Just leave them for a moment and come here!"

After several minutes of yelling and argument, Bernice gave in against her better judgment. She closed the doors leading out to the terrace and told the twins to behave. "Pretend that you are the father and the boy looking for the bull in the labyrinth. Here, tie a string to this couch, and one of you go around the house and hide from the other one. See how many times you can hide from each other."

Eumen and Attalay felt elated. Any excuse was made to get alone, away from Bernice's watchful eye because she always had them in her sight.

"Let's pretend we are those people who flew from Crete to Sicily," said Eumen. He opened the doors to the terrace, something he was not allowed to do. He knew he was taking a risk. "We can walk along the wall now and pretend to fly to the sun."

A sudden cry through the bedroom door startled Omphale and Bernice.

"He's fallen over the edge!" shouted Eumen. "Come! Attalay fell down!"

The frantic mother screamed and tore her hair out of

Bernice's hand. Both women raced to the door and entered the living room. The entrance to the terrace was open. Eumen held onto his mother's tunic.

"Attalay pretended he was flying to the sun," he whimpered. "He just fell over."

It was Omphale's worst nightmare. "It's my fault!"

At the base of the thirty-five-foot cliff, the twin people said would be the pride of Pergamum's future lay limp on the rocks. Next to the cliff, the seats of the ancient theater were empty in the bright morning. A loud and mournful cry went up from both the distraught mother and Bernice. The cliffs of Pergamum had claimed the life of another child, although people had vowed it would never happen again.

THE CAVE, ANTIPAS'S VILLAGE

Two weeks had passed since Florbella had begun to speak. Marcella and Marcos, wanting to understand more of the power behind the miraculous occurrence, came to the cave with Florbella. It was a Sunday night and a distinct time of preparation before Pentecost. However, Marcos didn't understand anything about the Jewish calendar and the religious holidays that seemed to be so important to them.

People were gathering, and the same bearded Jewish man whom he had seen debating with the Egyptians in the marketplace greeted and talked to them at the door. Lamps placed along the wall of the cave lit the large room with a dull yellow glow. This man was obviously the leader here.

He spoke to Antipas in a low voice. "My daughter wants to come here all the time. She is beginning to talk a little more each day. Something extraordinary is happening here.

It was his custom to introduce himself to the host when he came to an unfamiliar meeting place. "Thank you for taking my daughter into your community. I work for the city council as a lawyer."

He added, "Florbella had a terrible experience several years ago, and she had not spoken since that day. But something happened here recently. I'm not sure what it was, but she started speaking again. I want to find out more."

"You may join us anytime. You are always welcome. We believe that God hears the prayers of everyone, even a child such as your daughter."

"I don't believe in prayers. I'm a cautious man, and to be honest, I don't trust others easily. I suppose it comes from being a lawyer." He smiled at the light humor.

"What kind of law do you practice? Whom do you serve?"

"I am counsel to the city council, and I also work in the District Court of Pergamum. Outside of that, I help execute the wills of families. I tragically lost my whole family, and I'm still working on the details of everything involved in those matters."

At first, Marcella and Marcos moved to sit with the other visitors at the back. However, Florbella pulled her mother to the front to sit with her beside Miriam. Marcos watched his daughter during the meeting; she was actually singing the words of some of the songs, and it took his breath away.

Later, he mulled over the events of the evening as they walked home. He held one of Florbella's hands, and Marcella held the other. Florbella skipped along between them.

He pondered his two brief discussions with Antipas, one before the meeting and one afterward.

"My dear, I don't understand Antipas's words. He told me, 'Florbella is being healed by the loving-kindness of the Almighty. Nothing that we do can force God to do this or that; God is not like the gods of the people around us. He alone decides, and what he does is ultimately to our blessing. We wait in patience. Sometimes the Lord clearly shows his power. However, at all times, we bring him our praise and adoration.' I like that phrase, 'is being healed.' It tells me that something more than just a physical change is going on.

"Antipas believes in asking, in making petitions, as if his God is personally interested in our daughter. He has a strange way of talking about his God. In one way, his God seems so far away, and yet at the same time, he seems so close."

Florbella ran ahead, and he took Marcella's arm, talking to her quietly. "Florbella says she felt heat when Antipas put his hand on her and prayed for her. I told Antipas that I was grateful for him healing her—a miracle—but he replied, 'No, I don't heal; only God can do that.' Strange. Everyone else I know wants to get the glory, not give it to another.

"The funniest thing of all was his answer to my question

151

before we left. I asked, 'Are you singing about a person when you say, 'The One and Only, the Lion yet the Lamb?'

"Antipas answered, 'Oh, one of the names of Yeshua is the Lamb. He became our sacrifice. Through him, because of the cross and his death, we are healed, forgiven of our sins.' Funny! Imagine calling a man 'a lamb'!"

ANTIPAS'S HOME, PERGAMUM

Entering his home that night, Antipas felt excitement. He had been praying for a miracle and needed a lawyer to help him with administering the will. Since Eliab, bless the memory of his father, had passed away, he had prayed to the King of the universe, *send a lawyer to help me!*

"Miriam, I'm wondering if Marcos is God's answer to a prayer. Before they left for their homes after the funeral, I promised my brothers that I would find a lawyer to straighten out the will. I have nothing to report to them. After two and a half months, they will want to hear something!

"The will left by my father is, like everything else in his life, far too complicated. The estate is to be distributed among the surviving children. Marcos has the training to help us execute the will."

Antipas walked to his library. It was a large, square room located to the right of the great room used for family events. The four walls of the room were covered with shelves, each lovingly built. Each little square box was secured several inches from the walls and held small, rolled-up scrolls. Carpenters had formed squares with four corners. One was at the top, another at the bottom, and the other two on the sides. A few squares were full, indicating Antipas's keen interest in that subject.

On one of the walls, the shelves were full of business journals from Alexandria. They dealt with the Ben Shelah business there.

Shelves on another wall stored correspondence related to the work he shared with each of his brothers. Each brother's accounts were easy to find, reference, and add to. Two long, narrow windows high on the wall provided light in the library, where he spent many hours a day. Now it was dark outside, and the soft light from two lamps above his desk welcomed him.

The third wall stored business items related to his work in

Pergamum.

And on the fourth wall were scrolls relating to the covenant. Antipas had also been making a collection of newer writings: those of Paul, Peter, Luke, and Matthew. He had heard of several other writers and wanted their copies too.

The story of Yeshua written by John lay open on his dark oak desk. It was a long scroll and had recently come as a copy of the original document in Ephesus. It had the faint, almost-sweet scent of a newly created parchment, and he ran his fingers over the edges of the scroll. Antipas sat at his writing desk trying to bring his thoughts together. He ended each of his days in this much-loved room.

Miriam dropped into the room to say, "Good night, Grandpa!"

She gave him a kiss and left him to write notes about his day. The light seemed dimmer than usual. He blinked hard several times and then went to the kitchen and brought two more little lamps back to his desk.

Why am I having trouble seeing things tonight?

He wrote down some of his reminders for the next day and a few impressions of the day.

> *Tonight, several visitors came to the meeting, among them, Marcos, a lawyer, with his wife and daughter. The little girl who loves birds and who started to talk recently is Marcos's daughter! What happened to the girl? What was the 'bad experience'? How severe was their tragedy? Marcos may be the answer to my problems with my father's will.*

He was slow completing his notes tonight, blinking his eyes several times while writing.

> *My granddaughter's recent songs run through my mind. The melodies come quickly because I often hear them being sung in the marketplace but to other words. Is it wrong for Miriam to lead singing in the cave?*
>
> *Some would object, especially Jaron if he ever came to our meetings. I almost burst out laughing at the thought. How angry Jaron would become if he saw all those Gentiles worshiping God together with us!*

I am planning to improve the training of others as potential leaders. Previously, I taught the whole story of the covenant when meeting with five or six men. A new group should be trained to be more accurate while copying scrolls to minimize corrections. I wonder who I should choose for a new group of leaders.

The newest of the young men, Diotrephes, deeply concerns me. Several weeks ago, he started coming to meetings in the cave and introduced himself as a teacher at the gymnasium trained in rhetoric. Something about this man makes me bristle. My first impression is not to trust the stranger. I have seen too many sophists, or individual teachers, sway their listeners in the marketplaces. Those hucksters didn't need to be truthful to be successful. They only needed the power of persuasion. Is Diotrephes that kind of a person?

The time for evening prayers was at hand. Antipas covered his head with his prayer shawl. Thoughts came thick and fast.

How he missed his father's wisdom! He closed his eyes and watched a lifetime of memories pass by him. He wiped his eyes in grief for the loss of his parents.

Two issues gripped him as a Jew in Pergamum. One concern lay in submission to the empire; the other was giving recognition to the city's specific traditions.

Words came back to him, spoken by Isaiah centuries before, and he took them as a promise of comfort.

"I am with you, fear not, for I have redeemed you, I have summoned you by name, you are mine. When you pass through the waters, I will be with you; and when you pass through the rivers, they will not sweep over you. When you walk through the fires, you will not be burned. Do not be afraid, for I am with you."[34]

---

[34] Isaiah 43:1–5

Chapter 20
Decisions

THE CAVE, ANTIPAS'S VILLAGE

Marcella and Marcos were gradually getting used to the way meetings happened in the cave. These people prayed with their hands outstretched in front, with their palms upward to heaven and facing the front. None of this seemed so strange to them now.

They had been attending for five weeks, listening to music and meeting people. They were baffled by the strange prayers spoken to a God who required no images or animal sacrifices. He could not be seen. As Marcos listened to Antipas, his spirit moved between contradictory emotions. One moment he would reject the teaching, and another moment Antipas would say something that made perfect sense.

As Marcos looked at the people around him in the worship time, he saw that many were crying. One lady near the black rock cliff at the side of the cave had wet cheeks. A man sitting in front of him wiped his eyes. Antipas clearly had them in his grip as his talk reached their hearts.

After the music stopped, Antipas opened his scroll to a psalm that read, "Some sat in darkness..." As always, Antipas sat on a small chair when it was time to give his teaching. "This is a song that speaks to us of people from the north, south, east, and west."[35] Miriam and Antipas had prepared the evening's presentation together. This psalm would form the basis for his message and for Miriam's song later on.

He invited them to turn around. "Look at us: Some are from the north, from towns in Pontus around the Black Sea. Five families were born in the north, in Scythia. Then, from the south, Miriam and our steward, Onias, and his family and several other families came from Alexandria and other places in Egypt.

"People call us Grecian Jews. We speak Greek but worship like

---

[35] Psalm 107

the Jews from Jerusalem; however, we dress differently from other Jews, and we trim our beards. Now two families are from the east, from Syria. One family was born in Zeugma, much farther east. Also, a few families had their origins in the west, in Gaul and Spain.

"Why are we gathered together here? God is the one who builds his community. Our desire is to grow into a new kind of community, one built on love. No one is here by mistake. God's purpose brought us together."

Antipas looked at the two former slaves he had recently bought. He would always remember how Arpoxa started to tell her story and Ateas took over, acting out his life. That community party had lasted well into the night. Everyone still laughed at the strange picture of the white-skinned and blond-haired crippled people from the north emerging from their house in early summer wearing winter clothes.

Since that time, Antipas had come to appreciate Ateas's fascinating abilities. He painted scenes onto the pottery to be sold in the market. His pottery showed stags fighting each other and eagles fighting for food in mid-air. The moment these jugs or vessels were offered for sale in the Upper Agora shop, someone eagerly grabbed one for their home. Many were willing to pay more than the regular price being asked.

Arpoxa, the young woman, was just as gifted. In addition to her beautiful embroidery work, she could sing a song with the correct rhythm, pitch, and words after having heard the music only once or twice. It was their choice to become part of the Household of Faith, and tonight their newfound joy caused Antipas to speak on one of his favorite psalms.

Antipas spread his arms far apart to include them all.

"The psalmist used four examples of God saving people in difficult times; they came from four directions. Some wandered in desert wastelands; that is clearly a reference to places in the east. Some sat in darkness and deepest gloom, a deliverance from slavery, from Egypt. Some became fools through their rebellious ways, and some went out on the sea in ships; that's a reference to the Mediterranean Sea."

Antipas spoke of God and explained slowly and carefully. "God is the Creator. He is not the same as his creation. No, the creation is separate from his being. The Almighty is different from the gods of Greece and Rome. Why do the gods take on evil human motives, emotions, and activities? Because myths tell of gods who are the same as people in the world.

"Our scriptures say that God, the Creator, made everything right. But in the Greek myths, gods interfere with each other in unholy ways. The ungodliness of the gods, their rebellion, and their complicated lives are nothing but a mirror of our lives as humans.

"There is another story, one that stretches from the very beginning through to our day. It is about the God who is over all the gods created by man. Early on, he made a covenant and invited us, his creation, to come into it. This story of our faith is one of relationship with God.

"The Lord wants to be known by his people. He is the Creator but talks with his creatures through the scriptures and our prayers. God wants a relationship. He is eager for a covenant with the people that he created. As he reveals himself, he says, 'You will be my people, and I will be your God,' a concept often repeated in our scriptures.

"Listen to the last part of this psalm: 'Wanderers found a city where they could settle. He blessed them, and their numbers greatly increased. He lifted the needy out of their afflictions. Whoever is wise, let him heed these things and consider the great love of the Lord.'

"Look at us! All of us have been wounded or are flawed in one way or another. Yet whatever our background, God wants us to belong to his community. That means taking responsibility for each other in the good moments and the bad. Being a healthy community involves developing character traits of patience, forgiveness, acceptance, and generosity. The Lord describes his relationship with his people. We are to be 'holy,' set apart from the world and precious to God. Only he can make us holy. We cannot make ourselves pure."

Nowhere in the Roman Empire, in any library, law course, or theatrical performance, had Marcos heard anything like this. He knew he was in the presence of something completely different. His mind, although trained to think critically, couldn't take it all in.

Marcos closed his eyes, imagining the details of the different scenes, each story different, coming from north and south, from east and west.

Antipas had finished his teaching, and he stepped to the side. Miriam rose to sing one of her new songs. Beside her, Nessat strummed the harp softly. Talia and Aliza, the other daughters of Onias and Abijah, played flutes.

Our souls melted in the face of trouble.
Our son was gone; life's work turned to stubble.
Father's face was pale, repeating his laments.
Then mother cried, "He's home, and he repents!"
On our knees, faces to the floor,
Those in all our homes will praise you more.
    Everlasting Lord, Creator,
    Reassuring us, our Comforter.

Hungry, thirsty, no water in the bag,
Men stumbled, children cried, and camels lagged.
Over there, their guide saw an oasis.
All rejoiced, "Look! The land is spacious!"
Though trials come, we'll not keep score.
From the east, we will praise you more.
    Everlasting Lord, Creator,
    Sustaining us, our Renovator.

Sitting in great darkness, they longed for light.
Prison's shadows grew longer every night.
A rescuer came, threw away the chain.
They sang! No longer would they feel that pain.
Draw the curtains, pull wide the door!
From the south, we will praise you more.
    Everlasting Lord, Creator,
    Freeing us, our Illuminator.

Slaves shouted, stretched out on floors of ships.
Festering wounds, no relief for parched lips.
Then a helping hand took away distress.
"Redemption's here, and God's name, we will bless."
From open hearts, our praises pour,
From the north, we will praise you more.
    Everlasting Lord, Creator,
    Releasing us, our Lord and Savior.

Ships did business on far, distant waters.
Storms blew. Parents prayed for sons and daughters.
Winds howled; masts fell. "The rudder's no good now!"
Then came the question: "Safe in port...but how?"
From every coast and every shore,
From the west, we will praise you more.
 Everlasting Lord, Creator,
 Directing us, our Navigator.

We're here from east and west, the north and south,
Joyful praises rise from every mouth.
We love you, Lord, our Creator.
We worship you, Great Liberator.

Miriam's song was simple and, as usual, was repeated twice. When it was finished, people formed a long line from the front to the back. One at a time, they came forward quietly, knelt down, and broke off a piece from a loaf of bread that Antipas held. They took the bread in their mouths and then sipped from the communal cup of wine, staying on their knees for a moment and giving thanks at this time of remembrance of Yeshua's sacrifice. No one spoke. A deep silence prevailed—the silence of peace, the stillness of shalom.

MARCOS'S HOME, PERGAMUM

Arriving home an hour later, Marcella waited for Marcos to speak. However, he was still lost in the memories of the evening. After Florbella had gone to bed, they sat across from each other in their large room.

"I have many things to tell you," he began, "but I don't know where to begin. So many thoughts came as I listened to Antipas; memories flashed back from the earthquake.

"I missed much of Antipas's message because of my own thoughts. When my attention returned to the meeting, I wanted to stand up and say, 'Yes, I agree! We, too, were sitting in darkness and deepest gloom. My daughter was in darkness...trapped...and all alone! Our house was swallowed up, and the ground would not stop shaking. I was helpless!

159

"I could do nothing! We saw it when we were up on a hill, looking down. The Marmara Sea danced with tiny waves, and Hades called with deep groans—calling my brothers and families to their deaths as they slide under the waters.

"I closed my eyes, remembering those two days when we struggled to move the stone slab that had trapped Florbella beneath the debris. We did not know if we could get her out. My heart pounded as it still does sometimes at night."

Marcella nodded at remembering the event as he gently opened up his soul to her.

"Tonight, as I heard Antipas's voice, I opened my eyes. I was breathing hard like during the nightmares I've never mentioned to anyone." He glanced sideways at his wife, but she showed no surprise at his confession of nightmares.

"I wanted to shout, 'No one in Nicomedia came to help us! Their houses were destroyed too, everyone searching for survivors! The horror of trying to lift up that broken wall collapsed on our daughter. I will never see my four brothers again—below the waters, snatched away by a cruel god.'

"I drifted through memories. My mind was a jumble: patterns of clouds and light, that sunny day and then storms of grief, the never-ending screams in the face of death.

"But I was there...with many people...in what they call the Cave. My mind snapped back into the present. Joyful songs of young men and women brought me back to Pergamum. Most are day workers. None wear the clothing of the wealthy. They suffer from the common troubles of all people: illness, hard work, insufficient diet, and cold weather during the winter months."

He paused, about to explain something so new, so different, it took his breath away. His hands trembled. His sentences were somewhat scrambled, but his meaning was clear.

"Then I began...I entered a new path. This is what I wanted to say to you at home, my dear. How can I explain the sense of joy hovering in that place? These people are different. What is it? The singing...living together during hard times? Antipas cares for people no matter what their social class."

More assured, he explained, "Rome trained my intellect, but this new place reaches deep inside of me. A mystery... How was it that our daughter ever found this place or even entered a dark shed? To come into that cave—a dark place—even though she was always so scared of gloomy places after the earthquake... Wasn't Hades the one who trapped her in the earth and took away her speech? So I took a deep breath and tore myself away from thoughts of that earthquake, forcing myself to listen carefully to what was being explained."

A long, deep breath came. Marcos closed his eyes for something new was stirring him. "The grinding of the earth swallowing many buildings, my brothers, their families, slaves, and animals. I can't stop thinking about it, but another sound, a quiet, calming echo, began to overpower me: 'You will be my people and I will be your God.'

"My mind swayed back and forth between the earthquake in Nicomedia that took our entire family and Florbella's unexpected healing. I wanted to ask, 'How can an invisible God reveal himself? What does this invisible God look like?'"

Several seconds passed before Marcos continued. "I have no idea where these new revelations will take me. These concepts conflict with everything I have been taught about Greek and Roman cultures. While Antipas was speaking, I surrendered to the calling that was nagging at my conscience."

The tension in his face was gone; new words burst from his mouth. Marcella held her breath, afraid for what it might mean for her husband as he searched out these new truths. She was rejoicing in this new understanding; her daughter's healing was somehow related to Antipas's teaching.

"What is going on there?" Marcos asked. "I see joy rooted in love, but I can't explain it fully. Where does their love come from? There seems to be no single basis for their community, but Antipas said, 'God binds our community together.' They are so different: different backgrounds, languages, skills, and professions. Yet God is among them! I want to be part of this Household of Faith. I want to know all about Yeshua, the Messiah.

"A silent prayer came to my lips. 'I call out to you. I am one of those open hearts.' But what will others think? Can I really become a follower of Yeshua? What would that mean? What would we be getting into?

"I wanted to laugh from my sense of joy, but I couldn't, not there, not while everyone was taking the bread! I, as a visitor, could not go to the front for the Holy Bread. I remained seated, echoing Miriam's song in my heart but making it personal."

"You have never explained things so plainly, Marcos."

"Well, I see things clearly now. Two voices are clashing in my mind. One is Hades grinding deep in the earth, the Destroyer who sucked everyone in my extended family into a watery grave. The other voice belongs to Antipas. He is explaining a Jewish poem about people coming from the four corners of the earth. I hear him inviting people to belong, to be part of a new community, one that says, 'You will be my people and I will be your God.'

"Miriam is genuine in her affection for our little girl. Do you think Miriam could be the older sister Florbella never really knew? The older sister who was swallowed up, the older sister Florbella will never see again?

He sighed and smiled. "I didn't want to leave the cave tonight, even though they are people I hardly know. I wished that the moment would never be over. That thought came when Antipas described the relationship of these humble people to his God. He said they are holy, set apart from the world, and precious to God. Even in a dark place, in a cave, God can speak to me!

"The meeting ended, and I went slowly to the door, not rushing. My own thoughts were making me laugh."

"Laugh? Why? What were you thinking, my husband?"

He folded his hands and fingers together. "I made a mental note. 'Just wait until Marcella hears all this from me! Whatever will she say?'"

He kissed her and said, "For my part, I will always remember June 14 in the eighth year of Domitian."

Marcella placed her hands over his. Her bittersweet tears spoke of long years of grief and loss as well as a newfound joy and a sense of belonging.

LYDIA-NAQ'S HOUSE, THE ACROPOLIS

Lydia-Naq was elated by the news that she had brought back to Pergamum for Zoticos. Even though he was late coming for breakfast at her house, that did not bother her. As her slave poured him a drink of water, she reclined on the couch. She once again played over in her mind the arguments she had used before the leaders in Ephesus to promote Zoticos. She ran a hand over her knee and her shapely calf.

I won the coveted position of Chief Librarian of Pergamum for my brother!

She pictured her victory again, wearing her golden earrings shaped like the crescent moon. The matching bracelets and necklaces came from her most expensive set. There she was, standing in the Basilica of Ephesus, at the center of the government offices. She was granted access to the acropolis in the upper section of the city. Keeping her face calm and not betraying the tension in her heart, she had explained why her brother should be appointed as Chief Librarian.

Her heart was beating wildly as she made her case to the senior civic leaders of Ephesus. In her hand, she held the scroll from the city council in Pergamum, sealed with red wax. One man opened the scroll and read the recommendation for Zoticos to be the next chief librarian of Pergamum.

When Zoticos was comfortably reclined on the couch, she said, "My brother, I submitted the petition for you at Ephesus, and they accepted my recommendation. You will be the new chief librarian. Zeus has heard our prayers."

They discussed how this meant that he would now have more authority in implementing Lydia-Naq's desire to bring back the Lydian culture and language to the area around Pergamum.

"Now something else has come up," she said. "On Friday, when the morning business at the library is finished, I want you to be at the New Forum. I invited that Jew, Antipas, to publicly debate me. Yesterday a priest read the signs on the entrails of a sheep I sacrificed. He said the most auspicious time to debate the Jew was June 24."

They discussed the debate and then departed to begin their daily activities. Lydia-Naq knew secrets and was planning her attack against the Jewish businessman.

Her son Diotrephes had been passing information to her about Antipas and the village. Her last words to him came back, "Antipas is a successful foreigner who came into our city with business connections from Alexandria. He has many people working and living in his little village. None of them are slaves. There's something dangerous about that."

"You, my son, have brought me good news—well done for these first several weeks—helping me in my desire to stamp out this atheist."

Zoticos smiled, and his face lit up as he walked back to the library. He knew how significant the appointment was. Wouldn't his name be carved in stone? Distant generations would recognize him for having brought Lydian culture and its language back from the brink of extinction.

His chest swelled with pride at the thought, and suddenly, he realized he had gained something for which he was seeking.

"Well, I have discovered my life's purpose!" he said to himself. "All my life, I've wondered why I had these skills and abilities, but now I know!"

THE GARRISON OF PERGAMUM

During the past months, Anthony had noticed that Cassius had begun to question his training methods. The commander of the garrison had not said a word of appreciation, yet Anthony was convinced his instruction was providing army recruits with the experience they would need in Dacia.

A recent conversation he had with Cassius came back to him on a cloudless summer day. "You spend too much time with your scouts in the forests up above Pergamum," fumed Cassius. "Soldiers must fight in formation!"

Anthony knew that his recruits had grown robust, resilient, and ready for battle. They were confident in their newfound scouting skills. He replied, "Your men are to be congratulated. They carry out battle formations quickly, but as scouts in Dacia, they also need other skills.

"Sir, I fought in the dense forests of Europe, where trees grow close together. Enemies hide behind them and on the branches above, wearing dark clothing. They aren't seen until they attack. Do you know when they will draw you into swamps where they have an advantage? Our scouts will need specialized skills for Europe in addition to normal training. On the shores of the Euphrates River, you prepared soldiers for that terrain. Trees there are small and far between. In contrast, our scouts will have to defend themselves in dense forests."

Cassius shook his head as if to say, "That's nonsense," and walked away.

Precise information could enable troops to attack and gain an advantage through surprise. That was how Anthony and his team of scouts had successfully subdued many small villages, leading to Roman victory in Upper Germanica. They had overwhelmed communities in valleys between the Neckar River and the Rhine. Six years ago, his legion had fought against the Chatti tribe and won. They pushed the Alamanni tribe back from the low hills east of the Neckar and built a defendable Roman fort in Cannstatt.[36] How could Cassius understand the significance of the scouts' contribution if he would not listen?

Since Anthony feared further arguments with Cassius, he avoided more discussion. His scar would always remind him of the battle taking place inside his mind. He was sworn to true loyalty, devotion, and allegiance to the emperor—an oath he declared on the first day of every new year. That meant being faithful in battle with other soldiers. His continuing struggle, more than that with his commanding officer, was to keep his inner life secret. That battle was fought at night in his dreams.

THE LIBRARY OF PERGAMUM, THE ACROPOLIS

Zoticos set to work immediately. Everyone in Pergamum would soon know of his plans. Once the harvest season was over, his new study course would begin at the acropolis. Scribes were making copies of notices to be displayed in each marketplace, and announcements would be made in the surrounding towns and villages about the new course of study.

Several questions with Lydia-Naq kept returning: "What do I need for an adequate curriculum? How can I lead these people to once again walk the ancient paths? How can I motivate people to speak their ancient language? This is going to be a challenge."

---

[36] Stuttgart was founded late in the first century as Cannstatt, a Roman fort. The fort was a garrison, one of several along the Neckar River.

Chapter 21
The Debate

THE NEW FORUM, PERGAMUM

The night before the public debate, Lydia-Naq dreamed that a man was pushing her into a pool of water. The man in the dream wore a mask. It was the same one she had seen in Diodorus's home when she asked him to support the Lydian language expansion.

To her, dreams were a gift from Zeus, and they could not be ignored. She finished her preparations for debating Antipas, believing that Zeus had given her a clue about something that Antipas was hiding.

Diotrephes had learned so much while attending the meetings at the cave. She would use the information against Antipas, while he knew nothing about her. Diotrephes said she should not argue against Antipas' character and to stay away from his personal life.

My son says everything Antipas does is because he believes that there is only one god. This should not be difficult. What idiocy!

Word about the debate spread quickly throughout the marketplaces. From the start, she would find a way to force Antipas to criticize Rome. Putting pressure on him to recognize the authority of governments was her initial strategy.

She prepared several questions. Why had Antipas started to free slaves? Why didn't he accept the gods of Pergamum? His actions showed how alien his thinking must be. By the end of the debate, everyone would understand that he had become an evil presence in the city. And if left unchecked, his influence could spread.

As she climbed the four steps to the wooden platform at the New Forum, Lydia-Naq took several deep breaths. Her hands

166

were clasped as if she had already won the contest.

She saw in Antipas a short, dark-skinned man. His beard was neatly trimmed in the style of Grecian Jews, and he wore a brown tunic. Her appearance was so different from his; her bright white linen tunic, complete with gold ornaments, set her apart both socially and religiously. Gold threads sparkled in her black hair, and she tossed her head back with confidence.

Lydia-Naq and Antipas looked at each other. A moderator introduced the two speakers and said they would be arguing on civic responsibility. She was looking around, confident that she held an edge. The growing crowd gathered in the warm sun.

As soon as the moderator turned to go, Lydia-Naq asked the first question. Wanting to crush him immediately, she turned to Antipas, and the crowd quieted. "Are you a Roman citizen?"

Antipas replied, "Yes, I am a citizen of Rome, and I respect the authority of Rome."

I can't believe how easily he set himself up for defeat.

"So you are a good citizen. Doesn't that mean submission to the authority of the city where one lives?"

He answered, "God made human authority. He established governments. Different powers and various nations were raised up only to later fall away. Consider my people. In the time of my forefathers, Babylon conquered my city, Jerusalem. Assyrian kings harassed our people for generations. Then the Chaldeans came and led our people into exile. The Persians, the same people that attacked your city in those distant times, took us captive only to later permit our people to return to Jerusalem.

"Alexander the Great brought the language we now use every day. My father was born in Alexandria, the city Alexander the Great founded. There, both Greeks and Romans imposed laws. We respect Roman authority, and yes, I do want to be a good citizen. For me, that means knowing the laws and following them. I follow principles that determine good laws."

Lydia-Naq smiled with satisfaction. *Within the first few minutes, I forced him to say he is a good citizen and will follow the laws. I will win the debate by showing that he selects which rules to support. I will demonstrate that he isn't really a good citizen.*

"Did your forefathers submit to the demands of Antiochus and all his descendants?"

Antipas responded just as she thought he would. "You mean

167

to imply that we choose when to obey some laws and when not to follow others. We come from a race of people that love to discuss the finer points of legislation, so we talk about rules endlessly.

"Now, in the time to which you refer, the laws imposed by Antiochus IV were cruel. Our forefathers rebelled. Judas Maccabeus and his brothers fought against unjust laws and cruelty, and they recaptured Jerusalem. Like anyone here, they wanted to return to a previous age when they ruled themselves."

She blinked repeatedly. *My advantage won after his first response has disappeared. Jews cherish their traditions like I do, and so in a way, both of us want to keep languages, practices, and beliefs alive that come down from distant times.*

Antipas continued, "Jews went to Rome to establish friendly relations with the Senate. At that time, Rome wanted to block the ambitions of the Seleucid kings in Antioch. We teach this to all our children. The Romans were well disposed toward all who made an alliance with them.

"So two of our ambassadors, Eupolemus, the son of John, and Jason, the son of Eleazar, were sent to Rome. The purpose of their trip was to establish a friendship and an alliance. They perceived things this way: If they didn't create an agreement with Rome, the kingdom of the Greeks would eventually enslave Israel.

"In our treaty with the Romans and in the Decree of Pergamum, and other cities as well, we Jews were granted the privilege of friendship, confederacy, and proper rewards for service. Our enemies were the Seleucids."

"No one wants to hear about those ancient days!"

He ignored her interruption. "Thus, the House of Jacob went to Rome in the time of Bacchides, and Jews obtained the treaty with Rome. That established us as a nation. The Seleucid kings were the same enemies you confronted for generations.

"The records tell what happened here in Pergamum. At that time, Cratippus was the *prytanis*, or senior executive, of the city council. Cratippus attested that Abraham was the father of the Hebrews and that Pergamum was, in the oldest times, the friend of those Hebrews. At that meeting, the Decree of Pergamum was signed by all eight on the Senior Executive Committee in the city council: Cratippus, Hyrcanus, Strato, Theodatus, Apollonius, Enaus, Aristobulus, and Sosipater. The same thing happened in other cities in Asia Minor. These documents are well known.[37]

"Later, the king of Pergamum willed his city to Rome, accepting a distant authority and all treaties Rome had signed. So, yes, Jews do respect the laws of Rome. Even today, after our city is destroyed, we as Jews still obey the laws of Rome."[38]

This man is clever. He knows more history than I do. His mastery of details covers up something else. I will not prevail by debating political facts about his people, so I will bring him around to taxes.

She pointed her index finger sharply at his feet.

"Enough! Everyone knows the history of your people gaining certain rights unique in the world. Here in Pergamum, you developed a village with craftsmen and industries. You honor Rome, but you do not pay taxes as other citizens do."

Her tone was accusing, inviting condemnation.

He smiled. "Oh yes, we Jews do pay taxes. I pay the temple tax, which used to go to Jerusalem but now goes to Rome. Also, I pay heavy taxes because I have a shop in each of the two marketplaces. The House of Ben Shelah contributes heavily to the operation of the city. In fact, I pay more taxes than most people."

For him, it's all about shops and money but never what else goes on in the city! In the amphitheater, it's the stronger who is the victor. The champion is the one who draws blood first. Antisocial and taxes...here is the vulnerable spot in his armor to rally the people against him.

"You say that you submit. However, you do not do that. Why don't you join in social activities: the theater, games, fights, or processions? It's because you are antisocial."

A few people thought they saw what was coming. "Bravo!" was their response.

Antipas paused for a moment. "Submission, for us, is our

---

[37] Josephus 14.10.22 Josephus quoted from documents to which he had access. In these, Jews were given the honor by Rome, and other nations also acknowledged the Jews. Here, Antipas is using the same reference that Josephus had. The ancient relationship between Rome and the Jews was a matter of common knowledge to the Jews in the Diaspora.

[38] I Maccabees 8:1–31 is written in a way that infers the Roman–Israel Treaty, signed in 162 BC, was between equals. Thus, until the completion of Herod's temple, in AD 64–65, many Jews understood the relationship with Rome as one between equal nations. This changed entirely after AD 70.

whole way of life. Our way of life evolved as men and women came to know God. They have faith in him. The Lord wants a real community, one based on knowing God. Permit me to tell you about our God."

Once again, he's slipped out of my control! If I question him further on his beliefs, the crowd will want to know more about his god. I don't want to see ignorant people swayed by his ideas. I will accuse him of being an "atheist."

She went on the offensive. "Do you believe in Zeus? We worship and reverence many gods and goddesses. Our whole way of life constantly takes account of them."

He responded, "I believe that there is only one God, while you believe in many gods. I do not believe in gods made by the hands of men. I believe in the Almighty, the one true God, the Lord of hosts. He created the world from a plan before time began.

"We had a famous writer who wrote about the beauty of creation even though he lived during times of great suffering. God made the earth by his power. He founded the world by his wisdom and stretched out the heavens by his understanding.

"'When he thunders, the waters in the heavens roar. He makes clouds rise from the ends of the earth; he sends lightning with the rain and brings out the wind from his storehouses.'[39] Your poets, like ours, longed to know the mysteries of life, of summer and winter."

Lydia-Naq frowned. *Help me, Zeus! He has shifted back to his strange beliefs, and I must counter his fables with our stories. If only I could teach him about the altar and show him the whole story!*

"You are mistaken, Antipas. Before mankind was on earth, there was Tartarus, the god of the Black Sea. Before he was born, the dark depths held only death.

"Then came Gaia; she created Uranus, her firstborn. And then she made Pontus with its snow-capped mountains. Next, with the help of her son Uranus, Gaia filled the universe with creatures. She had twelve more children, and she called them the Titans. Then she gave birth to the three cyclopes, creatures that had only one eye."

Antipas spoke slowly, deliberately. "Yes, you have many gods, each one with his or her name. But we worship the one God—one

---

[39] Jeremiah 10:12–13

God with many names and many virtues. He is the source of goodness, loving-kindness, and mercy.

"Here is our story of the beginning: He created the seas and the dry land and called them good. He created the fish in the sea, the birds of the air, and the animals on dry land and called them good. He made man and woman and said they were very good. He did all this using only the power of his word. He did not need wars in the heavens to show his own superior power. He spoke, and the world came into being. His word is powerful."

Lydia-Naq had not heard his creation story before. She was surprised. "What? You believe that power is found only in words?"

She hesitated before saying more. *In my world, words are potent. I use secret, powerful words every day. A single word, like a name, lasts forever. Imagine him speaking of a god who cannot be seen!*

But I've found three weak points: He avoids social interaction within the city, so I need to develop this argument. And he rejects the social values of the city but uses people for his financial gain. If I can also show that he is an atheist, disrespecting our gods, the people will reject him.

"So you do not believe in the gods!" she taunted him. "Is that what you are confessing? Then you are an atheist, the worst type of humanity!"

He said, "I'm loyal to the everlasting kingdom of God."

I've got him! He has condemned himself!

She spoke her next words carefully, jabbing her finger at him as if to stab him with the words. "You are loyal to that kingdom. As a Jew, are you not loyal to Rome? Is Rome your kingdom or is it not?"

"There are many kinds of power. You refer to this yourself every day simply by talking about your gods. Rome is not responsible for everything, but you talk about gods who send the lightning or thunder, rain, or fertility. Those are powers over which Rome has no authority. We, however, know that all those things are in the hands of God."

She shot back, "But if you cannot see your God, if you no longer have your altar in Jerusalem, how can you make sacrifices? Why would he pay any attention to you if you don't sacrifice to him?"

He turned and looked her straight in the eye. "Your gods need dancing, drums, myth, and magic. When the frenzy is at its height, then your god comes alive. God, the one who watches over all of us day and night, does not need sacrifices, because he does not come alive through our sacrifices. Yes, our Holy City lies in ruins, and our temple is destroyed. So, naturally, we ask, 'What do we give him as a sacrifice?' God wants a broken spirit, humility, a repentant heart, prayers, a holy life, love, and kindness in our community. He wants us to be part of his covenant."

Lydia-Naq scowled. *What a meaningless religion! No processions, no animal sacrifices!*

"Pathetic! You have no animals being led to sacrifice by singing children, no priests or priestesses! How can you even think of that as worship?"

He answered calmly. "No, you don't understand. Everything we do is worship; our whole life is a sacrifice. We give ourselves as a sacrifice that is alive. To die to our selfish wishes is the greatest sacrifice there is. That sacrifice is the way to know God."

She turned toward him with narrowed eyes. "You are nothing but an atheist!" she said venomously, using the unkindest name she knew.

She left the platform and stepped onto the white marble pavement of the New Forum. Antipas stood on the platform and smiled as he watched Lydia-Naq walk toward the acropolis and up the steps to her house.

The voices of the people filled the New Forum, with many asking questions about Antipas's responses and opinions.

When Marcos had heard about the upcoming contest, he had wanted to listen to the debate and thought of asking Anthony to join him. The soldier had just completed the last teaching exercise for the morning, so he accepted the offer to come to the New Forum for the debate. Anthony and Marcos stood together, close to the platform so they could hear every word.

Anthony heard the entire debate and was impressed. The short, energetic Egyptian had courage, something he, a legionary, understood very well.

He was pleased that Antipas had withstood the verbal assault of the priestess. "I will search out this Antipas after I return from Philippi," he told Marcos, opening and closing his fist. "A little old man alone in the public place debating—speaking of a broken spirit, humility, and a changed heart. How strange! Even if the priestess described him as an atheist, it was evident that Antipas knows things about the unseen world that Lydia-Naq has never imagined."

Going to sleep that night, Anthony continued to think about the debate and his future.

THE ALTAR OF ZEUS, THE ACROPOLIS

On her way to her brother's house, Lydia-Naq sent a slave to prepare a sacrifice. This time a lamb would be sacrificed in gratitude to Zeus. No one knew it yet, but she was convinced that she had found a way to permanently defeat that Jew.

Zoticos was waiting and welcomed her in.

She raised both hands above her head as if in victory. "I wasn't able to trip him about taxes; he dodged that topic the whole time. When gladiators prepare to fight, they are given equipment for proper protection. Just one vital part of their body—a shoulder, a knee, or their face—is left exposed. The only possible strategy is to attack their opponent while protecting their weakest point.

"Zoticos, I have exposed his soft spot! It will make the Roman authorities step in and destroy him. He speaks of another kingdom, and therefore he cannot confess true allegiance to Rome. This is the path that will lead to his downfall."

ANTIPAS'S VILLAGE, PERGAMUM

At the synagogue that evening, the rabbi, Jaron Ben Pashhur, led the service. Although no one in the congregation said a word to Miriam or Antipas about the debate, she was sure that everyone in the group knew about it. She interpreted the glances from their friends as a general feeling of acceptance.

Going home, she overheard one woman: "Antipas projected a sense of hospitality, sincerity, and dependability in the city today."

Following their worship time, Miriam and Antipas returned home, and she hugged her grandfather for a very long moment. Her anxiety had been deep earlier in the day, not knowing what would happen after the debate.

Their evening meal was his favorite, lamb, and she reclined at the table with him, calmed by his presence and confidence. She gazed at her grandfather and lovingly said, "In the New Forum, I was so afraid for you, Grandpa. But now we are home safely, and I am so glad."

He put down his flatbread and the bone he had just taken in his fingers. The wrinkles around his eyes hinted at a quiet joy.

"While debating the high priestess, I noticed something changing inside my heart. That gut-wrenching dread, which I have been unable to shake since the fires consumed our house and burned my sisters, was much less noticeable. I recalled the words of Yeshua to simply be a witness to what I knew."

MARCOS'S VILLA AT KISTHENE

After the debate at the New Forum, Marcos returned to his home, pondering the summer break. Like many other wealthy families, he owned a summer villa along the Aegean Sea, which was more relaxed.

Many families spent July and August beside the sea, strolling along white sandy beaches, leaving behind their exhausting responsibilities.

He called to his servant, "I'm leaving Pergamum with Marcella and Florbella, taking our household to our villa in Kisthene, the City of Quince Fruit.[40] We will be enjoying pleasant breezes on one of the many beaches. While I'm gone, you are in charge of the house. If anything comes up, send for me. Send a message by horseback."

Florbella shouted when she learned they were going the next day. He explained, "During our holiday period, we'll sit down to a late breakfast. As the sun's rays penetrate our skin, we'll swim in the shallow waters. I'll walk with you in the evening and spend hours exploring lengthy stretches of sand."

"Will we see our friends there again, Daddy?"

"Oh yes, we'll make visits to friends in other villas." Marcos saw gladness in Marcella's eyes. "I've borrowed several valuable scrolls from Antipas, who had no concerns about lending them to me. I want to spend a lot of time reading during the hot summer days."

Many days they watched sunrises reflected in the bay to

---

[40] Kisthene is today known as Ayvalik, a well-known destination for summer visitors.

the east. Before dark, they sat enthralled by the vivid colors as the sun went down over the Aegean Sea.

His brothers' villas in Kisthene were legally his now. He owned and administered them, and he spent hours changing the registration of each one into his name.

The family walked barefooted along the white sands, listening to the waves and watching the gulls.

Marcos and Marcella were elated with Florbella's progress. She was speaking more each day. She enjoyed their vacation at the villa, where he told her stories in the evenings.

He walked hand in hand with Marcella one evening at the beginning of August. Florbella had run ahead, and he could whisper to his wife.

"I marvel that Florbella didn't die during the earthquake. Two days later, another earthquake moved the stones that covered her. During that second quake, I pulled her back from certain death.

"Then, full of fear, she lost her voice, and we moved to this province. She became friends with Miriam and Antipas at the cave. She's speaking again! Hades tried to kill her, but she is alive and improving every day."

He laughed. Only Marcella and the waves heard him in the late evening light. "Florbella has led us into a dark place—into the cave—and now she is singing!

"A question still occupies me though: What should I do with the properties left by my brothers here and in the province of Bithynia?"

He returned to his love for his daughter. "Marcella, Florbella said to Miriam, 'I love you,' and Miriam replied, 'I love you too, Florbella. I want you to come back to meet with us at the cave at the end of summer!' So much has changed this past year."

The conversation he had overheard still stirred him.

Chapter 22
Mithrida

TANAIS, THE BOSPORAN KINGDOM

Months had gone by since Flavius and Sesba had abducted the young woman, Arpoxa. That predawn raid resulted in her being taken to the docks in Tanais. Although they were disappointed in the price they received for her, they both realized that capturing, transporting, and selling slaves could be a profitable occupation.

Flavius carefully placed a large jug of beer on the table, covering the large knots on the roughly sawn wooden boards. He looked around at other men gathering for an evening meal. All told stories and spoke of events taking place in the Bosporan Kingdom. Many were shipbuilders who had worked all day long under the hot sun.

He wiped his mouth with the back of a dirty hand. "Three months ago, we made a costly mistake by breaking into that house. We might have been reported. Scum! Told us his sister was worth the price of a male slave! But it led to us taking hold of this opportunity, and since then, you and I have made money—lots of it."

Fingering his freshly shaved face, he raised a large mug to his lips. Both his tunic and his cloak had been washed, and his Roman soldier's uniform gave him a sense of superiority.

Flavius Memucan Parshandatha, like his companion, Sesba Bartacus Sheshbazzar, was proud of his Persian descent. They had met in the army, fought Germanic tribes together, and then, in defiance of Domitian's orders from Rome, they had deserted. Rarely did a tribune do what they had done, relinquishing the glorious honor of status in the Roman army.

"Three months with good success," Flavius bragged. "Recruited several new companions to capture Scythians, men and women alike. We send slaves south, and wealthy men buy them in the far-off cities. They pay huge sums for healthy slaves."

Sesba smiled and nodded in agreement. "Our tactic of looking like army soldiers has protected us from the authorities. I'm glad we never disposed of our uniforms. I applaud the way you approached the kingdom's regional treasurer from Tanais and brought him in as a partner!"

He spoke quietly so that others could not hear their conversation. "How easily we can obtain forged documents! As a soldier with documents, I can fool anyone now, Flavius. I'm used to saying that I am part of a specialized cohort transporting slaves to Sinop on the southern coast of the Black Sea."

Flavius nodded in agreement. "Yes, delivering twenty captives from the farms up the Don River, twelve from towns along the Dnieper River... We've been fortunate getting them to the harbor close by with little fuss. They brought a good sum. It feels good to have no debts. Sesba, you did well when you recruited six 'auxiliaries' to help us. But we need to do several things over the next few months. This is going to be our business."

"You have a larger plan, Flavius? That's what you were known for when we were fighting against Germanic tribes. You were always successful in designing strategies."

"We successfully changed our identities thanks to the money under the table—all eight of us. And new forged signet rings. That's because the kingdom's regional treasurer led their chief treasurer to join us. He gets his cut of the profits, so he's happy to look the other way. Consequently, we look like legitimate soldiers going about their duties. Now, Sesba, who was the greatest enemy Rome ever faced? Where did he come from?"

"That's easy! King Mithradates VI. Born in Tanais and brought up on the waves of the Black Sea, he inspired the rebellion in Asia Minor and instigated the Night of Rebellion when eighty thousand Roman migrants and citizens were killed. He outfoxed the best Roman generals for a quarter of a century."

"Exactly. Mithradates had a plan, and he started a rebellion. We'll do the same. Start speaking of Nero's return. Tell our potential recruits in taverns that you've heard Nero is ready to cross the Tigris and Euphrates Rivers. Tell them he is coming with an army. If they want to know more, then speak to them about what we are doing. Be like a fisherman. Pull them in. Let them bite the hook."

Sesba looked thoughtful as he considered the scenario. "Yes, we could do that."

"Our papers now show us as belonging to the Tanais Garrison but assigned to colonies along coastal areas. No one will challenge us! Our 'soldiers' will march along the roads, use fresh horses at relay stations, and even be paid by garrisons along the way.

"Now, regarding sea transportation, remember that I was born near Sinop. I know the shorelines of the Black Sea, both the dangerous rocks and good harbors. Here's what we need to do. Find someone who will work with us—a shipowner. That shouldn't be too difficult. I'll be looking for a ship. I want a captain willing to transport slaves and need a ship that can carry at least twenty in the hold, hopefully forty."

Sesba closed his eyes and smiled. "I see how you are going to expand our business. Instead of getting owners of other ships to take our captives to the market, we'll do it ourselves. But we need someone we can trust to manage what happens from the time the ship is loaded until it is unloaded in the South."

A cloud passed over Sesba's face. "How will we maintain security in our little army?"

"We'll be seen by others as soldiers following orders— simply taking slaves to markets. But to identify ourselves with one another, we need secret names. We'll find a way. We have to disguise ourselves. None of those loyal to us can have the same name as another person. We'll be a unique little army. We now have falsified Roman army names, and we can circulate openly. We'll easily recruit more followers."

"It sounds good, but how will this army be controlled? I don't want to die like the three governors that the emperor executed five months ago for rebellion! Domitian was as angry as a cornered lion!"

Flavius leaned back, satisfied to have convinced his friend. "I have a plan. For starters, we must be organized like a legion. We'll appoint tribunes, centurions, legionaries, and auxiliaries. There are big profits from slaves and wild animals for entertainment at the Games. Great profits!"

Sesba remained quiet for a while as he stared out the window, thinking about Flavius's plan. "It just might work. How long before we get rich?"

"Within two years. We'll have to think ahead and keep tight security to avoid being arrested. Local garrisons won't discover our real purpose."

"I like the sound of it. Our little army. What will we call ourselves?"

"A new sound around the Black Sea. The Faithful."

Sesba closed his eyes and thought for a moment. "Yes, I like that. We are the Faithful. It has an ironic ring to it."

"Now think about our names! Our first names are unusual. Both of us had Persian ancestors, so our names are linked to historical figures. One of my ancestors, Mithredath, was the treasurer for King Cyrus.[41] Rome's greatest foe was King Mithradates VI.[42] We worship Mithra, our Persian god. So, between ourselves, I will be Mithrida, a name no one else knows. My new name reminds me of my heroes. Now what about you?"

"My first name is Sesba. I told you that my ancestor was Sheshbazzar, a Persian governor, a satrap in Syria."

"We'll call you Sexta. No one else can have the same name. Each name will be unique. It should be impossible to infiltrate our gang or penetrate our secrets."

Sesba leaned back, putting it all together. "All right. Two tribunes of the Faithful are Mithrida and Sexta. But don't we need at least one more? The Black Sea region and Asia Minor...it's an immense region."

"I have someone in mind. My friend has the skills. He'll direct an operation. Remember when we were in the army together? Who was First Javelin in Legion XXI?"

"Of course! Claudius Carshena Datis! Where is he?"

"He's in Sinop. I'm going there. We'll get Claudius to join our little 'army.'"

---

[41] Ezra 1:8

[42] Mithradates VI of Bithynia and Pontus became Rome's greatest foe. Mithradates, a long line of local kings, claimed roots in both the Persian and Greek worlds. He eventually captured much of the area known as modern Turkey and controlled the Black Sea. In 88 BC he led a slaughter of Romans in Asia Minor, with about 80,000 Romans, Italians, and other foreigners being killed. Three wars followed. Mithradates was finally defeated, and his kingdom was destroyed in 63 BC. Rome created several new provinces in Asia Minor.

"But he's still angry with us, Flavius."

"Yes, but we need him. We'll go to Sinop and speak to Claudius. From what I've heard, he'll be interested in what we have to offer. He has not been living a happy life."

SINOP, PROVINCE OF BITHYNIA AND PONTUS

A week later, Flavius Memucan Parshandatha (Mithrida) and Sesba Bartacus Sheshbazzar (Sexta), the deserter tribunes from Legion XXI, had found accommodation in a small inn at the port in Sinop.

Several vessels had already entered the harbor that morning, having come from many ports around the Black Sea. Some arrived from the Sea of Marmara. Ships were even there from the Mediterranean Sea. Flavius started asking around in search of the one man he knew would make an excellent recruiter for their new army.

Blustery winds blew sand along the rocky northern shore that protected Sinop Harbor. Searching from house to house in the nearby fishing village, Flavius found Claudius, the other deserter critical to the plans for his secret army.

"How did you find me? Get out of my sight!" growled Claudius. "I never want to see your face again. The last time I trusted you for anything, I ended up having to run for my life. Twice, your ideas have turned my life upside down."

They stared at each other, former friends who had become enemies. First, Flavius and Sesba, two of the best tribunes in Legion XXI, the Predators, had disagreed with Emperor Domitian's decision to send their legionaries eastward to fight in Pannonia. Their secret plans to support the rebel governor of Germania Superior, Lucius Antonius Saturninus, were discovered. Flavius, Sesba, and Claudius saved their necks only by fleeing.

"What a way to treat an old friend!" exclaimed Flavius. "So good to see you after three long years."

"How did you find me here?" Claudius tried to shut the door, but Flavius's foot was in the way.

"Come, walk with me along the beach. Something special has come up. I need your help."

"You don't need my help! By Jove, your head never stops churning, always dreaming up complex plans that never work out."

"Claudius, you are needed. Let me explain how you can live a good life again."

Claudius grunted a reluctant note of agreement, pulled the door against the wind to shut it tight, and limped a short distance down to the narrow beach.

"Sesba is with me. He's back at the inn where we're staying. We were careful not to be followed," Flavius said as they walked beside the Black Sea. "You remember our discussions in the officers' tent, don't you? We were trying to stop our legion being sent to the province of Pannonia."

Claudius grimaced with pain as his foot slipped on a wet stone. "Yes, it was amusing to think we could confront the emperor—until our general learned about the plans. Flavius, leave me alone! I don't want to get into more trouble. Execution awaits all of us."

Flavius understood that his old army friend had lost his self-confidence. "Claudius, I have a plan, and it requires your abilities. You are needed."

Claudius shook his head and kicked the sand with his strong right leg. During these windstorms beside the Black Sea, his left leg was a painful reminder of what his own treachery had brought him.

He raised his head and looked across the dark waves of the Black Sea. "I'm no good to anyone now. I'm barely keeping alive by petty theft." He paused. "I can never return to Lower Germanica."

Flavius gently placed his hand on Claudius's shoulders. "You are descended from one of the most celebrated Persian princes. Wasn't Datis your ancestor, the one who fought against the Greeks and destroyed the Greek navy?"

"You remember well. Yes, Datis, he is my hero!" Claudius raised his face and looked at the roiling waves. "How I would love to repeat my ancestor's triumph. Destroying Greek ships and killing thousands of soldiers! My leg, this wound—it prevents me from even dreaming about such adventures."

"I have a job for you, and those wounds can work to our advantage, Claudius. You will tell stories of battles. Soldiers and officers alike will hold us up as heroes, and they will ask you to repeat the stories of how we overcame the barbarians."

Claudius stopped abruptly. "What do you have in mind?"

"Sesba is waiting for us at a tavern. We are getting into the slave trade."

"Isn't it dangerous for us to be seen together? After everything that happened in Upper Germanica..."

"Not anymore. We have a plan."

"Which is?"

"We are assembling a secret army in plain sight. We have a new name for it—the Faithful. It will operate out in the open. We will look like ordinary troops of Roman soldiers protecting the slavers. To confuse them, we will present documents showing we are assigned to a garrison in the North. No one will learn the real story. We have secured the best cover possible."

"I don't believe you. It's not possible. The Roman authorities are too clever for that."

"Sesba and I have falsified documents and new identities. We also have new signet rings. Only one kingdom could help us achieve this, and we know the treasurer! There is a new identity for you too...if you're interested in joining us."

Claudius couldn't help but ask, "What would you want me to do?"

"During the coming winter, you would stay in Chalcedon to gather new recruits. Then, next summer, you will begin transporting slaves to the South—slaves we will be sending you from the Black Sea area. I am going to find a ship and make it our means of becoming very, very rich."

Grudgingly, Claudius listened as Flavius explained more about the Faithful. The more he heard, the more willing he was to consider the prospects of something better than petty thefts and odd jobs at the harbor.

"Come with me. Meet with Sesba. I will explain everything. Within one year, we will be very wealthy."

"But...if we are caught, found out, tried, and executed?"

"If I imagined for a minute that anyone could break apart the secrets of the Faithful, I wouldn't be doing this. No, the army's bureaucracy will help us avoid being caught. We will use secret names and carefully falsified documents. We'll travel without being questioned. If we are, we'll say, 'We are following our instructions as issued by our garrison commander.'

"The Roman Army is spread out across a vast region. No one in the South will learn the truth. Besides, other soldiers are legitimately taking Scythians to market all the time. Ships leave Tanais all the time, and each one needs guards. And if someone becomes suspicious, we'll present authentic documents from the king's authorities in the Bosporan Kingdom."

Claudius stood tall on his strong leg. "So you have a plan."

"Yes, and remember, as First Javelin in the army, the most able centurion, you led soldiers well. In our little military, you will be one of three tribunes. We need recruits, and that's what you are good at, motivating people and sharing a vision.

"Isn't that what Datis, your ancestor, had to do before sinking the Greek fleet—convince people to follow him and follow instructions? Come join us, and we will explain everything to you. And we'll choose your unique name, only known to the Faithful."

Chapter 23
Trouble at the Synagogue

THE SYNAGOGUE, PERGAMUM

Jaron had long stopped asking Antipas to take an active part in the services. It was apparent to everyone that their relationship was strained. Jaron had only broached the conflict with mild rebukes before, but Antipas was concerned that the meeting Jaron had requested for Saturday evening was going to be much more than that.

Antipas always tried to attend synagogue services in the city. Many Jews lived on his property, occupying twelve of the thirty-eight houses. They walked to and from their place of worship as a group. He approached the synagogue as the sun was setting.

Jaron stood at the back of the building with Hanani. This was going to be a small meeting. Nadav opened the door before he got there. They were expecting his arrival.

"Good evening. May peace be upon your homes!" Antipas greeted his friends. "Hello, Nadav, Hanani, and Jaron."

Nadav had been asked to state the purpose of the meeting, and he wore a somewhat sour look. He stretched to his full height. A little black phylactery was strapped in place on his forehead. He fingered the long salt-and-pepper beard that reached to his waist.

"We are meeting with you tonight to insist that you cease being divisive to our Jewish community." His words were to the point, abrupt. "As leaders of our community, we want you to change. You know the Shema, 'There is but one God.' There is but one way to worship him as well.

"We know from discussions with others that you have been teaching that the Nazarene carpenter is our Messiah! You are changing our covenant and don't follow the tradition of the elders!"

Hanani added. "Look at all those foreign people coming to

184

your home."

Jaron asked, "Antipas, how can you teach these ideas? A Messiah would have delivered us from the hands of our enemies. Look at us! For almost twenty years, we have been without our temple and without a capital city. That carpenter did not deliver us from our oppressors."

Antipas realized how emotional the topic was when Jaron's voice tightened. "In three days, we mark *Tish'a B'Av*, the day when our temple was burned. We will be covered with sackcloth and ashes again when we remember. Twenty years ago, the Roman army burned the temple and tore down Jerusalem. Now we must remember, teach, and keep the law as received by our fathers. We will not have followers of the Nazarene spreading false teachings!"

Jaron put his right hand on Antipas's shoulder. Stubborn calluses formed by his carpenter's tools long ago thickened Jaron's fingers and the palm of his hand.

Once they had been good friends but no longer. "Antipas, you must publicly reject this teaching that the Nazarene is the Messiah. I am responsible for guarding the purity of our teachings. You are leading those of your community off the path of truth. I want our families to be happy together and welcome each other into their homes. We need to celebrate each time a boy becomes a man, to remember our rituals, and not be divided by differences of opinions."

Jaron declared the meeting over.

Antipas's parting blessing was brief. All was quiet at home; Miriam was asleep. He would not tell her of this night's conversation.

The synagogue council of elders met on Monday evening. Supper was over, and as the twelve elders gathered, their mood was somber.

Jaron, as usual, led the meeting. "The issue to be addressed is serious. What should our Jewish community do about Antipas? His teaching about a messiah is causing confusion."

"We were correct in our decision to allow his father to be buried in the cemetery. Eliab Ben Shelah was a Jew, the patriarch of a large family. But Antipas has gone much further astray than his father in his meetings during the week."

Elieonai was another member of the council. He was a child of original Jewish settlers brought to Asia by the ancient kings of Syria, the Seleucids. "One thing is clear about Antipas. He is obviously no longer one of us. Our cemetery is almost two hundred fifty years old, and everyone from our synagogue whose final home is there has been a Jew."

Jaron motioned to Nekoda to give an opinion on a suitable punishment for Antipas. Rebellion would not be tolerated.

Nekoda, a tall, thin man, came from Jerusalem and was a student of human nature, especially concerning leadership. He had moved to Antioch before Titus and Vespasian invaded the Holy City. Later, he watched men in Titus's army digging the mighty channel near Antioch. It was called the Titus Tunnel, a project to redirect a stream that historically flowed into the inner harbor of Seleucia Piera, the capital of the Seleucid Kingdom.

More than twenty thousand soldiers forced Judean slaves to cut through solid rock. Much work still had to be done before changing the watercourse of the creek that had been silting up the harbor during the annual floods.

Titus's impressive successes in destroying Jerusalem and his tunnel project demonstrated to Nekoda what strong leadership could accomplish.

His opinions mattered, and he had a clear plan worked out. "My friends, discipline calls for clarity, compassion, and honor. Antipas needs time to understand his error, to make changes without bringing dishonor to his family. He must change.

"How will we achieve that? First, we will clearly warn him about this new teaching. We will tell him to cease the meetings of his Household of Faith. Because his activities are contrary to our traditions, we should give him a verbal warning. He will suffer *midduy,* or temporary discipline, for sixty days, in August and September.

"Second, we need to show compassion. If Antipas does not conform to our verbal demands, we will be generous. We will give him another thirty days' warning to the end of October. Then we will call a meeting to authorize giving him a written warning on November 11.

"This is more serious because it will carry legal weight in the event of our having to remove his name from the Book of Life, the list of families in our congregation. This date comes six months before Pentecost, when we count the *omer*.[43]

"After Pentecost next year, if he still resists, he will suffer *hçrem*—we will expel him from all social dealings. He will be cut off. We will declare to the city magistrates that Antipas is not a Jew. To us, he will be a non-Jew. The consequences—social, legal, moral, and ethical—will be his responsibility."

The twelve men sat in silence. They had expected a harsh judgment from Nekoda, a Pharisee. But to think that they might pronounce *hçrem*, cutting Antipas off and declaring him a non-Jew!

The consequences could not be contemplated.

Rather lose an arm or a leg as a punishment but never, ever, could a Jew be considered a Gentile!

Tuesday evening, August 2, at sundown, the congregation gathered for the Tish'a B'Av service, the Day of Remembrance.[44]

Antipas, Miriam, and the other Jewish members of the synagogue fell on their knees, weeping with heartfelt emotion. Many were assembled to mourn. Only one garment was genuinely appropriate. They had put aside their regular clothes, and everyone wore sackcloth on this day of tragedy, the day of horror. They remembered the loss of their city, their temple, their kingdom, and their place of comfort.

"Has God forgotten us?" whispered one man to his friend.

Parosh, the owner of camel trains from Persia, was the reader of the scrolls. He was given the book of Lamentations by an attendant. Everyone knew those shattering words by heart, and

---

[43] Counting the omer is the Jewish way of counting the days from the Feast of First Fruits to Shavuot, or Pentecost, which falls on the sixth day of the Hebrew month of Sivan. It commemorates the day when God gave the Torah at Mount Sinai. See Exodus 34:22 and Deuteronomy 16:10. Jewish observance of the harvest of barley and the Christian interpretation of the coming of the Holy Spirit mark significant differences in theology associated with Pentecost.

[44] Tish'a B'Av, commemorated on the ninth day of the month of Av, is the day when the temple of Solomon was destroyed by Nebuchadnezzar in 586 BC. Herod's temple was destroyed on the same date in AD 70. The unique events of Tish'a B'Av bring Jews together in annual mourning. This day of fasting and sackcloth is commemorated with a reading of the book of Lamentations and various psalms.

the book was read slowly. "How deserted is the city, once so full of people! How like a widow is she, who once was great among the nations! She, who was queen among the provinces, has now become a slave."[45]

Jaron lifted his face, tears pouring down his cheeks. "Why did the Almighty permit our city to be destroyed—burned twice? First by the Babylonians and then by the Romans! And on the same day of the year, on the ninth day of the month of Av! The Almighty punished the sins of our fathers by allowing the burning of Herod's temple on the same day and month as the burning of Solomon's temple."

They wept bitter tears as deep grief enveloped them.

Early the next day, Antipas was back at the synagogue with the others, fasting and praying. No water and no food would pass his lips. His mind drifted to the death of his father and then to the ultimatum he was facing. As the effect of the fasting took hold, he was drawn to the past, when he lived in Jerusalem with its crowded, noisy streets.

A strange thought came. *What would Messiah do if given this ultimatum?*

By the afternoon, his mind was numb because of fasting. He had not slept well.

Yeshua did not resist violence, scourging, jeering, or crucifixion. He kept on doing what he had done before, avoiding arrest for months, until his trial before the Sanhedrin. Should I...could I...dissolve the Household of Faith? If I gave it up, it would only be for my comfort and convenience. No, I will stay the course.

His workers came to mind. One slave had been from Cyprus. Unable to pay his debts, he had been sold into slavery. After Antipas purchased him at the slave market, the man changed. He no longer got drunk, although he said the passion for strong drink pulled at him daily. That man had been touched deeply by the stories about Yeshua.

The two new slaves are free, learning to get around on their own. They are working and learning to be part of our community. That's what I want to do—set people free. Today, once again, we mourn the destruction of our city, but I will not repent of my

---

[45] Lamentations 1:1

teaching. I will continue.
The annual observance of Tish'a B'Av was over.

The next day they told Antipas he was wanted by the council. The men, some of whom had been his best friends, were grim-faced as they gathered around him in the sanctuary.

Again, it was Jaron who spoke. "We have never assembled like this before, Brother Antipas. This is an exceptional situation."

He paused, aware of the seriousness of the issues that brought them together. "These council members met for deliberation, and we decided that we must give you a warning about the sins that have been explained to you.

"This is your first warning. As part of that warning, you will not be allowed to join us for sixty days, including the meetings of Yom Kippur next month.

"During this time of midduy, of temporary discipline, you will be alone to contemplate your sins and the shame that you are bringing upon our community. You must renounce and repent of your ways by the end of September. If not, you will be allowed a second warning period until the end of October, another thirty days.

"The third warning will be formally given to you in writing on November 11. The council will provide a final chance to repent, until the Feast of Pentecost next year. At that time, if you still resist the council's requirements, you will be brought before the whole congregation, and you will know the pain of ex-communication, of being cast out, of suffering hçrem.

"You must stop teaching falsehood. You confuse people by your teaching, saying the Messiah has come and was crucified, that he was victorious over death. This is not a messiah for the Jewish people! When he comes, the Messiah will save us from our enemies, and he certainly will not die on a Roman cross!"

Trudging home, Antipas pondered the grim words. He knew it was the last time he would be part of the synagogue worship. It hurt him to realize this, and the sharp pang of rejection took his breath away.

The council, of which he had at one time been a part, was now taking the first steps to expel him. The image of the circle of friends returned. He looked at each one quietly, without a word.

He would never worship with them again, and a new thought struck him.

These men have been my best friends, but I can never give up the teachings of Yeshua. God Almighty, protect Miriam! If I am cut off from my community, no one will want to marry her, and if she does not have a husband, then my line in the Ben Shelah family will die out. Keep me from this shame, Lord!

The fear of midduy was already upon him. That was temporary, and he could be reinstated as a Jew in good fellowship if he would bow to their demands. But *hçrem*...social ostracism...a living death? *And yet, how could I live with myself if I abandoned my Messiah and my community? Gracious God, show me the way.*

Chapter 24
Walls

ANTIPAS'S VILLAGE, PERGAMUM

Miriam was talking with Arpoxa early one evening. She waved her hand back and forth, cooling the back of her neck. "How I love the evening sunsets of late August skies! This evening is beginning to bring relief from days of blistering heat. Was it ever this hot in your home country?"

After many months, Arpoxa was beginning to master the language. "Yes, at home, I also wore my hair up high like you do. I left my neck free to catch the slightest breeze, from the middle of June to the middle of August. People here in Pergamum sleep on the flat roofs of their homes. But we only stayed indoors to sleep. My father's house had a sloping roof."

Miriam wondered why Antipas did not say anything about problems at the synagogue. After the second Sabbath had come and gone and he had said nothing about not worshiping with his friends, she knew that something was wrong.

She wanted her grandfather to speak because she had heard a rumor that was circulating. "Is everything all right?" she asked him one evening.

"Have you noticed how some people are speaking against us?" he answered, asking another question.

Miriam had been wondering how to talk to her grandfather. "Divisions just seem to happen between people!" She was trying to draw him out.

"Look at our establishment, Miriam! A row erupted today over the Scythian young man. Ateas has great artistic talents. Although he isn't twenty years old, Ateas was the cause of jealousy in the potter's house. He has an unusual ability to blend his form of Scythian art with what we are doing. His pots have been selling well in the shops, and customers are bragging about

191

their new goods. The six other potters who make our usual goods are upset. They are surprised that a lame man can shape and then decorate pottery so well and are jealous even though they benefit from the additional sales."

Miriam sat back and pulled her knees tightly against her chest. "I know what you mean, Grandpa. People have disagreements over everything: what they wear, how they style their hair, what others wear, or the color of the dyes used in the tunics at the merchant's store. Gossip divides people!"

Antipas sighed. "What can we do when these little things happen? And what will happen now that walls are going up between the leaders of the synagogue and..."

She looked straight at him, knowing he was ready to listen to her suggestion. "People fear what they don't understand about others. Could we serve a small meal for the community? Tell the details of your life. Most have never heard your story.

"When your brothers were here for Great-grandpa's funeral, we laughed and cried together. Let the people in our village know the facts, and let them know your emotions as well. I will write a song and teach it to the younger people."

Then she added, "Grandfather," using her most formal address, "when you have that expression on your face, it makes me think that maybe I've said something terrible!"

"You are almost reading my mind! No, not terrible, just the shock of imagining what it would be like for everyone to know what has happened to me over all these years."

Miriam put her hand on his arm. "Do you know why I want to write a song? Ever since Passover, I realized that putting my thoughts to music helps take away my fears. Sometimes I am so terribly afraid. I try to block the bad things in our past from my mind. I want Mommy and Daddy to be alive again, and when I think of their loss, the fear makes me hurt deep inside.

"Last night, I had a dream. In it, many people were coming for a meal. I was looking for Mommy and Daddy in the crowd, but I never found them."

Once she started talking about her fears, it was so much easier to address her deepest emotions. She drew a deep breath. "Grandpa, what do you do when you are afraid? Do you just block out the fear in your mind?"

"I write down my thoughts because I'm often lonely, or

sometimes I'm planning events. At other times, I'm worried about what will happen next. However, I'll go along with your suggestion. Yes, Miriam, it's time to tell our story to everyone in the village."

She smiled. "Tell me what you'll say, and I'll write a song to match it."

THE GARRISON OF PERGAMUM

Marcos had come back from his villa in Kisthene. A warm sun shone behind fluffy white clouds as he knocked on Antipas's door. "Thank you for loaning me these five scrolls at the beginning of the summer. I'm here to return them."

"You're welcome! What did you think as you read them?"

"I need to have a long talk about the meaning of some of the things contained in the scrolls."

"Certainly. I'd like to invite you to attend a special meeting and meal at the village two days from now. We could set up a future meeting date then."

"May I bring a friend, Antipas?"

"Yes, I think lots of people will be there. I'm going to tell my life story, from Alexandria to Jerusalem to Pergamum. Who do you want to bring?"

"I have an acquaintance at the garrison. He is known as a demanding instructor, and his recruits are being trained for a mission in the army."

"Of course you can invite him!"

Leaving Antipas's home, Marcos walked to the garrison camp, where Anthony was completing the day's lessons with his men. A soldier was sent to tell the instructor that a visitor was standing at the gate.

Marcos had to wait only a few minutes for him to arrive. "Anthony, I'm here to ask you to come with me on Thursday night. Remember the old man who argued with the Egyptians about their gods and then debated with the high priestess of Zeus?"

"Of course," Anthony replied.

"His name is Antipas, and he healed my daughter. The physician at the Asclepius Hospital could not help her. I went to the Altar of Zeus, but nothing happened, even after a sacrifice was made for the miracle I expected.

"But Antipas did something. He doesn't take credit for it, but he healed my daughter. He's going to tell the story of what happened during the destruction of Jerusalem. You may bring some of your men too, if you like."

"I'd be happy to join you. Jerusalem was where my father fought and was killed. Antipas may have been inside the walls during the days when my father was trying to enter! Father's regiment paid for a special tombstone to their fallen trumpeter."[46]

THE CAVE, ANTIPAS'S VILLAGE

Thursday evening found Antipas with a much larger crowd than usual. The long shed that served as the cool space to dry the unfired pottery had been transformed into a small banqueting hall. Everyone sat on carpets, their sandals lined up inside the door.

Antipas whispered to Miriam. "Look at everyone eating. They are sitting in lines on the floor. The carpets are going to get sticky from the juice from the ripe fruit. Look at the selection of figs, peaches, and other fruits artistically laid out on the trays."

"We can wash the carpets! But look! Grandpa, there's hardly an empty space left. The place is full!"

"Thank goodness that the women bought plenty of fruit at the market earlier in the day!"

"Are you feeling nervous? Are you ready to tell your story?"

"Have I ever had this sensation? My legs are weak, and there's a ball in my stomach. The synagogue leaders are demanding that I stop having gatherings like this, but instead, I'm starting the fall season by feeding a large group of people."

"Tell your story. You've heard my song, and I'm ready to sing it. This evening, our whole reason is to bless them and to remove any misunderstandings about who you are."

Antipas looked at her and knew a personal truth.

Life can start again.... Miriam's song says it all. Hostility can be transformed constructively to build safe walls. Hateful walls tumble down when children are involved. Amazing! Miriam will tell our family's long story in only a few words!

---

[46] During the clash and noise of battle, trumpeters in the Roman army directed troops into position. They indicated if the time had come to move forward or retreat.

The long shed was full. People sat shoulder to shoulder, crowded together. Antipas raised his hands to indicate that it was time to quiet down. "Welcome to this special evening. The food tonight was wonderful, and I give heartfelt thanks to the members of this village who went to the market to choose it. Thank you for doing so well!"

Everyone applauded.

"This is not an ordinary meeting. Usually I read from our sacred scrolls that speak of our history, but tonight I want to talk about what may seem to be a strange subject: walls. I have seen many walls in my life. Some are made of natural materials, like the gray and black stone on your left. It is a natural wall, helpful, giving support so that we could build this long shed, which benefits us in so many ways.

"Some walls are built for a purpose. These could be useful walls, for homes or for protection. Look at the smooth wall on your right, built with bricks that we make here on our establishment. Together these two walls hold up the roof. But consider this: Some barriers are invisible. They divide people.

"Tonight I will tell you our story and of the walls that played an important part in it. Our family, the House of Ben Shelah, comes from the southern part of our land, from a place called Judea. We trace our family back many generations."

He walked back and forth across the front and realized the weakness had left his legs.

"Our people were tradesmen, skilled in pottery, weaving cloth, and working with metals. Before that, they were well known as a recognized clan. More than a thousand years ago, King David made us official suppliers to his household. We had constant contact with Egyptian merchants.

"David's son, King Solomon, loved everything: wine and women, song and dance, proverbs and puzzles, exotic animals and plants. At the time, the king of Egypt, Pharaoh Siamun, proposed a marriage of his daughter to King Solomon as one way to bring down walls, to keep the peace. The best kind of diplomacy!"

The crowd laughed, relishing the idea of marriage as diplomacy.

"Solomon agreed to the marriage, permitting Pharaoh to

come into his land and fight against the city of Gezer. Pharaoh quickly took this city, and the conquered city became the dowry of his daughter. Diplomatic relations improved, and members of our family traveled far up the Nile for trade.

"Some in the Ben Shelah family moved permanently to Africa, way up the Nile River, forming what was called the Elephantine Community. Other Pharaohs even let them build a temple to our God deep in the heart of Egypt. It took many days to travel up the Nile River to the only temple of our God outside of Jerusalem.

"Many years passed, and the kings of Babylon invaded our land and broke down the outer walls; our city was laid low. Solomon had built a magnificent temple to the one God. In the destruction caused by soldiers from Babylon, everything was burned. The city was destroyed, and our enemies took all the sacred objects used for worship, things made from gold, silver, brass, and precious stones.

"That day was like the death of a child. We still feel it. You see, as we protect our children from harm, so the walls protected our Holy City. Those walls were built to protect families, but the walls were destroyed. Many people died."

For a moment, Antipas felt confused. There was so much to tell them about the past. All of it was precious to him, but not all would be remembered by his listeners.

"Our family kept meticulous records of births, dates of marriages, deaths, and the ownership of title deeds. We all learned to read, write, and study in the Hebrew, Aramaic, and Egyptian languages. Then Greek was brought by the soldiers of Alexander, who founded the city in Egypt where we settled.

"I must tell you now about an invisible kind of wall: It has to do with our clothing. We kept our Judean traditions in Egypt. Men wore long beards and a pointed cap on their heads, especially those from the northern parts. We used to wear long tunics and, over our shoulders, a mantle with fringes, or tassels, down the front on both sides.[47] However, when our family moved to Egypt, we began wearing short tunics and cutting our beards. While we looked a bit more Egyptian, inwardly we kept the demands of the

---

[47] The Black Obelisk of Shalmaneser II, housed in the British Museum, shows King Jehu, of the House of Omri (Israel), with 14 Israelites dressed in this way.

covenant. We are called Grecian Jews because of the way we dress.

"Like other Jewish boys, I was trained by my father, just as his father trained him. We were taught to obey our covenant, to be disciplined, and to keep the family line of commerce."

A murmur rippled through the gathered crowd. It was no secret that to live on the Ben Shelah establishment meant acquiring discipline. He had purchased many slaves at the auction, and all, except Yorick, had acquired skills they never imagined before.

"Eliab Ben Shelah, my father, was successful in the family business of building and purchasing ships. Pax Romana brought by Emperor Caesar Augustus made shipping safe. Camels crossed the deserts, and pirates were wiped from the seas. Then highways were built, and as a result, trade flourished. My father and mother had twelve children."

He looked up and saw Marcos seated with a legionary he had never seen before. Behind this man were almost a dozen others. From their uniforms, he knew they were recruits.

Is this the man that Marcos asked me about? he wondered.

"When I was thirteen years old, I realized that there can be invisible walls between human beings. It was the second year of Emperor Caligula. Aulus Avilius Flaccus was the governor of Egypt.[48] We Jews were living in all five districts of Alexandria, totaling fifteen percent of one million residents.

"My oldest sister, Anna, was to be married, and my sisters Deborah and Zibiah were preparing the betrothal party. Anna never saw her future husband because he was one of the first men killed in the riots, stoned by a mob. Beautiful gardens were destroyed; buildings and businesses were burned. More than four hundred homes went up in flames as fires spread. My sisters were burned alive. Anna was eighteen years old, Deborah was fifteen, and Zibiah was eleven.

"I was alone on the street outside, walking to meet Anna, when I saw a group of boys next to the wall of our house. They

---

[48] Aulus Avilius Flaccus was the Roman governor in Egypt from AD 32–38. The pogrom in Alexandria took place in his last year. Estimates vary, ranging from as few as four hundred people to thousands burned to death. Caligula was emperor from AD 37–41.

threw a large jar of olive oil onto the roof and then tossed a flaming torch. I felt helpless. What could I do? They were all bigger.... I could have tried to save my sisters, but I didn't."

Walls...I couldn't get over them. Fire spreading...screams from inside...flames consuming...the smell of human flesh burning...bigger boys shouting, 'You will burn!'...the slaughter of family members...cries of grief all night long...

He paused, swallowing hard. "Five days later, we gathered in a walled section of the city. That wall was a good thing, protecting us, but our freedom was gone. Those divisive walls would never come down. We were crammed into one section of Alexandria. Some were orphans, having lost everyone in their family."

Antipas paused again, taking time to look at the intense expressions all around.

"I was married at the age of twenty to Ruth, a distant cousin of my mother, from another traditional Jewish family of Alexandria. I was taught in the history and beliefs of our people and trained by my father to run his shops in various parts of Alexandria. Our daughter, Tamara, was born a year later. There was another attempt, less successful, to burn our section of the city. My wife, Ruth, was attacked and hurt. She could never have children after that.

"Concerned with the turmoil around us, Eliab, my father, talked about going to Jerusalem. 'The temple in the Holy City is almost finished,' he said. 'Besides, it is no longer safe here!'

"I wanted to go to Jerusalem with my father and my mother, may God rest their souls. However, Ruth did not want to leave her parents behind. 'How can I leave them?' she wailed.

"'Don't go to Jerusalem!' Ruth's parents pleaded. 'It's not safe there either! Egypt has been our security for centuries. Alexandria is our city. These walls will defend us. How can they attack us if we defend one another?'

"We talked it over and decided it was better to leave. Before we went by ship to Judea, my daughter, Tamara, gave birth to our first and only grandchild, Miriam.[49] Johanan, my son-in-law, and Tamara gave their newborn the name Miriam in memory of one of the greatest women in our history. She was a poet and singer, the sister of Moses. They said, 'Just like Miriam of old, we are

---

[49] April 14, AD 65, is Miriam's birthday.

leaving Egypt.'

"Two months later, we were settled in Judea and worked as potters, as our ancestors had a thousand years before. We went to the temple for each festival, and people would say, 'Oh, you must be from Egypt! You speak with a strange accent!' But they didn't think our temple tax money was strange, and the coins we brought with us for pilgrimage were acceptable!"

It was funny how people laughed when the topic of money came up. Antipas needed a pause because to speak about the next chapter of his life was unthinkably painful.

"At that time, we lived as a family on a small farm near Bethlehem, outside Jerusalem, but it was not a time of peace. Jewish civil servants had been crucified after protests against the procurator, Gessius Florus.[50] Zealots, inflamed by the governor's actions, ruined everything the Jewish people wanted. Zealots wanted a separate Jewish state, but they could not see that if they fought against Rome, all their dreams would be destroyed.[51]

"Roman reinforcements came from Syria, squelching a growing rebellious spirit. General Cestius marched Legion XII from Antioch. After his soldiers reached the city of Zebulun, Zealots launched a brilliant attack against Cestius at a vulnerable point on the road. When the attack was over, five thousand three hundred Roman footmen and three hundred eighty horsemen lay dead. Not only were the horses taken but the Roman eagle standard had been captured; it was one of Rome's worst defeats.

"To the Roman soldiers, the eagle insignia is a rallying object of great importance. It is decorated with awards and honors the legion gained in momentous battles, and it must never be lost. This event, the loss of the eagle standard, caused Nero to send General Vespasian and his son, General Titus, to Judea. Rome would not be satisfied with less than Jerusalem's total defeat.

"After news came of the rebellion started by the Zealots in Galilee, my father sold part of his business, which gave him enough money to buy two houses. They were built side by side,

---

[50] Gessius Florus was *procurator*, the governor of Syria and Judea from AD 65 to 67, when Nero replaced him with Vespasian, one of Rome's most celebrated marshals.

[51] This story follows Josephus's accounts, including estimates of deaths and dates of events.

inside the walls of Jerusalem, in the northern section of the city. We moved from our farm near Bethlehem and lived on a crowded, narrow street close to the walls. We believed those high walls would protect us.

"Then the news came of our defeat at Jotapata![52] Town after town was burned as every man, woman, and child was slaughtered by Vespasian's army. People fled from Galilee for safety inside Jerusalem. Thousands arrived from Galilee, filling every corner of the city. They were exhausted, weak, and sick, and many had already been wounded or were dying. Poor folk, they had no food! At that moment, there was no doubt that the Romans would strike against Jerusalem.

"We had food and a secret place for provisions. One of the rooms had no windows, so my father dug an underground storage area. We stored food so that we could outlast a siege. Or so we thought. But Jewish soldiers heard that we had food stored. They came to search our house and confiscated all of it.

"We were a large family: Ruth, both my parents, Tamara, Johanan, and Miriam. Then there was Amos, my brother, with Abigail, his wife, and their seven children as well as Abigail's mother and father. I was the eighteenth person. What eventually happened to Amos and his family was terrible. I cannot bear to include their story, only ours."

Abigail has not recovered, and she mourns six of her seven children. Almighty One, bind up broken hearts. She and Amos, my brother...they lost so much, so many children.

He paused to gather strength.

"We had not expected fighting inside the walls of Jerusalem. In fact, a civil war, a terrible scene, lasted three years. Everyone was against someone else. The civil war started because John of Gischala and Simon Ben Giora separately demanded the right to control the battle against the Roman legions. They came from

---

[52] The siege and defeat of Jotapata, from May 21 to July 1, AD 67, demonstrated the discipline of the Roman army. About forty thousand Jews were killed. Josephus was taken captive, being the last officer alive. Others committed suicide rather than be taken as prisoners. Josephus later worked on the side of the Romans, attempting to persuade Jerusalem to surrender rather than be conquered. He was both praised and reviled for his part in the siege of Jerusalem.

different regions: John from the north in Galilee and Simon from the countryside to the south. Both leaders led factions composed of thousands of men.

"The priests, led by Eleazar, controlled the temple precincts. John and Simon demanded control of everyone else. All believed that the walls of Jerusalem would keep the Romans out. Those walls were amazing, more substantial than these walls in Pergamum. In Jerusalem, there were three walls, each inside the other. One was sixty feet high and fifteen feet thick. What could knock it down? But hatred, tyranny, war, distrust, and fear—that yearning for total power—these weakened our people. Meanwhile, outside the walls were legionaries preparing their attack.

"When Nero died, Vespasian was made emperor by his legions. Before he left for Rome, he promoted his son, General Titus, as commander of the legions, saying, 'Take Jerusalem and hand the temple over to the Senate as a gift.'

"Three legions arrived first, the strongest legions of the empire. Legion V came from Macedonia, Legion X from the Jordan River, and the third, Legion XII, from Syria. Finally, Legion XV came from Egypt to support the siege. I looked over the wall with Johanan, my son-in-law, one day, and we saw a quarter of Rome's fighting force lined up against us in the level area north of the wall. More than forty thousand soldiers and auxiliaries were there to break down our protective fortifications.

"But inside the parapets, a civil war was devastating our people. Simon's men controlled the upper part of the city, and John's men commanded the lower half. On one day alone, eighty-five hundred Jewish men died as the two factions fought for control of our city. In the following days, another twelve thousand were killed in the civil war. Always it was about who would control the outside access to the temple.[53]

"Three towering strongholds protected the northwest corner of the city. We trusted those walls to keep us safe from invaders. John's army, to create a secure area around themselves, burned houses, but as the fires spread out of control, the city's food

---

[53] February of AD 68: Josephus (4.5.2. 318-325) dates the downfall of the Jewish state to this date when the Jews "beheld their high priest, the captain of their salvation, butchered in the heart of Jerusalem."

supply went up in flames. Those grain supplies could have kept our city alive for years, but they were destroyed by the fires set by our own soldiers. Fortunately, running water was abundant, coming from springs that bubbled up inside our city.

"Every night our men went out to damage the Roman army's machines. My nephew went outside the walls with others through a tunnel. They burned the ramps being built up against our walls. Unfortunately, he was caught and crucified with many others, a terrible punishment.

"There was only one thing that John and Simon agreed on: No one could leave the city. That meant we could not bury our dead. Gradually it dawned on us: We were going to die from starvation or from the swords of the Roman legionaries.

Oh, God, Simon and John, each saying they protected Jerusalem... They inflicted great cruelty upon our people! What treachery!

"The final siege led to the destruction of our city. It started after Passover. General Titus knew that pilgrims were coming for Passover, so he gave safe passage to those coming to Jerusalem for the celebration. Eleazar, the high priest fighting the other two factions, opened the gates of the inner court of the temple to admit pilgrims.

"John, taking advantage of Eleazar, sent his men in as pilgrims, with street clothing covering their armor. They attacked Eleazar's men, who fled to underground caverns. Why did our own people kill our high priest? This was the beginning of the end.

"Our city was bursting with too many people when Titus started the final siege. We were doomed because pilgrims could not return home. We cried to the Lord for deliverance. Some went out at night to obtain food. More than five hundred men were caught searching for food and crucified. All could watch their agonies as we stood on the walls, watching the dreadful scene. The army even ran out of wood to make more crosses.

"However, the Roman army was becoming desperate since they had to conquer us before the end of July or their food supplies would soon run out. They had too many men to feed.

"By July 1, people were dying from starvation. Bodies were being dropped over the walls at night without a decent burial. There were no funerals. Mothers went crazy from grief, and one woman ate her own baby after it died. We were afraid. If soldiers entered the city, we could expect no mercy.

"We were all going to die. Finally, on July 17, when our family was reduced to twelve from eighteen people, we learned some priests were going to ask for mercy. A small unattended gate was going to be opened. At that moment, we rushed, limping and dragging ourselves. We made a pathetic dash toward the enemy, hoping for mercy.

"Just then, when we were outside the city walls, Johanan, my son-in-law, was shot from behind, killed by his own people. Tamara, my daughter, saw him fall to the ground and stopped to help, but our soldiers shot more arrows, and she was struck in the leg. A second arrow found its mark. We helped her limp away from her husband, who lay lifeless on the ground. Miriam was only five years old, and I held her tightly as she screamed with grief.

"We were surprised to find that the soldiers showed us mercy, taking us to Gophna, a city close by. They said, 'You must not gobble the food. Eat slowly! Get used to having food in your stomach again,' but Abigail's parents didn't listen. They were so hungry that they ate too much too fast. Unfortunately, they were too weak to survive. Three years earlier, we had been eighteen persons. Now we were nine.

"We asked for permission to go to the city of Philadelphia, on the eastern side of the Jordan River.[54] By that time, an infection was setting in on Tamara's leg. In Philadelphia, we were taken into the home of people who called themselves the 'Household of Faith.' They gave us food and water. We made new friends, which was our first acquaintance with people who believed that Yeshua came as the promised Messiah. They were Jews helping people like us who escaped from the Roman army. My father, Eliab, and the rest of our family spent many days learning about the teachings of Yeshua.

---

[54] Philadelphia, founded by Greeks after the victories of Alexander the Great, is known today as Amman, the capital of the Hashemite Kingdom of Jordan. It was not the same Philadelphia as in Asia Minor.

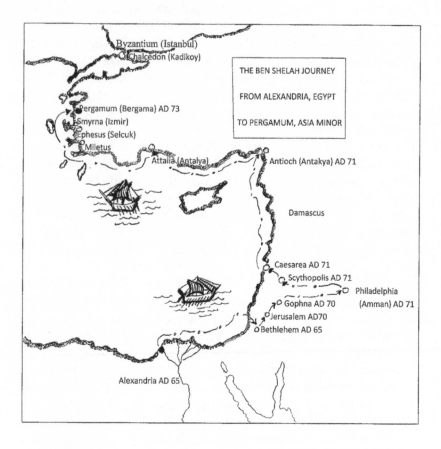

THE BEN SHELAH JOURNEY

FROM ALEXANDRIA, EGYPT

TO PERGAMUM, ASIA MINOR

"We heard that the temple had been destroyed and our city lay in ruins, and we wept. The date on the calendar was the same as hundreds of years before, when the army of Nebuchadnezzar destroyed Solomon's temple. We call it Tish'a B'Av, and it falls on the ninth day of the month of Av. In your calendar, it comes during the hottest time of the summer.

"God permitted our enemies to destroy our center of worship a second time. It happened on the same day. Why? God judged us. His message could not be more explicit. Greed, divisiveness, and fighting against each other—these were the walls dividing us. While we were safe in Philadelphia, in Trans-Jordan, we knew this: Walls alone cannot keep you safe.

"When he entered the city, General Titus said, 'Don't burn Herod's temple! I want it as a gift to Rome!' However, a fire had already started. Before it was destroyed, the gold, silver, and precious stones were gathered, and later Titus took them to Rome. Our temple's wealth was displayed in a victory march there, and Titus was celebrated. Then he built an enormous arch to commemorate this conquest. Our temple's treasure provided the funds for building Rome's most massive structure, the Coliseum. Even now, Emperor Domitian is adding a substantial new addition, space for another fifteen thousand spectators.

"Back in Judea, Jews were sold as slaves, and thousands were used by General Titus for sport, fighting animals in the arena. Other Jewish slaves were taken to Egypt to work in mines.

"I learned several lessons about real treasure. Our greatest treasure is Adonai, our Holy God. When we identify ourselves by his name, he changes our character. We act in new ways. I do not want to hoard my wealth. This is why I buy a slave each year and give freedom to that person. Instead of building walls that divide, we should build friendship and love; that is a treasure without price. We need protection for our children and for poor people and widows.

"Another lesson I learned: Our lives pass so quickly."

He paused, calming his emotions as he drank from a cup of water. His mouth was dry from speaking for so long.

"Returning to our family's story, we were in Philadelphia, which used to be called Rabbah. Our daughter, Tamara, could not walk, so we bought a donkey to take her from Philadelphia to the Gentile city of Scythopolis, south of the Lake of Galilee. We were afraid of being rounded up as escapees from Jerusalem, so we kept on until we arrived at the coast, at Caesarea. We could not go back to Alexandria, and we no longer had walls to protect us. Many families we knew in Jerusalem were completely wiped out.

"By now, Tamara was very weak, but she improved slightly, and we boarded a ship bound for Antioch. Days later, Tamara died from her wound. My parents, Ruth, Miriam, and I came here to Pergamum. Amos, Abigail, and their son Arom came two years later.

"My greatest fear is that we might accidentally build new walls separating us from one another. God allowed us to create a new community, one built on reconciliation between the peoples from the east and west, from the north and south. Walls can keep us safe, but sometimes they destroy us too."

He pursed his lips, having arrived at the climax of his talk.

"Our Messiah came to tear down the walls between people. Divisions, like the one between Jews and Gentiles, are almost impossible to remove! And there are others too, between masters and slaves, rich and poor.

"The Household of Faith stands for many things. In the Messiah, we find something we've never found before. It is said, 'He would not break a bruised reed.' That means he doesn't throw us away, doesn't discard us like a broken pot, and Yeshua doesn't reject us when we fail. He takes down walls that divide people. Amazingly, he made peace for us, not with a display of power but through weakness. He was strong like a lion, but he died as quietly as a lamb. Now people who never thought they could be friends are being brought together.

"He reconciled us, Jews with non-Jews. If we are one in the Messiah, we are no longer strangers to one another, living as aliens. We're fellow citizens of a new kingdom. God wants us to experience redemption and forgiveness, to be a light among people who live in darkness.[55]

"Let us work together to build this community based on sharing. In our village, there should be no walls dividing us. Instead, we will show love and compassion to one another. That's why I teach you about protective walls built with righteousness, justice, love, and faithfulness.

"Please help me to build this new community, one built on the knowledge of the Lord, where all are known for being compassionate. There's only one way to keep the wrong kind of walls from being built. That is by loving one another."

Their appreciation for his story came out, with some smiling and nodding agreement. Others clapped, and a few said, "We love you, Antipas."

His intensity had held them captive, and his message was uncomfortable, contrasting cruelty and generosity. His account both fascinated and repelled, and at the end, he had asked people to change their way of looking at life.

As Antipas sat down, the gathered crowd remained quiet. Miriam stood and said, "Grandpa tells many details about ancient families, armies, and wars, but my story is short. It will only take

---

[55] Ephesians 2:11–22

a few minutes."

She was dressed beautifully, and the many lamps in the cave showed her at her best. Her olive complexion glowed, and her long black hair was swept back with soft, bouncy curls.

Her eyes sparkled. "This song is called 'Broken Walls.' The first part is about my home near Bethlehem before we moved into the city of Jerusalem. I was too small to know that dangers lurked around the outside of our home. Walls protected me.

"The third stanza is about the story you heard from my grandfather. We came through fires. I was five years old when my father was killed. Those were terrible days and nights, but now we live in safety. The last part is about new walls—our community and the blessing God gave to us together here in Pergamum."

Miriam and her young friends brought harp, flute, drum, and tambourines together in various musical combinations during their practice time. A harp and a flute played together to portray a picture of longing, discouragement, and pain.

> I sat on my mama's knee,
>   freshly picked flowers in hand.
> My cat looked up, stretched,
>   and slept soundly by the wall.
> My fingers tugged her bracelet,
>   caressed Mama's wedding band.
> For me, a home at three years old,
>   the walls so strong and tall!
>
> My memories! Daddy kept horses,
>   working on the land.
> Mama served hot bread loaves.
>   I played for hours with my doll.
> Father held me in his arms,
>   his upturned face gently tanned.
> Bethlehem was home, and animals
>   slept within their stalls.

During the third verse, a mournful flute carried the tune, portraying the dreadful image of bodies piled on one another outside the walls.[56] Halfway through the third verse, Florbella leaped up to comfort Miriam. She leaned against her older friend and tightly wrapped her arms around Miriam's waist, her head turned down, her long black hair covering her face. Both Antipas's long story and Miriam's song spoke of profound grief.

> Trumpets blared! The food was gone,
>   and arrows flew above!
> Mama wept beside me!
>   Daddy's dead! Why couldn't I quell
> Wrenching, endless fears? People starved.
>   Flames of hate displaced love.
> Our city burned. Priests screamed
>   and wept as Herod's temple fell.

The flute stopped, and only the drumbeat continued, becoming softer, as if soldiers were leaving a field of battle. The speed of the drumbeat picked up again to indicate life beginning to return to normal. Miriam stopped singing so people could imagine the contrast. She looked down at the little girl's face pressed against her side and smiled. It made the perfect transition to the last verse of her song, the part about their new home.

On the final verse, the key went up a notch, and the harp played again.

> Oil lamps glow. New roofs and homes!
>   Around are pleasant places!
> Grace abounds. Slaves are friends.
>   We're home with pigeons and a dove.
> When Grandma died, Great-grandpa, too,
>   tears poured down our faces.

---

[56] The war lasted seven years, according to Josephus. Estimate of deaths in Jerusalem: 1,100,000; Jewish deaths in the countryside before the siege of Jerusalem: 250,000. After Roman troops entered Jerusalem, about 100,000 Jews were taken as slaves, many meeting their deaths in Caesarea Philippi. Many Jewish slaves, possibly 90,000, were taken to mines in Egypt. The best-looking male youths were taken to Rome and taunted for their weakness in the triumphal procession led by General Titus.

Transformed, redeemed,
  we hear the invitation of God's love.

Florbella continued to cling to Miriam.

Many people wiped their eyes with the backs of their hands. In the spontaneity of the moment, a story had been acted out with both music and drama.

A child wounded at age five by an earthquake, whose speech was now almost back to normal, hugged a Jewish orphan. Miriam was born in Africa and nearly starved to death in Jerusalem. Florbella came from the north, the young woman from the south. Miriam had helped in Florbella's healing.

The girl who loved pigeons and doves acted on impulse, showing to everyone that children, like adults, have deep feelings. Miriam kept her arm around Florbella long after the song was over.

People wanted to hear the song again so they could remember it for singing at home, so Miriam sang it again.

This time, people could match the verses with the long story Antipas had shared, and they understood it much better. And when Florbella sang along, Miriam looked down on her face to encourage her. The crowd wanted it a third time. Miriam and Florbella stood together, in mutual sympathy, an understanding that whispered a silent message to all the visitors.

Marcos would not usually take this risk. His whole training, outlook, and experience taught him to be careful in disclosing decisions. Tonight, though, he wanted to speak to thoughts flooding his mind since Florbella had started talking again. Together, he and Marcella waited for Antipas.

"May we speak with you for a minute, Antipas?" he asked.

"Of course."

"Six months ago, our daughter could not speak. Marcella and I were worried about her. The Asclepius Hospital was not the right place for her healing and neither was the Altar of Zeus. Suddenly, one evening, she came home from here and started speaking. We consider it a miracle, but you say that it is not a miracle, merely the grace of God. For four and a half months, we have been watching her to see what would happen. She is continuously improving.

"During the summer, I spent time with her at our villa in Kisthene. We walked, ran, and danced along the sandy shores. I read her stories. We started to talk about the earthquake and what happened to her in the ground.

"Her love for birds increased when she was trapped in the ground. The only thing that she could see was a branch of a tree, and a bird came and sat on it from time to time. That little bird gave her hope that she would be free again."

Antipas' eyes widened slightly. "I see. Keep going please," he said calmly, but inwardly, he was bubbling. He knew that the lawyer was starting to see the light of life.

Marcos continued. "Then we started coming to the cave. We saw the difference that comes into people's lives when they truly worship your God. I would never have thought that I could learn anything from you, but the way you include people from all over, the way that you explain things, all these started to make sense to me about a month ago."

"And now?" Antipas asked.

"I want to become a follower of Yeshua, the Messiah. Marcella, Florbella, and I want to belong to this Household of Faith community too."

"You are a wealthy man, are you not?"

"Yes, I have a good position."

Antipas spoke seriously. "If necessary, you must be ready to give up your life to follow the Master. Yeshua said, 'Give to Caesar the things that belong to Caesar and give to God the things that belong to God.' If you have hidden things, they must be cleaned, made new. He also said, 'Repent, for the kingdom of God is at hand.' It's a big decision."

"Yes, I understood that from what you said several weeks ago."

"And you, Marcella, what do you say?"

The words were on the tip of her tongue. "Since my daughter came home and said 'Jeshua' as her first word and started speaking again, I have had no doubts. The Asclepius Hospital, the best in the province of Asia Minor, and then the Altar of Zeus, did not heal her nor did all our prayers to Hera.

"Something is different here at the Household of Faith. I believe there is power for good here, and it has made a difference. I was ready to tell you of our decision before Marcos was, but I waited for him to tell me what he wanted to do."

Antipas nodded. "I am happy for you both. Marcos, you are a lawyer, and you would not be talking with me like this unless you had given it much thought. I must tell you, though, that being a part of the Household of Faith is not easy.

"The hardest part may be that this choice on your part will cost you. The authorities are not friendly to us. Are you prepared to lose much to gain more? For everything that you give up, you will receive many times over but in different ways."

His direct answer was reassuring. "Yes, I am willing to give up much. I have already gained back my daughter, and what these people have here cannot be bought with wealth. Antipas, we have talked about how it could affect us. Of course, I don't know exactly what this is going to cost. I influence the council. People love to hate lawyers, but they can't do without us!"

"All right, I will instruct you for a while before you make a public commitment, after which we will have an immersion in water to proclaim your decision. Starting now, you will tell people that you are a follower of the Master."

Marcos replied, "Unfortunately, I cannot join you for the next three weeks. The *Koinon,* the Annual Meeting of the Asiarchs, starts on Sunday morning, ten days from now. But Marcella and Florbella will be here."[57]

Antipas placed his worn hand on Florbella's head as a sign of blessing. Then, spontaneously, he reached forward and gave Marcos the holy kiss. It was the kiss that the people in the Household of Faith gave to each other before they left for home, lightly placing his cheek against his and then repeating the gesture on the other side.

"Good night, Brother Marcos. Peace be with you. Peace be with you too, Sister Marcella and Little Sister Florbella," said Antipas.

"Good night, Brother Antipas. Peace be with you," he replied.

Since he had lost his brothers in the earthquake, no one had called him brother.

---

[57] Each year, the *Koinon*, the Meeting of the Asiarchs, brought together officials in the province of Asia. The annual meeting rotated around the seven most important cities in Asia Minor.

After the meeting, Anthony sat in his place for a long time without moving. The recruits had left, and he sat alone. Deep emotions had been stirred within him as he listened to the story of the siege of Jerusalem.

Antipas would have been my enemy if I had been a soldier there.

He'd never heard the Jewish side of the story—people dying inside Jerusalem, starvation, and suffering. What a terrible event! Of course, they rebelled against Rome. But strange...Antipas told the story without hatred.

I wouldn't have done that. I think of revenge all the time. What would I do if I found the man who tried to kill me?

Miriam was a beautiful young woman. She sang about a cat, a little girl growing up and belonging to a family.

A sad story. What do those words mean—grace abounds, transformed, redeemed? What is this invitation to God's love?

He remembered his mother talking to him. She used to say that name, Yeshua, the Christus.

She told me to pay attention if I ever heard it again.

Anthony wasn't satisfied with the way his questions drove him in a new direction. He said very little when he returned to the barracks.

Through the Fire

Part 2

The White Stone

September AD 89

Chapter 25
The Acropolis

THE NEW FORUM, PERGAMUM

Excitement was growing day by day, and the city throbbed with a noisy, unfettered, escalating crescendo. The most recent wrestling hero in the Pergamum Spring Games was Vincenzo. This gave him the right to ride at the head of the Asiarch's procession. His task was to clear the road for the procession of the most elevated officials from eighteen cities of the province. A week later, he would again match his athletic skills against those of other contestants in the September Games.

Because he was a victor, an overcomer, he had been given a place of honor. Vincenzo's name was engraved on the entrance to the amphitheater, never to be forgotten. He had already left his mark on history. Heroes were recognized and honored here.

He wore his new necklace with an attached small white stone engraved with a new name, Treasured Son of Nike. No one else knew this name except the Asiarch of Pergamum, the mayor of the city. Nike, the goddess of speed and victory, had looked on Vincenzo with favor. The goddess had given him her greatest gift: victory. He had offered an expensive sacrifice to the goddess as a token of his gratitude.

Governor Marcus Fluvius Gillo was the chief magistrate of the Province of Asia Minor. He had been appointed by the Senate in Rome seven months before and approved by Domitian to represent Rome for two years as the province's head official. He was assigned to administer the province after a disgraceful legacy left by Celsus Ceriales. Domitian had condemned Celsus Ceriales for rebellion. It had been a great shock to the citizens of Asia Minor to learn that their highest official, a governor, had been executed.

The governor-raised his hand and lowered it suddenly as a sign for the twelve brass trumpets to split the air with regal resonance. People stopped talking, and everyone could hear the governor's voice.

"In the name of Domitian, lord and god, the Annual Meeting of Asiarchs is in session!"

The procession began. The Hero of the Games sat on a black horse holding the red banner that represented their city. The tall, narrow banner fluttered in the slight breeze. On the bright red background were embroidered three symbols of Pergamum: a flying white eagle, a golden lion, and a black ram. Bright yellow trim around the red banner set it off from all the others.

Vincenzo rode ahead shouting, "Prepare the way for the Asiarchs!" No one was going to obstruct the road as the procession passed.

Dignitaries rode behind the current governor. Each of the eighteen Asiarchs combined two positions of power and prestige. Mayors were magistrates and also had responsibilities as priests in the cult of emperor worship. Each city served as a regional administrative district, overseeing taxation and the welfare of twenty to thirty smaller towns and cities. Asia Minor counted on five million people in eighteen provincial subdivisions to enrich the empire.

The mayors of Miletus, Tralles, and Nysa rode side by side in the first row. Then came those of Aphrodisias, Ephesus, and Smyrna, followed by those of Pergamum, Magnesia, and Thyatira. In the fourth row came the Asiarchs of Sardis, Laodicea, and Hierapolis before the leaders of Ilium, Adramyttium, and Alexandria Troas. The last of the eighteen mayors represented Hypaepe,[58] Colossae, and Halicarnassus.[59]

The five hundred cities of Asia Minor made it one of the wealthiest, most productive provinces in the empire. Luxury goods flowed into Rome from distant reaches in eastern Asia. Each year ships sailed from as far away as India. Silver flowed out to purchase silk, spices, and carpets being transported from the

---

[58] Hypaepe, modern-day Odemish in western Turkey, was built on the road between Sardis and Ephesus

[59] Halicarnassus, modern Bodrum, Turkey, was home to Strabo, a student of Aristodemus in Nysa about 55 BC. He studied in Rome, traveled extensively, and wrote eighteen books on the world's geography as he knew it.

East.

The crowd applauded loudly as the procession passed by. The priests of temples in Pergamum followed the officials. Their brilliant colors identified their specific temple in the city.

Lydia-Naq led the priestesses and animals to be sacrificed. The young women had never looked more beautiful than they did this morning. The perfumes of the priestesses were part of the oblation, sacrifice, and dedication. Men came behind the priests and priestesses carrying censers of charcoal. They would soon fill each temple with the scent of burning incense.

Last came representatives of the guilds. The first were the stonemasons, who brought loud cries of approval. They were unmistakable as the physically strongest men who passed by and considered by all to be the most valuable workers in the city since their workmanship was permanent. Representatives from the other guilds walked behind them: carpenters and the makers of candles, clothing, metals, pottery, bread, oil, bricks, rope, and dyes.

THE ROAD UP TO THE ACROPOLIS

Since Pergamum's Imperial Temple provided limited space, the nearby Temple of Athena had been incorporated into the opening ceremony for the public figures, soldiers, and dignitaries. The procession, which included almost two thousand people, would take two hours before all reached the top of the acropolis. Starting at the gate of the New Forum, the procession wound its way slowly to the Selinos River, went across the bridge, and then marched upward past the lower hot baths. Farther on, at the east side of the acropolis hill, the road doubled back on itself. Then it climbed gradually westward to the lower edge of the city wall, just below the gymnasium.

At this point, the procession was a fully formed, mile-long chain of people, jubilant, colorful, and proud. All those involved knew what an honor it was to be included in the procession!

Thousands of ordinary people followed behind the procession dancing, jumping, singing songs, and welcoming the dignitaries to the grandest of all centers of government in Asia, the Acropolis of Pergamum. At the top of the acropolis, just before entering the open space leading to the most famous buildings, the commoners stopped at the security gate. They were turned back by guards, happy to have been able to follow the procession to this point.

THE IMPERIAL TEMPLE OF AUGUSTUS CAESAR, THE ACROPOLIS

Damon, the high priest of the Imperial Temple of Augustus Caesar, assisted by the high priest of the Imperial Temple in Smyrna, led the ox to the altar. Damon wore a white tunic and a white toga with two purple stripes. He slashed the throat of the ox at its jugular vein, and one of his assistants collected the blood in an unusual ceremonial bowl. The beast wobbled on its legs and then fell down, first on its front legs and later on its side as its lifeblood flowed out.

After the sacrifice of the ox in the Imperial Temple, a sheep and a pig were brought to the Temple of Athena. Receiving the dignitaries from across the province, the high priest of Athena bowed to them at the entrance to his two-story temple. He wore the colors universally ascribed to the goddess: a white tunic and a yellow toga with lines of orange.

He paused in front of the foundation stone and read, once again, the inscribed words: "From King Eumenes to the Victorious Athena." The temple was almost three hundred years old. Above him, on the second floor, the ancient armor of the defeated Galatian tribes was displayed, a tribute to Pergamum's ancient military victories.

THE CITY HALL MEETING PLACE

While the opening ceremony was taking place in the Temple of Athena, Marcos stayed outside the throng, beyond the commotion.

During the legislative year, the city council made decisions both important and minor. The body was made up of free citizens of the city, including wealthier merchants, lawyers, and professionals. When citizens became part of the august group, they were given a title of honor, *decurion*. These men controlled the finances and future of their city.

The central concern of the Asiarchs gathered today was the taxes required by Rome for the coming year and how they would be collected. Politicians, advisors, and decision-makers sat close together on the semicircular marble seating. The central seat in the Odeon was reserved for the governor. Beside him were the chief administrator and a benefactor, both from Ephesus. The mayor of Pergamum also occupied the front row.

Governor Marcus Fluvius Gillo stood to bring news from Rome. After waiting for the buzz to die down, he spoke in a loud, commanding voice.

He gave the traditional greeting to the assembled dignitaries. "Caesar is lord and god! Our most worthy Emperor Domitian sends his greetings to this distinguished group. He gives thanks to the gods that the province of Asia Minor is blessed with peace and many advantages. We thank you all for this fine hospitality. Greetings from the capital city of Asia, the well-built city of Ephesus."

The rivalry between Ephesus and Pergamum had become a source of endless jokes, both in Asia and beyond.

"Now you all know that I hate to speak about taxes."

He didn't mind the laughter that rang out. The crowd was expecting it because collecting taxes was a significant part of his life. He ended his speech regarding how Domitian expected additional funds to be raised: "...demanding that the property of those who do not obey the tax laws should be confiscated. Confiscations of property will pay for roads, bridges, and aqueducts in each province."

He then departed from his planned text. "When the sacrifice was being made at the Imperial Temple a short while ago, I noted that the space around the Imperial Temple is inadequate. Splendor and dignity should be awarded to our emperor. Will Pergamum contribute to a larger temple? Of course, a larger platform would have to be constructed, which would not be easy given your steeply sloping acropolis. I suggest you think about it."

Marcos had sat at the back of the room listening, and at home later that night, he talked with Marcella. "Since we started attending services at the cave, I increasingly dislike the rituals associated with each temple. So many of the activities and speeches involved the invocation of gods and goddesses.

"But that's not what I want to tell you, Marcella. Earlier today, I walked to the edge of the Greek theater. I looked down at the empty seats and then lifted my eyes to where the white bull's sacrifice had taken place less than an hour before. I think I understand the governor's intentions. Like a few others in the audience, I detected how the governor's generalized statements shed light on hidden motivations.

"Gillo is fully supporting the emperor's lust for money. He uses humor and fancy words, trying to be viewed as minimizing the impact on the province. He also wants to provide Pergamum with the hope of an upgraded Imperial Temple, but Pergamum will have to provide a place to put it.

"Support for Domitian has increased the power of the governor. But suddenly I saw an opportunity! The goal of my position in the city government is to benefit Pergamum.

"Marcella! An idea came this morning! Perhaps this city's provincial status can be raised. During these endless meetings, I'm going to work on this idea. My imagination has been stimulated by the events of the past several days."

Marcella knew him well and loved him. Once his face took on this expression, he became full of delightful energy—and he began planning another crazy idea.

She loved her husband and not just for his abilities to provide legal assistance to the city. She gave him a hug and made him feel welcome at home just as Florbella came running into the room.

Two more days passed, and after the final evening's entertainment, Marcos lingered at the gymnasium to think. He arrived home later than usual, and after the evening meal, they were sitting on the edge of their bed.

Marcella put her arm around his waist. "My dear, did you get more ideas about 'raising this city's status,' as you put it?"

"Yes, something is coming together. I'll admit it's a complicated plan. After the last speech, people went home. I stayed an extra hour and gazed at the acropolis during the last light of the day. Three houses sit on the edge of a cliff. Below them is the Temple of Dionisius. Those three aristocratic families practically govern the city. I've studied the cliff and the homes both at mid-day and in the dim light."

"What is so special about those three homes?"

"They are in the way."

"In the way of what? I don't understand."

"I'll have to explain how the world of men works in Asia Minor, Marcella. In Ephesus, the construction of a massive new Imperial Temple is almost complete. It's being built to honor

Domitian. The emperor will be worshiped there daily. That puts Pergamum even further at a disadvantage. This city can't influence important decisions because our voice isn't being heard. We are two days' journey by horseback from Ephesus, so we find it hard to directly influence our governor.

"I studied the governor's face the first day. I saw how irritated he became by the way that the procession was handled. The white paving stones around the small Imperial Temple became crammed to overflowing. The small temple structure there was constructed for Caesar Augustus a century ago.

"Maybe I was the only one who observed the look of annoyance on the governor's face. Anyway, I have an idea to provide the space needed for a new Imperial Temple! But to achieve my idea...well, it seems impossible. It would require Manes Tmolus, Atys Tantalus, and Atydos Lydus all agreeing to give up their historic aristocratic residences. That's the only way enough space could be provided to form a platform for a larger Imperial Temple"

"How could you convince three aristocratic families to move from their homes? You've had funny ideas before, but this one..."

"Their homes are built right at the edge of the cliff. Those mansions are the pride of their lives. Would even one of the families willingly sacrifice their historic, honored estates to advance the city's interests? I know this sounds impossible, so I need a plan! But removing those three residences...how would I go about seeing this through?"

"Marcos! I know how!" she said, inviting a smile. "It's simple! Why don't you simply call a meeting and tell each of those three men, 'I want you to move out of your home for the good of the city! You'll have to give up your homes so Pergamum can have a larger Imperial Temple!' No, my dear! That's ridiculous. You're dreaming!"

He laid back on the bed, his hands under his head. "Following the earthquake in Nicomedia, I inherited all of my brothers' homes, their orchards, and their summer villas.[60] It is no secret

---

[60] I based Marcos's loss of his family members on terrible destruction caused by two recent earthquakes along the Marmara Sea fault line. Marcos refers to a fictional event, on August 18, 85 AD, which mirrors the two disasters of August and November 1999.

that many of my brothers' properties were obtained with under-the-table activity and false evaluations. I wanted to make amends, not because I can easily afford it but because I have a new perception of true wealth."

"Just hang onto them. No one will know how wealthy we are."

He paused, and Marcella waited. "I will not allow those properties to be confiscated. I'm going to sell them."

"Why? You're a wealthy man now. Don't you want to hang onto villas and properties, orchards and lands?"

"Not really. I think I have a better use for what they're worth."

"So you already have a plan?"

"Perhaps I could also correct past wrongs. I'm not going to walk the hidden trails of dishonesty trodden by my brothers."

"My dear, you're changing! I've never heard you speak about money and wealth like this!"

"Yes, honesty is a narrow path. I'm going to walk along it."

"I see it beckoning you. Well, I'm beckoning you too. You've been home very late every evening during these meetings."

She passionately kissed the man she was learning to trust even more, and he responded to her with the warmth that was beginning to change his life.

Chapter 26
The Covenant

THE LIBRARY OF PERGAMUM

The goddess of fortune had been consulted to choose the day for Zoticos's first class, and on Friday morning, he met with his new students for the first time. The Annual Meeting of the Asiarchs was over, and the politicians had gone back to their respective cities.

On Saturday morning, Zoticos explained to Lydia-Naq, "The purpose of training this group is to provide teachers who will revive our mostly forgotten Lydian culture. I have enrolled twenty-four students. I'll train them, and they will teach others."

But he didn't tell his sister about Trifane. She was twenty-two years old and was the second person to register for his classes.

On the first day of classes, she sat on the right-hand side of the room, close to the front. He looked at her several times.

Trifane will do well—clear speech, commitment, and inner energy, and the Lydian language is spoken in her home!

He started his introductory remarks. "Welcome to these classes! Today is the first day of study, which is meant to equip you to teach others. The student who achieves the best results will receive a white stone, a sign of recognition of excellence. This course is designed to help you learn and teach so that you can pass on the language, culture, and pleasures of our Lydian ancestors."

I can't keep my eyes off you even if you are fifteen years younger than I am. Stunning Trifane! A lovely name... I must not let you see that I am interested in you.

ARMY GARRISON, PERGAMUM

New recruits for the year arrived and were already being trained under Anthony's direction.

"I'm pushing them beyond their limits, sir," he reported to

Commander Cassius. "During the first two weeks of their army experience, they stifle their groans. Within six months, these new soldiers will be on their way to Dacia."

Anthony knew that officers like his commander, calloused by the years of war, required that recruits be brought to the highest levels of endurance.

He explained the progress of his recruits to Cassius, pride coloring his words. "It is this fortitude—the instilled determination to conquer even when facing overwhelming odds—that forges men into a fighting community. Soldiers in a legion live together and fight together. These men are learning to lay down their lives for victory."

My father died in battle. He was considered 'victorious,' and there is a military tomb in his honor in Damascus.

It was three and a half weeks since Anthony had taken in Antipas's long story and Miriam's song. Since then, he has been driven by an indescribable need to go to the old man's door.

He entered the main gate of the little village and walked toward Antipas' homes, past the carpentry shop, the glass blowing shed, and the pottery workshops. The largest building had an open door, and he could see that it contained supplies: sand for glass, charcoal, and clay for the pottery. Wine, olive oil, dried fruit, and nuts were stored for the winter months.

A little farther on, he passed some houses. Each dwelling was well built and carefully maintained. Flowers and bushes decorated the outside walls of each home, lending a clean appearance to the village. Beside the door of each house was a stone bench. Men and women were visiting at the end of the day. Many people greeted him without concern as he walked past them for most of them had seen him at the cave.

Children played on the narrow paths between the houses. He also recognized several people from his earlier visit. Rather than curtains, these houses actually had solid doors and window shutters that fit tightly. Some of the homes in Antipas's village were in the process of adding a second story. All had a flat roof, a kind of terrace, which was useful at night in the heat of summer. As he observed the houses, he compared them to others in the city.

The houses in the poor sections of Pergamum are not like this.

There, garbage is tossed out onto the streets between the homes.
Old baskets, shards of pottery, and muck make narrow lanes
dangerous. Unpleasant smells assail the passersby everywhere
along those narrow, dirty streets. Antipas's village is different. It is
clean and well maintained.

Antipas heard the knocking at the door and found Anthony
standing in the courtyard. He recognized the legionary as one of
several at the cave on the night he had told his life story. A
question formed in his mind mirroring his general distrust of
Romans. *A soldier at my house? Why?*

"I would like to ask a few questions regarding your talk about
Jerusalem and your family. May I come in?"

The old man invited Anthony into the house and had a
servant remove the soldier's sandals and wash his feet. As the
soldier rose to enter the main room, Miriam covered her head
with a prayer shawl and quietly left the room.

Anthony stood beside a couch in the central room of Antipas's
house. His home was simple, large, and lightly furnished. Rugs
covered the floors, and brass lamps hung on the walls, ready for
the coming night. The three couches, one on each side of the small
table in the center, were covered with beautifully and intricately
crafted soft cloth. They looked like the Persian rugs but small,
delicate, and carefully embroidered. At one end of the room,
where Roman homes would typically have a statue of the goddess
Hera, a small table held a menorah, a framed candlestick with
places for seven candles.

Unlike a Roman or Greek house, with mosaics of inlaid stones,
the floor was made of well-polished inlaid white and pink stones,
the same kind used on the outer walls of the acropolis. The room
was simple, perhaps too simple, but it spoke of people who loved
to be together and who loved to read, learn, and discuss things.

"Is this the first time you have been in a Jewish home?" asked
Antipas.

"Yes," said Anthony, rubbing the scar on the right side of his
face. He quickly lowered his hand.

Antipas thought his guest did not know what he was going to
say. "You will see that we have no idols in our house. The
menorah's lamps signify the importance of light. In an hour, an
important Jewish event begins. It's a holy night known as Rosh

Hashanah. God is light, and he created light. We see because of light, and we refuse to walk in the darkness of the idols of the nations."

Antipas sensed in the young man a conflict, perhaps a need to learn. Or maybe he was uneasy in the house of a Jew.

"Please sit down on the couch and make yourself comfortable in my home. How may I be helpful to you?"

Taking a deep breath and letting it out slowly, Anthony said, "My name is Anthony Suros. My mother's ancestors came from Gaul and my father's family from Spain. My great-grandfather submitted to Julius Caesar, and for almost 150 years, we have had soldiers in our family. In fact, my father was a trumpeter in a legion fighting against Jerusalem. I heard your story, the struggles you had during the siege and how you escaped and came to live in Pergamum."

"Is your father still alive?" asked Antipas.

"No, my father died during the siege of Jerusalem."

"Sorry to hear that. Was he a good man?"

"My father was not with us much. He went to Damascus as a soldier. Once in a while, he would write a letter, and he sent money to us in Rome twice a year."

Anthony stroked the scar on his face. "My mother took care of me; she did not want me to enter the army. 'It's dangerous!' she kept saying. 'Wait until you are older!' I was sixteen and ready to take on the barbarian tribes of the Germanic forests."

Antipas watched the younger man rubbing his right cheek.

He estimated Anthony to be in his mid-thirties with big shoulders and well-developed arm muscles. He wore a soldier's tunic made of coarse cotton dyed a dark brown. His fingers moved from side to side. One moment, Anthony would rub his forehead. The next, he would rub his finger along the scar on the side of his face. Antipas examined the heavy red line from the corner of the soldier's eye to the edge of his jaw and back to his ear.

A soldier's nervous gesture, his way of thinking things through, trying to decide what to tell me...and what not to say to me. He's testing me out tonight. He's not here as a spy. If he were a spy... No, it's something personal in his life. That's why he is here.

A few seconds passed. Antipas picked up on the previous comment. "So you went to the forests of Germanica."

"Yes, as a scout. The black woods of Upper Germanica are dangerous, fearsome places for a legion. Scouts must search out extra information before a battle. There isn't space to camp as in North Africa or Mesopotamia. Did you hear about the great defeat of our three legions in the Teutoburg Forest during the reign of Caesar Augustus?"

Antipas replied, "Yes, we all heard about it when we lived in Alexandria. It happened when my father was just a boy. The story was passed down to us. Often when someone wanted to curse the Romans, they said, 'May it happen to them again!' We had many Jewish friends who hated Rome, and we made many bad comments about your armies."

Antipas had learned that humility and honesty shown early in a conversation encouraged a less secure person to open up about his life in a more profound way.

Anthony accepted the comment. "Well, it was partly to avenge that terrible defeat that I decided to go to Upper Germanica rather than join my father's Legion X in Damascus. I joined Legion XXI, the Predators, in January the next year. I was seventeen. That was three years after the fall of Jerusalem. I wouldn't have been fighting against your family there! You were already gone, and Jerusalem was a pile of rubble.

"My mother wanted me to learn about Yeshua, the Christus. You call him the 'Messiah.' She and my father, Aurelius, always got into discussions about Yeshua. Finally, they had a huge argument, and we went back to live with her brother in Rome. At first, he sent money to my mother, but after a while, he stopped sending any more. Her brother died, and my mother became poor. Sometimes we did not have food, and we lived in an impoverished section of Rome. I worked doing odd jobs with little pay."

Then he added slowly, "Mother died of the coughing sickness shortly after I went to train as a soldier. She said, 'Anthony, if you ever hear someone talk about Yeshua Christus, promise me that you will learn from him.' Over the years, I forgot what she had told me. In the forests, no one talks about the Messiah.

"After I got this wound on my face, I was required to rest and recover for a long time, and as I lay there, her words came back. You see, someone tried to cut my head off. My wound healed, sort of, but it means that I cannot fight on the battlefield. So I was sent here to the garrison to teach new recruits for my legion, teaching them how to be scouts. In the forests of Upper Germanica, that is a terribly difficult assignment. The main commander here, Cassius, doesn't accept just how important a scout is."

Anthony isn't a spy. What is he really thinking about? What does he need from me? And how did his mother learn about Yeshua, the Messiah? In Damascus?

Antipas swallowed hard. "When you were seventeen, our family members were arriving in Pergamum."

Anthony sat up straight. "Antipas, if I may call you by your name, please tell me more about what you believe. How does anyone, especially an old man who lost so many family members... How does a person put his life back together after a terrible event? Your community is different from anything I've seen. You talk differently and do things no one else does, like buying and freeing slaves. At the cave, I learned that you take in widows and trust them to run your shops in the market. Why do you do these things?"

Strong emotions swept over Antipas. He felt twin sensations: a fascination and also repulsion. For an instant, Antipas considered his desire for revenge.

This man's father was a legionary who fought against us in the siege of Jerusalem! Yet he wants to know God! He doesn't know how to put it into words. I don't want him to take my time. Tonight we will blow the shofar. It's the beginning of the new year. I could stop talking with him now... It would be the loss of only one person and an enemy at that. Could I have anticipated a legionary coming to the cave? No! Yet others go, listen, learn to sing...and worship. So why not this soldier?

'Love your enemies,' Yeshua said.

Tonight, Lord, we blow the shofar. Should I miss that important event so I can be at this one? Perhaps this is a lost sheep like the one Messiah spoke of....

He fought an inner battle, wanting to send the soldier away yet secretly thrilled that he could influence one of his "enemies."

He began to speak. "May I start at the beginning? We call our community the Household of Faith. We meet in the long shed we call the cave. It's an accident of sorts! Father bought this farm. After we moved here, Father became physically weaker with age. He told me, 'Do whatever you want to develop this place.

Whatever you build on the land will be yours.'

"Well, we started making bricks and pottery after Onias, my steward, found excellent clay up in the mountain. We take an ox cart up the river and bring the clay and charcoal back as supplies for the goods we make here.

"We needed a protected place for the clay pottery to dry before it went into the kiln. Onias suggested, 'Let's build a shed! Look, that long, straight rock rising out of the ground would form a solid wall. The sun is to the south of the cliff. All we need to do is build a long shed and cover the roof. It will store and dry our bricks and pottery before they go into the kiln.' So that's what we did!

"I already had some widows living here. The next year I bought two slaves and set them free. People were astonished! 'Why set slaves free?' they asked. It made some people angry, and they wanted to know why we did that. A few people started to join me in our home for worship, while others came to learn about the Messiah.

"Some of the people were Gentiles and not really welcome in the synagogue. At first, we met at my house, but one day it started to rain while we were meeting. Some people were standing outside because this house was too small, so I said, 'I wish we had a larger space.'

"Onias had an idea. 'Could we go to the shed?' At that time, it was smaller, but the next summer we expanded it. My father named our gathering when it was originally started. He said, 'It's the Household of Faith, a place of meeting and a place of community just like we had in Alexandria and then in Philadelphia, across the Jordan River in the Syrian Decapolis.'

"You saw the people. They come from across the empire. One slave came to us as an expert glassblower from Cyprus, so we added glass bottles to our shops. Shortly after my father asked me to develop this property, my brother Amos and Abigail, his wife, joined us. Four more brothers and their families moved to Asia Minor. However, two brothers and a sister remain in Alexandria. Each of us—we are six brothers in Asia—started manufacturing different items. My two brothers and sister in Alexandria run the shipping business but don't make any goods. They send us spices and products made in Egypt.

"Later, we spread out to other cities, and we now exchange products. Woolen clothing comes from Laodicea and rings, earrings, and bracelets of gold from my brother in Sardis. Brass lamps and linen clothing arrive from Thyatira. Another brother lives in Smyrna, and he brings spices, perfumes, carpets, and precious jewels in our ships. In turn, I send my brothers pottery, glassware, and some finished clothing.

"I free the slaves whom I buy, but I think it is better that I do none of the bidding. My servant does that. You saw the couple who came to us this year; Ateas and Arpoxa, his wife, are crippled. They work here now. Ateas makes and decorates pottery that sells well. His art is popular because of the motifs he paints. Arpoxa improves our clothing by embroidering colorful designs on tunics. People love her products. She also cooks and sings!"

Antipas was not satisfied with his own answer, and he added, "I have told you much of what we do, but all this is not what or who we are. We live under the covenant."

"What do you mean?" Anthony leaned forward.

"Well, the covenant is sort of a contract between God and us. If we worship him only and keep his commandments, we will be with him forever. We believe that God called us to know him. When we weep and feel pain, God knows about that.

"We come to know who God is by being part of the covenant. Through the covenant, we learn that God wants us to be in a right relationship with him. People could not understand or correctly practice the rules or the words of our ancient leaders. All that took place over hundreds of years, so he showed us what the kingdom is like that he wants. That's why Yeshua Messiah came to proclaim this new kingdom. The Lord is with us, making us into new people. Yeshua has another name, Emmanuel, which means God is with us. That's what I believe, but there is much more to it than this."

Anthony's face showed puzzlement. "Can you see your god? How does anyone know him? You talk as though you actually know this god and that he talks to you."

"We know him through the way that our ancestors learned. However, many of our ancestors did not follow God's purposes for us as redeemed people. So instead of living in peace with one another, showing love and mercy, they had malice and deceit toward one another. We had in our past, and still have, hypocrisy, envy, and slander, leading to violence. A nephew of mine was killed while bringing a sacrifice to the altar in our temple in

Jerusalem. I am witness to how civil war rips people apart. If we truly live by the covenant, then we become people with new goals and a clear purpose. We must not live for ourselves but for others."

Anthony hadn't said anything for several minutes. Slowly he raised his head to talk. "You call it the Household of Faith. What is faith? Why is it so important to you? How did you change from being a man under siege, who almost lost his life to starvation, to becoming a person who makes houses for slaves and widows?"

Antipas was surprised at the depth of Anthony's questions and put out of his mind the worship time he was committed to lead in a few minutes. Excusing himself, Antipas went to his granddaughter's room. He asked Miriam to go to meet with the others and tell them that he would not be coming tonight.

"Tell them I have a guest who wants to know about the light of the menorah. I want you to stay with them for worship tonight," he said.

"What does that mean—the light of the menorah?" asked Miriam.

"It's a new expression! A legionary must learn how to walk out of the darkness."

The question mark on her forehead suggested astonishment at his strange answer.

"Yes, I mean it! Now please, go quickly! Ask Onias to lead the group in worship. Please don't look at me like that! I did not plan this. Ask Onias to blow the shofar."

"But, Grandfather, you always lead the service to bring in the new year!"

He imagined a conversation with Jaron as if Jaron had come into his house just now.

Yes, Jaron. A legionary. In my house! A Roman soldier who wants to know about our story...yes, and our covenant too, our beliefs and our way of life! You're threatening to put me out of the synagogue because I meet socially with non-Jews! Well, this Gentile is hungry for God. And that will be my worship tonight—teaching a legionary.

Antipas repeated it. "Miriam, just tell them I won't be coming tonight. I believe that it is vital that I spend time with this man."

Anthony had listened carefully to all that Antipas had taught him. Leaning back, on his single bed at the barracks with his hands clasped around one knee, he thought about what he had just learned.

He would explain it all to Marcos. "This is excellent instruction. Antipas's humility, in which he admits the sins of his people, reinforces the truth of what he is saying. I am gradually learning the teaching given at the Household of Faith.

"This fits in with what Miriam sang about—redemption and restoration and putting the house back together. Community isn't merely a place to enjoy little things and be sad when losing a grandmother. This village is what they called their home. A home! That's what I've wanted most of my life. Maybe that's why I came to talk to Antipas. Nightmares are telling me I need a home. Philippi—my property—will never be a home like this. All day in Philippi soldiers brag of loyalty to Rome, but that ambush…

"Deception and betrayal lurk undetected. Antipas has inner peace and a strength I don't have, yet he, in a different way than I, has seen betrayal—a civil war in Jerusalem—but he didn't foster hatred. Instead, he came to this city and created a community."

Chapter 27
Seeds for a Future Harvest

THE TEMPLE OF DEMETER, PERGAMUM

The Festival of Thesmophoria was a celebration of the goddess Demeter and her daughter, Persephone. It was unlike any other day in the year for women, who anticipated this special event for weeks. Only married women or widows could attend, and they were welcome whatever their status: rich or poor, slaves or free, Greeks or Romans. This was the day when women came together as a community, as sisters related by everyday struggles.[61] For 370 years, the ritual had remained the same; Queen Apollonius first directed the temple construction and the first procession.[62]

The Temple of Demeter, enlarged several times during the development of Pergamum, occupied a space halfway up the acropolis. As devotion to the goddess Demeter grew, so too did the size of the courtyard around the temple. The entire complex devoted to the worship of Demeter was about fifty-two paces from east to west and twenty-six paces from north to south.[63] It was built into the side of the acropolis so that two matching stoa colonnades occupied the upper and lower slopes. The upper slope was called the Northern Colonnade.

---

[61] I have reduced the Festival of Thesmophoria from three days to one day and simplified the activities to make them suitable for younger readers. The celebration was probably three days long and involved the sacrifice of piglets and storing their remains afterward. The following year the remains of the piglets were retrieved. The three days and two nights included the Ascent, the Fast, and the Kalligeneia, a nighttime torch-lit ceremony of resurrection from the world of the dead. Aristophanes penned a famous Greek comedy about the Festival of Thesmophoria.

[62] Queen Apollonius was the wife of Attalos II, 241–197 BC.

[63] The complex measured 270 feet from east to west and 134 feet from north to south (or 90 m x 45 m.)

During this festival, a play would be presented where Persephone, daughter of the goddess Demeter, was kidnapped by the fierce god Hades, a brother of Zeus. Demeter, the goddess of fertility and agriculture, left the earth to find her, resulting in winter. Eventually Zeus negotiated with Hades and Persephone was returned to Demeter, bringing springtime, but she had to periodically return to Hades, bringing yet another winter.

Women sat under the Northern Colonnade to watch the theatrical presentation.

Women came to the Temple of Demeter after dawn. Dressed in their finest, they had their hair in braids, wearing bracelets, necklaces, and earrings. Perfume and laughter filled the air. Fall had come, and the harvest was over.

On this day, October 4, thousands arrived, each carrying some part of the recent harvest. Among the fruits and vegetables and the colors and songs, the sweet smell of baked foods and excitement filled the air.

Lydia-Naq, who had risen long before sunrise, carried a tray full of prepared figs on her head, balanced on perfectly placed braids.

The three most respected women, the mothers of the aristocracy, arrived together, walking slowly to accommodate Apolliana, the oldest of the three matriarchs. Their sacrifices included raisin cakes, date cakes, cookies, and pomegranates.

Women brought other gifts and prayers written on small pieces of white cloth, each representing the deepest fears, petitions, and concerns of the individual who brought the token. These were left as petitions to the goddess. Others brought a piece of handicraft or an elegant pot. Colors, odors, and textures, along with so much food and a feeling of community, all stimulated a sense of belonging to a unique community of sisters. The high priestess declared that Demeter had accepted the sacrifices of food, and many women wept for joy.

This festival was a feast, a communion, a dedication to life, and it would finish with a celebration of torches in the dark and erotic dances before they left for home that night.

After entering the temple gate, they bowed in front of the statue of Demeter. Women slowly placed their sacrifices at the base of the altar and quietly spoke their petition to Demeter. Already the space around the altar was filling with many offerings of different foods.

Lydia-Naq stood close to the front of the line; she was recognized as being one of the most important religious figures in Pergamum. She had her petition to pray: "Hear O Zeus, our father, and Demeter, our mother! We need an heir! Zoticos has never married. Give him a wife to make a home and give him an heir. May my son, Diotrephes, help restore the customs of our people!"

The three aristocratic friends stood together, each one with her petition. Omphale Tantalus brought her raisin cakes. She still mourned her precious son, the little five-year-old Attalay, who died a week before his sixth birthday. People stepped back in respect for they recognized the woman whose tragic loss had shocked the whole city. Omphale broke down weeping, and several women wrapped their arms around her.

She prayed, "O Demeter, you descended to Hades, searching for your daughter, taking from us all the gifts of the earth. I hoped for Eumen and Attalay to restore Pergamum. Long ago, the twin brothers established Philadelphia, which is still called the City of Brotherly Love. I prayed for a boy. I was here in front of your altar seven years ago, and you blessed me with twins. Hear the cry of my soul, O Demeter! I want a new place where there is no more danger to my remaining son, Eumen. He must not fall! We must move away from the cliff."

Bernice stood behind her mistress. She was still deeply troubled by the loss of the young boy she had cared for. "O Demeter! Bring back my little Attalay, so bright, devoted, fun-loving, full of zest, mischievous, and delightful. I am covered with shame; he died due to my neglect! What can I do to bring him back to life? I brought you pomegranates today. You bring new life every year. Please bring him back to life!"

Another aristocratic woman, Apolliana Lydus, wife of Atydos Lydus, mourned the loss of her youth. Long ago, she could play any instrument. Now her fingers curled in. Her knuckles were thick and ugly, and her feet were becoming sore. Even to come down the hill of the acropolis this morning had been a painful effort. She was close to the front of the line because women respected her status. She prayed and was amazed at the ridiculous prayer that came to her mind. She felt so old.

"Demeter, help me. My hip...my legs and feet—restore to me my health and take away my pains. Or do a miracle—move the cliff! I know it sounds impossible. Our family has lived in that villa overlooking the city below for almost four hundred years. We thought we had the finest place in Pergamum, yet we have lost too many children over the cliff. I can't walk up and down the steps of the acropolis anymore!"

It was noon before all the women had paraded in front of the statue of Demeter. Then the high priestess declared that all the sacrifices and prayers had been accepted. Women hugged each other with joy. Their prayers had been heard.

During this time, women mourned their lost ones, those who had gone down into Hades, and sympathized with others who had lost family members during the previous year. It was a day to cry, tell stories, and be a community of women who had loved and lost and who still lived, sometimes gripped by the fear of death. Their personal dramas would continue long after the festival night. Spring would return, bringing hope.

The first part of the mystery play was about the changing of the seasons, and it was acted out as the sun began to set. Women shuddered in the fearsome presence of the god Hades. They sat down, silent and mournful, pensive and excited, knowing fear and expecting deep emotion.

When the drama started, Demeter, the goddess of the harvest, appeared, played by a tall, stern woman. Beautiful Persephone, her daughter, walked around the courtyard, collecting flowers. Another woman played the role of the fierce Hades, who was hunched over. He was the cruel god, hard to see in the fading light, just as death was hard to foretell. Hades flitted from place to place, from pillar to pillar, slowly sneaking up on Persephone. Everyone knew Hades would capture the maiden. That was how winter came.

When Persephone looked around, Hades jumped on her, covering her mouth. She shrieked and struggled, but Hades was too powerful for her. He took her into the small eastern shrine, representing the Chamber of Hades, where the god lived underground. The event in the play was timed so that just as the sun sank below the horizon, Hades took Persephone into his underworld. Now it became darker and colder. Cold months would come, often bringing death.

While in the underworld, Hades offered Persephone every kind of food, but she refused. All knew that if anyone ate while in the land of the dead, they would never return to life. For months, Persephone grew thinner and weaker.

Months passed until Demeter, the mother, fell on her knees. While a choir composed of young women sang, she gathered presents to bribe Hades into releasing Persephone. She collected some of the gifts brought by the women earlier in the morning and wrapped up many of them in a sack. Demeter took the gifts and disappeared into the Chamber of Hades.

The chorus sang mournfully about the winter season, when there was no harvest and no fruit. Nothing grew, and animals died. Homes went without food, and children became sick. The chorus, sung by the twenty priestesses standing on the steps, told of hunger, famine, and pain. Mothers mourned. Above all else, hunger prevailed. At the end of the song, the chorus women slowly fell to the steps. They stayed motionless as if they, too, had died and been buried. Allegorically, the world was dead. The memory of family members lost during the previous year gripped women afresh as they watched the scene. It was a time of sadness, a time to remember friends and family members who had died.

From the top of the stairs, a new company of actors made their way into the drama. A severe conflict had broken out between the gods. Some were in favor of what Demeter had done, but others were against her. The confusion awakened Zeus, Hades' brother, from his distant dwelling place on Mount Olympus. He heard about the conflict and came to talk to Hades.

The chorus rose as the second part of the drama began. Someone began to sing a soft song but was interrupted by the loud voice of Zeus as he approached the small chamber.

"My brother Hades, you are as powerful as life and death. Give Persephone back to Demeter!" demanded Zeus.

The woman playing the part of Hades took her place in front of the small chamber. "Persephone can come back. When the sun rises in the south, I will send her back to the land of the living. Demeter will water the earth, and Persephone will live again with mortals."

Bargaining was an everyday activity. Negotiations in

marketplaces resulted in agreements by both parties. In this drama, Zeus finally agreed to Hades' proposal.

However, trickery was also a daily part of life, and Hades cleverly trapped Persephone. When she was almost faint from hunger and cold, he tempted her. "I'll send you back to your mother, but first taste this. It is delicious. It will give you beauty and strength and cause a man to fall in love with you."

Persephone had been tricked into eating the forbidden pomegranate seed, the food of the dead. Because of that, she would have to return to Hades every year. She could not break the magical bond Hades had forced upon her.

Spring would come again, so Demeter and Persephone emerged from the Chamber of Hades. They slowly climbed each step as two torches were lit. More torches shed light, and by the time Demeter reached the level of the stoa above, the courtyard was ablaze with light.

More songs broke out. Demeter was back, and spring's promise appeared in the chorus. A man by the name of Triptolen, again played by a woman, was waiting for her. Demeter showed him how to plant crops and taught him magic words to make plants grow faster. Every woman knew about mysterious, powerful, secret names. Married women could not even whisper a word about the drama of Persephone, Demeter, Hades, and Zeus to their husbands. Those were secrets known only to women, their own particular mystery.

ARPOXA'S HOUSE, ANTIPAS'S VILLAGE

The next day Miriam approached Arpoxa's house. A minute later, a broadly smiling Arpoxa opened the door. Today Arpoxa was ready to tell her whole story. It was the same story that she and Ateas told in pantomime several months ago. Now she knew enough Greek to fill in the missing details with Miriam helping her with the grammar.

"My grandfather, he starts the farm. He has good children, my father and my uncles. We had good land, good cows, good sheep, and rich harvest. Fresh, bubbling stream, mountains, fish, apples, nuts, and everything we needed."

"You can say, 'He started the farm,'" said Miriam. Scythians often had trouble with grammar and getting the past and present tenses sorted out.

"Then my grandfather die. No, you say he died, right? My father came to live in a big city. A big sickness came, and my father die, sorry, he died. Others died too, all the children. My mother was not in the city, and I had no father. Only my uncle was there. He is a bad man. He is an evil man."

She covered her face with her hands. Miriam wept inwardly for the painful memories Arpoxa could never or would never describe. Arpoxa's fingers pressed hard against her clear skin, her long blond hair falling down around her head. She straightened up, and Miriam could see the strain in Arpoxa's face.

"My brother, he is bad too, another kind of bad. He takes money food. No, you say, 'He took the food money.' He was every day at horse races. He came back with nothing, and worse, he owed horse racing people more money. We had no money, no winning from gambling. But we needed food."

Miriam understood despite the slightly confused grammar. She enjoyed helping her younger friend with the Greek way of telling her story. But now that she had become more emotional, Arpoxa forgot some of the grammar, and her story became harder to understand. Desperation sounded in her voice.

"We getting very hungry, and we yell at each other many times. We still need food for us, for me and him. One night two big mans is coming. They taking me. They give my brother money. Give him horse owe money he needed, but they not give him money for food. They take me on ship, and I meet Ateas. He comes from a big city, Bilsk."

Miriam's eyes were wide open as she began to understand the story. A cold feeling crept up her back. The hairs on her arm were on end.

She stared at Arpoxa. "Do you mean that your brother sold you as a slave because he had no money for food?"

"You are almost right. He has owing at horse place. He needs to pay horse owes or they hurt him bad."

Miriam's voice rose higher. "He sold you as a slave to pay off his debts at the races?" By the end of her sentence, she was almost screaming.

Arpoxa answered, "Yes, my brother says, 'You are crippled. You are not walking, so how can you earn money for what I am owing? You have bad feet so you are nothing worth. You eat much food. I not have money for food for you and me.' So I am sold to big man, man with ship. I think he not happy because he still needs more money for food after pay horse place."

Miriam's tears flowed for the attractive girl who sat beside her. This lovely woman, not yet twenty years old, had been sold as a slave! She had a beautiful face and a clear complexion. Could she help it if she had been born with clubbed feet?

Arpoxa is gifted. She takes a simple garment, the kind that people in Pergamum wear, and she makes it bright and attractive. Crippled from birth, abused by her uncle, and sold into slavery by her brother to pay for gambling debts!

As Miriam walked back up the hill to her home, questions formed in her mind. She prepared to talk to her grandfather.

"Why did Arpoxa not mention women? Were men the only ones in her life? Was there no one to help her? She met Ateas on the slave ship, but did they know each other before that? How did Scythians get married? Arpoxa is so in love with Ateas."

Again Miriam felt a pang of jealousy. Although Arpoxa was crippled, she had a husband to talk to her, to love her.

Feelings of pity mixed with those of jealousy.

Next birthday, I will be twenty-six, and I'm not married. No one in our community will marry me because of Grandpa and our beliefs. All the other synagogues are going to reject us too.

At supper, she said little, and she could not go to bed. Panic rose slowly within her. She knew she couldn't go to sleep when she was thinking about these things.

Antipas snored softly in his room. She took the small watch lamp from the kitchen and went to the library. She lit two lamps and put them on the stand, one on each side of the table.

Over the next hour, she wrote a song about what she had learned. Words flowed smoothly and fit a tune Arpoxa sang. It was a new melody from beyond the Black Sea.

Then she went to bed.

Chapter 28
Demetrius

ANTIPAS'S HOME, PERGAMUM

Onias handed Antipas a message from Demetrius that had just been delivered by courier from Smyrna.

October 16 in the 8th year of Domitian
From: Demetrius
To: Antipas Ben Shelah
   If you are well, then I am well. I write to let you
know that I hope to arrive in Pergamum in three days.
I left Ephesus almost two weeks ago and have enjoyed
a pleasant visit with the brothers in Smyrna. My work
here is nearly finished, and I look forward to being
with you shortly.

Demetrius was the representative of John the Elder, who lived in Ephesus. Previously, when he was younger, John made regular visits to the various cities. More recently, John had commissioned Demetrius to take his place in this annual tour of Asia Minor.

Demetrius's circular visit took him to the seven central districts: Ephesus, Smyrna, Pergamum, Thyatira, Sardis, Philadelphia, and Laodicea. Major roads connected these cities, and Demetrius brought news to each group, sharing John's letters. The whole circuit took about three months to complete.

When he had visited last year, Demetrius looked every day of his forty years of age. He was not a man to tolerate either exaggeration or falsehood.

After his wife had died in childbirth twelve years before, he did not remarry. The elders, fathers, and younger men in Asia Minor had become his extended family. His shop in Ephesus, specializing in water jugs, supplied him with enough income to carry out his trips.

He arrived on October 20, and Antipas grasped his hands, kissing him on each cheek. "Welcome to our home once again!" Antipas beamed.

"I am honored to be with you!" replied Demetrius with a genuine smile.

Antipas looked carefully at his guest. There were soft lines of stress on the face of this trusted elder. "Are you tired after your trip? Do you want to talk tonight?"

"Yes, Antipas, although we have two weeks to talk, we have much to discuss, and I want to hear how your people are learning the truth, how they are walking in the light."

"Very well, and I want to hear about Ephesus and your visit to Smyrna."

They sat together in the library after supper and passed from topic to topic until it was late.

Miriam listened in on the conversation, and Antipas asked her to continue learning from their guest during the next two weeks.

THE CAVE, ANTIPAS'S VILLAGE

It was a Saturday night with a new moon, making it a special evening that started a new Jewish month. Demetrius had agreed to speak to the Household of Faith, and the cave was full to overflowing. A dozen Jewish men drew their prayer shawls over their shoulders before the meeting began.

Marcos sat with Marcella and Florbella at the back with other families and their children. Anthony and some soldiers sat on the carpet across from them. Jewish women sat near the front, opposite their husbands.

Demetrius sat on a chair at the front and addressed the group.

"John the Elder sends his love, his prayers, and his affection. He is old and cannot easily move about, so it is my joyful duty to travel for him. I am his representative to the faithful. Harvest time in the fields has just finished. All over this province, farmers are rejoicing that crops have been taken in. Our lives are like a harvest field because we reap what we sow, and if we sow love, we receive it back in return. But we can also sow hate and resentment.

"These are some of the things we will discuss here for the next two weeks. We will spend much of our time on these topics: love and truth. Each evening we will meet here in the cave, just as we did last year."

People stood to begin the meeting with their frequent confession, the declaration they made each time they met together for worship.

"Our attitude should be the same
as that of Yeshua Messiah:
Who, being in very nature God,
did not consider equality with God
Something to be grasped,
but made himself nothing.
Taking the very nature of a servant,
being made in human likeness
and being found in appearance as a man,
He humbled himself and became obedient to death;
even death on a cross!

"Therefore, God exalted him to the highest place,
and gave him the name that is above every name,
that at the name of Yeshua every knee should bow,
in heaven and on earth and under the earth,
and every tongue confess that Yeshua Messiah is Lord,
to the glory of God the Father."[64]

When everyone was seated again, Demetrius spoke. "I have just come from Smyrna, where I read this letter from Brother John, and I will read it in all the other cities."

He opened the scroll and began. "That which was from the beginning, which we have heard, which we have seen with our eyes, which we have looked at and our hands have touched, this we proclaim concerning the Word of life."[65]

He talked for almost an hour, carefully reading aloud each sentence of John's letter. No one moved. Demetrius explained truth with unusual clarity. The tensions between light and

---

[64] Philippians 2:6–11
[65] 1 John 1:1

darkness, truth and falsehood, were clearly spelled out, and the people listened attentively.

He reminded them of the illustration of the sap in the vine. It flowed up effortlessly from the roots and flowed all the way to the very end of each branch. Fruit could only be found on a plant if every part was healthy and connected.

He then said that he would be explaining many of the letter's teachings during his visit. It would take several meetings like this to go through the letter John had written to the congregations. Many people asked questions, and the meeting went on until late at night.

The next evening, Antipas said Miriam and her friends were going to sing a song. Marcella and Marcos knew the young men and women who faced each other at the front of the cave. They were holding their instruments: drums, tambourines, harps, and flutes. It was not precisely like the chorus at the Greek dramas, but the musicians would reinforce Demetrius's teaching.

Miriam stood between the musicians, ready to sing her new song. "This song, called 'Harvest,' fits with what our friend from Ephesus taught us. It is about a friend of mine, and her story is about God showing his love and remaking us bit by bit."

Arpoxa rose from the back and inched her way slowly, painfully, to the front and stood beside Miriam. The young woman knew her story was going to be explained to everyone tonight. Still, Miriam had no idea that Arpoxa would walk to the front from the very back.

"This is my song," Arpoxa said. "Miriam wrote it a month ago after I talked to her. This song is about my life. I am, I *was* a slave from my home country. I am receiving hope in this new community. My brother wanted to be rich. He always gambled on many horses, and finally, he lost all his money. He sold me to get money to pay his debt."

Arpoxa beamed, knowing her storytelling had improved a lot, even if it wasn't yet perfect. "A few men were important in my life, and this song is telling about them. Miriam listened to my story last month, and now she is singing about me."

Miriam sang, imagining the years of suffering that Arpoxa had endured.

Our promised spring brings more than figs.
With sweaty brow, my grandpa digs.
He plants a seed. "This work is mine!"
He grins while every muscle aches.

Calves and lambs dance on soft, fresh soil.
Leaves of wheat appear. Father's toil
Means food and fruits from off the vine.
We relish fresh, hot raisin cakes.

Harvest's joy complete: steaming bread,
The calves are fat, the children fed.
Our pantry's full and stocked with wine.
With joy and song, each one partakes.

Brother buys things he doesn't need.
He gambles endlessly. I plead!
Character's gone wrong, bent on crime.
Debts! My life pays for his mistakes!

Harvest reaps seeds that were sown.
Motives watered, like wheat that's grown.
The Lord redeemed me just in time.
Agape love my life remakes.

Marcos had prearranged with Antipas that he would come to the front to address the gathering at the end of the song. He stood up and took his wife's hand, and they walked with Florbella to the front.

He said, "A year ago I didn't know anything about the Messiah, about the covenant, or about any of the promises you talk about. I am a counselor, a lawyer up there." He pointed to the top of the acropolis. "I'm supposed to keep things honest on the top of the hill."

Everyone laughed.

Marcos waited until the laughter died down. "I confess today that the Household of Faith is my new community. You have a love that I have never seen before. It started when Florbella came here. She had been deeply wounded and unable to speak. You should see her now! She wakes up singing, and she sings all day!

She's even teaching her dolls to sing!"

Again, laughter rolled quietly across the room. Antipas saw in him not just another cold lawyer. This man loved his daughter. The love of a concerned father for his daughter drew him into the hearts of these people.

"At home, she repeats all the songs she learns here. For a Roman lawyer to be together with Jewish families, listening to and believing the stories from Judea, isn't the best thing to keep my career alive, especially in Pergamum!"

People laughed again but this time quietly and nervously, understanding that he had begun to count the cost of his decision.

"I believe your teaching, Antipas. A miracle took place here with our daughter, and she has been completely healed. She is normal and healthy, and I accept the teaching of Yeshua Messiah. Great changes are taking place in our lives. I ask you to accept us into the Household of Faith."

Before anyone could move, Anthony stood up. This was not prearranged with Antipas, and his eyes widened slightly as the soldier walked purposely from the back of the cave to stand beside Marcos.

Anthony was wearing his soldier's tunic but had no weapons. He had left his sword and other symbols of power in his barracks.

Most Jewish men in Antipas's village had agreed to eat with and share meals with Gentiles providing that the non-Jews would respect their way of worship. The steps to this accommodation of different ethnic customs had cost Antipas many sleepless nights. Yet no one had ever seen a soldier at the front during a meeting.

Anthony began by saying, "Marcos invited me here to hear Antipas speak two months ago. I wondered what a Jew would have to say about the fall of Jerusalem, so I listened to his story. Since then, I have been watching his life. He is serious about something that seems impossible to me. He can love his enemies."

He paused, apparently not sure of how he wanted to express himself in his next thought. "As a legionary, I should be a natural enemy to him. Notice, I didn't say, 'I am his enemy.'"

Several people sucked in their breath, not knowing what to expect next.

"Two months ago, he told us his life story: how he came to be here and how he began this community. I don't know what I expected to hear. I don't understand all that he teaches, because some of the things he says are strange to me. It will take me time to learn. I am a scout with the army. Now I have to study with my eyes and mind to learn about faith. I don't deserve to even ask to be part of this community, as Marcos and Marcella just did. I know Yeshua the Messiah taught sacrificial love, and I have seen agape love alive here. If you could tolerate having me in your midst, I would have what I always wanted—a home."

Total silence met Anthony's remarks, a silence born of expectancy.

Antipas watched, trying to interpret the atmosphere. Something precious was happening. It was a sacred moment. Slowly people began to spontaneously clap in appreciation of Anthony's humbling yet bold speech, and then the clapping died down. The cave was just a simple shed, a place for protection, a dimly lit building on a Saturday night where the cold of winter would soon arrive.

Outside on a chilly, cloudy night, a drizzle started to fall. Inside, however, a promise of reconciliation awakened hope.

Ateas started to walk forward even before Anthony was finished speaking. He walked slowly, deliberately. It took him a while to limp to the front to stand beside Arpoxa. She sat beside Miriam. Ateas put his hand on Anthony's shoulder. Balancing himself on his stronger leg and resting on his crutches, he reached down and coaxed Arpoxa to stand beside him. His other arm was around Arpoxa's waist, drawing his wife close.

His speech was concise but said everything he needed to say. "I say also, here my new home. I like you people. You very kind people. Antipas, he is good man. The speaking here, tonight and before, it is all good, all truth. This is my home, new home for me." It wasn't perfect Greek, but his meaning was perfectly clear.

Antipas wasn't able to close with the usual prayers. Quietly, unexpectedly people moved forward, embracing their new friends. The cave was alive with people talking and chatting. In the darkness of night, a new light shone brightly. Antipas opened his arms as he faced them: Anthony, Ateas and Arpoxa, Marcella, Florbella, and Marcos.

"This is an evening I will never forget," he said, embracing them one by one.

Miriam saw Diotrephes pulling at Antipas's sleeve. She didn't like that young man. For months, Miriam had become more uneasy about his presence. She would glance at him and see that he was staring at her. During the last month, his attention was an embarrassment to her, so she simply stopped looking at him.

Antipas told her an hour later what had happened. "Miriam, I want you to know that Diotrephes spoke to me in a low voice, not loud enough for anyone else to hear. He said, 'Antipas, I want to be included in your community too. But my mother is the high priestess of Zeus, and I thought people would reject me if I spoke to them all like Marcos did. What do you think? Can I join your group too?'

"I'm worried by something in Diotrephes's words, but my, what a wonderful evening we had today!"

As Anthony walked back to the garrison in the rain, tension eased in his stomach; the ever-present need for revenge seemed to lessen. He paused, running his hand over the scar on the side of his face, where his beard would never grow again. He had stated that Romans and Jews were assumed to be enemies, but no rancor had tinged his words.

Chapter 29
Marcos's Entertainment

MARCOS'S HOME, NEW VIEW AREA, PERGAMUM

For a month, Marcos had worked on his plan. In the middle of October, he called Marcella aside.

"I've been asking about the three aristocratic families. The more questions I threw at the men giving me a back rub at the hot baths each day, the more details came out. I learned about their traditions. Each of the six adults has the pure blood of ancient kingdoms flowing through their veins."

"What kind of questions do you ask, my dear?"

"I asked about their day-to-day activities. I wanted to learn about their emotions and what is essential to them. I posed some carefully worded questions in the hot baths during the afternoons."

"And now what?"

"I'm ready to invite these three families to an evening meal at our home. I want to *give to Caesar what belongs to Caesar.*"

"You keep saying new things! Some hardly make any sense. Of course you give Caesar what he demands."

"The time has come to put many things right. Remember when I talked about selling my brothers' villas in Nicomedia that now belong to me? I will use the proceeds from that sale to benefit both Pergamum and Caesar. I think I can use my brothers' wealth to encourage three families to move away from the edge of the cliff. Now here's the next step in my plan. I want our servants to deliver a handwritten invitation for a full-course banquet four days from now."

The purpose of the evening had occupied Marcos's thoughts for many nights, and he had planned his after-dinner speech carefully for these important guests.

His whole future might depend on how well his plan was

presented at this banquet.

Marcella and Marcos lived in one of the new Roman villas overlooking the New Forum on a gradually sloping hill suitable for spacious gardens. Wealthy people occupied the villas between the army's garrison and New Forum.

In the time of Caesar Augustus, the lots along the hill had been divided into twenty generous acreages. On each property a stately villa rose offering a magnificent panorama of the acropolis.

A road at the bottom of each property ran level along the small hill, connecting the homes. Each villa had access to the Sacred Way by following this road. The paths leading to the villas were paved with fine granite paving stones. Horses' hooves, clapping on the pavement, created a staccato echo, announcing arrivals.

The six guests invited to their home arrived in two horse-drawn wagons, suitable for the dignity of their status as three aristocratic families in the city. They connected a glorious past with the present busyness and grandeur of Pergamum.

As the wagons descended the long, gradual slope around the back of the acropolis heading for the lower part of the city, Lady Omphale Tantalus spoke to Lady Apolliana Lydus of the day's events. Eumen sat at the back, and his nurse, Bernice, had her arm around the child's shoulders. Atys and Atydos, their husbands, chatted about business concerns.

Behind them, in another horse-drawn carriage, came Manes and Clytemnestra Tmolus.

Leaving the top of the acropolis, Omphale gazed over the side of the cart at torch lights that flickered in the streets below. Her lips pursed in a frown, an unusual expression on her normally happy countenance.

"What do you think this lawyer meant when he wrote in his invitation, 'Memorable entertainment after dinner'? I sent my slave to ask about it, and his reply was 'I am the entertainment tonight. You will laugh a little tonight and then laugh forever.' What a strange comment! What in the world does he mean?"

Apolliana gazed at the passing acropolis scenery and massaged her hands. "I have no idea what Marcos means when he talks about entertainment. I can only think that he is going to sing a song to us or do some magic tricks. Atydos says he's made a positive difference at the city council. His insightful comments are appreciated. This man was a good addition to our city, but he will always be a foreigner. He came from Nicomedia in Bithynia you know.

"My fingers ached today. My joints, hands, and feet, one of the worst days ever... It seems that every step I take is painful. Nothing I've bought in the marketplace has helped."

"Not even tea made from dried livers of African monkeys?" asked Omphale.

"No, and I paid a lot for that medicine. Why do you think this lawyer and his wife invited us but asked us not to tell anyone where we are going?"

"I'm not happy to have to guess at people's motives or actions. That's why I was a little grumpy about accepting the invitation," Omphale answered. The loss of her son six months before was not brought up during their half-hour ride down the acropolis into the Villa Nova district. Nothing would ever take away the pain of the tragic loss.

When Omphale got down from the wagon, she reached back up for Apolliana's hand in order to steady her.

Apolliana grimaced as she stepped down from the wagon. "I have no idea why all the secrecy is necessary. It's a little bit exciting though. We never have unplanned things like this in our lives anymore."

The horses tossed their heads as the women walked around the wagon to the front door of the home.

Omphale was greeted at the front door by Marcos and Marcella. Water in decorated ceramic basins was placed in front of the guests after they sat in the entryway to have the dust rinsed from their feet. A slave bent down on his knees and used a white cotton towel to dry them. The sandals of the six guests lay in a neat row beside the door.

Once inside the door, Omphale smiled. Familiar Greek myths brightened the home. Dazzling images sprang to life in each room, portraying a critical moment in each god's story. Gods and goddesses covered the floor, looking like real people. Some images stretched from wall to wall.

She examined the lawyer's home. Colored marble panels

three feet high, some with a greenish tone and others with a reddish tinge, formed a base along each wall. Each room had its own individual motif. A small fountain in the entry room splashed water into the square pond around it.

The niche where a statue of Hera usually stood in each home was empty. This was the first clue that something was different.

Next, Omphale looked into the entryway with the fountain and saw the empty sacrifice niche where Demeter would typically receive a small votive offering each day. She had a puzzled look on her face.

This home feels empty without the statue of Hera. Not even Demeter is honored. Why?

The entry room gave way to the largest room, on the right, where guests would spend the whole evening. Three matching leather-covered couches, on which they would recline for their meal, invited them to enjoy the hospitality of the home. Expensive purple carpets embroidered with motifs of animals lay draped over each of the three couches.

"Welcome, Honorable Manes Tmolus," Marcos said to the senior man, the leader of the three families. Marcella and Marcos's respect for the dignity of this historical family showed clearly.

"Welcome, Honorable Atys and Lady Omphale Tantalus," Marcos said, recognizing the family who had lost their young boy earlier in the year.

"Marcella, we brought Eumen and his nurse, Bernice. We don't let him out of our sight," Omphale explained, a touch of sadness clouding her smile.

"I think that was very wise, Omphale. Thank you for bringing him. He can play with our daughter, Florbella." Marcella called Florbella's slave, Marcosanus, to lead them near the kitchen. "They will be with Bernice and take their meal in the children's area."

Marcos continued, "We are so pleased to have you in our home, respected Atydos Lydus and Lady Apolliana Lydus."

Omphale observed, "I think the preparation of this feast has occupied several slaves the whole day. This is no ordinary meal."

Later that evening, as the guests left for their homes at the top of the acropolis, Marcos pulled Marcella close to him. They stood in their doorway and waved as both wagons pulled away to the rhythmic sound of hooves on a stone-paved street.

He turned from the entrance and slowly closed the door. He began to laugh, at first a gentle chuckle, which soon was transformed into tears rolling down his cheeks.

"You are an absolute scamp!" Marcella exclaimed, her fingers pushing against his waist.

"I wasn't sure I could pull it off. Imagine their surprise when I described each of their deepest fears."

"I see now that you learned a lot about them at the hot baths. I'm very impressed!"

"What do you think happens each afternoon? The hot baths are not only called that because of steam sweeping up from the hot stones, flooding a person with sweat! Hot gossip goes around, and who better to gossip about than the richest families in the city?"

"Well, these guests were indeed surprised by how much you knew about them, and for a while, I thought they were angry enough to get up and leave, but you quickly showed them that what you wanted was for their benefit. What made you think they would ever abandon their privileged places, with the best views in the city, and agree to move to a new location on the acropolis?"

Marcos smiled. "Actually, it was fairly simple. Through the rumors at the baths, I learned that each family had well-defined reasons for wanting to leave the cliff but that each was either fearful of losing their status of being in such an exclusive location or just ashamed that it was necessary.

"It was easy to discover that Lady Omphale Tantalus and her husband Atys are living in constant fear. They are petrified that the other little boy might be killed by a fall. They hate the cliff but have a weakness for popularity and fame. It wasn't hard to figure that out. Everyone was talking about both things when the little lad was laid to rest."

"And what about Lady Apolliana Lydus and her husband, Atydos? I know Apolliana lives in a lot of pain."

"Exactly right, Marcella! I've often watched Lady Apolliana walking from her house, down the steep steps of the theater, around the Altar of Zeus, and to the Upper Agora. It often takes an hour for her to make the trip. She lives in constant pain from her feet and knees. Everyone can see how painful it is for her to move about. She was ashamed to admit her need—or rather her fear of ending her days unable to get out of her house."

"How did you get her to listen to you? Pain like that is so personal, and many people won't talk about it openly."

"I appealed to their pride. Apolliana's family, the Lydus clan, uses the emblem of the eagle, the bird that soars higher than any other. It's symbolic of their family's far-flung trade throughout the Aegean Sea, their fleet of ships, and wealth created through trading. They have a reputation for taking advantage of new opportunities. I knew that letting them talk about their future prospects would give me a chance to bring the topic around to the disadvantages for Apolliana of living on the edge of the cliff and the advantage to finding a better place for a new home."

'The third family...did you see Manes's face when you started talking about him?"

"Yes, it was convincing Manes and Clytemnestra Tmolus that intimidated me. When I first started my little investigation, I didn't think they would agree to give up their home beside the cliff and move to a new house."

Marcos chuckled and repeated the statement he had made earlier in the evening. "Respected Manes Tmolus, we understand that your house is built back from the cliff just enough so that there is not the same danger to your family. However, I have been told that your family is weary because of the noise coming from below. Everyone knows that during festivals, loud noises continue all night from the Temple of Dionysius. At other times, it comes from the Greek Theater. Thousands of people scream, groan, laugh, and enjoy the dramas, but noise like that can cause stress. Some people have trouble sleeping during the festivals."

"Oh, did you see his eyes? He looked like an owl! His jaw fell open!" It was Marcella's turn to laugh.

"Yes, that bit of news was hard to come by. I had Florbella's slave come with me to the hot baths and make friends with Manes's slave. When I learned that Manes Tmolus really was at wit's end with the noise from below the cliff, I knew that all three families were ready for a banquet at our home."

Marcella smiled. "Even I was captivated when you said, 'Imagine it! There, right on the top of the most beautiful acropolis in the world, sits an Imperial Temple built to honor the next emperor of Rome. Built of white, polished marble, it's huge.

Maybe you will be alive when it is finished, maybe not. However, your children and your children's children will be part of the celebration! The world will marvel that anything so massive, so perfect, could be built! Gossip like this will circulate around the world. Pergamum has risen to become a famous city again. But that will happen only if there is the space for that temple to be built. For many years, you three families will be applauded and praised for sacrificing your cliffside locations to Pergamum!' Oh, you sounded like an experienced lawyer when you talked that way! But now, my dear husband, how do you propose to pay for getting the three families to move?"

"I still intend to use the money from selling my brothers' estates. They rarely paid the taxes they should have handed over to the authorities. I believe the value of their summer villas, homes, businesses, and orchards in the provinces of Bithynia and Pontus are enough to cover the expenses for three new homes to be built on the nearly flat eastern area close to the top of the acropolis. Moving them to new homes is the only way to free up space for a new Imperial Temple. Tonight, three families agreed to move. Over the next years, the city should be able to pay for the guild of masons to build the base for an enormous platform. It must be large enough to support a grand Imperial Temple.

"Apolliana won't have to walk far to the Upper Forum market or to the temples, the Tantalus family won't have to worry about their son falling, and Manes Tmolus can sleep peacefully during festivals at the Temple of Dionysius. And all three families will receive many honors for their 'sacrifice.'"

Florbella had been watching and listening. "Daddy, I'm happy when I see you laughing. What is the joke?"

"Someday, my child, I will explain how people who are already wealthy far beyond the rest of the city are only too glad to become even richer!"

He took Florbella's hand, and Marcella completed the circle. Laughing and running in a circle, they danced for joy.

Chapter 30
The Coldest Month

ANTIPAS'S HOME, PERGAMUM

Antipas found his mind full of conflict. He started to write his concerns from the day in a diary but couldn't find words to explain his unease. The unusual events tonight at the cave went unrecorded, and he went to sleep mulling over his many thoughts.

What should I do about Diotrephes? Can I trust the sincerity of someone who speaks that way—who doesn't confess his faith openly and speaks slyly? He has come faithfully to our meetings, but does he really trust in the Messiah?

In the morning, Demetrius sat with Antipas discussing the events of the previous evening. Miriam singing her composed songs was a new and exciting concept for worship. He wanted to tell the other assemblies about what had been presented.

He had already spent each evening of the past week teaching during meetings at the cave. He returned with Antipas after the evening's gathering.

"John is old and somewhat discouraged. He sees himself as standing between two worlds. The first is that of the initial enthusiasm that believers had in Ephesus. It seems that the first blush of youthful joy is disappearing, and a new set of ideas is taking over. He's urging everyone, 'Be wary! Keep to the true teachings of the Messiah and all he stands for. Don't let your beliefs be twisted and changed. Don't let anyone lead you astray!' That's the message I'm sharing with the Messiah's followers in Asia Minor."

Antipas knew that Demetrius had been talking with different people in the Household of Faith to determine if false teaching was entering their community. He asked Demetrius, "How can we tell the difference between the true ones and the false ones?"

Demetrius answered, "False teachers say salvation comes

from acquiring secret knowledge from chosen teachers, special books, and secret initiations. These new masters ask the question, 'Where does evil come from?' 'The material world is evil and from the flesh,' they answer, thus teaching that the flesh is evil. So if the material world is evil, and if it is our flesh that causes us to sin, then the flesh is sinful.

"Consequently, salvation has to come from that which is not of the flesh. That makes the mind the channel of salvation. Thus, they seek 'special knowledge.' This has broad implications. It causes people to say that Yeshua, the Messiah, did not come in the flesh."

Demetrius was earnest in his concern. "My dear friend Antipas, I'm troubled because I believe several families in your community don't follow John's teaching. They are susceptible to accepting heretical doctrines. Be careful, Antipas, when you hear false teaching. People hunger for secrets and for specialized knowledge. It's tempting. This kind of teaching does not demand repentance or personal sacrifice. This is what the Gnostics teach.

"Another aspect of false teaching entices a naïve and receptive person. False teachers declare that sinning is not problematic. Why? Because they say when you repent, you receive more of God's forgiveness. People called Nicolaitans are the primary source of these ideas. They tolerate sin and encourage compromise. False doctrines can be very alluring but lead to much evil."

During his many talks with Demetrius, the topic of Antipas's business came up. "My brothers are starting to complain that I am not supplying them with enough products to sell in their shops. I know it's because I opened three shops of my own in cities north of Pergamum."

After hearing all of the details, Demetrius advised him, "Close down the least productive of these new stores. You need to meet your obligations to your brothers."

"Another problem I'm having is the almost certain loss of two of my elderly widow salespeople. This is a new difficulty. It's come because of my problems with the synagogue."

"How bad is it going to be? Is it only the loss of salespeople or of sales as well?"

"Hmm, probably both. Solving this problem is going to

involve Miriam since she can fill one of the empty positions."

Following this discussion with Demetrius, Antipas knew that it was time to talk to his granddaughter. "Miriam, here is what I decided about our shops. I am struggling to keep everything going, so I must make a few changes. I must close our shop in Assos on the Aegean coast to send more goods to my brothers. So at the end of November, I'll have all those goods brought back here by horse and wagon."

"I'm sorry that you have to close down one of your shops, Grandfather. Can I help you in any way?"

"Since I started being 'disciplined' by the synagogue, some Jewish customers and friends are avoiding our stores. Sadly, sales have fallen off. Therefore, we must consolidate our work in Pergamum as well as along the Aegean Sea. This will have a substantial effect on how we do things."

He let out a deep sigh, reluctant to make changes but feeling forced to do so. "Two of the Jewish widows, Sheva and Damaris, will almost certainly leave my village if the elders banish me from their community. These two women have many friends in the congregation, and they will be supported by them living elsewhere. I can shift the other women around to staff the Upper Agora shop. It will leave Nikasa, the Samaritan woman, to run the store in the Lower Agora, but I can't ask her to work alone."

He took a long breath before continuing. "So, my dear child, I would like you to start helping Nikasa in the shop in the Lower Agora. Sorry, my dear, but you will have to work like the other women in our village."

THE GARRISON OF PERGAMUM

Cassius called Anthony to a private meeting in the garrison office. "What is this news that I heard about you?" he demanded, a sharp rebuke sounding in his words. "Three weeks ago, you went to a meeting at Antipas's village! What is this all about?"

"I can explain it to you, sir," he answered.

"You came here to train men to do battle in Dacia. You will not deviate from this purpose! I have been told that there is teaching about some Nazarene who said to turn the other cheek if someone strikes you on your face. Do you want a scar on the other side of your face? What a stupid man he must have been—

'Turn the other cheek!' Soldiers do not stay alive by following rules like that! I demand that you live like a man going to war, not gathering with ignorant people who refuse to fight!"

"Yes sir."

Already this teaching of Antipas was leading to confrontation and confusion for Anthony.

THE SYNAGOGUE OF PERGAMUM

The coldest time of the year had arrived. Trees stood with bare branches forlornly poking up toward the sky. Jewish families gathered each night to light the Chanukah candles, remembering the eight nights during which the temple in Jerusalem was rededicated. Parents told their children the story of the sacrilege when soldiers of Antiochus IV had desecrated their Holy Place by sacrificing a pig on the temple altar.[66]

That insult resulted in the Maccabees raising an army that won many battles against the Seleucid army that occupied Israel. The subsequent rededication of the temple carried great significance, and such an event could not be commemorated in just one day! During the dedication, the oil for the lamps in the temple kept burning day after day, even though initially there was enough liquid for only one night. The miracle became a confirmation of God's approval of the forces of light against those living in the darkness. Starting on Tuesday, December 13, and lasting until Tuesday, December 20, the *shammosh,* or extra candle, was used to light one additional lamp each evening. Every evening the light from the menorah shone brighter. On the eighth evening, when the last lamp was lit, a unique service of thanksgiving took place.

Jaron noted the pressure of Antipas's exclusion had already caused two widows to return to the synagogue.

"Even Antipas's granddaughter, Miriam, has to work now!

---

[66] Antiochus IV Epiphanes, meaning "God is present," sacrificed a pig on the altar of the temple in Jerusalem in 168 BC, driving the Jews to rebellion. The Maccabees, under Judas and his brothers, responded with a call to arms. Six years later, after driving out the Seleucid armies, the temple was rededicated. The Feast called *Chanukah,* or Feast of Rededication, is celebrated in November or December.

She has never worked before, but he is suffering as fewer people go to his shops." Jaron's voice was full of hope. "We are forcing him to come back to us. By next year at the time of Chanukah, Antipas will have joined us once again. No one can face the agony of rejection."

THE ACROPOLIS OF PERGAMUM

In the Upper City, nights were a time for intense revelry during the Winter Festivals of Dionysius and Saturnalia. Day and night, people ran through the streets, warmed by too much wine. Some nights it rained. Wide woven hats that reached almost to the shoulders protected individuals out in the open from a cold drizzle. People danced to popular songs. Others laughed, making fun of those who were drunk. They sang as loudly as they could.

> Dionysius pours out wine;
> I sacrifice my health!
> Dionysius, here's my time,
> To you, I give my wealth!
>
> Come, one and all, come dine with us,
> To you, I give my all,
> Drink long while in the prime of life;
> Dance hard, sing loud, stand tall.
>
> Celebrations so glorious!
> Banish all your sorrow!
> Join in song and shout the rhyme.
> Never mind tomorrow!

In some homes, loud cries were heard as fathers, upon arriving home, beat their children. Wines that had come by wagon from Philadelphia and Sardis filled cups around the city. Silver coins earned by workers during the harvest now filled the pockets of merchants. Crowds poured into the Greek Theater on the acropolis and into the Roman Theater near the New Forum.

Chapter 31
Surprises

THE GARRISON OF PERGAMUM

On Sunday morning, January 1, in the eighth year of Domitian, Anthony stood at attention with the soldiers that were being trained to conquer the King of Dacia.

As he had done on New Year's Day for each of the last seventeen years, he stood beside fellow soldiers for the annual declaration of loyalty to Caesar. They stood in the rain, lined up in the ready-for-battle formation. As Cassius bellowed out the words of the oath, the soldiers repeated them with loud affirmation.

The morning had dawned on the garrison with a weak light, the sun barely showing through a gray, overcast sky. As they gathered on the hill, cold winds penetrated the soldiers' cloaks.

Anthony followed each step to initiate his new recruits.

Cassius shouted aloud, "Caesar is lord and god!" He then performed a meaningful symbolic gesture.

One by one, Cassius cut a clump of hair from each new recruit with his sword, handing it to one of the centurions. The young recruit and the centurion walked over to a small fire where the hair was dropped into hot flames.

"With this, you are consecrated to Caesar," the centurion declared as each recruit smelled his hair being burned.

"By this act, you are now dedicated to the service of the army, living or dying. The odor of burning hair brings a gulp to your throat. The meaning is clear and each of you will forever remember this: Loyalty to Caesar means yielding body and soul for the defense of the empire."

Another recruit stepped forward, and the same initiation rite was carried out.

"Caesar is lord and god! We serve the empire with loyalty to Emperor Domitian!" the recruits shouted together at the end of their first Solemn Oath of Loyalty ceremony.

The words were familiar to Anthony, yet something was different this year. He had repeated the same solemn oath many times, but today he felt disconnected from the act of loyalty.

Anthony thought about what he had declared when repeating the words of the solemn oath.

The first day of the new year had come and with it the swearing of loyalty to Caesar. Would he repeat those words again the following new year?

Cassius called Anthony aside the next morning. From the look on Cassius's face, he knew that this was intended to be a confrontation.

"I have been watching your men during the defensive fighting training. It's obvious to me that they are less prepared than the other men. I want them to be more under my training command to improve their capability in face-to-face fighting. I'm reducing your time with them to two mornings a week."

Anthony began to say, "But fighting in forests, not in the open plains like you have done against the Persians... Commander, you have never fought for your life in the dense forests of Europe!"

However, those words stuck in his throat. A soldier never spoke back to his commander.

ANTIPAS'S SHOP IN THE LOWER AGORA, THE ACROPOLIS

Anthony wanted to argue but knew it would be futile. He left the garrison at noon. As he walked past the New Forum, he thought of the birthday celebration tonight for Antipas.

One thought kept going through his mind: *I should buy a gift for Antipas! What could I get for him? He has everything he needs. I have no idea.*

Instead of making his way directly to the hot baths, he walked a little higher, through the lower gates and to the Lower Agora.

Anthony walked around the long stoa, the overhanging roof protecting him from the light rain. He looked in at one store after another. Most were empty; customers had gone home for lunch or were already heading for their daily hot bath. He walked along the narrow end on the east side. Just before he turned to walk back along the north side of the marketplace, he saw Miriam.

She stood under the protective shade of the roof, talking to a saleswoman from the store next to the Ben Shelah shop. Anthony approached them. "Hello, do you have anything I might buy for a sixty-five-year-old man? I'm going to a birthday party tonight."

He followed Miriam into the Ben Shelah shop. As they entered, Miriam spoke politely. "Thank you for coming to our shop. I have seen you at the meetings in the cave."

"Young lady, I had heard that your little village has shops in the city but didn't know where they were. I'm pleased that I have found one so easily. Have you always worked in this shop? I thought you took care of your home in the village."

"Please call me Miriam," she said, taking in the long scar on his face and lowering her gaze. "Actually, I only started working here about five weeks ago. We had a change in our salespeople, and Grandfather asked me to help out here."

She felt an unfamiliar flutter in her stomach. Between glances, she took in every detail of his soldier's uniform.

Anthony noticed that one wall was covered with cotton, linen, and woolen clothing for men and women. Some products clearly showed Arpoxa's handiwork. Shelves at the back were stacked with pots and cooking vessels, goblets and cups for drinking, and jugs for wine and water. A small section displayed jewelry: earrings, nose and finger rings, bracelets, and necklaces. Some were made of silver, others of gold, and still others of burnished bronze.

"And please call me Anthony; my full name is Anthony Suros. My, you have a lot of intricate necklaces and bracelets!" he said. She noticed that he stole several quick looks at her, and then she turned with her back toward him.

Miriam reached for several necklaces. She held one up for him to see. "We call these the Black Sea set, necklaces made of different colors with a touch of black in them. This one, for example, is called Sinop, the city far north on the Black Sea, because of the shape of the pendant. That set is called the Aegean Sea, with tiny seashells interspersed between sea-green beads. Our most popular right now is the White Sea set. All the shells, small stones, and other objects are light colors. Women never get tired of coming in and trying them on, even if they don't buy them."

He had trouble breathing, and on impulse, he mentioned her singing at the cave. "I wanted to tell you after the service, Miriam, but it seemed inappropriate. Your songs stay with me after I have heard them. I keep thinking of them. The words and the meaning you put into them speak to me. Antipas's teaching stays with me too. He makes it easy to learn because he uses everyday objects to teach. He is disciplined and expects discipline from us."

Miriam tried to control the expression on her face, but her heart had started beating faster. *He's thinking of my songs. My words mean something to him!*

"Miriam, you are an excellent salesperson." He saw her cheeks take on a pink hue. "What excellent products! I'm looking for something unusual. Antipas's party is tonight. Not a tunic or a ring. Maybe a white stone... I would want something special written on it, something that only he would understand."

Miriam forced herself to control her breathing. "There is a stonemason up the road on the right about a hundred paces. He engraves names on small stones."

"Good, I need his help." On the spur of the moment, remembering the new free time he had because of Cassius's change to his training schedule, he asked, "Do you always work here?"

Why would he ask that? "Yes, every day except Saturdays; that is our Sabbath."

"Why are you alone now? All the shops usually have two people."

He's taken in all the details. Why is he asking?

"On certain days, the widow who works with me, Nikasa, goes back home at noon so she can feed children in our village. Tuesdays are her turn."

"So you are here alone...on Tuesdays?"

Her heart raced faster. She didn't trust her voice, so she simply nodded her head. *I've let him know I'm here every Tuesday...alone and ready to talk.*

"Thank you for your help, Miriam!" he said, placing his broad straw hat over his head to protect himself from the rain. Anthony then hurried to the stonemason's shop.

THE CAVE, ANTIPAS'S VILLAGE

Wet sandals were lined up beside the door while rain lashed the trees and bushes outside. The cave resounded with people enjoying themselves. Anthony could hardly wait for the opportunity to give his gift to Antipas.

Gales of laughter lightened the winter atmosphere. Marcos took upon himself the task of introducing each person who wanted to sing a song or tell a story. Some people gave Antipas simple gifts.

Anthony didn't trust himself to look at Miriam. His feelings about the conversation with her earlier in the afternoon left him light-headed. He wondered why it was so easy to talk to her. Was he too bold as to ask her if she worked alone? And why did she let him know when he could meet her without the other woman being there?

Just before the close of the evening, Anthony stood up and walked to stand beside Antipas. "I have a small birthday gift for you, Antipas."

Antipas took the gift in his hand and opened the carefully worked, brown leather pouch. He took out a small white stone. He read the new name, written in small Latin letters: No Shame in Scars. Antipas read it carefully again. He had been laughing, but now he looked intense, and Anthony wondered if he had done something offensive. Seeing the unusual look on Antipas's face, people stopped laughing.

"Can I read it aloud? Can others know what you wrote?" asked Antipas.

Anthony shrugged and nodded his agreement. To him, it was clearly a name meant as a private gift, but Antipas obviously wanted to share it with the others. "This is a gift our legionary friend just gave me. My new name is No Shame in Scars."

The effect on the people in the cave was immediate because it was a descriptive name. Everyone fell silent because they recognized that the white stone perfectly expressed the deep respect that Anthony had toward Antipas.

"My new name! A perfect one for a sixty-five-year-old man who holds so many scars inside. If I have wounds and can overlook them, then why can't I do that with others?"

Impulsively, Antipas reached for the younger man, carrying out the Jewish custom of kissing on the cheek. He kissed Anthony on his left cheek then leaned over to the right side and kissed him on the scar. Shame meant rejection and abandonment, but Antipas's gesture implied belonging and acceptance. Antipas felt something growing inside, a genuine emotion for this brave man whose gift summarized so much in a few words.

"I will keep my new name forever. I never thought of myself like that, but I believe it is true. I like my new name!" exclaimed

Antipas, and he felt compassion and curiosity for the legionary with the red welt.

Why is a mark so important to Anthony? He connected my new name with his scar. Does he know how many times I felt cut by words or that I am about to be given the ultimate "scar of shame"— being cut off from my people?

Antipas asked Marcos to stay after everyone else had left the birthday gathering.

"I have a difficult legal matter to deal with," he stated. "My father, Eliab Ben Shelah, left us one year ago. His will has certain complications, and I need help. Can you assist me please?" He shared the problem of how to distribute Eliab's estate without selling the village.

THE LIBRARY OF PERGAMUM

Following a week of holiday time, customary for classes in the gymnasium in Pergamum at the end of January, Zoticos was happy to see his students again. "My congratulations on your studies, questions, interaction, and conclusions you have come to during the first half of our course."

He looked over his students. "You will be asking about my plan for the next four months," Zoticos continued. "Of course, we have the two-week Festival of Zeus in April, so our history lessons take us to the middle of June."

Only at the end of December did I get my first long gaze from Trifane, and now…I'm half-crazy over her!

He paused as though in deep thought, walked around the table at the front of the reading room, and then took in all his students.

During the Festival of Zeus, I will offer Trifane individual lessons so that she will get to know me. What can I plan to help her trust me, to have her beside me?

"During our last few weeks together, from May 26 to June 15, each of you will make a presentation to show how you intend to pass all this knowledge along to others. Why is this important? Well, I know that some of you may have creative ideas that will help your fellow students."

ANTIPAS'S SHOP IN THE LOWER AGORA, THE ACROPOLIS

Anthony was free again from his duties of training the scouts.

He was genuinely concerned, knowing that the garrison commander Cassius was causing his training to be less effective. Domitian wanted a vast number of soldiers to cross the Danube River. If that were the case, then the invasion, the long-awaited battle, would happen next year or perhaps two years later.

He approached Cassius. "My instruction today is finished at high noon. I would like to be gone for the rest of the day, getting a gift for someone."

He quickly walked the two miles from the garrison to the Lower Agora. It was lunchtime, and Miriam was standing inside her shop, reading a scroll from her grandfather's library. "Hail, Miriam!" he said, surprising her.

"Hail, Anthony. Another gift?" she asked, unable to hold back a wide smile.

He looked at her again, admiring the beauty of her face. Her smile lines promised hidden layers of personality. Her light olive-brown face was a study in gracefulness. Light seemed to radiate from her eyes. Her black hair hung down past her shoulders.

He searched for a reason to talk with her. "Suppose I am buying a gift for my mother. What would you recommend?"

She couldn't swallow for a moment, but then she showed him the clothing along the back wall and looked up at him. "This is a soft stola. Women love these. See the embroidery Arpoxa added to it? What size is your mother?"

"I can't buy anything for her, Miriam. She died before I joined the Legion."

I don't know anything about his family.

"Oh, I'm sorry! I didn't know. Tell me about your mother." She blushed.

"I will if you tell me about your mother afterward."

She leaned forward, wishing she could slow her heartbeat. "I agree. You tell me first."

Anthony began, "My mother's name was Marti, daughter of Lahai. Her father served in the legion, just as his father had before. She didn't want me to join it because, as she said, 'Too many people die in wars.' Actually, she wanted to go back to her home in Gaul. We lived in Syria at that time, and she had a big quarrel with my father when I was six years old."

Miriam furrowed her brow. *She really cared for Anthony.*

"That was the last time I saw my father. She took me to Rome, and my father sent us money for a few years. He served as a trumpeter in Legion X. Being at the head of his cohort put him at the front of the battle. Still, it was not dangerous because the province of Syria was peaceful. Guess where the only resistance came from?"

"From the Jews!" said Miriam. As they both chuckled, he took a half-step closer.

He continued, "My mother and father were married in Damascus during the second year of Nero's reign. I was born on January 14, in the third year of Nero's reign. She made nutritious food, rich brown bread. Sometimes she put honey on it. She would sing me songs, and I enjoyed music. Even though she loved to draw, we usually didn't have enough money to buy materials. Sometimes she would draw pictures in the sand outside our apartment.

"Before she died, she made me promise her something. She had started going to meetings in caves. There are big caves under the ground in Rome. 'Promise me two things: Don't go into the legion like everyone in your family has for generations. And if you ever hear of anyone speaking of Yeshua Christus, go and learn from him.' I became a soldier, so I would not have pleased her with that."

Miriam's breath caught in her throat. *His mother was a follower of Yeshua Messiah....*

He looked away, out the door, as he remembered his mother's death and his promise to her. "Recently I heard Antipas speaking in the marketplace about Yeshua. I started attending meetings in the cave after Marcos invited me. I sought your grandfather out and had a private talk with him. I told him about my mother, that we lived in a small apartment in Rome. I earned a little by taking wood to homes or carrying things from the markets. After I turned seventeen, I joined the army. Shortly afterward, my mother became sick and started to cough. I found out later that she died from the coughing disease in Rome on July 5, three years after the siege of your city, Jerusalem."

"So you are thirty-four years old!" Miriam exclaimed, delighted that she had followed all the details of his story. "Your mother died when you were seventeen years old, and it has been seventeen years since the fall of Jerusalem."

"My, you have a quick mind for facts and figures!"

Now it was Miriam's turn. "Let's see how quick your mind is! My mother gave birth to me at an agitated time when we lived in Alexandria. Father wanted to go to Jerusalem, but my mother was determined to stay in Egypt. I was born on April 14 in the eleventh year of Nero."

"So you are twenty-five!" Anthony felt his pulse pounding in his throat. "Well, what kind of a gift would you think my mother would want from this shop?"

Grandpa started me working in his shop. Why? Was it because he gave up on finding me a husband? No, I don't want to believe that. So why am I here alone on Tuesdays?

Talking about birthdays and families came quickly as they discussed family tales. He told her what it was like to be in Rome at the age of seventeen, and she told him about her mother dying in Antioch from gangrene in her leg.

"So you've lived in Pergamum since you were six years old? Did your grandfather bring slaves with him when he came here?"

"No, but he bought one each year. He had never done anything like that before. Every year he sets one free, but last April he brought home two slaves, Ateas and Arpoxa."

The topic of freeing slaves was uncomfortable, and he said, "I have to leave now. I hope we can talk again."

Miriam smiled as she watched him leave. *He wants to talk with me again, but this is dangerous. What will Grandpa say if he ever learns that I was talking with Anthony without a chaperone?*

After he left, the saleswoman from the adjoining store came to talk to Miriam. "Well, that was a long conversation! What did he come for? What did he buy?"

"He didn't buy anything," said Miriam. "He talked about his mother, but he didn't buy a present for her."

"Well, you may have talked a lot about his mother, but I'm sure that wasn't all you talked about!" teased the lady. "That's the second time he's come here, and I think he will be back again!"

On her way home, after closing the shop, Miriam started to hum. She offered to pray at supper, and she sat at a table to write down some thoughts. Antipas said to her, "You are singing a lot tonight. Did you have a good day at the shop?"

"Yes, Grandpa, I had a very good day at the store today."

"Did you sell a lot of items?"

"No, just about normal, but I talked with someone who might become a customer." She hummed some more and started to write a new song, a song of joy.

Chapter 32
Deceptions Revealed

ANTIPAS'S HOME, PERGAMUM

The time had come for Antipas to test his students to see how much of his teaching they had retained. Marcos was one of them. For weeks he had instructed the group, and he felt that various aspects of the covenant should now be clear to them. They had started well, yet there was so much more to teach.

"Tonight, Diotrephes, it is your turn to tell us how you would explain what you have learned. Speak as though you were teaching the people gathered in the cave."

Diotrephes stood up to speak, in the fashion of Pergamum, instead of sitting. Coming to the meeting, he was determined to show the followers of Antipas, as he called them, that they were too timid in how they spoke at the cave. He would show them the right way!

"Antipas and friends, I believe in most of the teachings of Yeshua. However, I cannot agree with the teaching brought to us by Demetrius, which really comes down from John the Elder. People should not be told to avoid superior knowledge. We in Pergamum have always sought to know more. This is why the Library of Pergamum is our historic treasure.

"I speak as a Gentile, as you like to call me. Mostly I perceive that the law that you follow causes conflict from one unresolved issue. A large part of the problem of your religion is that you cannot see your God. Thus, everyone holds a different image in their mind. Take Zeus for example. Simply walk around the altar, and you know what he looks like!

"I understand your teaching. I started coming to the cave almost a year ago. You are correct to say that knowledge is passed from one generation to another. But your covenant does not indicate how to get the specialized knowledge everyone needs. When I asked, 'Where can wisdom be found?' I heard your answer: 'The fear of the Lord: that is the beginning of wisdom.' But that is unsatisfactory.

"Strive for more knowledge, not less! Demetrius says, 'If we claim to be without sin, we deceive ourselves, and the truth is not in us.'[67] We should be humble enough to confess, 'Yes, we do sin by transgressing the law,' but that does not mean it is shameful to sin. We do it both intentionally and unintentionally. Repeated sin provides us with the experience of forgiveness over and over, so forgiveness rescues us from ignorance. Didn't Yeshua say mercy should be extended seventy times seven? This means we can sin without fear and sin repeatedly. Knowledge like this, of this kind of forgiveness, is good for the soul."

Antipas's eyes opened wide.

Diotrephes did not learn this from me! Where does he get these ideas? Yeshua forgiving sins that are intentionally committed over and over again? What utter falsehood! He doesn't understand anything about Yeshua Messiah!

Marcos saw Antipas struggling to breathe calmly. The older man spoke quietly and slowly. "I explained to you why Demetrius came. He brought a warning about false teaching. Diotrephes, I see that your ideas are the same as those of Cerinthus in Ephesus.[68] You didn't tell me that you believe all this."

"You never asked me! You want us to accept all your ideas, but you never allow us to explain ours."

Antipas's lips were stretched as tightly as the drums used in the cave. "Diotrephes, the teaching I give to this group is no longer for you. You cannot stay in a group that will be the source of future leaders. Your present beliefs do not agree with the covenant."

Diotrephes was stung by the rebuke and Antipas's quick rejection. "What? Are you expelling me from this group because I gave you my opinion?"

Antipas struggled to keep his composure. "Your ideas reflect the teaching of the Nicolaitans, a false teaching, and I don't want it coming into my community!"

---

[67] 1 John 1:8

[68] Cerinthus of Ephesus was an early teacher of primitive forms of Gnosticism in the late 1st century. He was alive during the time of John and was shunned by the Apostle.

Diotrephes looked stunned. "I am not teaching falsehood!" When he became disturbed, his face became very red. "Antipas, did you know that the ideas I just expressed are also in the minds of a number of the people who sit with you in the cave?"

He picked up his cloak and writing materials and turned to leave the room. At the door, he turned. "I am leaving, but you will hear more from me about this!"

Silence fell on the room as Antipas looked around. He had stumbled into the real beliefs of the young man, and Diotrephes would not be returning. He could never be a leader in the Household of Faith. Antipas spent the next hour with his friends discussing the many errors that Diotrephes had expressed.

LYDIA-NAQ'S HOME, THE ACROPOLIS

Diotrephes opened the door of his mother's home. In a few words, he told Lydia-Naq what had happened. He had been barred from the leadership group at the cave. "He sent me away because of my beliefs, saying I am a false teacher! Imagine that! Who does this old man think he is, coming to our city and becoming my judge?"

Lydia-Naq took the opportunity to pry out as much information about the cave as she could. She asked her son many questions, and he was willing to talk. He related the ideas taught by Antipas and then told her all about the people in the Household of Faith. She gathered the information and began to make a plan.

Before the end of the evening, Lydia-Naq had all she needed. She was ready to go on the attack against Antipas.

ANTIPAS'S HOME, PERGAMUM

Antipas had just finished his noon meal, and his mind flitted from one situation to another.

So many decisions... The synagogue will soon disown me. Then there are my day-to-day problems of keeping my villagers happy. I have to decide what to speak on each time we meet at the cave... And Diotrephes! Help me, O Lord! Across the valley, I count several temples devoted to false gods, and here my village seems so small. My witness, too, is minor, and few accept the covenant, but I have chosen your path in which to walk.

Antipas was at peace. He had drawn a line to define his

beliefs. He knew that the worst lay ahead, but he could not turn back. He comforted himself by repeating the words he had read at dawn: "The sorrows of those will increase who run after other gods. I will not pour out their libations of blood or take up their names on my lips."[69]

He went to his library and counted the money saved during the first three months of the year. There was not enough to begin building another house. He only had a hundred fifty denarii put aside to buy another slave. That represented almost a worker's daily wages for five months, nowhere near enough to bid again at the slave auction. His plans for this year had been changed by events beyond his control. He would not be able to set another slave free.

Late in the afternoon, Onias announced the arrival of a family from Gambreion, a village sixteen miles up the valley on the other side of the Bakir River.

"Yes, I'll talk to them," said Antipas. "How many people have come?" Onias noted that a group of six had arrived: five on foot and a woman on a donkey.

"We don't know what to do," said the distraught woman a few minutes later. Her five sons were timid and looked scared.

"Our house burned when strong winds came up two weeks ago in the late winter storm. Afterward, we asked people for help. No one would lend me money, and I'm a widow with five children. We owe money on the seed we borrowed last year. I could pay it off if you loan me the money. In our village in Gambreion, your name is whispered as a man who helps widows. I came here because you are the only hope I have."

"You must eat the evening meal with us," said Antipas. "I want to know the details. How did the fire start? How much do you owe? Who loaned you money last year? Can your boys work? Tell me about your family."

They took off their sandals, and Antipas's servant washed their feet. The boys had never seen a home like this before. Ahead of them was the large room, complete with reclining couches for meals. Off to the left, they stared open-mouthed at the library for they had never seen so many scrolls in one place. To the right,

---

[69] Psalm 16:4

beside the kitchen, was the bathroom.

"Look, everyone!" a child cried. "A bathroom with running water!"

They laughed at the idea of such a luxury.

Antipas talked with the widow while they waited for the meal to be prepared.

When Miriam came home from the shop, she took over the details. They would host the family until decisions were made. "My grandfather is pleased that you gave him the full story about what happened to your husband and how you became a widow. He is working on how best to help you.

"You must have been up very early to come all this way. Grandfather will talk more after the supper meal. You cannot go back to your village this evening, so your family will stay here tonight and sleep in this big room where we eat our meals. We will lay carpets on the floor, and then we will loan you our wagon so you can go back home early tomorrow morning. Your donkey will be fed along with our animals."

Late that night, Antipas went back to his desk. He took up the scroll he had started reading early in the morning, before sunrise. He continued reading. "Lord, who may dwell in your sanctuary? Who may live on your holy hill?"

His eyes glanced down at the psalm written in neat Greek letters. The Septuagint asked questions, and Antipas finished his day with answers. "He who lends his money without usury and does not accept a bribe against the innocent. He who does these things will never be shaken."[70]

He rubbed his sore eyes. It was getting harder to read late at night. He squeezed his eyelids shut tight as if to renew his usually clear vision. With eyes closed, he reviewed the story of the widow and prayed for wisdom. Should the money he had saved be used to help this poor woman and her boys?

The next day, the family was sent back to Gambreion in one of Antipas's spare wagons. Part of the money he had saved was now a loan, enabling her to buy the materials for rebuilding her house. She would pay off her existing loan for seed, and later this month, Antipas would send a group from his village to Gambreion

---

[70] Psalm 15:5

to work on rebuilding the widow's house. She would pay it back when she could.

THE LIBRARY OF PERGAMUM, THE ACROPOLIS

Zoticos's study course was the talk of the acropolis, and now it was time for Lydia-Naq to teach one of the lessons. She took the students to the altar and explained each sculptured scene around the outside base.

"You gain pride in your city and the Lydian culture when you understand the details of the greatest Altar of Zeus in the world. You know about the wars of Zeus in *The Iliad* and other classical Greek volumes. Here he is! Zeus, so strong, winning the fight against every opponent he faces!"

Her eyes seemed to be on fire. As high priestess, one of her greatest privileges was explaining the story of her great hero. "He is the god of the gods, the father of the gods."

Her whole body acted out her words. "Fighting and winning—this is the heart and identity of Pergamum. Winning against impossible odds—isn't that our history, what made our city famous? In two weeks, when the Festival of Zeus starts, I want all twenty-four students to join me for the sacrifice of the white bull. You will be teachers in the future! You will renew our language, our legacy, our and honor!"

Zoticos had formed an idea of how to get Trifane close—very close—to him. He smiled broadly, his eyes constantly darting back to the lovely young woman. He explained, "After each lesson, you will come in groups of four to my office to observe the work of the chief librarian. You will see my new acquisitions. Here are the groups I want for each of the days next week."

Trifane will come on Sunday, and she'll enjoy my office.

THE SELINOS RIVER, UPRIVER FROM PERGAMUM

Antipas gave Saturday, April 1, as a holiday to all his workers. Because of Passover, his shops in the Upper Agora and Lower Agora were closed for two days, Saturday and Sunday, even though it meant the loss of badly needed income. His competitors in the marketplace did business every day, but Antipas closed his shops on Saturdays.

Early on Saturday morning, a small caravan of wagons set off, going up the Selinos River with Antipas leading the way in the first wagon. As they rumbled along the road, children shouted and jumped from one wagon to another and then back into the first one to be with their friends.

Four miles up the river, they came to where it was joined by a small brook fed by one of the many mountain streams. A flat grassy area around a curve in the river presented itself as an ideal place to spend the day. It was a much loved place for the Household of Faith where they had been in previous years. Soft white clouds moved slowly overhead. Small farm fields were covered in white flowers, giving the appearance of fresh snow. Wildflowers were everywhere, and red, yellow, and white flowers exploded colorfully in the warm spring weather.

Marcella and Marcos sat together with Florbella. Children laughed and shouted as they jumped into the cold water then quickly dashed out shivering. Everyone watched as Onias and his sons killed and skinned two sheep. The other men gathered wood and lit a fire between three large stones halfway up an embankment, near the place that yielded the clay for the potters in Antipas's village. Meat sizzled as the flames consumed the fat.

Antipas said, "Lots of people went through the Red Sea with Moses, except they didn't get water on their heads or feet. Now a few people will be dripping wet from head to toe because they have asked to be baptized by immersion." He invited them to come down with him into the water. People chuckled. They knew how cold the water was here...and how hot the water of the Red Sea was said to be.

Anthony arrived at the camp just as Antipas was preparing to start the baptisms. He had only a short time off during the afternoon and needed to return to the garrison soon after.

Antipas gathered the little group at the water's edge and asked them a few questions to affirm their beliefs. He explained that as the Messiah had died and been placed in a grave and then come back to life, so these people would be buried in the water. Coming up, each one was symbolically a new creature, clean from sin and ready to live a new life. Many people had become part of the Household of Faith in the last twelve months.

Marcella and Marcos went first, and Anthony followed. He made a funny face as he felt the ice-cold water flow over his body and jumped out quickly, lost his footing on a smooth stone, and fell on his back into the water, creating a big splash.

Everyone laughed. No one was ever prepared for cold mountain water. Their surprised expressions became part of the enjoyment as spectators took many memories home with them. As Antipas came out of the water, he looked over the gathered group and saw Yorick standing at the back. The young man seemed as dejected as ever.

Miriam had worked on a song with Antipas so that it would fit with his teaching for the day. The words were set to a children's melody that was popular in Pergamum, and they had practiced the song for the last two weeks. Two of the young men sounded trumpets between each verse.

As she began, she said, "I call this song 'The Cost of Freedom.'" The instruments began. Most of the families already knew the new song since their children had been singing it as their older siblings practiced at home.

Quietly, across a grassy plain,
Abel brings a firstborn lamb.
His brother sneers with scorn,
"Why would God accept a creature slain?"
A lamb has shed its blood.

Shouting loudly, "No!" across the sand
Pharaoh shouts, "Bend your knee!
These slaves must not go free!"
He raises his staff. "Let them be damned!
These slaves must shed their blood!"

Moses and Aaron stand on the shore.
There's blood within the Nile!
Pharaoh asks, "What is this trial?"
He will face much more!
He swears he'll shed slaves' blood.

Many plagues confound the angry king.
Locusts, flies, gnats, and hail;
"Frogs jumped into our water pail!
Lice and boils! We can't clean a thing!"
Animals will shed their blood.

One more plague, the worst! The firstborn son.
"Let them go!" Words of dread!
"Firstborn sons will soon be dead!
We'll leave. No more building will be done,
Or your son will shed his blood."

Unleavened bread is made; lambs are found.
Blood is smeared on the door.
Freedom demands much more.
Death's Angel passes by without a sound.
These lambs have shed their blood.

Worship! Adore! Praise the King of Love.
He paid the highest price:
My willing sacrifice.
It means we fear no more. The Lamb of
God paid sin's cost with blood.

Anthony stayed to hear Miriam's song before leaving to return to the garrison. The song had ended, but the harps and tambourines, flutes, and drums continued playing. No one wanted to stop singing or leave the grassy field beside the mountain stream.

While the camp was being taken down in preparation for their return to the village, Sheva, one of the three Jewish widows, took Antipas aside. She repeatedly jabbed at the ground with her index finger. "You are making a mistake! We shouldn't be teaching all these things to non-Jews! I didn't grumble the last time you did something strange, but now I cannot remain in your village. You have gone too far for me to feel comfortable in the Household of Faith."

There was a twinge of anger mixed with sadness in her voice. Antipas knew she would not stay with his community but would return to the fellowship of families in the synagogue.

Chapter 33
Acceptance and Rejection

ANTIPAS'S SHOP IN THE LOWER AGORA, THE ACROPOLIS

Three days later, Miriam waited in her shop with an air of expectation; it was Tuesday. Anthony would come today. When he appeared in the doorway, her heart sped up. *Of course, Anthony doesn't know what happened at home, but I'll surprise him.*

"You know what my Grandpa did today?" she asked.

"No, tell me," said Anthony with a much wider grin than her question warranted. He stood just inside the door, letting his eyes adjust to the dim interior of the shop.

"He closed down all the workshops, the potters, the clothing, and the glass-blowing, and he left early for the little village of Gambreion. Most of the people in our village went there. Only a few of us stayed; I'm in the shop here, and Chavvah is in the Upper Agora store. Some are looking after the animals. A glassblower is looking after the fires in the furnaces and the kilns." She looked at the scar on his face.

"I have been to Gambreion," Anthony said. "It's the little village about half a day's journey from here. I took my new scouts there once when we went into the mountains for training. We stayed there overnight and slept under the trees."

Miriam nodded. "Yes, that's the place. A widow lives there. She lost her house in a fire and had debts. Grandpa has loaned her money to buy timber for a new roof. He says we need to be generous because the Feast of Unleavened Bread is about helping others. He took most of the village to help rebuild her house and will pay his helpers for time spent away from their workshops."

Something about helping a widow momentarily took his breath away. His mother had been alone for years.

If Nikasa, the widow who typically would be returning to the shop midafternoon, was away too, then he could stay longer today. That would give him plenty of time to tell Miriam his recent news. He leaned against the doorpost.

He's feeling comfortable, Miriam thought. *I can tease him a little.*

"Your face when you slipped in the cold water! You should have seen yourself. Such a surprised look! People laughed so much when you fell."

Anthony's heart rose. "Well, it was cold!" he said. "That water comes down from melting snow on top of the mountain! But I meant to ask you, how do you write songs? How did you get the idea to write Arpoxa's story and mix her story with your grandfather's teaching? How do you decide which tune to use?"

Miriam leaned on the counter; her eyes were wide open. *He wants to know my thoughts!*

"Music has always filled our home, but since my grandmother died, our house seems quiet. Grandma taught me songs, hundreds from the psalms, from Egypt and Jerusalem. We laughed and sang while making food for Grandpa. I write some songs when I'm sad and others when I'm happy. Grandpa asked me to write a new song for the occasion. I wanted to write a song with the tune from the Temple of Dionysius. You must know it; everyone was singing it."

Anthony grimaced and hung his head. "Years ago, I would have sung that."

She nodded. "Festival tunes are so catchy. Everyone in Pergamum has been singing that song since December. However, I decided against using that tune. It comes from a pagan temple, and it praises the wrong ideas. After all, Dionysius really does take people's health and wealth. That tune just wouldn't fit the story of Moses at all."

"So how did you choose the little tune you taught the children?"

Miriam smiled. "I hear children singing in the agora or down the streets where they play. The tune stays in my mind. Some of the songs they sing have words that are not suitable for me, but then I find those that fit what I want to say."

"There is a lot of emotion in your songs. I can hear it in your voice."

He isn't satisfied with only a few answers. I think he really wants to get to know me.

"I was feeling lonely for my mother and father, depressed as I thought of myself as an orphan girl. I get down sometimes, Anthony, I really do. I hate feeling alone! One day, Grandpa asked me to comfort Arpoxa, but I didn't want to at all. However, I went to her, and she talked to me. I didn't have to do anything, just listen to her story."

Her trust in Anthony was growing through the questions he asked. And he loved music!

She closed her eyes before saying, "Now it is my turn to ask you questions, soldier! How do you take a new recruit and train him to become a scout? Does a soldier have to show special talent? Is it true that they have to be good with the bow and arrow? That's what I heard."

"You know a lot already! No, not just anyone can become a scout. Yes, they need to be master archers, and they need to have a natural sense about when to take a chance but not get killed in the process! You have to have patience to wait and watch. If you don't have patience, if you can't concentrate, you can't become a scout."

Miriam nodded eagerly.

"The lives and safety of your legion constantly depend on understanding the terrain. You fight in the hills and valleys of Europe, going through many magnificent mountain passes, walking along beautiful lakes. You think you are safe, but the beauty is deceptive. Danger may be just ahead! Your enemy may be waiting for you. He won't be generous or show mercy, and he won't spare your life either!"

He explained to her the Battle of Teutoburg. "I went into my legion because of that terrible defeat. Three legions were destroyed."

She gasped. "Was revenge going through your mind?"

He closed his eyes, recalling moments from long ago. "Yes, I wanted revenge—before I knew what war does to a man. I was seventeen. I thought victory simply meant marching into Lower Germanica. I bragged, 'We will fight them and make them pay for what they did!'

"Miriam, on my way to Mainz, while we were going through the Alps, we marched through a mountain pass, and there in front of us, I saw a lake glistening in the sunlight. Reflections of the mountain made mirror images in the water. The day was gorgeous. The air was still, with not a bit of wind. We seemed so small with the tall mountains above us with snow on the peaks. The big trees looked so tiny high up on those green slopes. Trees and endless forests...that's what we became used to. We were to find out later that a volley of arrows could come against us at any time. We were small in the mountains, yet we felt that we were so strong."

He wondered how to describe it to her. Suddenly he wanted to share his memory of that stunning beauty—and other memories and experiences too. If Miriam saw that scene, would she write a poem...or put it to music? He wanted to show it to her, not just describe it. Better yet to have her sitting there beside him, enjoying the scene for days, not marching by quickly as soldiers did at several miles every hour. He wanted to be there with her...and this time, the army would be far away. He was stunned by his daydream.

She noticed his quick silence, the faraway look in his eyes. *He is trying to tell me something. He has more on his mind than the mountain pass! Tell me more, Anthony! I am so excited to hear you open your heart to me!*

"You were thinking about the mountains, weren't you, Anthony? I've heard about them. People told me about tall trees and mountains towering up. Romans think the edge of the world is surrounded by forests on all sides."

"Yes, I was thinking about mountains because...I wanted you to enjoy them too."

He stiffened slightly and stood up straight. He closed his eyes and then opened them, speaking freely about his conflict at the garrison. "My commander comes from an area where there are no forests. He knows only of flatlands, wide rivers, and Persians who would like to cross those rivers to attack. He and other soldiers do not realize that wars in Upper Germanica and in Dacia have to be fought in forests!

"I was in the garrison on Sunday night. Cassius, my commanding officer, called me. 'Stand at attention, soldier!' He has no use for what I am teaching the scouts. 'I hear you are still friendly with the old Jewish man, Antipas. Is that right?'

"I said, 'Yes sir, that is right.' "He glared at me and said, 'A soldier who goes to those cave meetings with you told me that a gathering outside the city was an attempt to act out ancient myths. He says Antipas acted out a rebellion of the Jews against the King of Egypt a long time ago and reports that a whole army was destroyed. Then he drowned you in the water while everyone laughed. He says this new leader, Yeshua, is greater than the old leader, Moses. Now, soldier, is his report right or not? Answer me!'

"Miriam, I didn't know what to say! Obviously, he doesn't know about the history of the Jews. He would take it to mean that Antipas was somehow using an ancient myth to make fun of Caesar and the Roman Army."

A shiver went down her shoulders and arms.

"I told Cassius, 'Jews tell stories about their ancient religious events. The purpose of Antipas telling the story was not to incite Jews in Pergamum to rebellion! Quite the opposite, this little group of Jews wants to help the people of the city, especially poor families, widows, and slaves. They have no interest in swords or bows and arrows. That gathering was just a place to tell one of their stories,' I explained. 'You see, their festivals are times to celebrate things people value the most, not to incite people to war.'"

Anthony stood close to the door where he had stood for almost an hour. "Cassius said, 'You are too involved with that group. I fear you are developing double loyalties, just what a scout is always told to avoid.'"

Miriam sucked in her breath, held it, and breathed out very slowly.

"I want you to know, Miriam, that I am already involved. I believe the story of the defeat of Pharaoh's army. I am happy that Adonai, the God of your fathers, brought us..."

Anthony seemed to freeze, unable to finish the sentence.

"Yes, this God brought all the people in your grandfather's village together. This has now become a problem for me since I want to belong to your community, yet Cassius is on the verge of stopping me from attending the meetings. I am caught between two loyalties. One is to my garrison and my commander. On the other hand, I love and appreciate Antipas and all he stands for."

He moved as if he were going to step closer to her but stayed near the door. Thoughts tumbled around in his mind. He wanted to say, "He brought us together." He should have said that. No, maybe he had already said too much. Would Miriam think he was too forward? Perhaps it was because he was a scout. Waiting was bound up with being a scout. He taught new recruits about being cautious. Was he waiting too long to tell her his thoughts?

The storeowner from next door stepped into the Ben Shelah shop. She had been listening to the conversation, as she always did, often not understanding what they were talking about. She heard the words 'I want to belong...' and decided it was finally the right moment to slip her head in through the open door.

Inside she saw Anthony standing beside the door and was a little disappointed.

My, he acts slowly, this soldier! When is he going to tell her something personal, something that will fire up her heart? Even I can see that the poor girl is waiting for his kiss!

"I have to be getting back to the garrison after I have been to the baths, so I really must leave now," said Anthony a little bit too loudly.

After he left, the gossipy lady said to Miriam, "You really have an admirer, don't you? My, doesn't he hurry over here! Every Tuesday, I've noticed. Just after the Samaritan lady goes to feed children in your village! Regular, like the sun coming up and going down! You can trust that young man, you know. He has a lot of self-discipline."

Miriam watched Anthony walk down the crowded colonnade toward the baths.

I've noticed too! Every Tuesday when he has free time. God, he used your name, Adonai. He said, "The God of your fathers brought us..." but why didn't he finish his thought? What was he going to say? What is happening? Am I crazy to notice him, to look forward to his coming to talk to me each week, to think we could talk the whole afternoon? I'm afraid I am falling in love. Grandpa would never let me marry a Roman, and this one is a legionary! O God, what should I do? Why does he have to be a Roman? If only he were Jewish!

She didn't know if she should laugh or cry. Later, Miriam was at home alone in her house for the first time she could remember, waiting for her grandfather to return from rebuilding the widow's house. She laughed and then cried, finding consolation as she made the dough that would be baked as flat bread.

She laughed for the joy of music and the beauty of the white, pink, and red oleander bushes and the endless fields of wildflowers. She sighed, remembering his face, slightly too big for his body and with that long red scar that he never talked about. She cried for Anthony's curly black hair, for his mother, for the widow, and for herself.

THE SYNAGOGUE OF PERGAMUM

Tuesday night was a special night of sadness for all the faithful Jews in Pergamum. Zattu, the synagogue's historian, was a descendent of Jews in the second deportation by the Babylonians. Almost six hundred years before, Zattu, his namesake, had returned from Babylon. He walked to Jerusalem with 1,254 men from the same clan. All of those formerly deported had long since died, but his name had been preserved throughout generations.

Tonight Zattu said, "It was twenty years ago today that the doors of Jerusalem were sealed shut against the troops under Commander Titus. Over a million people were crowded into our city for the festival. The legions moved into position and would not let anyone out when the city was full. Jerusalem could hold no more people.

"That was the beginning of the end, the final siege. Tonight is not just a night to commemorate the passage of our people from Egypt. It is the third night of the Feast of Unleavened Bread. We rejoice that the Lord Almighty set us free from Egypt, yet we mourn because of Rome's domination."

Jaron looked around the group as they stood at the synagogue door, ready to go home. His heart was heavy, and he wished that Antipas could be won over bit by bit. Would dialogue make him see his error?

ANTIPAS'S SHOP IN THE LOWER AGORA, THE ACROPOLIS

Miriam tapped her fingers on the table, counting off the days.

Five, six, seven days. Is he coming again today? He always finds a different excuse to come. This should be the day.

"It's your birthday soon," Anthony said as he greeted her, smiling at the door.

He remembered! He's considerate.

"Yes, I guess I'm getting older like everyone else," she said, unable to hide her grin.

"Time goes by, sometimes slowly and sometimes fast. I used to think about how slowly time went by. We were fighting in forests, waiting for enemies to show themselves. But we were afraid to make a sound because that would let them know we were watching them."

"What was it like?"

"Germanic tribes are fierce and independent, determined not to give up their lands. We had to go into a forest, a small group of us; I went with another fifteen men to find where a clan had its village and to make sure they were not preparing to fight us. They had agreed to live in peace with us, but they were difficult to trust."

I'm glad nothing more happened than his scar, she thought. "And did they fight you?" she said aloud.

"Sometimes they did! Once we had been directed to ensure that a whole section of the Black Forest remained peaceful. The army built long wooden forts with towers all along the tops of the hills. We cut down a wide swath of forest around each fort so they couldn't spring surprise attacks. More than once, they shot flaming arrows."

"So that's when you got your scar...."

Anthony stopped. It was the first time she had commented on his face. He would eventually have to tell her the details about how he received his wound, but he wasn't sure if she could ever understand his thirst for revenge.

He wondered if he was in love with this Jewish woman. If so, what could become of it? He was a Roman, a soldier! Should he be talking to her about his hurts and disappointments? Could he reveal to her his love for the army? But what of his hatred for the officer who left him unfit for active duty? What was he doing—to her and to himself?

"I didn't get the cut on my face at that time, no. That came later."

"I'm glad that you did get back alive."

A rippling sensation spread down the back of his neck.

She noticed the quiver in his shoulders. "So it was later on?"

"That's right, only three years ago actually. It didn't happen until..." He could not tell her about being ambushed under the bridge at the Neckar River. How could she understand his pain and confusion these last three years?

She tilted her head to one side, as she often did when listening intently.

"That was a painful time in my life. It's hard to talk about."

Miriam leaned forward, closer to him than before. "I understand your feelings. I have had painful moments in my life too. Sometimes I try to remember what my mother looked like, but I can't even remember her face. She turned back to help my father when we were escaping Jerusalem. An arrow killed my father before he could get out of range of the archers up on the wall behind us. Another soldier shot my mother, hitting her in the leg. Grandpa carried her and me to safety in a town where the Romans took us. An infection crippled my mother's leg, and it took her life several months later. I was young when Daddy died, and I didn't know what was happening! I was so scared. I still have bad dreams where I'm looking for my mother and can never find her. This overwhelms me and robs me of my peace. Not until..."

She didn't know what to say, how to tell him of the turmoil she felt so often. *How can he possibly understand how empty I feel longing for my mother and father? The Roman army was responsible for the siege. Yet Romans offered us protection when our group of refugees ran out through the gates!*

Anthony pressed his hands against his face and looked down. He wanted to understand her, but too many awkward questions were an invisible wall between them. How could they talk about the past when love and hate lived side by side? Who was the real enemy? The Romans were her enemy, but their soldiers had let her family live. How could Simon's soldiers, her own people, be so cruel to her mother and father and to Amos and Abigail?

Both were silent, not knowing how to go on. They both wanted to speak but were afraid to break the spell of the moment. One wrong word could hurt so much.

Anthony said, "Please don't try to tell me now, Miriam. You aren't ready to tell me yet. Wait. Wait until..."

But wait until when? Would he ever understand the pain of losing both her parents? Those men in the forest—he had to burn their houses. All of them lived, though, because that was a legitimate defense of the empire. Legion XXI tried to stop the killing by making barbarians fearful. Could Miriam understand what it was like to be a scout and put his life at risk every day as he went into dense underbrush to learn the enemy's secrets?

He couldn't think clearly. He lifted his eyes from the floor and felt genuinely awed by the beauty of her brown eyes, her olive skin, and the tiny movements on her cheeks.

What is he thinking? He is very considerate of me. He is trying to show me that he cares—a soldier, a legionary and yet so gentle. He wants to understand.

Her thoughts left her confused. She looked at Anthony's curly black hair, his big square jaw, and the scar that would mark him for life. His eyelids were a bit too puffy, and his lips were cracked from military exercises in every kind of weather. Standing this close, she could see he was a full head taller than she was.

I don't know what to think. The visits you make to my shop every week... I count the days until you come to talk to me again. I think I am falling in love with you...and yet I don't want to fall in love with a Roman legionary! Dear God! My father would reject you instantly if he were alive...and dear Jaron, can you or anyone in the synagogue imagine me even talking to a legionary?

Again, she wanted both to laugh and to cry. Her grandfather and Jaron would have at least one thing in common. Both would disapprove of Anthony being here!

He spoke. "You aren't ready to try to explain all those things. Do you have anyone else to listen to you? In a few days, I'm going to go back to Philippi. This is a trip I must make to see the commander of the garrison there. But in the meantime, I will wait, and I will learn what is behind your word, 'until....'"

She didn't know if they were her own thoughts, if she was praying, or if her mind was just racing ahead. *God, are you playing a joke on me? Why is it that the only person who wants to know what is behind the "until" moments in my life is a Roman legionary?*

THE ACROPOLIS

The annual festivities in Pergamum were making the already noisy streets of the city louder; they were the sounds of future hopes growing in the city. Multitudes came from far and wide for the Festival of Zeus. Ships sailed into Elaia, the nearby port, bringing pilgrims from distant towns. Farmers from up the river filled the roads with wagons. Camels, donkeys, horses, and carts clogged the postal route from Thyatira. The inns in the city were full, and relatives crowded into small houses.

Zoticos enjoyed the benefit of his position. The library owned five seats at the Greek Theater, four rows up, behind Mayor Quintus Rufus. All significant figures working on the acropolis had places close to the front of the theater and could attend each production there. He chose the students who would attend, planning carefully and having his secretary send invitations to each of the students in the course. Unknown to the others, Trifane received an invitation to each evening's performance. She quickly realized he was favoring her above the others.

This year, for sixteen days of the festival, until April 30, the Altar of Zeus received sacrifices. Live animals, taken up the hill on the long winding road around the acropolis, arrived with colorful wildflowers on their heads placed there by children. Dark smoke and wishful prayers curled their way into the heavens.

Ordinary people in the city heard surprising news. The three aristocratic families had promised to leave their homes on the acropolis and move to a less prestigious, but safer, place. They were giving up their homes to provide space for a future temple.

Each of these three families was held up as a model for all citizens to follow. Common people commented on the generosity and self-sacrifice needed to give up the highly desired property overlooking the theater.

Each night the Greek Theater overflowed with more than ten thousand people. All were delighted to hear announcements that the three thousand voting citizens of Pergamum had voiced their approval of the most critical change to the acropolis in decades.

THE LIBRARY OF PERGAMUM

Trifane quickly warmed to the special attention of her teacher. Zoticos seemed so learned, so important. The chief librarian was one of the most significant men in the city. Each night she noticed the respect people gave to him.

Her instincts of quiet womanhood kept her cautious though. Zoticos had not said anything about his feelings toward her. He looked at her far too often during his lectures and later said too little. And now he had invited her each evening to the Festival of Zeus and for supper afterward, partaking of the best meat of the first sacrifice offered that morning. She could not submit to him, not yet. She needed to know he truly cared for her.

Noticing her reserve and frustrated that she resisted the

overt gestures of favoritism, Zoticos refined his approach. He created a new position in the library. After the festival, lectures resumed, and Zoticos invited her to be his new assistant.

He explained his offer to her. "We have many scrolls, many books from all over the world. You work carefully, easily distinguishing between various scripts from Corinth or Thessalonica, Rome or Carthage. You accurately evaluate the age of a scroll by its color or quality of papyrus or parchment. And you work so naturally. Well, it must be a gift from Athena, the goddess who protects the library, who inspires people to gain more knowledge.

"Now, these are my plans. First, I want to revise the schedule of classes for my course next year. I'm going to dictate some ideas and would like you to write these down and suggest how best to implement them.

"Second, I need a new system to classify books. We'll note each author and manuscripts copied at different times. This project will start in June or July. Would you like to help me, to be with me?" His yearning increased as he spoke gently, unable to avoid looking at her beautiful face and innocent eyes.

I want her to start saying more about herself. It might take a few months. Before the end of summer, though, I will ask her to marry me.

Trifane was flattered. It was the first time the chief librarian had used the words "to be with me." She hung onto them with the hope that a deeper commitment would be forthcoming.

"Trifane, please make a list of the students who are finishing these studies and the smaller cities and towns where they will be working. Use this parchment. I want to work out changes to the curriculum for the coming year. The course will be over in the middle of June, and then, well, I will have you work every day in the new office. Prepare your readings every day, and continue your work. Then you will come and be with me."

Once again, he had not said anything of his feelings for her. She tried to read between the lines, asking, "What do you mean when you say, 'be with me'?"

He could only say, "I'm delighted to have you close by. When you are near me, I feel completely different, and I hope you feel the same way. Listen, the course is almost over. I am going to have several banquets just for you."

Finally, she was flattered by the scholarly man with the black hair and carefully cut beard. She found herself thinking of him more and more each day. *What will it be like to be the wife of the chief librarian?*

Over the next two days, Zoticos rearranged the desks in one of the four rooms off his own office. By moving copyists into the room with those who looked after the repair of older volumes, he was able to make space for her. The new office was called Office of Assistant to the Chief Librarian.

It was the first time in the library's history that a woman was designated to work with this degree of responsibility.

When asked why no women were working in the building, everyone quipped, "The last time this happened, Queen Cleopatra walked off with our scrolls as well as the arsenal money, nine thousand denarii! No one wants our treasures controlled by the whims of a woman ever again!"

ANTIPAS'S HOME

It was the Feast of Pentecost, Shavuot, starting at sundown on the sixth day of Sivan, May 20—on a Sabbath day this year. Antipas had just returned from the synagogue and the dreaded final meeting with the elders. He had been officially expelled from the synagogue. It seemed as if an impossible obstacle had been placed in front of him. Even though he knew everything that would happen, it was still a day he had feared since last September.

Miriam sang as she came to the table for the evening meal. *In three more days, he will be back to talk with me. Will he tell me more about his scar? I want to explain all about Pentecost, our special day, and what it means to us.*

She realized Antipas was not going to offer grace before the meal. "Shall I thank the King of universe for our food?"

He didn't answer.

"Grandpa! Are you well?"

Silence met her question.

Miriam! Oh, my precious granddaughter! What will ever become of you now? They covered their ears not to hear my voice. I went in a Jew and left feeling naked. To them, I have become a non-Jew. I am cast off. What can I say? Oh, my people!

Chapter 34
Hopes and Disappointments

THE UPPER AGORA, THE ACROPOLIS

One morning after the Games in early May, Zoticos invited Trifane to his office in the library.

"What a lovely surprise to see you here!"

"Thank you. I thought I would come early, Zoticos."

"Arriving early! I like that in a future employee. Look, here is your new desk. It's made of dark, expensive wood from far up the Nile. Skilled carpenters associated with the new Egyptian Temple crafted it."

"Oh, and you've placed an inkstand with feathers from rare birds on the edge of the desk! That's very thoughtful."

"Well, if you like lovely things, come to my office. Here, now, look at the city from this balcony." He stood close behind her, pointing out the city's famous buildings. "Here we are, looking down on the Greek Theater. Only two other structures on the acropolis are higher up, the Palace of the Kings, there to the right, now occupied by Quintus Rufus, and the military arsenals behind us."

"Stunning! The view from your office is amazing!"

"I told you that I'd have some special banquets just for you. I am asking that you please come to my house for supper tonight. It's halfway down the acropolis, near the famous Peristyle House."

"I'm not sure that I should accept such a kind offer...."

"Well, I was going to have my kitchen slaves prepare your favorite dishes—unless you don't want to come, but you have already told me about all of your favorite foods."

"Yes, we talked about food a lot during the festival."

"I like being with you. And I want you to be with me, and I want you to like being with me."

After the second evening sharing a meal at his home, Trifane

293

felt increasingly reassured of his good intentions toward her. She was finally convinced that he wanted her to join with him forever and share in his busy life, his richly decorated house, and their intelligent dinner conversations.

Trifane walked into a store looking at new stolas. In the middle of June, the hot weather made it uncomfortable to walk outside at midday. She wiped her brow and reviewed her relationship with Zoticos during the previous six weeks.

I'm not completely happy with the way things have worked out, but my life is beginning to take a positive turn. My fifth dinner with Zoticos on Saturday night was more romantic than I could have hoped for. After the festival ended, he took me to the Games. How we cheered for our favorite athletes! And he has begun to introduce me to many of his friends.

THE GARRISON OF PERGAMUM

Anthony was given permission by Cassius for a seven-week break in duties to visit his farm in Philippi. The next group of recruits would begin their training in September.

As he began to prepare for his trip to Philippi, he considered the tasks he needed to complete there. The rent money from his farm was being paid to the army since he was not living there. He needed to verify that Atticus was being faithful in his rent payments and that the documentation was in place for him to reclaim the farm upon retirement from being an instructor of scouts. He had just gone into his tent on the training grounds when a messenger came to tell him that the garrison commander wanted to talk to him.

Cassius was standing in his office as Anthony entered.

"At your service, sir."

The commander modeled the discipline expected of officers, and he came straight to the point. "I learned that you continue to attend the meetings of that Greek Jew, the one who teaches erroneous concepts. These are the same meetings that I talked to you about months ago."

"Yes, I have been attending those meetings, sir. What are this man's errors?"

"He buys slaves and sets them free."

"That is true, sir, but many of the greatest men in Rome

started their lives as poor men, and they became rich and made great contributions to the empire."

Cassius would have none of it. "This is different! This Jew buys slaves and sets them free immediately. He doesn't even require that they buy their freedom. What would happen if everyone were to do that?"

"I have never heard him suggest that anyone should follow his example."

Cassius glowered. "One soldier told me that Antipas gave his workers time off to build some widow a house—for free! He says that Antipas isn't going to charge interest on her loan. What are his intentions toward widows and poor people?"

"Sir, there are very few people who would offer any help to widows."

"This man's teaching is a problem, and it has now reached the garrison! He brings people together from subjugated lands and says all are equal. I don't like the sound of this. Giving power to slaves is dangerous. If it were to spread, this could become a threat to the empire."

Anthony wanted Cassius to have an accurate picture of Antipas's village. "You know that I have been attending these meetings for almost a year, sir. I have never heard him be discourteous to the emperor. Not once has he so much as breathed a word against the authorities. In fact, quite the opposite, he encourages people to pay their taxes and obey the laws."

"Who taught this Antipas?" Cassius was vicious now and was not going to retreat.

"His master was a man who lived and died and came back to life."

Incredulous, Cassius added, "Impossible! How did he die?"

"He was crucified, sir."

At this, Cassius exploded. "Crucified? Crucified! You say he follows the teachings of some crucified criminal? Where? When?" His voice trembled with disbelief. "Soldier, you are being misled! Reject these teachings. That will be all. You are dismissed!"

THE UPPER AGORA, THE ACROPOLIS

As she walked from one shop to another, Trifane was dancing inside. Not only had she had several banquets given for her by

Zoticos but she also had a new responsibility.

The first parchment was finished, indicating which students were to go to other cities and towns to pass on what they had been taught.

Her work on the second parchment was almost finished too. Zoticos wanted to revise the schedule a bit for the next year, and he depended on her intelligent observations. She had made two suggestions on how to improve the curriculum. Her next job would begin in a few days as she cataloged some recently acquired manuscripts.

Her heart was so light. She wanted to skip like a child.

Zoticos is kind, paying so much attention to me. He has not yet said that he wants to marry me, at least not in those words, but the way he said he wanted me to be with him forever made me understand his final meaning.

Her mother had been angry at her spending time with the chief librarian. "You will get into trouble with a man you know nothing about!" her mother said every evening when she came home late. Her mother knew that her daughter was susceptible to flattery, but Trifane did not want to listen to her mother's warnings.

Trifane walked into another store to look at their selection of new stolas.

What will I wear when my special day comes along?

The sales lady, Eugenia, sized her up and decided to try to sell her one of her most expensive stolas, a blue one with colorful embroidery on the short sleeves. The more she looked at Trifane, the more she realized that she had seen her before.

"I saw you yesterday...and each previous day during the last week," said Eugenia.

"When did you see me?" Trifane suddenly felt anxious.

"A friend and I saw you walking and talking with the chief librarian. My friend said she saw you going to his house. Someone else said you were the new girl at his house."

"Yes," Trifane said slowly, "I went to his house."

Eugenia said, "I hope you know what you are doing!"

The saleslady was known in the Upper Agora as a gossip. She had destroyed more than one person's hopes with a well-phrased bit of chinwag, but this time her intentions were more from a place of concern.

Trifane's heart was beating so quickly she could hardly breathe. She nodded.

"He has hosted many pretty faces in this city. They say that Zoticos chases anything lovely: faces, figures, or legs. You are clearly a lovely woman in every way. My friend says, 'Zoticos finds a lovely face and a shapely body quicker than he orders an expensive scroll from Greece.'"

Eugenia's own daughter had been one of Zoticos's earlier conquests.

Trifane put down the stola she was going to buy without speaking another word. She didn't look at Eugenia or acknowledge her. She walked out into the marketplace, willing herself not to run. Hardly able to catch her breath, she forced herself to step into another shop. Her legs shook. For a moment, she could scarcely breathe.

An elaborate hoax just to seduce me? I'm just another conquest to him!

She entered the library and dashed up the steps to the second level, turning right into the hallway to the office where only two weeks ago she began to acknowledge her feelings for him. His office was empty, and she felt a deep rage.

I've been taken in like any other woman! Oh, Zeus! He said, 'Sweets after a meal, the best part of the feast,' and that he wanted me to be with him for special dinners. But he never said he loves me!

Trifane wanted to do something to hurt Zoticos as much as he had hurt her. She felt used, sick, empty, and disappointed, and she was angry at herself for giving in to him and even more upset at him.

Her resentment grew as she looked at his expensive inlaid desk covered with parchments. Some were orders for new books, and others were statements of shipments coming from Africa or Spain.

A pile on the left side of his desk awaited his attention, and in the center of the desk were two parchments, the ones she had worked on. Zoticos's secretary came in. By now, he was used to seeing her coming and going.

"Looking for Zoticos today, Trifane? He went to the port to receive those shipments, so he won't be back until Monday morning. Only one more lecture with him, then you'll be finished with the lectures! Have you completed all the readings? Just a few more days…"

"Yes, the course is almost over," she replied, forcing her voice to remain calm.

Zoticos doesn't know it, but I will miss that last class.

She added quickly, "I still have something to do to finish my work on this parchment." The secretary bowed slightly as Trifane took it. She rolled up the new parchment and tucked it into her shoulder bag.

Everyone in the market knows that he looks for pretty faces and attractive bodies. He has had a long list of lovely women. I admit that I love him…but the futility! He has used me, and I hate him for it. I want to scream, and I will never see him again. He betrayed me.

Without saying anything to his secretary, she walked slowly out the door. She felt dizzy and went down the steps and out of the building. Trifane arrived home, went straight to her room, sat on her bed, and held her head in her hands.

THE LIBRARY OF PERGAMUM, THE ACROPOLIS

Zoticos arrived early on Monday, having brought several new scrolls. He greeted the staff and sat down at his desk, but after a few moments, he called his secretary. "Do you know where I put the parchment I was beginning to work on? I intended to list revisions for next term."

"Yes," said the man, "Trifane came on Saturday morning. She seemed upset, not her usual self. She came into your office, looking for you. I told her you would be back today. She didn't say a word but walked around your desk, took the document you are talking about, rolled it up, and walked out of the building. She didn't even greet me or say goodbye properly."

"Well, never mind, I'm sure she'll be working on some ideas I gave her, writing them down at home. She is a bright young woman."

"Yes, and if you don't mind me saying so, she is gorgeous."

Zoticos sat down and smiled. "Yes, she is pretty and intelligent."

ANTIPAS'S HOME

Antipas and Miriam settled into a new schedule. Thankfully, the volume of business in the shops had stayed the same since the adverse actions taken by some Jewish customers against his shops did not spread. Miriam looked at the Hebrew calendar.

Anthony's last visit had been on Tuesday, June 27. That also was a sad day. He had said a sincere goodbye to Miriam and left for Philippi. He would not be back in Pergamum for seven weeks, until almost the end of August.

THE GARRISON OF PERGAMUM

Cassius, the commander, had been thinking about the ten recruits who had become interested in Antipas's teaching. Anthony was the person who was inviting these recruits to Antipas's weekly meetings. Cassius decided that Anthony must immediately be expelled from the garrison until this growing problem could be understood and eliminated.

Some research needs to be done. How did he get the scar on his face? What really happened when he was in Upper Germanica? What else don't I know about him, and why has he started believing in a Jewish Messiah?

Realizing that a backup plan would be helpful in case of complications with the army's top authorities in Philippi, Cassius invited Diodorus to a meeting.

"I'm having difficulty with one of my soldiers," Cassius began, not sure of Diodorus's personal convictions or political inclinations. "Recruit Instructor Anthony Suros is away for the summer, but when he returns, I have decided that he must immediately be isolated from the recruits at the garrison. I was wondering if you could use him at the gymnasium."

"What kind of an instructor is he?" asked Diodorus, who was anxious to improve the quality of teachers, especially for training athletes for the Games the next year.

"Anthony Suros is an excellent archer, and he could be a help in training young athletes. Understand, though, he is a bit rebellious. He says he is a follower of Yeshua, that so-called Jewish Messiah we've been hearing about."

Both men laughed at the concept.

"I've written to some retired generals in Philippi asking for further information about him. While waiting for their answers, I don't want him teaching my recruits."

Diodorus rubbed his hands together in anticipation. "I'm determined to improve the sports training program. I'm practical, a bit of an opportunist, and just between the two of us,

I'm delighted that Anthony might be assigned to the gymnasium upon his return to Pergamum."

"What could you do to change his mind about this Jewish Messiah?"

"As director of the gymnasium, I will easily persuade this legionary that his newly formed ideas about Yeshua are misdirected. All that is needed is for Suros to understand Cicero's foundational concepts and commit to being a faithful citizen of Rome. In a short while, he will recover from this lapse in judgment. After one year, you will have him back at the garrison, but I will have an instructor of physical training in the meantime."

A SUMMER VILLA AT KISTHENE

Trifane waited, keeping her secret until the middle of July. She rested under the shade of a tree at the beach in Kisthene as her mother was gathering up the remains of their picnic. Horacio, her father, was walking on the beach.

"Mother, I need to tell you that you were right. I should have listened to you."

"What are you talking about?" her mother asked.

"I don't know how else to tell you, so I will just say it. I am going to have a baby."

Her mother was stunned. She sputtered in surprise, "But, but how? When? Who?" and then, in a moment, Cratia put it all together. "Did you fall for that man, the rich man in the library?" She struggled to control her voice.

It was as bad a situation as she had feared. She had warned her daughter.

"Yes, I did. I was so foolish! He paid attention to me and promised me a job in the office room next to him. He even made me his special assistant."

"When did this happen?" Cratia's stomach churned.

"He started paying attention to me last year. First, he showed special kindness and gave me a privileged seat each evening at the theater during the Festival of Zeus. He promised me a position in the library. Then he introduced me to people in the most important areas of the acropolis. Finally, he started giving me dinners. Oh, I fell for it!"

"Maybe he really loves you. Maybe he wants you, and maybe you want him." Her statement was really a question.

"About five weeks ago, I learned that he has fooled other women too. No! Mother, I never want to see him again! I loved him, but now I hate him, and I can never trust him again!"

Cratia didn't know what to say. "You don't want him to know you are pregnant?"

"No! Mother, I really don't. Will you promise me two difficult things?"

"I will try to do anything that you wish, dear, if it's at all possible."

"First, I want to stay here in Kisthene after the summer is over. I'll stay until February. I think that's when my baby is due. I've decided that it will be best if I give my baby away. Eventually I want to get married properly, and then I will have other babies. Can you stay with me?" she pleaded with her mother.

Cratia came to sit beside Trifane. "Oh, my dear child, of course I will stay with you! We'll stay in this rented villa until the end of summer. I will care for you, and we'll see your father once in a while, but he'll have to come back here from the city. I'm so sorry you got taken in like that!"

She held Trifane in her arms, emotions of love and protection pouring out as she stroked the wavy black hair of her beautiful daughter.

"Second, don't tell anyone who the father is, not even Dad. Promise me?"

"I promise you, my child. You can trust me. If someone ever did find out you had a baby, they would likely think the father was one of your fellow students. No, I won't tell any of our slaves either. Just you and me, we are the only ones who know. Your father and I will work something out, but we will stay in this house only until the end of August. After that, we'll find somewhere else to stay. You can count on me."

Cratia thought about her plans for the rest of the year and for the coming winter. They would find a way to stay in Kisthene.

Her daughter's secret would be safe, but how could they stay on all winter at the beach? After all, they could barely afford the rent for the expensive villa during two months of the summer.

LYDIA-NAQ'S HOME, THE ACROPOLIS

Lydia-Naq had taken the fortunate lull in her duties to have a meal prepared for her brother. In the middle of August, the heat was so intense that making slaves work often seemed cruel. Humidity in the warm air crushed one's lungs. Even Egyptians, who were used to the hot weather, had trouble working a long day while finishing the foundations of the New Temple.

"My brother, I am anxious about you. You have not been the same since the end of June. It was a fantastic event to see your first students graduate, but I have been watching you, and I think something is wrong.

"You had no energy at the graduation, and you have become sullen when you should be full of joy over what you have accomplished. You don't talk, you go for long walks alone along the streets of the city, and you have become withdrawn. Something is bothering you; I can tell."

He looked at her with a blank expression on his face.

"Today, on your behalf, I made a sacrifice at the Temple of Hera. As I made the libation offering on Hera's altar, the goddess put a thought in my mind: Zoticos lost something. I think it was Hera's message to me.

"What have you lost, my brother? You gained much by training your first twenty-four students, and now you have recruited the next group for instruction this fall. Have you lost something?"

She waited for his answer. He almost seemed to ignore her as he walked around the room and looked out a window. "You are perceptive but not accurate, my sister! You are correct in saying there is some loss in my life. You did not notice, did you? You said twenty-four students finished the course. Twenty-four began, but only twenty-three finished."

"What does that mean? Why is this important?" asked Lydia-Naq.

"It means this: I fell in love with one of the students. Her name is Trifane, our most capable researcher and one of our best debaters. She is beautiful and had her twenty-third birthday in July. She's too young for me, perhaps, but I fell in love with her and had her to my home. She loves me also.

"Over the last three months, I came to the decision that I need a wife. I no longer want other women in my life. I was going to ask her for her hand in marriage the next time I saw her. But first, I was going to find out how to approach her father and mother. However, she never came back. She seems to have left the city.

Why was I walking along the streets in the evenings? I was trying to find her. She left suddenly. I don't know where she has gone."

Lydia-Naq's perceptive skills came into full focus, a special gift she had of reading the minds of other people. When people brought their sacrifices to Zeus, they would often tell her their innermost feelings and fears.

She felt the presence of Zeus as she said, "I promise you one thing, my brother. You will learn why your woman left, and you will find out the reason in an unexpected manner. I will ask Zeus for this, and he will show us where she is. I am sure that this young woman wants to talk with you again, Zoticos."

Through the Fire

Part 3

The White Robe

September AD 90

Chapter 35
Proposals

It was a hot and muggy afternoon in late August when the little shop was suddenly darkened as someone stood in the doorway. Miriam looked up from stitching with a thread and needle. It was Anthony. His hair was longer and curlier than when he had left for Macedonia. Her heart raced as a joyful smile spread over her face.

"Hello, Miriam," he said by way of greeting, his voice lively. "Are you still selling your grandfather's items?"

He was tanned and healthy. Clearly he had been working in the sun!

She answered with a soft voice. "Oh, I am so glad to see you!"

"I have lots of news from my farm property near Philippi." He lowered his voice. Only Miriam could hear him, no one else. "I have to tell you how much I missed you," he said. He looked directly at her; he had to know her reaction to his surprise return.

She blinked several times. "I missed you too. I thought about you every day."

He smiled and took a step into the shop, and she took a step toward him. He was within reach of her, and he longed to take her hand or to kiss her. "All summer long, I helped my friend harvesting grain on my farm. I thought of you and wanted to share with you the things I saw, like a little colt dancing around the field. When it was so active, I instantly thought of you and wanted you to be there. It was brown and white with a white patch around its eyes. There were little calves, too, running and jumping. After the noon hour in Philippi, when the sun is high, it's impossible to work. A shade tree marks the entrance to my farm. I would lie on my back and remember your music and your singing."

She needed to sit down. Her legs were giving out. *How many nights have I felt lonely, staying awake long after Grandpa went to bed, tossing and turning during the long, hot summer? I dreamed of you saying this to me, telling me of your love.*

He took a deep breath, let it out, and took another. "I don't know how else to say this, Miriam. I've said it over and over to myself a thousand times as I was coming back over the Aegean from Philippi. As I was there for so long without you, I realized my need for you. I want you to marry me. I want to spend our lives together, and I want our own family, to grow old together. I can't live in peace without you."

"I'm so glad to hear this from your own lips, Anthony. I'm so happy you are back here! I want to say yes, but I'm not sure I can." Her fear of abandonment was gone, but in its place, a chasm formed, something that would keep them apart.

Anthony reached out and enfolded her into his arms. The two of them held each other tightly for a long time, and both found their eyes watering with joy.

He slowly pulled back and looked down at his sandals, with the military thongs wrapped several times around each leg. He rubbed his right hand down the front of his soldier's tunic. They both knew that the army uniform kept them apart.

"What will your grandfather say? You are Jewish, and I am a non-Jew. Worse, I'm Roman, a legionary! Will we have to wait until I am no longer a soldier?"

Her fears were coming to life again. So many questions had no answer. Something might happen to him while they waited. What if she could never be with him?

As she was wrapped in his arms, a dream had come back from the summer. Her dream included Anthony's face, but she was running in her dream, trying to catch up to him. He was ahead of her on a long road and then in a dark forest. He slipped out of sight before she could catch up to him and reach out to take hold of his outstretched hand.

Another night she had dreamed that she was on a broad, open plain when she saw Anthony take a path into the mountains. She had become lost while trying to find where he had gone. Every time she woke, she felt caught between hope and frustration.

But now, she looked down at her hands that had just held him so tightly. "Anthony, I want to become your wife. You are in my dreams at night, and I think of you in the daytime. I've even written songs about you!"

Anthony turned his head and gazed out through the open door as if trying to see into the future. "I have been a soldier in my legion for seventeen years, serving sixteen years as a legionary and this last year training scouts. I hope your grandfather won't make us wait until I retire. By then, I'll be forty-two years old with twenty-five years in the army. Perhaps we could settle here, or you could come with me to Philippi, but I think it would be better to stay near your friends. Do you think he would make us wait eight years until I could leave my present assignment?"

Miriam bit her lips. *Grandpa may not agree to this at all. He digs in and holds onto a position like your soldiers defending a field of battle. Nothing will make him change his mind if he thinks he is right. He may not let me marry you!*

But she looked at him with a smile. "I want us to be together. I have dreamed of it. But you are right; it cannot happen quickly. I know in my heart that I must have my grandfather's approval or our whole future would never be at peace."

Reaching up, she ran her finger along the long red line from his eye, down his right cheek, under his jaw, and to the base of his ear lobe. He didn't move. It was the first time she had touched him like this.

"Miriam, I will come back next Tuesday. The drillmaster has a garrison full of new soldiers. He will probably keep the same regimen that Cassius has had for the last six months. If he does, then I can see you as we have been doing. Maybe you will find a way to convince your grandfather. Maybe he'll let us be married sooner. I'll be posted here for a long time as the instructor of scouts. Think of every possible way to tell him so he agrees to our marriage." He added, half in jest, "If not, then we would have to wait until he dies! I can't wait that long!"

She caught her breath. "I can't wait that long, and I won't! What you don't know about my family is that the Ben Shelah men live a long time! Eliab was my great-grandfather. Would you believe that he died at eighty-six years of age? Three days more and he would have been eighty-seven. Grandpa is sixty-five years old—only sixty-five! How could we wait another twenty years if he said no? I couldn't live like that, wanting to marry you and not being allowed to."

"Thank you for giving me something exceptional to hope for. I am not foolish enough to think that everything will happen exactly as we want, but at least we agree with each other." With that, he tenderly kissed her on the forehead and let out a great sigh.

After Anthony had left, Miriam sat down in her chair, her head in her hands. She chuckled. Then she laughed out loud. She was loved. He loved her. Their voices had been low and could not have been heard outside. Her gossipy neighbor would have nothing to talk about.

MARCOS'S VILLA AT KISTHENE

Marcos knocked on the outside door of the villa he had rented to Horacio and was greeted by a slave. "Is Horacio at home?" he asked. "I need to speak to him."

Trifane walked to the door and then turned away, leaving him with their slave.

"Sir, my master is watching the waves come in" was the reply, which simply meant that Horacio was out on the beach and had no expected time to return. Marcos went around the house to the shore and saw him sitting on a rock, enjoying the white sand and cool breeze while watching the shorebirds search for food.

As he approached, Horacio heard the crunch of the sand and turned to see who was coming. He smiled and waved. Marcos sat down beside him and said, "Good evening! What a beautiful way to end a summer day! I come with a strange request."

"Certainly, Marcos. How can I help you?" asked Horacio, his gaze fixed on the beautiful dark orange glow after the sun had set.

"Last week I sold properties here, but the new owners cannot occupy them yet. Could you keep an eye on all my properties close to the sea?" To show the extent of the land, he pointed up the shore to where a small hill met the sea. "They used to belong to my brothers; when they died, the properties were transferred to me. I had an employee caring for them, but he told me that he is going to another city for a new job. I need someone to watch over them and keep drifters out."

"And you want me to take care of these villas?"

"Exactly. I would be most pleased if you took the job. You'll continue to stay in the villa, and I want you to look in on the others to make sure everything stays safe."

He let a handful of sand fall slowly as he gradually opened his closed fist. "I would let your family stay on here for free during the winter, and I will pay you some money as well. I know that it is an unusual request, but I don't want any damage to these buildings. Vagrants did some damage to someone else's villa recently. Free lodging all winter and spring for looking after my properties—this is my proposal."

When Horacio entered the house some time later, he hugged his wife and could not speak. "What has happened?" asked Cratia suspiciously. For the first time in weeks, a smile shone from his face.

He answered, "I think Hera answered our prayers." He briefly told Cratia about Marcos's business arrangement. Together they poured out a drink offering to Hera in thanks that their prayers for Trifane had been answered in the most remarkable way. Cratia and Trifane would stay in Kisthene for the whole winter, and it wouldn't cost Horacio anything. Better yet, Trifane would be kept from the shame of nosy neighbors and hurtful gossip in Pergamum.

She would give birth to her baby during the winter months a long way from her home.

THE ROAD BACK TO PERGAMUM

Traveling back to Pergamum, Marcella, Florbella, and Marcos watched as their summer home disappeared into the distant blue horizon. The two horses' black coats shone with sweat from the exertion of pulling their wagon full of baggage down the long coastal road and back home.

"I love coming home after spending the summer at the seaside," sighed Marcella. "This has been a wonderful summer. The sunsets over the Aegean this year were the richest reds and oranges into dark purple."

She had enjoyed the cool of the evenings spent walking with her husband along the smooth white sand. She felt loved and cared for, and for the first time in years, she began to accept the loss of her children from the plague and his family members during the earthquake. She added, "I'm content to be getting back to Pergamum today. It's the first day of September, which always gives me mixed emotions, both sad and happy."

Marcos answered, "I was delayed by finishing the negotiations to sell properties, but that's all done now." For several minutes, he described how he had managed the sale of his brothers' properties and the transfer of funds to Pergamum to pay for the aristocrats' future homes.

Marcella enjoyed seeing the change in him since the healing of their daughter. She appreciated his new attention to her and Florbella. Additionally, he had begun to care for others and to show a love for people that was entirely different from his general selfishness when they were first married. She knew that this kind of transformation could only be the result of one thing. The teaching at the cave was changing both of them.

He was keeping his promises to the three families on the acropolis. Furthermore, during the summer, he had also started to comment on the practical needs of poor families in Kisthene. They owned houses and lands, but their wealth was now more of a resource to help others instead of a source of snobbish pride.

"Wasn't it amazing? Cratia and Trifane, who are going to watch over our properties, wanted to stay there this winter!" Marcella exclaimed. "It's a comfort to know that they will look after the houses, even keeping the orchards and gardens cared for until next summer. Cratia is a capable woman. And that lovely, quiet, well-mannered young woman! Weren't we lucky to have had a well-trained woman as a private tutor for our daughter this summer!"

THE GARRISON OF PERGAMUM

As soon as Commander Cassius had returned from Ephesus, Anthony reported for duty to him. However, he wasn't prepared for the implications of their conversation.

"Anthony, during the past year, I saw you falter in the allegiance you owe Rome. Consequently, I have decided that this next year you will not be an instructor in this garrison."

"Are you sending me away just when I have...?" He could not finish his question.

"You are a quiet man and say little about yourself, so I have been investigating your background. A retired friend of mine told me a little bit about you. He confirmed you were a scout in the conquest of lands along the Neckar River. I learned you discovered villagers' plots against your legion. This happened on two occasions, I believe."

"Yes sir, this happened twice, as you say."

"Clearly you were effective on the battlefield, but here you are supposed to be a teacher under my authority. I want to acknowledge your service to Legion XXI, so I will allow you to continue as a reservist. But you will not serve this garrison until we settle the present loyalty question. I am assigning you to train young men for the Pergamum Games next May at the request of the gymnasium master, Diodorus."

Anthony stood at attention, saying nothing.

"An interesting bit of information also came to me from Philippi this week. I wrote to the army division that cares for the wounded, asking for information about you. I was told that you were wounded while attempting to discover a possible location of attack from across the river. I was also informed that two tribunes from your legion disappeared shortly afterward. Nothing has been heard of these deserters since, but a rumor is circulating in Philippi that they have gone into criminal activities. Do you know their names?"

Anthony attempted to keep a blank look on his face. Distant memories flooded back. "Their names were Flavius Memucan Parshandatha...and Claudius Carshena Datis. Those two...but there was another.... What was his name?" he said in a quieter voice.

The tone from the commanding officer was cold and demanding. "I will take note of these names. Another strange thing about your legion is this." He stopped and began reading from another scroll. "Shortly after your patrol was ambushed, about twenty soldiers from your cohort disappeared. That was after a small group of enemy soldiers from Dacia crossed the Danube in the winter to attack the camp. It is believed that those twenty soldiers are deserters afraid they would be punished for not guarding the legion's camp area well during that night."

"Do you know anything about the whereabouts of those tribunes or the twenty soldiers from your own cohort?"

Anthony let out his breath slowly. "Sir, I know nothing about where they might have gone. Their disappearance is new information to me. I was in a hospital for months after the ambush."

A deep sigh of relief welled up. He had not been asked about his relationship with the two tribunes, only about their names. He would not have to explain how his face was slashed open, and he knew nothing about the twenty others who had disappeared.

Cassius's tone changed, now slightly less authoritarian. "You cannot continue to live in the garrison. You are no longer serving here. Therefore, you will have to find your own accommodations from funds paid by the gymnasium. Perhaps you can help young men to do better in the games...at least I hope so. Diodorus will begin teaching you the basics of Roman civilian life, lecturing from the writings of Cicero. To maintain your reservist status, I require that you attend those lectures and come to the garrison every two weeks to report on what you have learned."

Suddenly Cassius's voice was harsh again. "Soldier, you have been led astray, but we will set you right. The teaching of this man Antipas is a disgrace!" Cassius stopped for a moment and looked out of the window. "This blemish must be removed from the city before it infects others. You are dismissed."

"Yes sir!" said Anthony.

Cassius and Diodorus had conspired behind his back, and he was being hemmed in. But he was also comforted since as a reservist, he hadn't completely lost his position. Most importantly, no disciplinary action had been taken. He could still live close to Miriam. He planned to see her at the shop and at the cave.

He breathed a sigh of relief. Only yesterday he had been elated at Miriam's response, her affirmation of love. What would this sudden change in status mean to Antipas? Would it cast him in a poor light, implying that he would be unable to support Miriam if he married her? And did Cassius's outburst against Antipas mean he was in danger?

DIODORUS'S OFFICE, THE GYMNASIUM, THE ACROPOLIS

Diodorus waited in his office. It was a spacious room with two windows overlooking the inner court where students did their exercises. The courtyard was large enough for instruction to be given to over five hundred boys at once.[71] Everyone in Pergamum

---

[71] Tour groups rarely visit Pergamum's lower acropolis. The best way to see it is to descend a steep path from the Upper Agora by foot. The gymnasium ruins and several other sites are well worth the extra time.

wanted the city to be committed to regaining its original position of being highly favored by Rome. They were excited that the acropolis was going to be significantly improved. In the same spirit, the city leaders had demanded that Diodorus train the young men of the city to the best of their abilities. After this order had been issued, Diodorus agreed with Cassius to have Anthony transferred to the gymnasium.

The western wall of the pillared courtyard held water in three small pools. They were not large enough for swimming, but boys bathed in them during breaks from strenuous sports. The day started off with classes, and each boy had a period of physical fitness training. Those who showed the most promise received specialized instruction, and it was to this group of budding athletes that Anthony had been assigned.

The largest room in the gymnasium was simply called the hall and was used for school activities as well as public events for the community. Almost every evening, some kind of entertainment took place. It was especially important from November to February because the cold rainy season made outdoor activities difficult.

The southern exposure of Diodorus's office gave an unimpeded view of the long footrace track. It was as long as the running track in a stadium and occupied one of the few flat areas on the acropolis.

Anthony arrived at Diodorus's door.

"So you received your orders from Commander Cassius. I have been waiting for you. You are late."

"I would like to know how I can be useful in the gymnasium. How do you want me to refer to you, as 'sir,' or Diodorus, or some other way? As a legionary, I always address my commander as 'sir.'"

Diodorus studied him. He looked disciplined, but it might not be as easy to change his mind as he had told Commander Cassius. He was determined to dominate this insubordinate soldier.

"'Sir' will be fine until we get to know each other better. As for your assignment to the gymnasium, I want you to work with young men ages fourteen to sixteen. Your job is to train our best athletes. Work with them extra hours, preparing for the Games in

May next year.

"I have plans for a class in Roman law beginning next week after hours, twice a week, and as Cassius has told you, you are required to attend these classes. Let's see. What nights shall we meet? Perhaps Tuesday and Thursday? Diotrephes tells me that the Jew has been teaching you on those nights. Let's make those evening hours our commitment to learn Roman customs, shall we?"

The schoolmaster's voice was spiced with sarcasm. Anthony immediately recognized this salvo of requirements as a well-contrived plan to keep him from the cave. He closed his eyes; the memory of a volley of arrows shot from behind the cover of a dark, dense forest came back to him. This time one of the highest authorities in the city was endangering his future.

He rapidly blinked and blinked again. Diodorus examined his face. He could see Anthony didn't like losing those evenings. Good!

"This year, you will not learn about Yeshua or Christus, whatever you call him. Instead, I will teach you and a handful of others about our greatest hero in Roman civil law. You will become a disciple of Cicero, as I am. You may not be a follower of the Jewish Messiah. Do you understand? Now repeat to me the intention of our decision."

Ever the teacher, Diodorus was determined to gain the upper hand immediately.

Anthony responded in crisp sentences, the way a Roman centurion liked to hear a subordinate talk. "You called me to be an assistant, sir. I am under your authority most days. Cassius continues as my commanding officer. You and he and the citizens of the city made a decision. The young men must be better prepared for the sports events in May next year. You want more victories each year, and I will work under you while I am in the gymnasium.

"You will teach me the lessons of Cicero on the nights that I previously studied with Antipas. Your intention is to make me understand what makes a person loyal to Rome. While you teach me, I will remain attached to the garrison as a reservist.

"I will no longer teach men scouting skills. Once every two weeks, I will report to Cassius what I have learned. He wants to know how true loyalty to Roman principles affects the life of a citizen. In short, you teach me, and I report to my commanding officer. That is what I understand, sir!"

"You are dismissed." Diodorus pulled at his chin.

Diodorus's job was to bring him back to full loyalty to Domitian. Anthony would remember this painful interview, and he knew the soldier's pride was wounded. Obviously he was a capable instructor. For now, he heard submission in every word of the soldier's quick little speech. Anthony must have been a good scout, but that scar must drive him away from the ladies! Too bad he was so visibly flawed!

After Anthony was well out of the building, Diodorus realized what had happened. The legionary had left out the most critical part. The man had neglected to completely repeat all of what Diodorus wanted. Anthony did not say he intended to give up that business about being a follower of the Jewish Messiah.

Diodorus stood at the open window and watched Anthony walking down the acropolis steps to the nearby Lower Agora. He suddenly realized that working with this man was going to be harder than he thought.

ANTIPAS'S SHOP IN THE LOWER AGORA, THE ACROPOLIS

As soon as Nikasa left the shop, Anthony strolled along the colonnade. Miriam was inside with a customer. A few minutes later, the shop was empty again.

"You look wonderful!" he said. "I have lots of news, some good, some not."

"You look...exasperated! I haven't seen you look like this before. What's happened?"

"Yes, let me tell you. I was called into the office of my commanding officer. He told me I will not teach scouts this year. He said I am bringing false ideas into the legion by taking soldiers to hear Antipas speak. Next he had me go to Diodorus's office, in the gymnasium. My new assignment is to train boys and make Pergamum more competitive in Asia Minor's sports events."

She couldn't see how this would be a problem. "Is that all? It actually sounds terrific! Where will you live? Will you still be paid? Is it all daytime work?" She had so many questions!

"Not so fast! I will be paid as a teacher and rent a room near the Lower Agora somewhere because I cannot stay in the garrison any longer. They don't want me mingling with the soldiers. In fact, they want me to learn to be a truly loyal Roman. Apparently that can only be done by Diodorus teaching me in the gymnasium on Tuesday and Thursday evenings!"

"But those are our evenings for study with Grandpa! That means..." She began to understand that a systematic effort had begun to bring Anthony back into the legion, to reform him, and to redirect his loyalty. They talked, and the more she learned, the more she felt the authorities were being unfair. But at the moment, she couldn't see a way out.

Anthony was being trapped!

TRIFANE'S HOME, PERGAMUM

Zoticos made one inquiry after another and learned from one of his students where Trifane lived. He found the address, and his knock at the door was shortly answered by Trifane's father.

"My name is Zoticos-Naq Milon," he said, attempting to impress the man with his full Lydian name. "May I talk with you for a moment? I am here on important business."

After a few minutes of social talk, Zoticos learned that Horacio worked as a salaried senior clerk in the customs house. Zoticos was somewhat reassured by this information because it meant Trifane's family's status would be compatible with the high standards demanded of a marriage into the Milon family.

Horacio was the assistant to the Asiarch and responsible for purchasing adequate supplies of wood, charcoal, wine, oil, and grain. This meant working with many people in the city and the surrounding regions.

Five of Horacio's colleagues worked at the same level of administration: the storage of supplies, taxation, care of animals, water and sewers, and management of slaves.

These men, responsible for Pergamum's smooth administration, often faced citizens that came to them with hidden motives. "How can I help you, Honorable Zoticos? You must be a busy man, and I'm sure you don't have a lot of time for extra socializing."

"Last year, your daughter, Trifane, studied with us on the acropolis. It included a course on Lydian life and times. I was one of her teachers."

"Certainly, I have heard all about it."

"Since the middle of June, she has stopped attending. She was to become my assistant at the library. Scrolls come from different sources: Corinth, Athens, Rome, and many other places. She is competent in keeping track of the various copyists. We need her help. Please ask her to return to the library right away."

Horacio considered in silence, wondering if this was leading to some attempt at deception of the customs office. If so, it would be nothing new. Suddenly his eyes opened a little wider. He had a suspicion about this man. Trifane refused to reveal who the father of her unborn child was, but very possibly, this was the man who had seduced her.

Zoticos became uncomfortable at the long silence. He turned his head, looked down to the floor, and twisted his hands. "Do you know where she is?" Zoticos asked, suddenly looking up at Trifane's father.

Horacio was sure there was far more to Zoticos's story than he had told. "I will tell Trifane your news the next time I see her and that you asked her to work in the library." He was determined not to let this man know where she was.

Zoticos left slowly. What had he said to irritate this quiet little man? He felt indignation and disappointment. He muttered to himself, "Trifane is a lovely soul. She doesn't deserve a father who is so unfeeling. Such a beautiful young girl deserves a more caring father!"

THE HOT BATHS

Listening to the men talk at the hot baths, Marcos formed a much larger picture of what was taking place in Rome. Topics under discussion were sometimes carried on in hushed tones. Just now, information leaking out of the empire's capital spoke of dark activities in the closed rooms of government. Hidden in the cloudy mist of the steam room, men were prone to say things that would be dangerous to mention in other places.

One administrator spoke openly to a colleague while perspiration poured down both their faces. "Domitian is furious over intrigues in his palace. Remember how his infidelities and scandals were exposed two years after he became emperor?" The two men gave a hearty laugh.

Another man in the room replied, "All the building projects Domitian undertakes in Rome are leading to a bankrupt empire. He wants to contribute even more to the arts and architecture

319

than Nero! Imagine! Fifty huge, new buildings! Further, he's expanding the Coliseum. The only thing he can do to prevent a crisis is charge more taxes and expropriate properties. He has to add revenue. The long-term effects of the fire in Nero's day are not over yet."

"Next year, in Sardis," said a third, "the number one topic of the Asiarchs will again be about taxes. Anyone want to make a bet we won't be affected?"

They laughed hilariously at the thought of making a bet about the erratic actions of their emperor. That was just as crazy as betting that Thyatira would be the winner of the Games next spring.

Chapter 36
Anthony's Request

ANTIPAS'S SHOP IN THE LOWER AGORA, THE ACROPOLIS

It was Miriam who made the decision. "We have to speak to Grandpa," she said to Anthony. "Two days from now is Yom Kippur, a day of fasting and mourning. Also, tomorrow is your day off. Come to our house tomorrow so we can talk to him before Yom Kippur begins and tell him we want to get married. Afterward, he will work out the details."

ANTIPAS'S HOME

Antipas sat deep in thought. The sunlight from an upper window shone on the matrix of small boxes whose scrolls were kept away from the wall to prevent humidity from affecting their quality. In his spare time, he was beginning to work on a codex, a new kind of document with sheets of parchment held together along one side by stitches instead of being rolled up in a scroll. That was eventually going to require another means of storage. Little square boxes worked so well for scrolls.

He was at first perplexed when he heard Miriam had invited Anthony for dinner this evening. He had wanted to dictate scrolls to the four men who were learning to make new copies of the ancient scriptures. There would be no dictation tonight.

After the food was placed on the table, Antipas asked his servant to go home early. He said a quick prayer to thank God for the food, and as soon as the "amen" left his lips, Miriam said, "Grandpa, Anthony has a question for you."

Anthony cleared his throat and looked directly at Antipas. "This is a special time with you, Grandfather Antipas." He glanced at Miriam. "Everyone calls you Grandfather, a term of great respect. I want to call you Grandfather Antipas in a new way."

Antipas pushed the food away. *Now, that's a strange*

comment!

Anthony began, "Let me explain. When I first came to the cave, I remembered that I heard you speak publicly in the marketplace to the people of the city. You argued there is only one God. I came to the cave and heard more about the story of your lives and how you came to believe in the Messiah. Over the next four months, I visited you in your home and at the cave. I understood more. You invited me into a smaller circle of people so that I could teach and train other men in the future."

He paused. "Also, I noticed how your granddaughter, Miriam, conducted herself. I visited her every week in the marketplace, at your shop, after you put her in charge of the afternoon duty."

Antipas slowly repeated what he had just heard. "You visited her every week in the marketplace, at my shop, after I put her in charge of the afternoon duty?"

"Yes. Gradually I came to understand her, to value her, to know her. After I came back to Pergamum from Philippi, where I have a farm, my commander told me he does not want me to train recruits any more. He thinks I am contaminating the soldiers who come to the cave because of your teaching. Now I have been assigned to work at the gymnasium to prepare young men for the games next year."

Antipas had not eaten a bite more. "What does all this have to do with Miriam and being here for supper?"

"When I returned from Philippi, where I helped with the harvest, I told Miriam that I loved her. She said the same thing to me, that she loves me. We want to get married, and we very much want you to approve. So yes, I am asking to marry Miriam."

Antipas tried desperately to keep a blank expression on his face. *Did I ever see anything between them—a look of admiration or a questioning furrow on their forehead? Could my granddaughter ever hide something like this from me?*

He had to say something. "I see," he said. "You want to marry Miriam." She was beaming as he had not seen her smile for a long time.

I can't respond joyfully. The man is a Roman citizen, a legionary, a Gentile—and Miriam needs my protection. I have investigated so many eligible men for her, in many places, but not one of them was good enough for her.

Anthony, I accepted you as part of the Household of Faith, but

322

that didn't mean you could be part of my family! I don't have anyone else besides her. Oh, soldier! People in my family died because of what your army did to us in Jerusalem!

He drew in his breath. "I will think about this. I know you would like to have an immediate answer, but this brings up unasked questions that I must think about. Yes, I will have to think and pray about it."

Anthony interrupted. "If it would help, Grandfather Antipas, you need to know this: I've been in my legion for seventeen years. Eight more years and I will have served for twenty-five years. I'm a reservist now, but then I will no longer be in the legion."

Antipas looked at Miriam. She hadn't said a word, so he asked, "How much do you know about him? Do you know him well enough to marry him? Do you trust him?"

Miriam's face turned pale, and Antipas was determined to make this very difficult for her.

Then he turned to Anthony. "Have you ever been married? Excuse this question, but have you ever lain with a woman? Have you been like all the other soldiers? Aren't they all the same? How much stability can you give her?"

Anthony replied slowly, "No, I have never been married, Grandfather Antipas. And I have never lain with a woman. I wanted to marry a young woman when I was sixteen, but we were too young to get married. She was the daughter of a friend in Rome, but she died from a coughing disease; after that, I went into the Legion.

"As you know, my mother was a believer in the Messiah. She spent many hours with me in her last year of life speaking of these things. She said, 'One day you will think you are ready for marriage. What does it mean to be ready?' She explained, 'The easiest thing in the world is to live for your own needs and wants, but when you start a family, you have to be dedicated to providing for the needs and wants of your wife and children.'

"She made me examine everyone we knew. 'Let me teach you about the importance of decisions. Look at this family! What do you see? Look at that man's relationship!' Then she would say, 'Look again, more carefully! Can't you see a connection between what he did before and what is happening now? Can't you see the results of actions in the lives of people later on?' She would have been a better scout than I was if she were in the army! She taught me to always think of the consequences that follow actions. She taught me about life more than anyone. Can you imagine a woman in the army?"

It was the first humorous comment of the evening, but their laughter was forced.

"My mother said, 'If you have sexual relations with a girl before being married, she probably will not trust you during your marriage. If you take the broad path, then other women will walk with you, but you won't find the narrow path back to your home.' She explained how my father had left her for another woman. She said, 'Rome is full of filth, and it smells everywhere. People here think only of themselves and not of others.' Her words have come back to me many times since then."

"Did he tell you this about his mother?" Antipas asked.

"No," she replied softly.

"Did you know about the young woman who died from some disease?"

"No," she confessed.

"How can you marry a man if you don't know him? I think I have illustrated that there are many questions even you have not asked that need to be well answered before I can approve such a marriage."

Antipas had made his point. Questions without answers hung in the air. "I will think about this, and when I am ready, I will give you a decision."

A solid knot weighed down the old man's stomach. He couldn't eat anything more with his mind in turmoil. The supper Miriam hoped would be a happy occasion had turned into a time of silent torture.

Anthony finished and asked to be dismissed. "Thank you for listening to me, Grandfather Antipas. I pray to God that you will listen to him for direction. I trust you more than anyone I've ever met. I love your granddaughter, and I believe she will be able to trust me all her life. I will not rush you, and I will not ask you about this again. I know you love her much more than I do. She is a precious person, and I want the best for her. A scout is trained not to do foolish things when in the forest. He waits until he has heard what was most important, not what he was afraid to hear. I will wait until you are ready to speak to me. Goodnight."

Anthony and Miriam looked at each other for a couple of

seconds. Once again, he admired the feelings shown in her face. Her cheeks revealed tender emotions, and tiny fluctuations on her lips indicated she was in deep thought. Her eyes spoke of both hope and fear. She was deeply moved by the conversation yet had concerns about the possible results.

Then he was gone. He left their home and descended to his small and sparse rented room on the western edge of the city.

Chapter 37
The Wilderness Path

ANTIPAS'S HOME

Antipas sat down slowly on the most comfortable chair. Two lamps burned, one on each side of his desk. The smell of old parchments and lamp oil, the comforting sight of scrolls rolled up and stashed away in their places, and the smooth armrests of his chair would generally have been enough to set his mind at peace.

Tonight, though, he felt agitated. Yom Kippur had come around once more, the day for the atonement of sins. Twenty-five years ago, when they first arrived in Jerusalem, he went to Herod's temple to sacrifice a lamb. How much had changed! He no longer had fellowship with his friends at the synagogue, and last night his granddaughter had told him she wanted to get married to a legionary!

He began a new scroll, one he would typically use at the end of a year to summarize his accounts. He had a new account in mind, one that needed to be thoroughly reviewed. He always calculated the balance of income and expenditures or amounts owed to him from his customers. This new scroll would trace his journey through the most difficult decision he'd ever faced. Calculating his granddaughter's safety and happiness would be much more complicated than adding and subtracting columns of figures. He began the new scroll:

> *Wednesday, September 20. Miriam wants to marry the legionary! Lord God of my fathers, I don't know how to pray tonight. My mind and heart are empty. I feel numb. How can I be sensitive to what is going on around me?*
>
> *Yom Kippur, in the ninth year of Domitian: These are the records of my soul. This is perhaps the most difficult decision of my life. Leaving Alexandria to go to Jerusalem almost tore my family apart, and fleeing Jerusalem to surrender to the Romans was terrible. Still, we were a family, so I had others to share the complexities of life.*
>
> *King of the universe, this is a day to confess my sins. I am humbled by the decision before me. How many times*

have I sought a husband for Miriam from my own people? Always I found a fault. Now my community has cut me off, so no one will consent to marry into my family. Miriam has found a man, a soldier, the one I cannot admit into my household.

He stood up and reached his hands toward the roof and then prostrated himself in prayer as he faced Jerusalem.

Miriam woke the next morning feeling rested. A confidence of joy spread through her as she dressed and put on her jewelry. She felt loved and accepted in a new way. She had learned much about Anthony through her grandfather's questions, and the more she came to know him, the more she felt she could trust him.

She went over her most recent dream: She was small again, five years old, and she wanted someone to hold her hand. "Tighter!" she called to her grandfather as they ran away from Jerusalem. Then she faced the enemies, the Roman army. A hand reached out to her. "Tighter!" she said again, and she realized that one of the Roman soldiers had taken her other hand. She looked at his face, and it was Anthony.

She combed her hair and braided it with red and blue ribbons. *I am loved,* she thought.

On Monday, Sukkoth, the Feast of Tabernacles, Antipas added to his new account:

September 25. The journeys of our fathers through the sands and wastelands of Sinai invariably led them to places never seen before. They ate manna, which nourished them every day. Reveal to my soul, Almighty One. Would Anthony have eaten that manna? No, enemy soldiers were not part of Moses' community. It's easy to follow this principle: "A friend of my enemies is my enemy, and a friend of my friend is my friend." Yet I learned these words: "Love your enemies." But I cannot love Anthony. I have found a command that I cannot obey.

ANTIPAS'S SHOP IN THE LOWER AGORA, THE ACROPOLIS

On Wednesday after the Feast of Tabernacles, Antipas rose early. He had to confirm a doubt in his mind.

How could they have talked all this time without him kissing her or doing anything more? After all, isn't he a military man?

As soon as the shops were open, he left his village, walking toward the Lower Agora. He found his store open and the Samaritan widow already talking to a customer.

The woman in the store next to his was willing to talk to Antipas. "Yes, we saw the young soldier come to your shop. We tried to listen in on his conversations. We saw him come and go, and it was always on Tuesday afternoons when he came. We used to comment on it because it seemed so strange."

The woman on the other side of the colonnade was even more forthcoming. "Oh, yes! What a story! He stands in the doorway. He is a considerate young man! He tells her about his farm in some place.... She tells him about her mother."

"He comes here often?"

"Every Tuesday, the same time every week."

"And he just stands in the doorway?"

"My, you are a funny old man! I know you are the owner of the shop, and I know she is your granddaughter. Are you trying to find out what they have been doing?"

"Yes," he answered.

She laughed. "You know that chinwag is all we do here in the agora. But in this case, there's nothing to gossip about! He comes, stands in the doorway, and barely takes a step inside. I always think, 'Today they are going to start kissing and carrying on.'

"You can spot that type right away, all those men who try to get an easy woman. But listen, I spied on them for almost a year. Nothing! Nothing, I tell you. Not even a kiss! So disappointing! I saw him step into the shop two weeks ago after he had been away for so long. I thought, 'Now this is it!' So I looked in. She was running her hand along the long red scar on his face. Sorry, no juicy gossip here! Sorry to disappoint you. That's all I ever saw!"

He went home with new information, and he didn't like it.

ANTIPAS'S HOME

Wednesday, October 4. I doubted Anthony, but the woman in the agora confirmed Anthony's story. He only stood in the doorway! They talked across the room! He has more discipline than Ruth and I, forty-five years ago, yet I still don't trust him. I know the temptations of a man. His word is proven...sort of. I will once again read the Law and the Prophets to find an answer to this matter. Since this is harvest season, I will return to the story of my forefather Jacob. He also suffered unmeasured worries in his home, he who harvested many unpredictable difficulties with women and children.

Antipas put down the quill he had used to write. His eyes hurt more than usual. He stood and held his hands upward to put his prayer shawl over his head and shoulders and bowed. It was not a bow of submission but of pain, a deeply wounded spirit, and profound sadness. During this struggle over Miriam's future, even the joy of belonging to the Household of Faith seemed to fade slightly.

THE CAVE, ANTIPAS'S VILLAGE

Antipas asked Marcos what he had been able to do in working on the Ben Shelah will left by Eliab. His brothers, especially in Thyatira and Laodicea, were anxious to get a resolution. He had received several curt, almost nasty letters from them. "It's more than a year since he died," wrote Daniel from Laodicea. "I don't want to wait another year to hear about the will."

"I have to explain that your father's will does not have an easy resolution," the lawyer said. "Your father bought the property, so it is in his name, but it was you who developed it. According to Eliab's will, your buildings on the land are your property. They are separate from his estate. In addition, Eliab had many other assets in Alexandria, including ships. The will calls for the estate to be distributed among his heirs. Altogether, there are eight sons and one daughter, that is, nine persons. Amos, as the oldest son, is to receive two portions.

"This is where the problems begin: Two brothers and one sister live in Alexandria, in Egypt, far away. Now Asia, where we live, is a senatorial province, and Egypt is an imperial province.[72]

---

[72] Senatorial provinces were under the direct administration of the Senate in Rome; imperial provinces were administered through the Offices of the

I will have to propose a settlement in the Senatorial Court in Ephesus. The Imperial Court in Alexandria will have to agree to the final decisions. I will work on all provisions and tell your brothers when the two courts have declared that I can proceed.

"An entirely different matter has to be dealt with regarding the buildings you constructed on your father's property. You improved and developed the village, building three dozen houses, several workshops, and the cave. Part of the property includes fenced off areas for animals. It was your father's property, but you own all the buildings on his land, per the specification he put in his will. Here is the problem: Your father wanted the *value* of the property to be divided into ten portions, two in the case of Amos. The heirs will each receive a share. Yet concerning the houses and the buildings, you own all the improvements.

"So two different Roman jurisdictions are involved in applying the laws of inheritance, Asia Minor and Egypt, and this will take some time. I shall write a letter to each of your brothers to explain the complications and ask them to be patient for a resolution."

ANTIPAS'S HOME

Antipas put down the scroll. He was sure he had read the words dozens of times before, but tonight the story of the sons of Jacob shook him. His hand was trembling even though the cold winter winds and rains were still a couple of weeks away.

> *Saturday, October 28. 'The sons of Judah: Er, Onan, and Shelah. These three were born to him by a Canaanite woman, the daughter of Shua. Er, Judah's first-born, was wicked in the Lord's sight; so the Lord put him to death. Tamar, Judah's daughter-in-law, bore him Perez and Zerah. Judah had five sons.'[73]*
>
> *My attention goes to Tamar, the shameful way she treated Judah and the dishonorable way he acted toward her. How could Adonai allow her to be with child when she was his daughter-in-law?*
>
> *Tonight, O Mighty One, I realized how the head of our*

Emperor.

[73] Genesis 38:1–30 and 1 Chronicles 2:3–4

tribe of Judah came to form our clan through a Canaanite woman; she conceived his first three children. His wife...a Canaanite! You blessed my forefather Shelah although it was a pagan woman who brought him into the world. Shelah—my family name, my family—descended from the third of those three sons, from a woman not descended from Abraham! I don't like this story of my people's past. I don't want this story to influence my decision.

He put down his pen, prayed, blew out the reading lamps, and carried a single lamp with him to light the way to bed.

THE CAVE, ANTIPAS'S VILLAGE

Antipas looked out over the people in the cave. Miriam would sing a new song today. People would then participate in the Holy Meal. Everything was beginning to return to normal. It was clear now which families had chosen to stay with him and which had returned to the synagogue congregation. Antipas's mind still tended to concentrate on Anthony.

I am starting a series of studies, the names of God. My mind is divided, saying the words while my attention is wandering. Like the potter who makes the same wine jug for the hundredth time. Like the wheel that goes round and round, forming vessels. I'm constantly thinking of Anthony...but a potter's hands are productive, and I keep asking without finding an answer. How could he be part of my family?

Since Diodorus had forced Anthony to miss the evening instruction at the village, Marcos was noticing how much less challenging the discussions were in the group. He was at the meetings but did not want to be the only person asking questions of Antipas. The other men attending did not have the same sense of curiosity or urgency. Anthony had brightened up their group so much, and his absence made a big difference.

"I want to change our schedules starting this week," announced Antipas, looking around the large room in his home. "The groups meeting on Monday and Wednesday nights will now meet on Tuesday and Thursday nights in my home. The group that usually meets on Tuesday and Thursday nights will come here on Monday and Wednesday."

Antipas looked at Anthony and Miriam. They understood. It

was an invitation for Anthony to be in the leadership-training group once again. He would continue at the class taught by Diodorus about famous Roman statesmen on Tuesdays and Thursdays and attend Antipas's instruction on Mondays and Wednesdays.

After the meeting was over, Antipas and Miriam bid them goodbye. Anthony, Marcella, and Marcos went back to the city.

ANTIPAS'S HOME

Antipas said goodnight to Miriam and went into his library. Once more, he was shaken by the story unfolding before him, this time regarding the design of the first tabernacle.

> *Monday, October 30. How is it, Lord of Glory, that you chose Bezalel, son of Uri, the son of Hur, of the tribe of Judah? You filled him with your Spirit—with skill, ability, and knowledge in all kinds of crafts: artistic designs for work in gold, silver, and bronze, to cut and set stones and work in wood and do all sorts of craftsmanship. And you selected Oholiab, son of Ahisamach, of the tribe of Dan to be a helper. The tribe of Dan![74]*
>
> *These were artisans from opposite ends of our inheritance, Judah in the south and Dan in the north! You called these two workers together and later placed their tribes on opposite ends of the land. Why did you bring opposites together to create the place of worship in your tabernacle?*

By the middle of November, Antipas arrived at the story of Nehemiah, the wine taster of King Artaxerxes, who allowed the restoration of Jerusalem.[75]

> *Tuesday, November 14. It's crystal clear! We are to be married only to those of our race! Wasn't that determined by the reformers, Ezra and Nehemiah? Didn't Adonai forbid the children of Israel to marry outsiders?*

---

[74] Exodus 31:1–11
[75] Nehemiah 2:11 begins the story of Nehemiah in Jerusalem.

He slept well, secure in the belief he had found an answer to his dilemma.

THE CAVE, ANTIPAS'S VILLAGE

Chanukah came early in the ninth year of Domitian. Six weeks had gone by, and Antipas had not spoken to Anthony about his relationship with Miriam. Florbella was well integrated into a small group of young children. Ateas had become known for his abilities as an artist, and Arpoxa was expecting a baby. People were excited for her but worried about how she would manage with a toddler running around the home.

Miriam had written another song for this particular service; the "Song of the Lights" she called it. When the evening celebration in the cave was over, Antipas went very slowly back to his library. His mind returned to the construction of Solomon's temple and true worship.

> *Sunday, December 3. Almighty One, how did I miss this story before? The design for the temple of Solomon was made by Huram-Abi, a man of great skill. Huram-Abi's mother came from Dan, the most northern tribe of ancient Israel, and Huram-Abi's father was from Tyre—a pagan land! The man chosen to make the furnishings for Solomon's temple had a pagan father!*
>
> *Huram-Abi—trained to work in gold, silver, bronze, and iron, a specialist in stone and wood, could work with fabrics and purple, blue, and crimson yarn as well as fine linens—and was experienced in all kinds of engraving!*
>
> *How could a half-pagan man be selected for that task? Well, it didn't matter that much. Our faith in Adonai is passed through the mother, and Huram-Abi's mother was faithful to the covenant.*

Antipas had found no consistent answers in his search to support his desire to reject Anthony. As he held up his hands in prayer, he had a strange thought. *Perhaps I am seeking the answer I want to hear—not what God is saying.*

DIODORUS'S OFFICE, THE GYMNASIUM, THE ACROPOLIS

Diodorus continued to teach Cicero's principles of civil

responsibility and Roman social order. "They satisfy the essential requirements of human nature," he stated. "Material, moral, and intellectual problems in the Roman Empire find solutions within these principles."

To Anthony, it sounded as though Diodorus was teaching that the world would become perfect by applying these values.

"Could the empire stay perfect after the death of Augustus Caesar?" he asked with a look of innocence covering his face.

The question intensely annoyed Diodorus. On the one hand, it was above suspicion, a natural follow-up considering the corrupt lives of Tiberius, Caligula, and Nero followed by "The Year of the Four Emperors."[76]

But Anthony's question was a clear challenge to the basic concepts of Cicero, who wanted leaders to be men of right-minded conduct and correct expression. He believed that the demands of right thought and measured action produced a balance in society.

"No," answered Diodorus slowly. "Cicero taught that courage, as a moral and intellectual virtue, is found in its supreme embodiment in a statesman. 'A statesman in the empire will be a man who never thinks of privately gaining wealth at the expense of his province. He makes the good of the governed his sole aim and remembers that the office he holds is a trust. Anything that is a half measure will be shunned.'"

He continued, "Cicero also taught, 'What does the ideal man look like in the Roman Empire? He is kind, affable, and leaves aside his passions. If a magistrate has to punish someone, he is lenient and observes a conscientious goodwill. He is courteous too. Improper cravings, wealth, power, and glory are put aside.' That is the ideal leader."

It was with that statement that Anthony saw the hypocrisy in the whole existing system. His next statement shocked Diodorus. "This is a wonderful description of a person who has the goodwill of the empire as his goal. Could you point me to such a person? I would love to study at his feet."

---

[76] The year AD 69–70 in Rome witnessed political turmoil as three army commanders claimed to be the rightful ruler; Galba, Otho, and Vitellius. Finally, Vespasian, who was leading the siege against Jerusalem, was acknowledged as the next emperor.

Anthony's question elicited a burst of laughter from the seven other men in the group. Diodorus marked it as the moment when he decided to bring about Anthony's destruction.

Imagine the danger if this man stays in the legion teaching soldiers. His questions shred arguments like a sharp, two-edged sword. Yet he has a point. I would like to find the perfect person about whom Cicero wrote, and I, too, would learn from him.... But as for Anthony, I wish the sword that left a scar had gone much deeper.

"Of course, Cicero is talking about an ideal person, not an actual magistrate," Diodorus explained, hiding his vindictive, destructive intention.

Anthony had thrown the schoolmaster off balance; he was not used to such questions from his students.

The next day Diodorus met with the commander of the garrison. "Cassius, I will hold an extra class on January 1. It's the day when all legionaries swear allegiance to Caesar. I will keep Anthony with me, implying he has not learned enough and must take some extra lessons. I'll prepare a challenging class to compare Cicero, Cato, Livy, Virgil, and a few other writers on the topic of 'Being a Good Citizen.'

"This means he will miss the required January 1 Solemn Oath of Loyalty, and he'll be guilty of a grave offense. Afterward, you'll tell him that if he admits to having made mistakes about this business of the Jewish Messiah, then he can return to the garrison next September. He'll continue teaching normally. If he doesn't admit to his errors, you can deal with him through the Roman Army's disciplinary process."

Cassius understood the subtle trap and approved instantly. Danger lay ahead for Anthony.

Chapter 38
Stormy Winds

MARCOS'S VILLA AT KISTHENE

It was January 1, and Trifane felt huge and heavy. She wanted to deliver any day now, not wait until the baby was full-sized. She walked into the kitchen with a question. "Mother, suppose I give up my baby, and then someone adopts the baby. What does the law say about that?"

Cratia stirred the onions and lentils as she answered. "Days on the calendar come and go, but Roman laws stay the same. According to the law on adoption, the father has the right to get his child back after an adoption and raise it as he wishes."

She stopped to let the impact of her statement sink in.

"Or the father can take the baby and give a slave in exchange to the mother if he is generous. Why do you ask, Trifane?" The kitchen was silent, with only the sound of the wooden spoon against the edges of the cooking pot.

Hearing no reply, Cratia continued, "The mother has no legal rights to keep the baby. Trifane, let's not think of these things just now. Here is a nice warm meal on a cold, windy day. Look at the waves against the rocks over there. My! I've never seen big waves like these; look at the foam on the sea! The god of the sea is angry today!"

Trifane felt uncomfortable, and her back hurt. Her breasts were tender too.

Zoticos is a manipulator! I hate him. I do not want my baby to be raised by a Lydian nationalist. I hope it's a boy, but how will I find care for my baby? Who could love my little boy—adopt him and raise him? But if he is adopted, would Zoticos take him and raise him as his child? I need someone who will care for my baby boy. Zoticos must never know a thing about him!

She vowed never to see her lover again. Trifane entered the main room and pulled the chair up beside the door, listening to the howling wind. She opened the door for a few minutes, watching towering waves leap over the lower reaches of the beach. The wind and storm surges pushed the water higher up to the road along the sand, where the waves turned and became tiny rivulets flowing back into the Aegean Sea.

Why did I ever let him take advantage of me? What was my first mistake? I think it was letting him know I cared so much about the festival. He made me feel proud to sit with him in the principal seats of the theater each night for two weeks to see all that entertainment. So he just takes women and showers them with attention? I won't have him!

Her mother came into the room and quickly made her way to the door. "Trifane! What are you doing? Don't let the wind blow through the house like this! Do you want to die from cold and exposure when you have this fine villa to stay in? I've been thinking about the baby. It must be about six weeks until you give birth. We really need to start finding a midwife to help at that time. I'll ask around at the market. Now come into the warm kitchen and eat our noon meal with me. Don't open the door like that again, not during this storm!"

ANTIPAS'S HOME

Antipas's scroll of notes had become a long prayer. He wrote again:

> *Monday, January 1. I have arrived at the life of Ruth, the great-grandmother of David and an ancestor of Yeshua, our Messiah. Tell me how you chose her? When I read her story, I am almost tempted to think Miriam could marry Anthony. Is the word "tempted", or is the right word "tested"?*
>
> *Naomi let her sons marry two women—pagans—of Moab. One of them was named Ruth. But I am not like Naomi. I am trying to protect my granddaughter from committing a sin. Ruth's background was one of worshiping idols. Yet she was respectful to her mother-in-law. And she turned away from her own kind—and her gods—to go to Bethlehem, where her kinsman-redeemer, Boaz, took her in. She became the mother of the line of King David.*

My granddaughter cannot make this decision for herself. As her grandfather, I am responsible for protecting her.

His prayer felt self-righteous tonight. He had a restless sleep as he started the new year.

The next night, on Tuesday, Antipas took more time in his study. The storm that had battered the Aegean coast for two days still blew with fierce winds. Rain now pelted the house. In the middle of a winter storm, he sought comfort in the scriptures once again.

He continued on from the previous night, rereading his notes. He wasn't happy with the tone of what he had written or the depth of his prayer. He turned to another story, the one he had avoided for months. It was the story of a woman named Rahab, a harlot. She helped deliver Jericho into the hands of its enemies, the Hebrews. He felt a growing perplexity as he started to write his prayer.

Tuesday, January 2. God of my fathers, I do not understand. You promised to take our forefathers out of Egypt, and the army of Pharaoh was destroyed. How many miracles in the wilderness did you bring about? Daily provision of manna...sandals not wearing out...finding water in a desert.

When the first battle was being planned against the Canaanites, a pagan woman was there to help the Israelite spies. Why choose a pagan, a prostitute? Why is Rahab listed in the lineage of Yeshua? Why was she permitted to marry into the tribe of Judah? The Scriptures sometimes do not support what I want to believe. I am more confused all the time, and I still don't know which path to take: to let Miriam be married to him or not.

Even after he went to bed, questions continued to disturb his mind.

Is it possible that God would bring a Roman man into our home? Rahab saved the people of Israel. She helped to bring about the destruction of a city of the unrighteous. Anthony... Could he save us from destruction? No! It was his army that destroyed not only the city of the righteous and the righteous people but our place of worship as well!

That night he dreamed of Jerusalem. In his dream, the city burned with bright orange flames. He was running, first up one side street and then down another. There in front of him was all the wheat for the city. He wanted to save the food for the people. The pile of grain started to burn, and he saw the Jewish military leader Simon—happy because he had destroyed the food of his own people!

He woke up, remembering the faces of Simon's men after the city's food had burned. "Now everyone will have to fight the Romans," they screamed at him. Antipas had shouted back, "You are our enemies, every bit as much as the Romans! Why did you burn our food supply?"

I don't know who my friends are...or my enemies. Who can I trust?

He turned over and prayed.

It all happened more than twenty years ago, and it is still alive in my mind, where no one else can see it. Only a few of us remain from the thousands of the faithful in Israel; we were delivered from the destruction of Jerusalem.

MARCOS'S VILLA AT KISTHENE

Going by horseback, Marcos made a brief trip to check on his properties in Kisthene. He wanted to see if the strong winds had caused any damage. A cold blue sky promised some calm days after the storm. "Hail!" he said as he knocked on the villa door. A voice bid him enter, and he pushed open the door of his seaside house.

He looked inside carefully. The lovely young woman he had left in charge four months before lay on one of the couches, eating dried figs. She didn't look the same as the last time he had seen her.

"Don't bother to get up! I'm here to talk to your mother," Marcos exclaimed.

"Mother went next door to see if the wind damaged any of the doors or shutters," Trifane answered without getting up.

"You are..." He looked at her stomach and didn't know what

to say next.

"Yes, I am expecting a baby. I'm due in less than a month, Mother says."

He tried to recover quickly and couldn't. "Have you been well, I mean, have you had any difficulties?"

"Like what?"

"Well, my wife and I had four children. When my wife was pregnant, each time she had trouble every morning. She vomited a lot, and she had to have proper rest."

Trifane clearly remembered Marcos and her joy in tutoring his daughter, the little girl who could watch seagulls endlessly.

"Tomorrow I have to be back in the city council. I help to implement the decisions of the citizens of the city, but today I'm here to see how my properties are after the storms."

"Are the people in the city council your best friends?"

"What an extraordinary, honest question, Trifane! All right, if you want to know, honestly, no, those men are not my close friends. I don't trust men if they are unfaithful to their wives and brag about it at the hot baths. No, my close friends come together in another place."

"Why are those other people your friends, not the ones you work with?"

Her question took him back to Florbella's plight. He had no idea how long he might talk to her or when her mother would come back. Small talk like this with Trifane was interesting. He decided to tell her a story: the time their daughter was healed.

"Remember how you enjoyed tutoring Florbella during the summer?"

"Yes, your daughter is a lovely girl!"

"You were teaching her how to improve her speech, but did she tell you the story of how she completely lost her voice?"

"No, she never told me. What happened?"

"Let me tell you the whole story. Several years ago, before you met Florbella, she was in a dreadful earthquake. We thought we had lost her; the earthquake near Nicomedia caused the seashore to open up, and I lost everyone in my family. My daughter was trapped by rubble, and we couldn't free her. Two days later, another tremor came. The ground moved in a way that she was freed. I was able to grab her and run. Sadly, after that, she could not speak. A spirit held her tongue. In other ways, she was perfectly normal. She spent much of her time watching birds. One day she found a little village close to Pergamum where there were tame pigeons and doves. She made friends in that village, and their kind actions brought her back to normal."

"What do you mean by 'their kind actions'? What kind of people are they?"

"Do you want me to tell you all that happened?"

"Oh, yes, please tell me the whole story. I don't have anything to do these days except wait for my baby to be born. Don't leave out any details please!"

He finished his story before Cratia came back, and Trifane asked, "Please tell me more about the young woman who became a friend to Florbella. What is her name? Where does she live?"

"She lives in that little village I mentioned on the west side of the river, under the shadow of the acropolis. From where she lives, looking up straight ahead, you can see the Altar of Zeus."

"What is the name of the man who is in charge of the village?"

"His name is Antipas, and he is Miriam's grandfather. She's about your age. She is friends with a lame woman who is about to have a child, just like you."

Cratia returned just then. She had found only minor damage to one part of a villa. She was delighted to see Marcos.

Trifane was excited to hear the story that he told. *This may be an answer for my baby. The people in that village genuinely care about others. I will remember this. Miriam is the one who befriended Florbella when she couldn't speak. I trust Marcos. The people in that village don't deceive people...not like Zoticos.*

After he left, she said, "Mother, I just heard about a woman who is almost the same age as me. She sounds like a person who is caring and compassionate. Remember Florbella? Well, this woman, Miriam, helped Florbella start talking again. I think she would know what to do with my baby, whether to keep it or know of a family that would love and care for it."

"What? You've decided already? You don't even know her!"

"I want a safe home for my baby. Marcos said these people changed his whole life. He trusted us to take care of his properties, so I'm going to trust him about Miriam."

THE GARRISON OF PERGAMUM

Anthony reported to Cassius again. The last time he had reported to the garrison, Cassius had said he was too busy.

"Come in, soldier," said the gruff voice of his commander. Anthony entered.

"You did not come on Monday, the first day of January. It is required of all legionaries for your Solemn Oath of Loyalty. Explain yourself!"

"Sir, Diodorus informed me the day would be given over to additional teaching. He said he wanted to compare several authors and what they taught about citizenship. He told me he had talked with you about this. His teaching took the whole day, from early morning up until evening. Do you want a general summary of his teaching?"

"Of course not, soldier! I want to know why you missed the Solemn Oath of Loyalty on January 1. It is compulsory for every legionary in the empire!"

"Sir, you told me to come only on days you had specifically mentioned. That was the arrangement that you required. For months now, I have worked with the staff at the gymnasium, training young men for the Games. That was to be my chief assignment."

"Nothing ever replaces the Solemn Oath of Loyalty! I am still continuing with the investigation into your background. You have a farm, don't you?"

"Yes, I do have a farm, sir. It is in Philippi."

"Where exactly is your farm? Under what circumstances did you get it?"

Anthony realized he may have fallen into a trap. It was evident that Cassius and Diodorus were working together against him. In a flash, his scouting instincts came back. His senses aroused and his mind alert, he looked around for clues.

"The complete record is in the city of Philippi, sir. Ask for the original information from Rome. Special circumstances were involved. As a result of certain actions in Upper Germanica, Legion XXI, the Predators, and Legion XIV were separated." A scroll with unopened seals was on the table, and he had an idea. "My situation was a direct order from the emperor."

Cassius's face looked threatening, but the mention of Domitian at the end of Anthony's explanation was unexpected.

This soldier's story is apparently more complex than I thought. If his orders came from the emperor, that complicates my plans considerably. I don't want anything hazardous. I need to be very careful. Is something hidden in the connection between this soldier and his legion? Am I dealing with a soldier who has influence? If so, how do I handle him? It has become dangerous to delve into any issue in which Domitian is involved.

In his frustration, Cassius yelled for the clerk in the next room to come and take notes. "I will investigate this situation so I can know how to determine your future association with the army! I want you to tell this clerk any important details about your previous cohort and events in Philippi after you were wounded. Continue to report to both Diodorus and to me. Otherwise, I will send for you when I need to see you."

ANTIPAS'S HOME

Antipas had been writing his thoughts down for more than four months. In his search for answers, he pulled out scrolls from ten years earlier. They were written with small, neat letters. He looked at them again and realized how much larger his writing had become. Before starting his prayers, he read over his previous entries, noting each date. He was meditating on the history of his heroes, and he had come to Hezekiah. That king had celebrated Passover, Judah's greatest feast.

However, Hezekiah celebrated one month later than Moses mandated, and it was not a sin! Men from Ephraim, Manasseh, Issachar, and Zebulon came to Jerusalem, and even though they had not been adequately consecrated, they were given permission to participate in the Passover! As if that were not enough, "even aliens participated." He read the words again and again. "May the Lord, who is good, pardon everyone who sets his heart on seeking God—the Lord, the God of his fathers—even if he is not clean according to the rules of the sanctuary."[77]

His entries were becoming shorter. Partly it was because his eyesight was beginning to fail him and partly because the questions kept finding answers that were unexpected and surprising. Tonight, his prayer was condensed into a few words.

---

[77] 2 Chronicles 30:18–20

Tuesday, February 6. Hezekiah had the people celebrate during the second, not the first month, and that wasn't a sin. Why didn't Hezekiah require people to act precisely as the law said? Please show me how men who were not correctly consecrated could celebrate the Passover. And how could even aliens participate? Why did King Hezekiah allow that? Surely he was disobedient in that detail. And what, if anything, does this have to do with Anthony?

Chapter 39
Chrysa, the Golden One

MARCOS'S VILLA AT KISTHENE

Once again, a winter storm battered the coast. Winds howled, pushing at doors and rattling the tightly sealed shutters.

Late in the afternoon, Trifane went into labor. She felt her first contraction as she watched the driving rain and the branches of trees bending in the wind. The storm gradually subsided as her contractions grew more intense. She lay on the couch in pain, and the delivery turned out to be long and difficult. Cratia had found a local midwife in the village of Kisthene who came to help. Trifane screamed during the intermittent pains that lasted throughout the night, but she rejoiced because the end of her long isolation in Kisthene brought her a new life.

"It's a girl, born on February 8!" exclaimed Cratia joyfully to her daughter.

Trifane wanted to give a name to her baby daughter that would help her remember the last difficult hours, so she tried to think of a name that meant "daughter of my pain" or "daughter of the storm."

The midwife came back from the kitchen, where she had opened the window's shutters. Cratia looked to the east and came quickly back to her daughter to describe what she had seen.

"It is a good omen! The morning sun is just coming up. It's a glorious sunrise after yesterday's storm. The sky is deep blue, and two bands of yellow clouds overflow with golden hope. The sun is shining with long shafts of yellow light coming through layers of clouds. I've never seen a lovelier sunrise than this in my whole life! And to the west, the band of clouds is pink, and the sea is growing calm."

Trifane held her precious daughter and realized that the light had just given her baby a name. *"Chrysa," the "Golden One." You are my "Daughter of the Golden Dawn," born after a big storm in my life. I will recover and learn to trust while your life is only starting. Precious one, may you bring a golden dawn to many people.*

"Her name is Chrysa," Trifane pronounced. "Do you think we can find a young mother around here who would like to earn some money by taking her into Pergamum? She is to take my baby to that family that I told you about that lives in the village across the valley from the Altar of Zeus."

ANTIPAS'S SHOP IN THE LOWER AGORA, THE ACROPOLIS

Anthony went to Miriam's shop to talk with her. "Hail, Miriam. I am so delighted to find you here. How is your grandfather?" he asked.

"Not happy," she said. "He is in a sour mood every day, he is not eating well, and he sometimes stays in his library and leaves all the work for Onias to do. Grandpa seldom checks into the glassmaking work anymore, and that's unusual. He sends Onias everywhere, even to the agora to restock the shops. Something is keeping him up every night, and I believe it's about us. I also think that's good news because if he were going to say no, he would have said it long ago. I know him, so don't be discouraged, Anthony. God is working to bring us together."

ANTIPAS'S HOME

Antipas had to make a choice, so tonight he decided to write down all the reasons why he could not accept Anthony into the Ben Shelah family. He had finally found the way to add up the columns of pluses and minuses. The minus column held sway on every question. He looked over the list several times after he had written it and realized he could never accept Anthony.

ANTIPAS'S VILLAGE

A knock at the front door brought Miriam from the kitchen. She opened the small shutter on the main door and looked out. The driver of the wagon bringing sand from the seashore for the glass workshop stood at the door with a stranger.

She opened the door with a puzzled look. "Do you want to see my grandfather?" she asked. "He is in the library right now."

The driver of the wagon said, "No, this man found me while I was getting sand, and he learned that I was from the village here. He has a message to deliver to you."

The stranger looked around nervously and said, "There is a woman who knows that you are a kind person. A little baby is coming, but you must not ask where it came from. The day after tomorrow, at high noon, I will leave a baby girl wrapped in a white blanket near the city dump. You have to go there. A woman will be with me, but she is not the mother. She is going to nurse the baby while we come to the city. The mother cannot keep her, and she wants you to care for it and find it a good home. Please do not ask any questions."

With that, the man turned and quickly walked back to the road toward Pergamum without even confirming that she would agree to come.

Miriam had no idea what to do with this news. In a few months, she would have her twenty-sixth birthday. *A baby is being given to me? Who would abandon a baby? What will I do with a baby? Arpoxa delivered her baby only a few days ago, and she is so happy about their son. But me? I'm not married! What will I do with an abandoned baby?*

Miriam continued to watch with her mouth open, and her body was paralyzed by her thoughts as the man retreated down the lane to River Road.

ANTIPAS'S HOME

Antipas wondered why his granddaughter was so quiet at supper. She said she wasn't feeling well and excused herself from the table. *Maybe Miriam is sick from all the work or because of something she ate.*

In his library, he turned to the new scrolls. One manuscript had come to him only recently. He discovered the passage Luke had written about the first convert to the Messiah from outside of the small circle of Jewish hearers. Antipas read Luke's account of Cornelius, a Roman centurion who had belonged to the Italian Regiment. [78]

Something very deep inside of Antipas began to break apart as he read the passage a second time. He lost his breath for a moment. He picked up his quill, and his hand was almost unable

---

[78] Acts 10:1-48

to keep up with the flow of ideas leaping from his mind. Something within his spirit had uncovered a deep spring. Ideas bubbled up that he had never considered before. He squinted, taking a long time to write with large letters.

Friday, February 9. The story about Cornelius breaks all my traditions. It's a story both attractive and repulsive. It shows that you are a God who knows the hearts of believers as well as unbelievers, providing a way for their salvation. However, it leaves me uncomfortable! That man was one of the first Gentiles to come to faith in Messiah—a Roman, a centurion!

What keeps Anthony and Miriam apart? Is it the will of the God of Abraham? Or is it the will of Antipas? Or is it the tradition of the elders?

But what if a tradition doesn't always make sense? If I examine everything honestly, many things in our past are not right. For example, that civil war about who would control the temple during the Roman siege didn't make sense. John of Gischala and Simon Ben Giora fought against each other, and everyone else fought against them. None of that was right, yet their convictions were built on our traditions. No one could even question John or Simon. In the end, both caused death to come to my family!

Which of the elders of the synagogue is willing to extend friendship or fellowship? Who loves the people I love? None! Why? Because of the traditions of the elders! Could it be that I am doing to Anthony what the elders of the congregation did to me? Is the Lord of Abraham, Isaac, and Jacob leading me on a new path? What is the right path? Yeshua Messiah spoke of the law of love. Have our traditions become more important than mercy?

However, if we don't retain all our old traditions, which ones can we let go of and still be men of righteousness? I am an old man. How could I learn to walk a new path? This would be a hidden path, hard to find. Yet am I not creating a new tradition by bringing people together in a village from so many different backgrounds?

MARCOS'S VILLA AT KISTHENE

Two weeks had gone by since the baby had been born, and Trifane left the door where she had been standing and watching the wagon as it moved slowly down the road beside the long, straight beach. She went to her room to get the parchment. It was time to burn it. She wanted to be rid of the memory of Zoticos.

"Mother, have you seen the parchment I brought from the library?"

"Yes," answered Cratia, "I took it."

"I was going to burn it! Why did you take it?"

"I thought it was wrong to give your baby to someone without them knowing her name."

"Why did you need that old parchment?"

"It was close at hand, so I cut off a piece and wrote her name on it with the day she was born. I hope you don't mind. I tucked it inside the little blanket I knitted for the baby."

"No, I'm sure it will be all right. The people in the village will know her by her real name. Thank you, Mother. That was very thoughtful."

ANTIPAS'S VILLAGE

Miriam knew her grandfather would be surprised, but she could never have anticipated the look on his face. "I can't go to the shop at noon to take over from Nikasa. Can you get someone else to go there?"

"Why? What is happening?" he asked at breakfast.

"When the sun is at the top of the sky, I'm going to get a baby."

He could not swallow his bread. He looked up with an expression on his face she had never seen before. "What? You are going to have a baby?"

"I did not say I was going to have a baby. I said, 'I am going to get a baby.'"

He stared at her blankly. She could not remember the last time he had nothing to say, but finally he blurted out, "Who is giving a baby to you?"

"I don't know. It's a baby coming from another city. The mother can't care for it. Somehow they heard about our village and sent a messenger to tell me it was coming."

"What will you do with it?"

"We'll bring the baby home, and then we'll find someone to

adopt it."

"Lord of the universe, as if we don't have enough problems right now, and now you bring me this news. A baby!" Antipas groaned and then started to laugh.

Miriam had to pass through the mighty gates that guarded the eastern entrance to get to the edge of the city. In the past, these tall structures controlled the traffic into and out of the city. She crossed over a bridge spanning the Selinos River. Close to the river, Miriam found the dump.

She was standing near the dump area when a driver came with two horses pulling a wagon. Sitting beside the driver was a woman with a shawl over her head. She gave a little bundle to the driver then carefully climbed down from the wagon and walked around to the side where the driver sat. He held the reins with one hand, and the horses neighed and tossed their heads. Pulling her scarf closely over her head so no one could see her face, the woman took the bundle from the driver and walked to the edge of the trash dump.

Miriam's heart pounded. She held both hands to her chest.

Would anyone actually give a baby away like this? I have heard of this happening before—when girls take a baby to the edge of the forest—but here I am watching it happen. And I'm supposed to pick it up, this baby that is a problem created by adults. I'm going to make sure that this baby grows up in a home where it will be loved and accepted.

She pushed the thoughts out of her mind to concentrate on what was happening. The woman climbed back onto the wagon. Miriam waved. The woman and the driver both waved in recognition, and the horses moved back onto the main road connecting Pergamum with the cities to the east and the shorelines to the north.

She ran to the little bundle and gently took it in her arms. The tiny girl was sleeping soundly.

What a sweet face! Oh, look at her little fist! And what lovely, soft black hair!

The baby stirred but continued sleeping. A little piece of parchment dropped out from inside the blanket. She read, "Her name is Chrysa, the Golden One. She was born on February 8. She is two weeks old." Miriam was delighted to know the baby's name and birth date.

Miriam took the baby in her arms. In her excitement, she wanted to run but forced herself to go slowly, carefully back through the massive Eastern Gate where several soldiers were on guard, watching travelers going in and out of the city. Many other young women walked along, some carrying a baby in the same way. Miriam was just another woman holding a young child.

"Look, Grandfather! It's a girl. Her name is Chrysa! Someone wrote her name on a parchment for classes in the gymnasium where Anthony teaches."

Antipas felt both shock and worry. He tried not to show it. "Well, at least we know what the mother wanted to call this child."

"In the meantime, I'm going to care for this baby," Miriam declared. "Here, you hold her, and see what a lovely little creature just came into our home!"

The old man held the baby girl for a few minutes and gave her back to Miriam. "Well, Chrysa, welcome here. You have a home with us until we can find a proper place for you."

Suddenly Antipas frowned. A new thought hit him.

What will we do with a baby in this home? People will begin to gossip about Miriam and Anthony even though they would be completely wrong! Lord Almighty, have mercy! People will whisper that Miriam and Anthony have had a child, causing our family name to be dishonored in Pergamum. This is even worse than...

Nothing could be worse than the timing of the arrival of this baby. At night he wrote in his scroll:

Saturday, February 24. Something unexpected happened today....

He squeezed his eyes, trying to think of something, anything, to express his surprise and concern over what others might think. Try as he might, he could not write anything else, and he had no words in prayer. He said the words over and over.

Something unexpected...

Chapter 40
Antipas's Reply

THE CAVE, ANTIPAS'S VILLAGE

On Sunday, Antipas knew what to do. He would announce the baby's arrival to everyone in the Household of Faith meeting to ensure that all had been told. This would also take care of the people who attended from outside the village.

Antipas drew a deep breath. "I have one more thing to tell you during the time set aside for announcements. Most of you already know that a child came to us yesterday. Children are a gift from the Lord, and this one seems to have fallen from heaven."

People laughed because the word had already circulated. "It is the Lord who puts children in families. I do not know whose child she is, but this baby will be staying with us until a home can be found. The child was left in the care of my granddaughter, Miriam. She has found a wet nurse for the baby; Arpoxa will help with the feeding.

"This child must have come from one of the nearby villages, and I believe that God Almighty brought this baby to us to care for. If you know of a home that wants a baby, someone praying for a child or a family that cannot have children, let me know."

Everyone knew that this year Antipas could not afford to buy more slaves or lend money to needy families. Still, he continued to show great love to people, and he was even willing to take in an unwanted baby.

The people left for their homes with a much lighter step after the Holy Meal. Seeing love in action made it easier to talk about God loving other people. However, some still had difficulty putting the worship of Greek gods behind them. Actions based on selfless love touched these people deeply. Women debated who would be willing to take in a baby that had been left at a trash dump. One woman said, "I'd take her for myself if she had been left at the edge of the forest. But she was left in a dirty place, where ashes and broken pots cover the land; this baby is sure to bring bad luck. Who would want to bring her up?"

ANTIPAS'S HOME

As they entered their house, Antipas asked, "Miriam, what do you see in Anthony?"

He had not talked with this degree of openness for many weeks, and she decided it would be best to respond in the same way. "I see dignity in him. He has an inner strength I have not often seen before in a man. He has good character and courage."

Antipas wanted to pursue the topic more closely. "Some women say the same thing and five years later exclaim, 'He's rot in my bones!' Anthony might become 'rot in your bones.'" It was a common expression referring to unhappy marriages.

"No, he teaches people well. He wants to learn. He is gentle."

"I don't understand how you can say that." Antipas didn't want easy answers, and she had no answer to his next question. "How can a legionary be 'gentle'?"

"I think he has a lot of self-discipline."

"How do we know he is sincere? Would he fall back on his word?"

Miriam was ready for this objection. "He says he wants to fear the Lord. He's been put out of the military camp. Remember what happened at the beginning of the year? His garrison commander and the gymnasium director played a very deceitful trick on him, causing him to be absent from the soldiers' loyalty ceremony."

"Would you be fulfilled in a home with him?"

"Yes, I would." Her voice was calm and assured, but her heart was pounding, wondering why he was asking her this.

"But how can I let you marry him? Consider who he is! I should have been able to recommend him to you from the beginning. This was never the way it was done in my home in Alexandria! And his father fought against our armies in Jerusalem!"

"Grandpa, you taught me marriage is holy. The first words in scripture after creation were about God bringing a man and a woman together."

Antipas was not ready to stop arguing. "Yes, but after the Garden, the first story is about a murder and death. I want to know this: Does he get angry? How many men has Anthony killed? How could I live with myself if I let you marry a military man who didn't treat you well? And I know my brothers. They would say you married the enemy!"

"You will see, Grandpa," she said. "He is not the enemy. He is a true friend."

THE CITY COUNCIL

Lydia-Naq was one of the organizers of a meeting in the city council to discuss the future of the city without Antipas. At a previous meeting, she had convinced the participants that Antipas was a danger to the future of the city. She argued that his setting slaves free would eventually encourage other slaves in the city to rebel. Today the specific means were to be decided for bringing him before the Roman authorities.

By the end of the discussion, an agreement had been reached. Antipas would be called before the city leaders in two meetings. Since he had spoken against all the temples and gods, he should face each temple's leader in his first appearance. The high priest of the Temple of Dionysius said, "I want the first event to take place in the New Theater."

In the second event, Lydia-Naq asked that Antipas be required to pay his taxes and publicly declare, as a non-Jew, "Caesar is lord and god." Damon said, "This will take place in the amphitheater. Leave it to me to organize it."

The only detail not clear to everyone was the date. Most argued for May 1, but that decision was left to the goddess of fortune. A sacrifice would be made later and the liver of the animal taken out. One of the priests would determine the message from the goddess, which would indicate the most suitable date for Antipas to be formally judged.

Marcos kept mental notes on all these conversations, saying nothing and keeping a blank face as the decisions were reached.

ANTIPAS'S HOME

Early on Monday morning, Marcos arrived in haste at the village storehouse and asked Onias about Antipas's whereabouts. "I need to talk to him now! It is very urgent."

"He is coming back soon from talking to our shepherds."

Onias was curious about his haste, but he wouldn't say any

more than "I will wait for him in his library. It's urgent."

When Antipas did return, he assumed that Marcos wanted to talk to him about the will. He was glad to see a friend. "Hail! Welcome!" he said cheerfully, but the lawyer's expression told him that this was urgent and serious.

"Antipas, my news is not good. I attended a meeting at the city council last night. The temple priests are demanding to have you removed from the city. As a group, they are calling for a formal confrontation. The priestess Lydia-Naq is the most vocal antagonist moving them to action. She is the mother of Diotrephes. He seems to be making good on his threat to avenge his dismissal from your classes. There is talk of a trial by the temple priests. Also, on the last day of the Feast of Zeus, Lydia-Naq is asking that you be called forward to pay your taxes in public as a common citizen. That alone will cause a problem because of the required oath to the emperor."

"And if I don't..."

"What are the punishments that might be given if you don't comply? They most likely would take away your property. So confiscation of property or possibly banishment. In the city council, I heard that Ephesus is asking Domitian to punish Elder John with deportation to Patmos. Our city council hasn't decided what to do with you, but all of them are concerned about the growing number of people who want to know more about what you believe. They fear your influence, and they would prefer you to be dead."

Antipas looked at him with compassion. "I am sorry that you had a hard message to convey. It must be difficult for you to say such things to an old man like me."

Marcos stared, wondering how Antipas could have peace when he had just received news of a possible death sentence. Antipas was not outwardly afraid.

THE CAVE, ANTIPAS'S VILLAGE

Antipas realized his life might be cut short at any time, so every day counted. Even before sunup, people flocked to the cave, which was now full of people standing around the edges and by the doors and windows. The news of the love shown by these people to one another was enough to awaken slaves, merchants, millers, bakers, leather workers, and masons early in the morning.

He turned to one of the most difficult of the psalms. "How blessed it is when there is unity between the brothers."[79]

He taught them the psalm and how it spoke of unity and division. "I want you to love one another. Water and oil cannot mix, yet in this psalm, unity is compared to their coming together. Why water and why oil? Oil is symbolic of Jerusalem. Imagine the scene. The new high priest is about to be anointed, so this is a daytime scene full of festivity, noise, gladness, and jubilation. The oil is poured onto the head of the new high priest, and he will hold that title for the rest of his life, or until he is fifty years old. It is a once-in-a-lifetime celebration for most people. A lot of you were never there, so let me describe it for you."

Antipas talked about the temple and the reason that Israel had a high priest. He led them slowly through all the duties required in the temple.

"The second scene in the psalm comes from the top of a mountain. It's a night scene, speaking of dew. So much moisture falls there at night that the land does not need rain. The dew is dense, and sheep eating the grass in the morning have enough water to stay healthy.

"So we have one scene that takes place during the day followed by a picture of a peaceful night. One is full of noisy worshipers; the other is quiet, with sheep sleeping in the fields. You are witnessing two remarkable events. The first is on Mount Zion, in the south of our homeland, called Judah. The other happens on Mount Hermon, in the north, where ten of our twelve tribes lived.

"Compare them further. Oil covers the beard of the priest. His responsibility is to the people, who act like sheep. The second part talks about sheep, who sometimes act like people."

People chuckled because Antipas often compared them to sheep.

"King David had come through a civil war, and now he wanted people to live in peace. Here is the main point: Oil and water do mix but only if you continually keep stirring them! Typically, people separate. We all know how small arguments result in angry feelings and finally in sharp divisions. That was true of our

_____

[79] Psalm 133

history—ten tribes in the north and two in the south.

"However, under the new covenant, we share our resources and our ideals in one another's best interests. The Holy Spirit unites us though we spring from various languages and tribes. It no longer matters what our families or traditions might have been.

"God gives unity as a gift. Unity comes down mysteriously, like the manna that came from heaven. Harmony is something precious. Yeshua Messiah showed us the way to live together. But better than being shaken about, as in a bottle, we actively serve one another and love one another.

"Dew forms at night. It arrives silently. Like dew, we can't see agape love coming down. It's better than manna because it allows us to forgive one another when little arguments begin.

"We are bound by this covenant. Our unity comes from sharing the same beliefs. We keep the covenant more easily when we remember that Yeshua promised to return. We should act, believing his return could happen at any time."

His friends did not know it, but Antipas was starting to prepare those who remained at the Household of Faith for whatever was going to happen to him.

Last year they had acted out the experiences of the Exodus at the curve in the river. This year they would be gathered in the cave with lamps, in the same way that the Jewish families huddled together in their homes when the Angel of Death passed over their houses. Their homes were safe because of the blood of the lamb smeared on the doorposts. This was another way of presenting the story, making it real to them.

"Now I will tell you a story of betrayal. I want to tell you about one of Yeshua's followers who betrayed him to the temple authorities. We have already learned that some of those who had been following him 'turned back and no longer went about with him.' Yeshua's group got smaller as people started to fall away."

Antipas asked, "Remember last month when we celebrated the Feast of Purim? That celebration marks the time when God used Esther to rescue His people from danger. She was willing to take a risk at the right time. Yet at other times, the Lord did not save people. Whatever happened then, or whatever happens now, Adonai is Lord.

"This year, we will keep the Passover and the Feast of

Unleavened Bread differently. During this week, I will not be giving individual classes in the evenings and neither will Onias. Instead, we will share in each other's homes; it will help develop the sense of community and make you strong. You will eat meals with people you don't normally spend time with. For the next eight days, I want you to share in hospitality. Take in people you don't know well. Learn to trust one another. What I've said to you before, I say again: Love one another."

ANTIPAS'S HOME

That night as he pondered the Scriptures after the service, a single sentence came back to him.

It was from the passage he had read early in the morning. Because it spoke so deeply to him, he wanted to avoid it as a basis for his decision, but now it had him pacing from one end of his library to the other.

He froze in mid-step, the words coming back to him: "Let no foreigner who has bound himself to the Lord say, 'The Lord will surely exclude me from the people.'"[80]

> *Wednesday, March 21. Here is the answer! I thought of Anthony as my enemy because he is a soldier. Aren't all Romans beyond God's grace? But does a person's profession exclude him from the covenant? Israel was to love aliens if they followed God. Lord Almighty, I have an alien in our midst, and he wants to follow Yeshua. You alone could make this scout instructor to be an instructor of your Law. Anthony, you are the alien I am ready to love, but I have one final test.*

He did not write anything else but lay awake thinking for a long time.

The next morning, Antipas was much closer to a sound decision. He sent one of the village boys to the gymnasium to ask Anthony to come see him. Word came back by the same messenger saying that Anthony would come to the village mid-afternoon after finishing at the baths. He found Antipas alone at

---

[80] Isaiah 56:3

home, and they went into the library.

"Have you ever worshiped an idol made by human hands?" Antipas asked.

Anthony searched his memories. "No, my mother had no interest in images. After she left my father and before she died in Rome, she became a follower of Yeshua Messiah. My father rejected Roman and Greek gods as simply stories. He told me once, 'I go to many places and find every city and town has its own god, each claiming to be more powerful than others. How can any one of them be more powerful than all the others?' He gave it all up. When he was excited, he used the expression 'By Jupiter!' as did most soldiers.

"I respect the glory, the majesty, and the power of Rome and the empire. As you know, I have to study Cicero and all the other writers of ancient Rome right now. No one can live up to the virtues they taught, because the darkness in the human heart prevents it. Rebellion and greed come into hearts and undermine the best ideals of Rome. Cicero does not grip me. Your Scriptures do. I have not found truth anywhere else."

Antipas had his answer. He would take one more night to sleep on it before acting on his decision.

On the following Monday, Antipas asked Anthony to come for supper. When he arrived, Miriam was directing the preparations for the meal. She looked lovely with her hair done up and her light blue prayer shawl partially covering her braids. They settled in to eat with Antipas reclining on the center couch. Miriam rested her head on the couch to Antipas's right. Anthony took his place on the left couch, breathing in the fragrance of her green olive soap.

At one point, Anthony tried to form the words with his mouth: *Why does he want us here with him for supper?* However, Miriam couldn't understand what he wanted to say.

While the food was being served, Antipas spoke with a glad heart. "Anthony, I have canceled tonight's Monday evening instruction that you usually attend. We will meet again with Marcos and the others on Wednesday. I needed a day to think. I've been pondering this question: What keeps peoples, nations, and languages apart?

"Last year, in September, you came to talk to me, asking me to allow your marriage. I needed to search my own heart. For months I have searched, trying to justify why I did not want you two to be joined together. Hence, every night I came before the Almighty, and I wrote my ideas to keep track of what I was learning.

"My problem was this: I freed slaves who before were strangers but who have now become part of our village. I loved these people in a general way, but I have to admit that I seldom trusted them. In my personality, I have a need to be in control of everything. But I found that sometimes I had taken the Almighty's place, seeking to keep everything according to my ideals. I wanted everything to be perfect.

"Your request to get married upset my attempts to control my little world. It was something that I had not anticipated, and it made me uncomfortable. I did not want you, a Roman soldier, to become part of my family. It upset everything in my upbringing. I would have said no if I had to give an answer when you asked me. It has taken me many months to explore my heart and my motives.

"Anthony, when you said, 'I will wait for your answer,' that struck me. You did not try to put yourself in a position of strength as other Roman soldiers do. You showed more humility to me than I deserved, and it gave me time to consider. As I took my time of meditation every night before sleeping, I saw changes the Almighty was producing inside of me.

"Let me tell you something as I open my heart to you both. My greatest weakness has been deep fears that I have kept hidden inside. I did not want to die like the Jews did in the fires of Alexandria or the destruction of Jerusalem. All my life, I've feared fires. Anything I could do to excel and be noticed, that is what I did. This zeal made me a successful businessman. I developed my property into a village with all these houses for the people we keep busy. Over a hundred people live in our village now. Over a hundred fifty people attend our gatherings in the cave, and I realize now that this was as much a business success as a success in pursuing God's purposes for my relationships.

"I came to realize it was fear keeping me from saying yes to your request to be married. I was afraid of what my brothers would say, especially Daniel and Jonathan. They caused me much trouble many years ago, and I didn't want them to come down hard again. I was afraid of what the men and women in the congregation would say to me or about me. I was afraid, most of all, that I would violate our covenant in some way. God wants pure lives. However, his mercy extends to the ungodly, to the non-Jew, and to the humble in heart."

Miriam looked at Anthony, and her eyes were big and round. Everything her grandfather had said in his lengthy introduction encouraged her, giving her hope that he would accept their love for each other and agree to their marriage. Her mouth was open, and she raised her hand to cover her lips, hoping she knew what was coming next.

"I could never agree to something until I looked at all the angles, and after doing that, I found that first of all, I had to change. Of course, I never stopped thinking about your request. I watched you to see what your attitude would be. I tried to make you lose interest by withholding consent. Then I tried to find every reason possible to say no, but as I prayed, the Holy One told me through his scriptures to love you."

It was a long speech, and he didn't know how to finish.

Miriam was no longer lying on her side on the couch. She was sitting straight up, her hands clenched in tight fists over her chest, ready for her grandfather to say he approved of their love for each other. She looked at Anthony, and the sparkle in his eyes told her he was also in a moment of suspense.

"So the request you made to me has an answer. Yes, I want you, Miriam, to be married to Anthony. As your grandfather, I choose to make this match. I will ask the Almighty to bless you and to give you peace."

They looked at each other in joy-filled amazement. Antipas wasn't finished talking yet. To make his decision, he first had to expose his deepest fears, the dread born in him when the pogrom consumed his three sisters. The old man was not just giving them his permission. He admitted his anxiety of the opinions of others and what the Romans, or Jews, or anyone, could do to him. By addressing his qualms, he had gained power over his deep, hidden apprehensions.

"Anthony, I have a very special place in my heart for you. I saw in you everything I wanted in a son, but the problem was that you are a legionary! You represented my enemies, Roman soldiers, those who destroyed my city and my history.

"However, I have to be honest and say it was the Roman

soldiers who saved me when I submitted to them. My nephews are dead because of Roman soldiers and because of Jewish soldiers. Jews, Greeks, and Romans—all have been my friends and, at times, my enemies. But you never personally hurt me. Instead, you showed respect and consideration. You probably have more self-discipline than I have, Anthony. You've done nothing but good since I met you. I asked Marcos and the others about you at the Monday and Wednesday group.

"Now, why am I talking so much about myself? I had bitterness and anger in my life, but God has been working in this heart for months, for years actually, to take them away. My life and outlook have been changed. The last thing you want to know is all this about me. You just want me to say, 'Yes, you will be married.' That is what you wanted to hear, not all the reasons why I'm saying yes."

Anthony could hardly believe the change in Antipas. Miriam's eyes flooded with tears as Antipas talked. Her heart leaped hearing her grandfather speak this way. She had seen the changes that had been taking place in him. He had chosen the hard path, the painful narrow way, which meant opening his deepest fears to them.

The pent-up grief and stress gave way as he confessed to Anthony that he now fully accepted him. He stood up with his arms outstretched, and Anthony came slowly to hug the old man. Miriam ran with him into her grandfather's arms. She put her face in his shoulder and hugged him.

I am sixty-six years old. What is the matter with me that I am crying? I know I have done the right thing. Last night I read that our Messiah has come to the scattered children of God to bring them together to make them one.[81] *The wall of division is broken down. My, Anthony is strong, so big! God, make him a good husband for Miriam.*

After his long speech, the meal was cooling off, so Antipas asked the servants to reheat the food. As they waited to be served again, Miriam thought of many questions that had immediately become relevant.

"Have you thought about a wedding, Grandpa? What about Chrysa? Do you think we could adopt the baby? What if another

---

[81] John 11:52

family wants to adopt her?"

Antipas laughed. "I've said enough for one night, Miriam. No more decisions tonight!"

He did not even go to his library after Anthony had left. Love was replacing his worries. Trepidation and panic were being lifted, and he sensed deep peace. Now instead of anxiety causing him to stay awake, he had many new activities to plan.

I will ask Onias to invite everyone in the establishment to the meeting on Saturday evening.

THE CAVE, ANTIPAS'S VILLAGE

Before going to the service, Antipas read from the scroll again to visit the passage that had allowed him to see the mercy of God.

"Let no foreigner who has bound himself to the Lord say, 'The Lord will surely exclude me from his people...and foreigners who bind themselves to the Lord, to serve him, to love the name of the Lord and to worship him, all who keep the Sabbath without desecrating it and who hold fast to my covenant: these I will bring to my holy mountain and give them joy in my house of prayer. My house will be called a house of prayer for all nations.'"[82]

As the evening was ending, he held up his hands before the group and said, "Tonight I have an announcement."

He called Anthony and Miriam to the front, and he took off his cloak, placing it over their shoulders as they stood side by side. They faced the group. Miriam's face was radiant, and Anthony smiled broadly. Antipas stood back and viewed the couple standing before him.

This is a faint sketch compared to the beautiful moment when we were covered by the wedding canopy. I was nineteen, betrothed to Ruth. Our engagement lasted a year, and all our family members gathered. The Ben Shelah clan was to be joined to the Ben Caleb family. What discussions! Families harping on every detail! Weeks of preparation! Opinions on everything! Those ways are lost, gone forever. I can never introduce the beauty of my traditions to Pergamum.

He rested his hands upon Anthony's shoulders. *A Roman, a soldier, will marry into my family. Love that comes from on high changes us. I am being changed.*

---

[82] Isaiah 56:3–7

He explained a Jewish betrothal to everyone. The bride-to-be was now promised in a solemn commitment by him as her grandfather to Anthony, there being no father to give her away. For Romans, this was the *spondee,* the formal declaration of intent of marriage, and in the law of Pergamum, she was now *sponsa,* a promised one, an engaged one.

Anthony took a slim ring from his pocket and put it on the third finger of her left hand. He gave her a nose ring and two matching earrings as well. Then he took a cord and wound it around his neck. He twisted it and made a loop that he placed over her neck. The symbol of eternity bound them together, joining them in hope. "I vow to be joined to her forever, just as this cord has no beginning and no end."

Anthony looked at Miriam and ignored the people around him. He concentrated on her soft beauty and the many events that had brought them to this time.

I count Rome as my family home. But here in Pergamum I found someone to whom I will be devoted all my life. Something from each place will be combined to form our home.

The people rose from where they were seated on the carpets and swarmed toward them. Ateas and Arpoxa beamed with joy for them. Marcos and Marcella waited until the crowd of well-wishers had dropped off, and then they approached them. Anthony and Miriam were engaged and accepted by all the people in the Household of Faith.

At home, Miriam hugged her grandfather and wiped away a tear. "My betrothal! The fear that I had of being left as an orphan is gone."

Chapter 41
Hopes and Fears

LYDIA-NAQ'S HOME, THE ACROPOLIS

That same evening, Lydia-Naq called her son and brother together for a meeting. "Diotrephes, my son, you must tell your uncle what you know about the atheists. They must be put to shame."

"Uncle Zoticos," Diotrephes began, "since I was expelled from the leader's classes, I have heard strange things about the Household of Faith. This year they cannot buy any more slaves because business has been bad for the Jewish man.

"I also learned that the Roman soldier who attended meetings there, Anthony, has angered the garrison's commander. He was required to participate in the classes of the gymnasium headmaster. Diodorus is teaching men a course on Roman civics, but he has not been able to change Anthony's beliefs. Diodorus told me two days ago that he cannot get this legionary to value Rome's high ideals.

"Recently I heard from my informant, Yorick. He says that a baby girl was taken in by the people of the village. Of course, many families get rid of their babies, especially girl babies. Usually they are taken to the edge of the forest. However, Miriam says that she found this baby at the edge of the city's trash dump.

"Now, this is what makes it worse. News about saving a baby circulates quickly among poor people in the city. People already talk about them: the healing of a little girl that couldn't talk, the freeing of slaves for no good reason, and loans being made to people with no interest being charged. These people built a house for a widow after she lost it in a fire. Atheists are helping out widows and not expecting anything in return. Poor people who have nothing can only dream of riches and love. Antipas and his dangerous atheistic teaching may delude them to demand more from the city."

Zoticos frowned. "What do you think is the most dangerous thing going on?"

"It's their teaching, Uncle Zoticos. I was there for almost six months. When Antipas teaches about this Messiah, he gives people false hope, telling them they will live forever and that they should not be afraid of death."

Lydia-Naq smiled at her son. "Thank you for explaining it so well to your uncle. Now hear me. I intend that Antipas will be dead. These atheists have no other leader in Pergamum. Their group will die out when he's gone. The army repeats the phrase, 'Eliminate the commander, and you will have scattered the enemy.' We will destroy their leader, and everyone in that little village will be scattered."

Lydia-Naq then changed the subject by giving her son some important news. "I heard some interesting information today that is also an opportunity for you, my son," she said. "News came from Sardis, from the biggest and most famous of all the schools. Five teachers are there who lecture students in history. A position has opened to supervise the Department of History. I will immediately make an offering to Zeus because I want to recommend you for taking that job in Sardis. You have the qualifications, and I think I have enough influence to get you appointed there."

Diotrephes grinned. He was ready for anything, especially a promotion!

"If I can get you into that position, my son, I will want you to keep two purposes in mind. First, influence the education in Sardis to be along the lines your uncle has been teaching here. That is, encourage citizens to speak Lydian again and restore our ancient ways.

"Second, find a way to infiltrate a group called the God-fearers that I've heard exists in Sardis, where followers of their Messiah gather in that city. You know enough of Antipas's teaching to fit in there. Who knows what Zeus would have you do in Sardis?"

ANTIPAS'S HOME

Marcos called on Antipas early Saturday morning. Bright colors exploded from flowering bushes planted on three sides of the house.

"Antipas, my friend, you must make new plans quickly. I

attended another meeting about you at the city council late last night. Whatever the outcome of the first trial by the temple priests, they will require you as a non-Jew to pay your normal citizens' taxes at the second trial. This is meant to be a trap. If you do confess that Caesar is lord and god, then that will destroy everything you stand for. If you don't confess using those words, they will punish you."

Antipas bent forward. "This is serious. What does it mean for me? What will happen to Anthony and Miriam? What does it mean for our Household of Faith?"

"You must have Anthony and Miriam married immediately. There's no time to lose. I would like to host that event at my house. Leave the legal details to me."

Antipas leaned back in his chair and looked at the ceiling for a moment before responding. "I suggest you set the wedding for Miriam's birthday, April 14. If possible, complete their adoption of Chrysa on the following day."

Marcos scratched his head. "That's perfect. It gives me time to draw up the legal documents for each event. I can host both ceremonies at my house. Last summer, I sold several properties. Some of the money I got from them let me acquire the two homes adjacent to my house. After Anthony and Miriam are married, they must go to one of these houses for a while to be out of the public eye. It probably will be dangerous for them to stay in your village because the authorities may come looking for Miriam. If they intend to expropriate all your property, they will want to make sure Miriam is in the city."

He saw a question forming in Antipas's mind. "Now, about your concern for the Household of Faith, Antipas, you teach that God led your ancestors out of Egypt and gave them deliverance. A door of opportunity will be opened for it to continue; I just don't know how."

THE CITY HALL MEETING PLACE, THE ACROPOLIS

"Pray for me," Marcos said quickly as he left his home. Unable to stop his heart from pounding, he worried about the speech he had planned to give to the city council.

Will I succeed in my plans? Can I continue to be honest and yet live in a world that seems so unfair?

His scheme was to pay his taxes before the Festival of Zeus

began. He had calculated the cost of covering the next six years of assessments. He had a plan that might get around the custom of bowing and declaring loyalty before the statue of Caesar. The officials were more relaxed and less attentive to details at this time because the council's agenda was frankly dull now. Generally, no one paid taxes early.

Today the one hundred twenty seats had been fully occupied. The council heard the plans for the festival and reviewed the plans to give the three aristocratic families final approval to build their new houses on the acropolis in the space with a spectacular view overlooking the eastern valley. Applause greeted these developments.

Marcos called out at the end of the meeting, "I'm aware of the sacrifice made by the three respected aristocratic families. They have decided to give up their privileged locations and rebuild on the less dangerous area above the gymnasium. As a newcomer to the city, I want to show my support by paying my taxes early. I will even pay a few years in advance to help start the project."

Expressions of surprise and delight came from the men who were still in the council chamber. Marcos handed a heavy leather pouch full of coins to the city treasurer.

Potitus Vinicius was a young aspiring lawyer. He had also applied for the position that Marcos was assigned when it became vacant several years ago. Potitus's uncle had been the governor of the province of Asia sixty years before under Emperor Gaius Caligula.

Hearing Marcos speak, Potitus objected. "When you pay taxes, you have to declare, 'Caesar is lord and god.' The proper place for your paying taxes is in the next room, not in here. Go to the altar in front of the statute of the emperor!"

Since Marcos had arrived in Pergamum, a running battle with Potitus, the disappointed lawyer, had been simmering. Potitus was quick to take every opportunity to defame him.

Marcos stood calmly. "Does anyone else want to pay their taxes early? The city treasurer is beside me right now, not in the next room! Three esteemed men have decided to give up their ancestral homes. Like them, I want to see this city restored to its greatness. Unless we all pay our taxes on time, and a bit extra if possible, how will we ever regain the majesty that has been lost to Smyrna and Ephesus? I want to help get this new project started—now!"

The overwhelming pro-city appeal of his argument, this unusual gesture, took Potitus Vinicius back for an instant. The leaders of the Guild of Stonemasons voiced their approval quickly and loudly, longing to get the massive renovation project underway. By now, it was common knowledge that Marcos had initiated the concept of a large new base at the top of the acropolis.

He smiled and felt his face brighten. "Potitus, look at this pouch full of coins! Have you ever handed over an amount like this to the empire? Do you doubt that I give to Caesar what belongs to Caesar? Oh, and by the way, would you consider paying your annual taxes early? We could use your support too."

Potitus stared at Marcos, who wore a smug smile and walked with the city treasurer to the Office of Tributes next to the Odeon.

Gossip spread immediately of an unusual willingness to pay many years' taxes in advance. Surprised civil servants accepted the large sum of money and provided a receipt. Marcos breathed much more easily for he had not made the declaration, 'Caesar is lord and god,' and would not have to think about taxes for years.

Most importantly, the powerful Guild of the Stonemasons was firmly on his side. They would do everything to defend the city's commitment to the immense task of changing the contours at the top of the acropolis. Years of work awaited them.

The second part of his plan was complete thanks to the success of his confrontation with Potitus, his younger opponent. The document firmly tucked into his belt stated that he did not owe taxes for six years.

Now the last part of his plan remained to be put into place.

THE MAYOR'S OFFICE, THE ACROPOLIS

Marcos left the city council and went straight to the mayor's office to secure permission for an army reservist soldier to marry. Consent was not always granted, but the mayor listened to his petition. He knew that Anthony had been relieved of his official duties at the garrison to teach at the gymnasium, so he granted the authorization without question. He also provided permission for the adoption the day after the wedding, telling Marcos he would be present for the adoption, as required by law.

As Antipas had wanted, the wedding was to be held on Miriam's birthday. He had a twinkle in his eye as he spoke with Miriam. "You will be twenty-six years old, my child, and your husband will never forget either your birthday or your anniversary!"

"Or he will forget both of them like most men do!"

They laughed together.

MARCOS'S HOME

Antipas didn't know whether to weep or laugh. On this Sabbath, it was April 14, and he had never participated in a wedding on a Saturday. With each new experience, he seemed to drift further from his traditions. He prayed that God would bless this marriage; it would have to be celebrated without a proper betrothal period.

The beautiful memory of Antipas's wedding in Alexandria with the seven days of the ceremony came back—days of feasting, joy, and dancing with the coming together of two families. Those celebrations were missing here. No one could imagine what images came to his mind when he said the word "wedding."

Marcos welcomed him to his home in the morning. Five people were already there as witnesses, even though only two were needed. Onias, the faithful steward of the Ben Shelah family, and several trusted friends were standing in their living room.

Marcella and Florbella held red roses and white lilies. Antipas nodded to twenty of his most trusted friends. Most of them would attend the ceremony but say nothing.

Antipas was distressed but realized that this had to be a quick wedding given the potential danger to his life and possibly to Miriam's. He stifled a laugh.

Anthony and Miriam are going to adopt the baby tomorrow. I already know the name of my great-granddaughter! Everything is so out of place, so many twists and turns in the road of life! I made a commitment to my daughter, Tamara, before she died in Antioch nineteen years ago. I promised, 'I will give Miriam the most wonderful Jewish wedding any girl ever had.' Forgive me, Tamara! I can't do that now.

Marcos instructed Anthony and Miriam where to stand. The five witnesses had to be told what to say and when to say it.

Nothing had been planned or rehearsed. No formality made the moment special.

Tears and laughter sprang from different emotions. Sadness came from thinking about Alexandria and the glorious moments of his wedding. Still, he would have to put those thoughts away on Miriam's special day.

Marcos and Marcella provided a meal at noon. There was much laughter throughout the small banquet, and Florbella started to sing.

Antipas had a shock when he realized Marcella was serving meat and a milk product, cheese. His eyes shut in protest, and he almost gagged. As a Jew, he would never have served meat and milk items together. How easily Gentiles could offend Jews, even unintentionally!

"I bought two villas next to ours," Marcos announced, "and for now, these new places will have a special use. For the next few nights, Ateas and Arpoxa have agreed to stay in the house closest to mine. It will be special for them to be in a villa for a few days, and Arpoxa will have the two babies to look after. Anthony and Miriam, you will be staying in the house farther away from us. This will be our gift to you, to be alone for a few days in the big new villa by yourselves. Miriam, if there is anything from your home at the village you need, Urbanus can bring it back here tomorrow."

Antipas hugged Miriam and accepted Anthony into his family.

He would see them tomorrow, early in the morning. But today was theirs as a couple, and they would experience the joy of two becoming one. Tomorrow Chrysa would legally become their child.

MARCOS'S NEWLY PURCHASED VILLA

Evening was coming on, and Anthony led Miriam to their villa, which had a large entryway. Four pillars on the edge of a shallow pool of water supported a high ceiling. The main room was almost as big as the cave; it could hold more than one hundred fifty people sitting on the floor. Scenes from Greek myths were inlaid on the floor with colorful mosaics.

Upstairs they found several rooms, each furnished with beds, a wooden wardrobe, and chairs. Anthony held Miriam close, hugging her. He drew her to him and slowly kissed her.

"Remember when I said 'until' to you in the shop? Then I didn't know I would hold you like this. I thought we would only be married..." he hesitated, "...much later."

Miriam was breathless. "Yes, I never dreamed it would be so soon."

"Tomorrow is the first day of the Pergamum Festival of Zeus. All teachers at the gymnasium have sixteen days of vacation. Tomorrow, late in the afternoon, I will report to the garrison to verify that I don't need to report again until the first day of the Games. Thankfully, I won't be meeting with Diodorus for two weeks. Several teachers went by ship to Ephesus today for the Festival of Artemis. Just think! I have all these days with you before I have to go back to the gymnasium."

"Until then, and always, my beloved, I will love you," said Miriam, her head on his shoulder, her body close to his.

"'Until!' That will be our particular word. And I repeated it again today. Did you hear it in the promise I made to you? 'Until'...we are parted by death—that is how long I will love you and be faithful to you."

"Oh, Anthony, I will always love you, and I will always care for you. No matter how many difficulties come our way, I will always be with you and only for you."

She pulled him closer, marveling at the joy of his arms around her. "Be a seal over my heart," she said. "I want you to always be close to me."

Chapter 42
Drama in the Roman Theater

MARCOS'S HOME

On Sunday morning, immediately after the meeting at the cave was over, Antipas hurried with Onias and his family to Marcos's villa for the adoption ceremony.

"Thank you for being prompt, Antipas," Marcos said. "I'm sorry that I had to arrange this event so early in the morning. Today marks the beginning of the Festival of Zeus, and the mayor cannot stay long to officiate at the adoption. Don't worry about people at the cave missing Miriam and Anthony this morning. Most of them know their marriage took place yesterday and understand their absence. I do think that this adoption should be known to only a very few people.

"We cannot make this into a big Jewish event like the ones you love! No! The adoption must happen now with as little time lost as possible! Anthony and Miriam will continue to stay at my villa for the time being. Miriam must not return to your house or be near the village until we know what's going to happen. Marcella and I will feed them for as long as necessary. The two-week holiday begins, so the adoption must be completed today."

Antipas knew that Marcos was privy to the plans of the priests and priestesses serving in the religious establishment. He knew there would be a trial before the end of the festival, Monday the thirtieth. They might arrest him at any time to prevent him from escaping. If that happened, Miriam might also be arrested.

Sometimes Marcos felt like a spy, but it was his way of handling the great injustice that was being planned in the city. The adoption ceremony would be completed this morning. All the scrolls in Antipas's library would be moved to his new property for safe keeping until the potential dangers were passed. They could take the scrolls back to the village later if no further problems arose.

Marcos didn't want to alarm Antipas, but for the next few days, Ateas and Arpoxa would have to stay close to Anthony and Miriam. Arpoxa was feeding Saulius and Chrysa both. He forced himself to think about the adoption preparations and to stop contemplating the latest decisions made by the authorities to rid the city of Antipas.

Marcos gave instructions about the formalities as they gathered in the main room for the ceremony. At completion, Mayor Quintus Rufus would have to leave quickly to start the festival procession. While they were waiting for Quintus, Antipas stood to one side.

"Here is how an adoption is done under Roman law," Marcos explained. "Anthony, you stand there, in front of me, on my left. Miriam, stand beside him, on my right. Antipas, stand beside Miriam and give the baby to her when I tell you to; then step back.

"Onias, you are one of the witnesses. Be ready to sign this document. Marcella cannot be a witness because I am the clerk for the law here, and it would be a conflict of interest for my wife to be a witness. Marcella, you can stand behind Miriam.

"Yes, Florbella, you can hold the flowers and kiss the baby after the adoption is finished.

"No, Antipas, it won't take long. We will speak just a few sentences. The other three witnesses are to stand behind Anthony and Miriam. I will stand in front of you."

A few minutes later, the mayor of Pergamum arrived at the house and was escorted into the room. Quintus Rufus wore an expensive white linen toga over his tunic. He greeted them and made a comment. "I'm happy to see rejected girl babies adopted into homes."

With an official-sounding voice, he said, "Important events like this are usually done in the city council with many people observing and approving. I'm just as pleased to be at a small family occasion. I am required to explain the law of adoption before I can say the words of adoption and give this little girl to you."

Anthony and Miriam nodded. They were ready for the ceremony.

"Do you know the mother or the father?"

"No, we don't," said Anthony.

Rufus looked at the adoption document through his big puffy eyes. "This says the baby's name is to be Chrysa Grace Suros. Is that correct?"

Miriam and Anthony both nodded yes. Marcos knew that her real mother had given her the name Chrysa, but Grace was the name they wanted to add. That was all he knew about the baby.

Rufus continued, "The law states that if the father wants the baby, he can come and take her from you at any time until the age of twenty-one. Do you understand this might happen if the father learns where this baby girl is living? You may grow to love this child as your own, but if the real father can prove the baby is his by obtaining a statement from the mother, then he can take the baby and raise it."

The expressions on their faces showed they didn't like this part. "Yes, I understand," said Anthony.

Miriam questioned, "Just come and take her?" She couldn't imagine growing to love Chrysa Grace and then having some unknown man—the father—claim her as his daughter. Ateas and Arpoxa, sitting on chairs, looked at each other; the possibilities raised by this Roman law made them nervous for Anthony and Miriam.

Quintus Rufus nodded. "He could give you, the adoptive mother, a slave in compensation, that is, if he is a compassionate man, or he could leave you empty-handed. You would have no legal right to keep the child. Do you understand and accept these conditions?"

It had to be a verbal affirmation with both the new father and mother agreeing. Miriam looked at Anthony. "Yes," said Miriam, "I understand. I will adopt the baby. We will raise her as our own child."

Anthony agreed. "Although she is not flesh of my flesh and not born to us, I will raise her as if I were her father. I will love her. She will never have reason to be sad that I'm her adoptive father, but if the real father comes for her, we will obey the law." His firm conviction and the warmth of his love for the child elicited an "ah" of admiration from everyone.

At this point, Marcos motioned for Antipas to give Chrysa physically to Miriam, and the mayor stated that Anthony and Miriam were then the legal parents of the child.

They signed the adoption document of Chrysa Grace Suros,

and the mayor added his name with a flourish. When he was satisfied that all was in order and that the legalities of the adoption were completed, Quintus Rufus hurried out to return to his offices. In an hour, he would be heading the festival procession up the hillside.

"We've completed the adoption," Marcos said. "You will be a good mother, Miriam, and I can see that you will be a loving father, Anthony."

Miriam hugged the little one whose eyes were wide open. She was now two months old. The baby looked at everything but could say nothing.

Miriam spoke up. "I wrote a song. What would a Roman home be without a legal document, and what would a Jewish home be without music for the occasion?"

She sang her song, "Adoption," telling of a wedding, a family, and a baby.

Mama wears a pure white wedding dress.
She says, "I do!" and warmly she responds
To Daddy's, "Others, we will bless."
Our home is known for healthy, loving bonds.

Before I felt Mama's warm embrace,
I could not tell her when my hands felt cold.
Mama says, "Look at her sweet face!
She has our care. There's nothing we'll withhold."

They will keep me safe through life's alarms.
Content, I'm family now. I have a name.
I'm resting in my daddy's arms.
Friends gather. "She's beautiful!" they exclaim.

I know nothing of the rights of heirs,
But I'm adopted, chosen, held with joy.
I see their smiles. I know I'm theirs.
I share a home that nothing will destroy.

The song was like those of the Pergamum singers. It was a simple song, put to the tune of a lullaby some women in Pergamum sang to help their children settle to sleep. While

Miriam sang, Chrysa Grace looked up into the face of her new mother, and a spontaneous smile broke out.

Pronouncing them to be the little girl's parents, Marcos raised his voice. "On April 15, Chrysa Grace Suros belongs to you. She has been adopted into your home." He took her in his hands, telling her how fortunate she was to have Anthony and Miriam as her parents. They had been married for one day, and they already had their first child.

"My sweet baby," said Miriam, "you are a little miracle. You will teach us of God's grace, our little Grace." Anthony grasped the adoption document as he held the child, and he said, "Look, little one! You have a home, a mother, and a father!"

Although joy overflowed in the home of Marcos and Marcella, elsewhere evil plans were beginning to form.

THE ACROPOLIS

Within the city of Pergamum, the great Festival of Zeus, the spring celebration, was gaining momentum. Crowds from the surrounding villages packed the city, and a sense of excitement filled the New Forum as the festival parade formed. Two hours later, a white bull was sacrificed on the Altar of Zeus. After the meat was cooked and distributed to the priests and priestesses, the haruspices called them together because they had read the signs regarding the trials for Antipas.

"We have examined and read the entrails of the sacrifice," they explained. "A trial held on the first days will be more auspicious than at the end of the festival.

"The gods' message for you is that the Trial of Character must be on Thursday, the fifth day of the festival. You should hold the Trial of Sacrifice two or three days later but not more than halfway through the festival."

Late on Wednesday evening, a messenger arrived at Antipas's door. "The authorities of Pergamum require your presence at the Roman Theater tomorrow night. You will be there before sunset."

ANTIPAS'S HOME

Antipas rose early. His heart was calm even though he knew he faced danger. He remembered the words of Yeshua: "They will lay hands on you and persecute you. They will deliver you to synagogues and prisons, and you will be brought before kings and governors, and all on account of my name. This will result in your being witnesses to them. But make up your mind not to worry beforehand how you will defend yourselves. For I will give you words and wisdom that none of your adversaries will be able to resist or contradict."[83]

He remembered his brothers and felt a twinge of guilt. He had not prayed for them for days. *Make Anthony an instrument of peace for my brothers. Lord, I bless him to have the wisdom to help in healing their deepest wounds.*

THE NEW THEATER

Four soldiers arrived at Antipas's house before sundown, and they brought him to the Roman Theater. His short black beard was neatly cut, his feet were freshly washed, and he smelled of fresh olive soap. He wore small black armbands around his wrists that he always put on when inspecting the quality of the workmanship in his workshops.

He breathed a prayer, the one his scroll was opened to in his library.

I am a dread to my friends; those who see me on the street flee from me. I have become like broken pottery. I hear the slander of many; there is terror on every side; they conspire against me and plot to take my life. But I trust in you, O Lord; I say, "You are my God. My times are in your hands. Save me in your unfailing love."[84]

Soldiers took him to the door leading onto the broad platform. He walked slowly, noting the expressions of people in the theater. In the gathering gloom of the spring evening, the theater was already full. He listened to people as they waited expectantly for a new form of entertainment. The jibes had already started.

"A Jew is accused of being an atheist!"

"Is he the man who debated the Egyptians? This will be different from the tragedies and comedies they constantly present."

Singers, dancers, musicians, and entertainers usually filled

---

[83] Luke 21:12–15
[84] Psalm 31:11–16

the platform, but tonight only temple priests waited for him. The buzzing in the crowd grew in volume.

The full theater was soon shrouded in darkness. More than fifteen thousand people had gathered, and many waited outside, hoping to get in. Torches placed along the main aisles permitted people to find the few remaining seats. The torches were rags soaked in olive oil wound around long poles placed in holes drilled into the theater seats along the edges of the aisles. When a torch stopped burning, the slaves took it down to pour more oil on the rags. Around the stage, several torches were also burning brightly, and they cast a flickering orange light.

Three more torch stands were brought to the stage, and torches were inserted to provide light. As the last rays of the sun disappeared, the din of the crowd grew in volume.

Antipas stood alone on one side, a small man on a wide stage. The contrast between him and the priests could not have been greater. Antipas wore a simple white linen tunic with a blue and white prayer shawl around his shoulders and a black skullcap on his head. Shorter in height than any of the men lined up against him, an unknown person, he appeared to be facing overbearing odds while standing alone against the distinguished figures on the stage.

Whereas he was simply dressed, the men and women against him wore their finest garb; their rings, bracelets, and ornaments were religious treasures. The priests wore elaborate garments bearing the colors of their temple. Their magnificent clothing brought Pergamum's symbols together: those of religious pride and unbroken tradition.

Nine high priests and high priestesses were gathered from centers of worship: the Imperial Altar of Caesar Augustus; the Altar of Zeus; the temples of Egypt, Athena, Dionysius, Hera, and Demeter; and the Asclepius Hospital. They whispered together, agreeing on what accusation would be brought by which priest.

Diodorus, the tall headmaster of the gymnasium with the deep voice, was in charge of the evening's event. He waved his hand and announced the purpose of the event. Silence gradually fell over the crowd.

Damon, the high priest of the Temple of the Imperial Cult, smiled from his position beside the seven high priests who were lined up shoulder to shoulder. The high priestesses of Demeter and Hera were there as well. "In the name of Domitian, lord and god, our highest authority, the emperor, I declare this evening's event open."

Diodorus waited as a roar of approval swelled from the people and gradually died down. He began, "Tonight, in this Trial of Character, a stranger who came to Pergamum twenty years ago as a refugee from Alexandria will defend himself. We are here to determine if Antipas Ben Shelah is worthy of being a citizen of our city. We took him in, gave him hospitality, and let him know our ways. He has been successful, building up a little village and running two shops in the city. He has several workshops too. However, instead of adapting to our ways, he is creating divisions. The authorities asked for this event. Antipas, you are called to defend your actions. Answer well, for your future depends on it. If you are not deemed worthy, then a second trial will follow."

The high priest of the Egyptian Temple stepped forward. His splendid robes of yellow, red, and black reflected the glory of his position representing many ancient Egyptian gods. "Antipas, you are accused of intolerance, a great sin, for no one may live anywhere in the empire unless they are tolerant and respectful of others' beliefs. Each city, each town has its own gods and goddesses. In Egypt, we have a pantheon of forty-two major gods as well as many minor ones. You upset our customs of this city by saying there is only one god."

Antipas looked over the spectators in the theater, noticing a few men who had purchased items from his shops. "I do not seek to offend anyone with my beliefs. All men fear death, and my teaching touches on being an overcomer, no longer trembling in fear."

"You teach that the gods have no power. This is false! We know their influence!"

Ignoring the statement, Antipas continued, "It is not intolerance to say that all people fear death. I know of your temples in Egypt and the attempts of the ancient pharaohs to live forever. My teaching has shown that the one God makes a difference in everything. Consequently, we no longer have to fear death."

The two men talked back and forth for a long time, with the Egyptian arguing for a multiplicity of gods and Antipas steadfastly refusing to admit either their existence or power.

The popular high priestess of the Temple of Demeter stepped forward. Her expensive brown and yellow robes and ornate turban showed that money flowed liberally into her temple. "You say you are loving and tolerant, but actually, you inspire animosity! You are not a good citizen. Good citizens attend public events: the Games and the theater. Why do you despise our society?"

Antipas searched for the right words.

Emmanuel, you are with me through deep waters, through flowing rivers, and through fires. Guide my lips. Give me your words.

"Your word 'despise' is not correct. I urge my workers to do the best they can, to bring out the best of their skills. You know that widows and orphans find a home in my village. My workers are treated with dignity. I feel genuine affection for all those around me."

"Have you ever come to this theater?"

"No, I have not. You accuse me of not attending public events, especially the Games. I know that the Games are important to this city. In two weeks, they will begin, and nothing is more important to the young men of Pergamum. Twice a year, the stadium and the amphitheater overflow with citizens cheering on the competitors. People cheer for the winners, and their prize is a wreath and public recognition."

At this, the crowd erupted in cheers.

"But for me, there is something more important. There is only one winner in each event, and the victor receives praise, glory, and honor. Instead, I am concerned with those who can't compete. I spend time with them. Some cannot overcome the hurdles of life. In our community, we teach each other to look after people who will never achieve public recognition."

"Nonsense! The grandeur of competition is becoming a victor!"

"That's because you share the common ideas of honor and glory. But watching out for poor people is also a mark of honor. We are overcomers when we learn to show selfless love. We are victorious when we serve our neighbors, even when they are not at all lovable."

He had used the words "victor" or "victorious" many times, and in saying those words, he had inadvertently alluded to the name of the Greek goddess Nike.

One man close to the front yelled, "How dare you use Nike's name this way!" Another cried out, "Victorious! What has he ever won? Never even been to the Games, and he thinks he knows something about victory!"

The high priestess of the Temple of Demeter followed up on the yells from the crowd. "Are you more powerful than Nike? Nike gives athletes their success, and we offer sacrifices to her. You must not falsely use her name! It's bad character!"

"Yeshua Messiah gives us victory over ourselves. It takes courage to learn to love people who are not lovable." He smiled.

Some spectators, annoyed at his references to the attributes of Nike, began to roar with the cheers generally heard during a race in the stadium. Antipas held up his hand after a time, but the crowd would not become silent.

The high priestess of Demeter moved back, unable to continue her accusations.

His next accuser, the high priestess of Hera, was a heavy-set woman dressed in purple and white with blue trim on her miter. "This man stirs up trouble. He teaches false hope. People of lower social status pay attention to him. Fellow citizens! Antipas teaches a heresy. He is trying to obliterate the privileged position of Roman citizens. He acts as if all racial and ethnic groups have equal status. Many people bear witness that he declares, 'There is no difference between Roman, Greek, Jew, or Scythian!' This must be stopped."

Her voice could be heard effortlessly by everyone in the theater, even those at the top, in the back row. Her face was twisted in a cruel snarl as she addressed them.

"Imagine! This man attempts to get rid of status and position, to turn natural authority upside down. His followers call each other 'brother' and 'sister.' He allows slaves and servants to live on the same social level. He doesn't say it this clearly, but those who by right of birth are of the highest social order are made to feel like slaves. I accuse you, Antipas, of rebellion! You want to establish a new social order, a new kingdom with a new king."

Antipas noted the anger in her face and answered in a calm and firm voice, "No, I do not want to establish a new kingdom. Rome governs the world in ways we observe every day. But Rome does not rule the hidden places of our hearts, where each of us has dominion over our will. I try to live as a good citizen. Did not even Cicero call for taking care of the poor and the weak?"

The high priestess held her chin high. "Look! His malicious character is on display, trying to deceive us with 'the hidden places of our hearts.' He wants to control the thoughts and wishes of each one and thereby form another kingdom. How foolish! He denies it, but by using this subterfuge, he has plans to destroy our gods. How? By teaching that his god is more powerful, he wants to control slaves. He intends to have them set free in high numbers and manipulate their emotions. Thus, he is dangerous and deserves the worst kind of punishment."

Antipas took a half step toward her. "Am I establishing another kingdom? No! Why do I set slaves free? Because, many years ago, my ancestors were slaves, and they were freed. But this is a different time and place. I set slaves free using my own resources. I am just one man in a city of more than a hundred fifty thousand people. I have purchased more than twenty slaves and set them all free, but I never instructed any other person to do the same thing. If I did tell them, let them come forward. Who is a witness against me?"

No one responded. With greater boldness, Antipas asked, "Will anyone here willingly give slaves their freedom? Anyone?" Complete silence met this question. "Look around! Who has been influenced by my actions? I am the only one to set slaves free. Who has heard me speak rebellious words about authorities?"

Antipas's courage in contradicting the words of the high priestess of Hera won him grudging support from many.

"You see, Esteemed Lady, no one believes your accusation."

She loudly addressed the audience while pointing her finger at Antipas again. "I declare that this man is a danger to the family structure of Pergamum. His teaching and pattern of life will result in divided families. We will rue his presence in our city. He even holds orgies called love feasts early on Sunday mornings. No one can go to his village—to that dark cave—unless they accept his teachings or have learned his false ways." Now she glared at him. "You must be anxious about sex!"

The crowd loved the talk about sex and love. Ribald jokes made them come alive all the more, and many clapped their hands. They were going to learn what he was really like!

He held his hand out, and voices died down. "The love we

have for one another is not erotic but a love expressing the worth we feel for one another. Our teaching elevates women so that we see a woman as a precious person. A woman is just as precious as a man. Further, we teach that sexual relations should be confined to marriage."

Many people were yelling, booing, and hissing at him.

"And we teach that within marriage there should be trust, happiness, and fulfillment of one's passions. We teach children to obey their parents. Your accusations about the love feast are false. It is only a simple meal of bread and wine held during a special moment on Sunday mornings before anyone goes to work. We remember Yeshua the Messiah because he has risen from the grave."

After each of the others had accused him, Diodorus took over for the last part of the trial. He had planned to use arguments about the excellence of Roman customs against this enemy of the city. Instead, he decided to talk about shame, honor, and rejection. Shaming students at the gymnasium was his most powerful tool. The pain of personal humiliation hurt more than intellectual opinions.

"No one wants you here, Antipas! Do the young men at my gymnasium, those learning Pliny and Cicero, Roman government and history, do they flock to you? What about worshipers at the huge New Temple? Why, not even your friends at the synagogue want you!"

Antipas had been calm while the priests brought accusations against him, but now his face had a strained look. Each of the priests had criticized his actions and beliefs. Diodorus was taking another path to demean him in front of Pergamum's citizens.

So your most persuasive argument, Diodorus, is all about shame! Hmm, 'Whenever you are arrested and brought to trial, do not worry beforehand what to say. Just say whatever is given you at the time, for it is not you speaking, but the Holy Spirit.'

He looked around the entire theater. A hush had come upon the spectators. While he was a short man, he stood tall and took a deep breath, trying to make out individual faces.

Eliab's final blessing came back to him. He saw his father lying on his deathbed, and every word of Eliab's blessing gave him courage.

Antipas, you are like a victorious lion, hunting for the truth. You

*are strong, but you have the heart of a gentle lamb. Because you
are strong, you do not cry out. When you become weak, like a lamb,
your enemy will be ashamed. You know much of fires; often you
walked through fires of affliction. Your strength is faithfulness. It
will keep you from the traps of your enemy. You will look the enemy
in the face, and you will be an overcomer.*

Before Diodorus could say another word, he spoke, "Let me
reply, Most Respected Diodorus, with a story." The formal use of
the esteemed title took Diodorus back for a second, but Antipas
had already begun to speak. "This theater is a place of stories, a
place where many of you have come scores of times. Stories
captivate us."

Antipas was at his best when he was telling a story or acting
out one about his ancestors. Now he captivated the throng with
the way he talked. He walked freely around the stage, gesturing
with his arms, acting out each of the stories that came to mind.

"Not far from here, you enter the gates of the Asclepius,
where you go when sick. Asclepius was the son of Apollo, the
grandson of Zeus. One day, as you remember, Asclepius found his
way into the earth, as snakes do, and he came back with the
greatest secret of all time: the secret of eternal life. If he shared it
with humans, as he wanted to, then all humans would live
forever! Thus, Asclepius had power over death. Zeus was furious
when he heard about Asclepius!

"'What has your son done, Apollo?' he cried out. 'If he tells the
secret, humans will live forever, and they will become like us!
This cannot be!' Zeus, therefore, had his own grandson killed
rather than bring eternal life to humans."

The crowd murmured. Everyone knew the story and in much
greater detail than Antipas had told it. "Now let me tell you
another story. It is also the story of a man who was killed, not to
stop people from living forever but so that people *could* live
forever. This man healed people from many illnesses. He was
born less than a hundred years ago into a poor family. An evil king
pursued him when he was a child. Instead of teaching hatred
against the king, this man used stories to teach people to love
others selflessly. For example, one day he went to a wedding, and
there was no wine. He asked the servants to pour water into pots,
and he turned the water into wine."

"Bring that man to my tavern!" someone yelled from the

crowd. "Have him turn dirty water into good beer!" People hollered and cheered.

Antipas bounced on his feet, acting out the stories he loved so much. "Another time, he met a blind man who was unfortunately born that way, and all his life he had lived in darkness. Then this good man spit on the ground, put a bit of the mud on the blind man's eyes, and sent him to a pool to wash his eyes. Shortly afterward, the man born blind came back, and now he could see! Another time a big crowd was gathered, but they had no food. He made five loaves and two fish multiply, and everyone was fed."

"Send that man to my house; I have lots of kids to feed!" a father called out.

Scores of people added, "Tell us more!"

The crowd was beginning to get what they wanted, entertainment and stories, especially tales about free food.

"One day a man called Lazarus became sick. He died and was buried. Four days later, this good man came as a friend of the family. The sisters were grieving. He went to the grave and said, 'Lazarus, come out of that grave!' The man who had died came back to life."

Antipas stopped while the crowd thought about that, and he looked at Diodorus. Silence fell over the crowd. Diodorus didn't know what to do. Should he stop the story now? Would the crowd complain? Much of the entertainment in the Roman theater came from storytellers. Usually loud, lewd comments poured out of the throng against them, but at this moment, they wanted more.

Antipas knew the fears of the working people in Pergamum. He told them many more stories: of people healed, demons cast out, and a violent windstorm that was stopped when men were afraid of their boat sinking. His stories struck their hearts, swaying them as he interacted with them.

Antipas had been shamed publicly by the religious leaders, but instead of cowering and running away, he told stories. The crowd was being bewitched. Diodorus realized that Antipas had tapped into the spectators' own fears of rejection, poverty, and loss. He walked close to Antipas and put his hand on the old man's arm to stop him from further swaying the crowd. He told himself, *This man is dangerous, and this is proof that we must be rid of him.*

But Antipas would not be stopped. "He went about healing the sick, making lepers well, and bringing the dead back to life.

His name was Yeshua, and he was from the town of Nazareth."

Everyone fell utterly silent. For most of them, it was the first time they had heard the name Yeshua. "The people wanted to make him king because he gave them free food." The crowd agreed with another roar of approval. "However, a week later, the people turned on him. During one of our festivals in Jerusalem, an event held about the same time as your Festival of Zeus, they killed him."

"How did they kill this man?" asked a man with a brash voice.

"They crucified him and put a sign over his head, 'The King of the Jews.' But this is what no one knew: His death was a sacrifice. When he came back to life, it showed that he had the power to give eternal life. To those who accept his teachings and his way of life, a new life is created. It's what I call 'overcoming love.'"

This time his use of the reference to Nike in the word "overcoming" didn't cause pandemonium. It brought about a profound silence. It was the first time "love" and "overcoming" had been joined together as a phrase for most. While he was finishing his words, some in the crowd sensed that maybe he wasn't an immoral influence.

The interchange between Antipas and the crowd infuriated Diodorus, who sensed that his command over the evening had slipped away. It began the moment Antipas started telling stories. Diodorus saw that it was time to end the trial. "That's enough, Antipas!" he said, walking to his side and pushing the old man's arm down.

"The first trial of Antipas Ben Shelah is over!" Diodorus declared loudly. "The second trial will be a bigger event. Come to the amphitheater three days from now." Looking at Antipas, he added, "You are to bring your tax money for the year."

The two-hour cross-examination had ended more or less in a draw. The points made by the priests' accusations would stick, but Antipas's defense, illustrated with stories, commanded respect. However, to the authorities present, the Trial of Character had proven beyond doubt that Antipas was a danger to the established social, religious, and imperial order.

Chapter 43
Mithrida, Sexta, and Craga

TANAIS, THE BOSPORAN KINGDOM

During the previous winter in the Bosporan Kingdom, north of the Black Sea, Mithrida had completed an agreement with the owner of a ship. Before they agreed on the purchase of the vessel, several long talks had taken place. At first, negotiations on the price almost broke down. "You should pay more for this ship. I've carried as many as forty-two slaves in this vessel." The elderly owner was a relative to one of the princes of the Bosporan Kingdom.

"But your new ships are already transporting slaves, and you don't need this old vessel any longer," urged Mithrida. "This vessel was slightly damaged in a storm at the port of Amastris on the Black Sea coast. We will pay for it in three equal payments to be made over three years."

An agreement was reached, and by the beginning of April, Sexta, as they called him now, had brought thirty-two slaves from small towns along the Dnieper River. He bragged, "It wasn't hard at all to get local men without work to go along with our scheme."

Claudius, whose name in the Faithful was now Craga, climbed aboard the ship the day after Mithrida had made the first of the three payments. He held his nose and breathed deeply, shutting his eyes from the smell before being able to speak. "Well, we'll be sailing in a few days. I can see that it will take me a long time to get used to the stench. But when it comes to making great profits, I guess it's possible to withstand anything." He grasped the hands of his friends, Mithrida and Sexta, and they slapped each other on the back, congratulating themselves on having achieved rapid success.

Mithrida turned to Claudius, the slightly lame soldier who had been the finest centurion in Legion XXI. "What plans have you

388

made, my first javelin?"

"I came across a man who quickly found three exceptional recruits for me who joined the Faithful. His name in the Roman army was Gergius, but our army name for him is Taba. He heard me speaking at a tavern in Chalcedon and gave me ideas. He is tall and thin and prides himself on the way he handles a sword. When he was still in the army, bringing barbarians into submission, he was known for successfully fighting against four men who tried to ambush him in the forest.

"After we arrive in Port Adramyttium and dispose of our slaves, Taba will stay in Asia Minor for a year. He wants to go to Sardis, which he calls the City of Gold, to recruit soldiers for our little army. According to him, there are lots of riches to be found there. In ancient times, when the Lydians ruled, gold was as common as stones on the street. And listen to this! Within a week of agreeing to join us, he recruited two more, Maza and Harpa."

The three leaders of the Faithful chuckled with glee. Their plans were working out superbly. Confident of future success, Mithrida, Craga, and Sexta headed for a meal and drinks at the tavern.

Chapter 44
Because of the Name

THE CITY HALL MEETING PLACE

On Friday evening, the entire civic establishment gathered in the city council. Each person wanted to give a personal opinion about what had happened at the theater.

Mehu, the Egyptian priest, began. "Diodorus, it was a good thing you closed off the evening when you did. You shamed Antipas by saying that he has no friends in the city. That was difficult for him to refute. Imagine a person without a community! But then he started telling his stories, and people forgot what you said. You shouldn't have let him start talking about his beliefs again. He's persuasive."

"Yes, and we didn't get a clear mandate to kill him," said another.

"He is small and old, but his debating skills were equal to yours," said the high priest of Athena. He believed he would have demolished Antipas if he had been given more time to attack. Never mind. He would have an opportunity two nights later.

Lydia-Naq spoke up. "I don't understand what any of you are afraid of. We won. Don't you see? Although no one came forward to defend him or back him up, it would have made no difference. We need no mandate of rejection from the citizens of Pergamum. Antipas's own words condemn him. Our job is done. When the high priest of the Imperial Temple of Augustus takes his turn, the poor little man will be finished!"

She walked down from her seat position and started to leave the long narrow room.

"What do you mean, 'When the priest takes his turn'? Why does that finish Antipas?" The high priestess of Demeter still did not understand Lydia-Naq's comments.

She looked around at them. "Don't any of you understand? In

the same way the Romans killed his messiah, they will kill Antipas. We didn't have to do anything except create the climate for the Roman authorities to require action. The Jewish Yeshua was said to be the King of the Jews. Don't you realize he sealed his death warrant by pointing that out? He lifted up the name of a man whose followers would resist our emperor. Antipas condemned himself!"

Lydia-Naq looked at the blank faces of some and exploded. "Rome will never accept anyone who refuses to say, 'Caesar is lord and god.'"

She stared belligerently at Diodorus. "I want to have a long talk with you tomorrow!" She marched out of the city council.

Saturday morning, another meeting took place at the city council. Diodorus was in charge, and again, Marcos was present. He took careful note of their tactics and formed a strategy so that Anthony and Miriam would be protected.

For the second trial, the high priest of the Imperial Temple of Augustus would be the single prosecutor. He would represent the Roman government. The full weight of Roman law would fall on Antipas. The civil authorities had denounced him as a detrimental influence, and they were confident that he would not recognize Domitian as a god.

Lydia-Naq called Diodorus aside after the plans had been worked out. "Mehu was right. You shouldn't have let Antipas carry on with his stories. Before you took over, the crowd was completely with us! When you told him he was no longer wanted, it was a perfect moment to close the circle, to get the crowd to yell for his death. Instead, you let him go on and on about a good person who did good things for everyone! Antipas made it sound as if this Yeshua was a perfect man. Why did you let him start talking about Asclepius wanting eternal life for humanity? How could you let the evening slip away like that?"

Diodorus simply looked at her. *All my life, I have wanted to find the perfect man described by Cicero. I thought maybe I had found him. I could have become a follower...until I found out that he had been crucified.*

After a few seconds, Diodorus responded to Lydia-Naq's tirade with a smile. "I'm sure the plans you have for Antipas on Sunday night will work out perfectly. Congratulations!" He examined the cold eyes of the high priestess once more and walked out without another word.

MARCOS'S HOME

Marcos talked with Anthony and Miriam at noon on Saturday. "Don't call Ateas and Arpoxa right now. We have some important decisions to make, and Arpoxa is busy nursing the babies. I must talk to you alone.

"Miriam, my intention is to get you and many of Antipas's scrolls safely away from the city. Soldiers have been posted at the bottom of the village property. Your grandfather is under house arrest. If Onias and Abijah leave the village with your things on a wagon, the soldiers watching Antipas won't know anything unusual is being planned. They will bring your clothes and anything else you want from your house today, but you can't personally go back there. Abijah will take everything you need. She'll transfer the clothes and the scrolls to a wagon and bring them here.

"Also, you can't go to the cave in the morning as you usually do. The group there won't miss you. Your very recent marriage was to your advantage. I want both of you to leave Pergamum tomorrow at noon. I'm arranging for you to go with a group of girls from the village to Thyatira. All of you will stay with your Uncle Jonathan. Tomorrow morning, four wagons will be packed by Urbanus.

"He will be in charge of them, and he will drive the first wagon. Because Chrysa needs to be fed, Ateas, Arpoxa, and Saulius will have to leave with you. They have already agreed to go but don't know the whole plan.

"The young people in your village enjoy going on a trip out of the city, so here is what we hope will happen. Tomorrow at noon, a group of active, singing girls from your village will go through the Eastern Gate in the first two wagons. The third wagon will have the scrolls inside together with enough supplies for the trip. You, Miriam and Anthony, along with Ateas, Arpoxa, and the babies, will be in the fourth wagon. I don't want you to be noticed as you leave the city."

After making sure they understood his plan, he continued. "In the afternoon, you will go as far as Gambreion and stay there one night. The widow whose house was rebuilt by Antipas will welcome all of you. The second day you should make it as far as the town of Forty Trees and stay there for the night at your Uncle Jonathan's farm.

"I am hoping you will arrive in Thyatira before the end of the third day. Going as a group means you'll have greater safety, but traveling with women and babies adds an extra day to the trip. Because of the festival, many young people are coming and going on the road. This is a great advantage to the plan. Miriam, I want you and Chrysa Grace to stay in Thyatira with your Uncle Jonathan Ben Shelah and Aunt Rebekah until things calm down. Urbanus will bring the village girls back to Pergamum after one week."

He stood up, ready to go to the village. "The Festival of Zeus lasts for two weeks, and people come and go freely, so getting through the Eastern Gate should not be difficult. Many citizens of Pergamum will be going to Ephesus for the Festival of Artemis. You will have two weeks for us to learn what the next part of the plan will be.

"Only Urbanus knows about this plan. He has already sent a trusted person to tell the widow to prepare for your arrival. But you must keep this to yourselves. Ateas and Arpoxa and all the young women going with you must think they are going on a holiday trip to get away from the Festival of Zeus."

Anthony expressed a question that had been forming. "I have two weeks off from classes. How will I know when to return? I must avoid being declared a deserter from the army."

"I agree that we must keep that from happening. I will let you know what is happening here by messenger pigeon to Jonathan," he said. "You may have to return to Pergamum alone for a while. At this moment, I simply want you both to leave the city without anyone noticing. Don't wear any military garb while going through the city gates, but take everything with you, all your armor and gear."

He withheld the rest of his thoughts. Antipas might get off with a light sentence; however, a worse punishment was possible. It might not be safe here for Miriam if the authorities called for the village to be expropriated. He was worried about the meeting tomorrow night. Their demands might put him in a problematic conflict of interest. If he was seen as biased, he might be replaced and lose his ability to protect the interests of the family and the village.

"Now excuse me. I have a lot to do before tomorrow night. Onias will send duplicate messages by carrier pigeons to your uncle in Thyatira. We'll tell him that several young people will arrive on Tuesday evening and that you two, Ateas, Arpoxa, and the babies will come with the girls.

"Please don't ask me for all the reasons why I say that. Onias knows my plans and is helping with the arrangements. Sorry to be so quick with you this morning. I can't tell you why, but you will soon know the reason."

Anthony was amazed at his ability to plan. He whispered to Miriam, "Marcos is a capable strategist. He could have been a scout for our legion."

He smiled at the thought. She asked why he was smiling and laughing after such a scary talk. She would soon get used to the little things that brought him laughter.

ANTIPAS'S HOME

Abijah busied herself in Antipas's home. She gathered Miriam's clothes, the perfumes, mementos, and her jewelry. She found a little scrap of parchment and laid it on the top of the clothes. It had the names of about two dozen people on one side, and on the other was written, "Her name is Chrysa, born on February 8." As she turned quickly to put clothes into a bag, she brushed against the parchment. It fell on the floor, at the end of Miriam's bed.

As was instructed, Abijah made several trips to her house, bringing Miriam's personal things with her. Shortly afterward, when other soldiers relieved the first ones guarding Antipas, she took the bags from her home and placed them in a wagon. Onias took the reins, and they made their way down the hill to River Road.

Abijah and Onias talked as they made their way to Marcos's home. "Do you really think Antipas has written a will that leaves everything he owns to his granddaughter?" asked Abijah.

"I don't know about that," responded Onias carefully, not wanting to reveal the main topic of his last conversation with Antipas. "I think we need to be careful to stop any gossip from spreading."

Later that night, sleep would not come to Antipas.

Tomorrow I will learn about my future, but tonight I am free in my own house. Miriam and Anthony and the dozen young people leave tomorrow by wagon. How could I have known that helping the widow woman and her sons in Gambreion would one day help my granddaughter? They may help me more than I helped them!

"Hear my prayer, O Lord, listen to my cry for help; be not deaf to my weeping. For I dwell with you as an alien, a stranger, as all my fathers were. Look away from me, that I may rejoice again before I depart and am no more."[85]

Sometime in the middle of the night he awoke and stood on the floor. His nightclothes hung around his frail frame; his hands were stretched upward.

"Do not fret because of evil men or be envious of those who do wrong; for like the grass they will soon wither, like green plants, they will soon die away. Trust in the Lord and do good; dwell in the land and enjoy safe pasture. Delight yourself in the Lord and he will give you the desires of your heart."[86]

He needed a deep sleep, but he still had a long list of other items on his mind. He prayed for the people in each household in his village. He knew them all by name, the widows and the orphans and the slaves who had received freedom and a new life. Scenes returned of his annual visits to the slave market as he remembered the purchase and redemption of each person.

He stayed awake for another hour, remembering how much his community loved him. He went over the immense outpouring of love at his sixty-fifth birthday and the practical jokes Urbanus, Philo, and Philogulos played on him at his sixty-sixth birthday. He slept well past his usual time to be up early for the Sunday morning Holy Meal. Onias was knocking on the front door just as dawn began to show in the east.

A bright moon hung over the sky, having just started to diminish in brightness. Clouds kept hiding the moon, and then it would appear again as they blew over the eastern sky in the

[85] Psalm 39:12–13; also Job 7:19, 10:20
[86] Psalm 37:1–4

confusion of weather patterns, common at this time of the year.

Antipas was calm as he led the prayers in the cave. Everyone had learned about his trial in the Roman Theater. A few started crying. Before the Holy Meal, he called them all to come forward one by one, even those who were not yet permitted to take the bread and wine. He laid hands on each of them, blessing each of them. This stretched out his time with his friends and made the meeting very long. His comforting words brought many tears. Soft sounds of sobbing were heard.

He read from Peter's letter.

> *"You are now a chosen people, a royal priesthood, a holy nation. You are a people who belong to God. Why? So you can declare the praises of him who called you out of darkness. You came into a wonderful light. Once you were not a people and now you are the people of God; once you had not received mercy, but now you have received mercy. Dear friends, I urge you, as aliens and strangers in the world, to abstain from sinful desires, which war against your soul. Live good lives among the pagans that, though they accuse you of doing wrong, they may see your good deeds and glorify God on the day he visits us."*[87]

Urbanus got up and left them quickly. Antipas knew that he was off to finish preparing the remaining wagons for the trip to Thyatira.

Dear God, you have fed my spirit every day through these people whom the world would call insignificant.

He thanked them for their acceptance and their love. He asked forgiveness because he could not do more for each household. They left, many going to their places of work.

The sky in the east had started to clear, and a golden sun was peeking out from behind rough black clouds. A new day had begun.

MARCOS'S HOME

Two hours later, the wagons with the young people arrived at Marcos's villa. Breakfast was served as they chattered wildly.

---

[87] 1 Peter 2:9–12

It was the beginning of a grand holiday. Going away to a different city was a treat more exciting than anything that had ever happened before. They would be away for the whole time that Pergamum was celebrating the Festival of Zeus.

When breakfast was finished, they all gathered in the main room for Marcos to give the girls their instructions. "When you get near the Eastern Gate of the city, some guards may be watching you. I want you to be singing songs, especially you, Aliza, Nessat, and Talia; you...uh...have louder voices."

He didn't say so, but they were also the group's cutest and more distracting for the guards.

"You girls will be in the front two wagons with six in the first and six in the second. All of you...lift your voices high; let them hear you sing! After all, it's festival time! It was Miriam who taught you songs, right? This time she has a little baby to care for, so she and Anthony won't be teaching songs to anyone. This is your opportunity to teach songs to people along the road!

"The third wagon will have your baggage, some of Antipas's personal records, and the food for the trip. Anthony and Miriam will come along in the fourth wagon with Ateas and Arpoxa.

"Sing for the soldiers, for the other young people on the road, and for one another! Soldiers won't bother you; I am sure of it. Urbanus will be sitting in the driver's seat of the first wagon, and I want one of you girls on either side of him."

The Eastern Gate, built in the days of Eumenes II, remained a marvel of engineering. Its triple gates permitted an enemy to come through only the first gate before realizing that they had been surrounded and blocked by a second and third gate. A tower stood over each entrance with guards looking down, ready to shoot deadly arrows. The Eastern Gate had never surrendered to an enemy army. It took five men on each of the massive gates to open them or close them, and no one could remember the last time they had been closed. Under Roman rule, the city was a safe place.

Twelve guards stood on duty, studying the crowd of travelers as they poured into the city. Marcos's four carriages left together when the sun reached its highest. The dark clouds of the morning were gone with the breezes. The warm spring air gave a sense of peaceful laziness to the city. Before noon, thousands of farmers and merchants, having come early in the day from scattered villages up the valley, began to pack up the mats they had placed on the ground to show off their items for sale and return home.

The flow of people through the Eastern Gate was so high at noon that the guards could not afford the time to inspect each wagon. A group of happy young people in wagons, playing tambourines and flutes, strumming on harps, and singing songs raised little suspicion.

With attractive young women to gaze at, the guards' attention was distracted for a few minutes. Urbanus pulled the horses up sharp and stopped as if innocently waiting for inspection. Other horses and carts in the line quickly piled up behind the four wagons, and a small uproar at the gate caused returning villagers to yell. People shouted, and a commotion started.

"Get a move on it, will you!" shouted one farmer angrily.

"What is the holdup?" A cry came from a merchant who obviously wanted to get home quickly. "We can't wait here all day!" he shouted in indignation.

Anthony and Miriam were protected from the sun by a cover over their wagon. Ateas and the regular wagon driver for the Ben Shelah family sat on the driver's seat. Arpoxa was breastfeeding her son.

Urbanus and the four wagons quickly passed through the gate and safely left the city of Pergamum. Several of this group had been part of the team that came to help the widow in Gambreion. It was going to be an excellent time away from home!

Anthony leaned over his daughter, the scar on his face resting on Grace's small, delicate cheek. He wanted to say the words out loud, but he couldn't, and he relished his precious thoughts. He both prayed for Grace and made a promise to her. "Little Grace, Miriam and I took you into our home. We rescued you, and while you sleep, we will protect you. There! The guards have let us pass. I will be the best father you could have, little one. I will always protect you."

Miriam looked at the baby sleeping in her arms, quiet and safe. *Grace just wants love and attention. We don't know her mother. Perhaps we will never meet her, but there is a big story behind the mother giving birth...and then giving this precious child away.*

They were soon on the Roman postal road. Many carts were coming into the city for the festivities, while others, like theirs, went eastward toward Thyatira. Miriam was relieved to successfully get away from the city. Suddenly she remembered something. "Anthony, remember the little piece of parchment with the name 'Chrysa' written on it? Have you seen it? I wanted to keep it for her to have someday."

"I'm sure it is here somewhere, tucked into your belongings. Don't worry. Abijah packed all your things very carefully."

"Even if her real father appears, she will still be..." She didn't finish her thought.

He sensed her anxiety. "Don't worry. No one is going to take Grace from us. We made it this far. We know where we will stay tonight, with the widow and her children. Tomorrow night we will stay at your uncle's olive farm near Forty Trees, and on the third day, we'll be safe in Thyatira. Three days of travel, and we will be safe. God is looking after us, and soon we'll be home again." He pulled her close to him, rested her head on his shoulder, and smelled the sweet, enticing perfume of her hair.

Across from them, Arpoxa and Ateas both smiled. She would not forget the sight of the little family huddled together in the back of the wagon. Ateas enjoyed being part of an exciting adventure.

THE AMPHITHEATER

Late on Sunday afternoon, four Roman soldiers dressed in full military attire came to take Antipas under guard to the amphitheater. Two of them carried ropes that they tied to their prisoners' wrists while two of them walked behind him. He wore his best cloak, a white cotton robe that covered his tunic. All the spectators would be dressed in Roman garb; Antipas had chosen to wear the clothes of his ancestors.

They led him up the carefully crafted, richly ornamented ramp leading into the amphitheater. He remembered the road from his wandering to the Jewish cemetery before his father had died.

They led him to a small building on the steep embankment. Constructed at the top of the hill, outside and above the amphitheater, it was part of the cemetery grounds that held the graves of the men who fought as gladiators. Those heroes had given their lives for entertainment for the crowds of mostly younger men. They died to the sounds of cheers and chants to the glory of victory and death.

His guards forced Antipas to sit in a dark room where none of the soldiers would speak to him.

Noise rose louder and louder as people assembled in the amphitheater and grew in intensity while the sun was setting. Somewhere a trumpet was blown three times, apparently a signal because the guards now led him out of the door and down a long flight of white polished marble stairs to the amphitheater.

At the eastern gate, they stopped. Antipas heard the water of the stream far below flowing under the vast sports complex, emerging at that spot under the massive arch holding up the gate.

Two men behind him held torches. In the flickering light, he was just able to make out the words carved in the archway: "Vincenzo: Hero of the Games of Asia, Thyatira; eighth year of Domitian." This was the third time that Vincenzo had won that honor.

Antipas folded his fingers together. *The entire world will remember his name, written in stone forever, but no one will remember mine.*

They pulled him roughly into the amphitheater and onto the platform. All of the seats were full, and the shouts and noise confounded him for a moment. A much larger crowd had gathered than the one three nights before. Twenty-five thousand spectators jammed into every space. The jeering and shouting quieted for a few seconds as they saw him enter; then the din started again, at a higher pitch.

He was pulled to the center of the platform, and the ropes binding his hands were removed. The four soldiers then backed away and stood behind him as he faced the dignitaries of the city. The seated audience was all around the ample oval space where gladiator fights were held. The crowd was becoming slightly irritated. People had been promised a satisfying evening's entertainment, but the platform full of city officials did not look promising. They were more interested in swords, spears, and clubs, with plenty of blood, than another debate.

The Pergamum Amphitheater, the largest coliseum in Asia Minor, was set in a massive, natural bowl between two hills. It came to life as the acoustics, perfected through centuries of Greco-Roman experience, amplified the growing noise.

The west side of the circular bowl was reserved for the

dignitaries. The eastern side was much higher and could seat many thousands more. Dignitaries such as Mayor Quintus Rufus and Vincenzo, the hero of the games from the previous year, sat in positions of honor.

The mayor stood up, turned to the crowd, raised his hand for silence, and declared, "Caesar is lord and god." Immediately, the whole crowd rose to reply with a mighty shout, "Caesar is lord and god!" Everyone knew that this assertion went to the core of whatever dramatic scenes would take place here tonight.

Quintus Rufus let the crowd grow quiet. Then he looked at Antipas, announcing, "Three nights ago, Antipas Ben Shelah, you were confirmed by this city to be an intolerant atheist. We are here tonight to witness the payment of your taxes to the empire and your declaration of loyalty to Caesar."

He nodded in the direction of the high priest of the Imperial Temple who represented the Roman government. Silence enveloped the mass of onlookers as they waited to see what would happen next.

Damon took over. "Come, Antipas. You are here to publicly pay your taxes. As a Jew, you did not have to pay personal taxes, only business taxes and the Jewish temple tax. Well, your own countrymen have disowned you. Your name was crossed out of the synagogue's Book of Life. You are not a Jew. Consequently, you must pay personal taxes like all other citizens."

Lydia-Naq sat in the second row and leaned forward.

Antipas was ready to pay. He took a large pouch off of the belt around his waist. "Over there," Damon said. "Take your tax to the table in front of the statue of Emperor Domitian. Put your money on the table!"

A statue of Domitian stood in the niche under the eastern gate. After walking across the arena, Antipas opened his pouch containing the money and poured a large pile of coins on the small table. Then he walked back to the platform.

Not a voice could be heard from the throng watching the event. Silence prevailed.

Damon stood to his full height. "As the high priest of the Imperial Temple and guardian of the customs of the Roman Empire, I require that you repeat the Solemn Oath."

Antipas looked directly at Damon. The old man's loud voice was heard by everyone. "I have paid my taxes, and I have given

401

honor to this city and to the empire."

A few people made a clicking noise with the tongue, showing their initial disapproval.

Damon took a step toward Antipas. "In your trial three days ago, it was determined that you practice customs that, if adopted by others, would threaten the empire. You teach people not to believe in any other gods than the one you follow. This makes you deserving of death for misleading others.

"However, we are not unmerciful, so we give you this chance to choose life. Now you must proclaim the power and deity of the emperor by doing what all men in the Roman Empire do. At this time of paying your taxes, you must take a pinch of this salt and sprinkle it over the flame while you declare, 'Caesar is lord and god.'"

Antipas stood as tall as he could. He was short, and beside Damon, he seemed very small indeed. The tall purple hat on the high priest's head accentuated the contrast. Antipas no longer felt frightened or speechless. A sense of peace surged through his heart. He spoke to the throng, understanding many wanted his life. He would give it to them...with perhaps a bit more than they were expecting.

"I am a loyal citizen of Rome and have served Rome. From the products we have made, I have paid far more business taxes than almost anyone here. I pay taxes on my shops, on my sales, on my establishment, and on the products that we manufacture, those of glass, pottery, and everything else. But, sir, the central question tonight is not about my taxes, is it? It is about my faith in God. He is the one who is the Lord of the lords; he the God of the gods."

The crowd was silent, following every word. "He is everlasting, and his ways are forever. Because he cannot die, he is not like the gods you worship. All men must die; that is why no man, no matter his earthly authority, can be a god."

Hundreds—no, thousands—sucked in their breath at his words, whether they were taken as an expression of courage, disrespect, or insanity. Everyone—even those crowded into the topmost rows—could hear his clear voice speaking slowly, deliberately, and persuasively.

"I have never denied the authority of our emperor. I have always paid my taxes and lived an open and honest life. I believe that Yeshua, the carpenter of Nazareth, is our promised Messiah.

He was crucified under the Roman governor Pontius Pilate. He loves those who trust in him, and he died as a sacrifice for them. His was a unique sacrifice, the sacrifice of his life. He died as a ransom for our sins. We are saved through his death as we are brought to understand the nature of the sacrifice that he became for us."

A growling sound swept over the crowd. Antipas was too confident. Some in the crowd began to jeer loudly. Here was a man who worshiped a dead man! He waited for the booing to die down, but loud calls were starting to be heard continuously.

"After three days, Yeshua came back to life. Hundreds saw him over many weeks. Then he went to heaven in a cloud, showing that he is the Lord of life and has power over death. I respect the authority of Emperor Domitian, who imposes order and laws on people in every province of the empire. But I will not make your confession."

Jeers erupted from all over the amphitheater.

Any possibility of bending his resolve, of imposing the will of Rome to force Antipas to comply, disappeared. The high priest held up his hands to quiet the crowd and demanded, "This is your last chance. Confess, 'Caesar is lord and god.'"

Antipas stood straight with his feet together. His posture was much like that of the soldiers standing at attention on January 1 as they declared the Solemn Oath.

"In this upside-down kingdom of which I speak, the poor are not oppressed, and slaves are treated kindly. If someone seeks to gain his own life, he loses it. If someone dies to himself, he comes alive. To Rome, I owe my taxes, my work, and my respect. To God, I owe my life."

The crowd was absolutely silent, breathless, listening to his answer. Didn't he know that death awaited him? Wasn't he afraid? He said nothing more.

Quintus Rufus, the mayor of the city, again stood up at his seat in the dignitaries' section in a display that seemed to have been rehearsed. "Citizens of Pergamum, you know we are men of honor, and Pergamum will not be brought to shame by this man's statements." Then, turning to face Antipas, he said, "You have chosen your fate. You will not be given another chance to recant your beliefs."

A shout of approval went up from the crowd. The mayor

turned to all the spectators, those before him and those behind him, before continuing in his denouncement of Antipas. "We will not permit you to bring dishonor upon our city. You will suffer tonight for the offensive words you have spoken. No one will ever remember this little rebellion of yours. Your own words of defiance have brought about your sentence. The sentence is death."

Now six soldiers took Antipas from the platform, two in front of him, two beside, and two behind. They led him up the stairs to the western gate, following the entourage of dignitaries, authorities, and priests. This was their victory march, for they had won, having overcome the little man's stubborn willfulness. Slaves carrying torches lit their path. He felt the grip of the soldiers beside him holding his wrists.

At the entrance to the unfinished New Egyptian Temple, the crowd was stopped. They were allowed to observe what was happening within by looking over the low unfinished walls of the temple. They wanted to enter the precincts of the great new sanctuary but were not permitted. Few words were uttered.

Antipas saw movement in the darkness ahead of him illuminated only by a hot fire burning in a brass grate under an ornate bronze cauldron shaped like a bull. The fire was being fed by slaves stacking logs under the kettle. He sucked in his breath as he heard the soldiers behind him exclaim, "The oil is starting to boil."

Slaves pulled a crane from the area where construction of a massive wall had occupied the bricklaying teams earlier in the day. The crane was used daily to lift timbers and massive stone blocks into place along the top of the walls. A large block of wood still sat atop the crane.

Antipas turned. The noise in the amphitheater had turned into a great silence within the New Temple. For more than a year, the foundations and outer walls of the new construction had been taking shape. The old Temple of Artemis had been torn down. The foundations of two round towers were buried in the ground, as were the stone blocks that would hold a massive edifice between them. In preparation for the previous year's Festival of Zeus, the old Artemis temple had been removed. Large tapestries were hung from poles behind the bronze bull cauldron, reminding the population of the goddess's central part in the season's festivities.

Crowds shoved and pushed along the outside of the western wall. All were trying to make out what was happening within the sanctuary. Even the roar of the fire seemed lost in the enormous space of the dark temple.

In the dim light of the fire, the crowd could see the small man dressed in a white robe now standing on the eastern side of the New Temple. He was close to a low, partially built, red brick wall. News spread quickly that Antipas would meet a painful death.

A loud voice asked, "How can anyone stay so calm in the face of death? Does he possess a power stronger than the fear of death? Maybe he is right about some things."

Vincenzo overheard the comment and sucked in his breath. He spoke through narrow lips. "Don't believe it! The authorities of our city were right to be swift in their response. Antipas is a rebel. Don't be sorry for him! His ideas make people value themselves above the authority of the government. Don't think his ideas aren't powerful. You don't understand the effect his kind of teachings can have on people. What would happen if these ideas spread? The city is right to get rid of him."

"He's a harmless old man" came the reply, but this time the man kept his voice low.

Vincenzo stopped in his tracks and forcibly took the man by his neck. "The weak ones die while the strongest triumph! Antipas denied the gods; he pays homage to another king! He is being sacrificed to appease all the gods he has offended. He's being put to death in the very place where the gods whose existence he has denied will be worshiped! Animals will be sacrificed here, lambs and goats, oxen and bulls!"

Antipas watched as the wooden crane, pulled by a dozen slaves, rolled slowly toward him on its four wooden wheels. He stood close to the entrance of what would eventually become the New Red Temple.

He heard a guard. "Earlier today, a lamb was sacrificed here without as much as a squeak! I wonder how much this man will yell and scream when he's being lowered into boiling oil."

Vincenzo spoke loudly so that everyone around him in the darkness of the night could hear him. "You lost, Antipas! You said you were an overcomer!"

The crowd, which had now filled the area along the partially built north wall, stood silently, waiting for an answer.

Although Antipas couldn't see Vincenzo in the dim light of the unfinished temple, he addressed the taunt in a loud voice. "I confess in the name of the One who conquers death: He has risen, and he is the Overcomer!" He spoke clearly, challenging the notion that the goddess Nike was victorious, the overcomer.

The intense heat from the fire under the hollow bull held the priests and the spectators back from the altar. The interior of the bull had been filled with oil, and now the pungent smell of burning pine logs mixed with that of boiling oil filled the area outside the unfinished temple.

Sweat poured down Antipas's face. He stood in front of a sculpture of the goddess Artemis, where an animal had been sacrificed.

He offered a quick prayer. *Help me to be faithful to the end. The lamb made no sound as it was slaughtered.*

With a loud prayer, he said, "May the God of the heavens, the Almighty Lord, forgive you."

Knowing there was no reason to resist, Antipas willingly placed his hands together. The guards holding Antipas laughed. They bound his hands behind his back with thick leather thongs. Next, soldiers from the garrison of Pergamum laid him on his back and tied his feet with more leather thongs.

Others moved the tall wooden crane into place and slowly lifted him high above the boiling oil and pushed the crane forward to place him over the bull. Then they started to lower him slowly, unwinding the rope. The priests had demanded that they take a long time to bring him into the oil.

Antipas closed his eyes against the searing heat rising from the bubbling oil. A sudden hush came over the whole crowd. They had never witnessed such a punishment.

Thousands held their breath. Imagining pain like this was beyond their abilities. The heat would be too intense to bear. He was being sacrificed inside a sculpture made to receive the sacrifices to their gods.

The last words of the old man as the crane lowered him were the same words he had said two nights before. "From everlasting to everlasting, the Lord's love is with those who fear him, and his righteousness to their children's children—with those who keep his covenant and remember to obey his precepts."[88]

He was still well above the boiling oil when the block of wood that had been sitting at the top of the crane shifted. It had needed reshaping to fit into place and had been left for the next day's construction crew. The block fell, narrowly missing Antipas and dropping into the oil below.

A wave of hot oil splashed over the side of the bronze cauldron. Immediately, a blaze from the fire below rushed up the path of the dripping hot oil. The surface of the oil in the cauldron burst into a fireball, and flames consumed Antipas instantly, making his death far quicker than the priests had wanted.

As the fire flared, the wooden crane caught on fire. It was in danger of falling onto the bronze bull. A temple servant quickly tossed a bucket of water onto the flaming oil in the cauldron to keep the nearby tapestries of Artemis from catching fire. The water hit the oil and turned to explosive steam that blew hot oil over the fabrics, the servant, and several of the priests standing in front of the sculpture. Covered with the hot flaming oil, the servant collapsed where he stood. The robes of several priests caught on fire, and they ran around the open sanctuary, casting off their burning clothing. Confusion spread around the unfinished foundations of the great temple.

Some wondered later if this was retribution by Antipas's God.

THE ACROPOLIS

Normally people looked up to the acropolis and admired the polished white marble blazing against a blue sky or shimmering under the scorching sun of midday. On this night, heavy dark clouds kept the bright full moon hidden, and the Altar of Zeus did not stand out as usual.

In history, in literature, and in their imaginations, Zeus would forever continue to fight the giants of the Underworld. Around the base of the altar, the father of the gods eternally and triumphantly thrashed his enemies in beautifully sculptured and colorfully painted scenes of their battles and defeats. This was the story of the beginning of the world. Zeus had to accept the help of Athena or else victory would not be his. In this world, the analogy continued with the high priest of Zeus depending on the support

---

[88] Psalm 103:17–18

of his high priestess.

Athens and Pergamum forever would be joined by the myths of the ages. Pergamum would eternally stand, proudly bringing the attention of the world to Zeus. The evening sacrifices offered to him in thanks for the death of Antipas made smoky black trails that rose slowly into the heavens.

Below them, in the sanctuary of the New Temple, the fire died down, and finally the flames caused by the boiling oil were extinguished. A pile of red-hot coals and ash remained. It would be tomorrow at midday before the ashes were cool enough to be cleared away. The body of Antipas had been consumed by the fire, and only a few bones remained.

The fire had cleansed their city by eliminating the rebellious atheist. Sacrifices made to Zeus always brought victory against enemies. To the high priestess, the high priest, the virgin priestesses, and all those who had instigated and then watched the trials of Antipas, this was a display of the power of Zeus. As she prepared for sleep, Lydia-Naq looked down on the scene from her home on the acropolis.

Thank you! You gave us victories in ancient times. You brought about another victory tonight, this time against a small, dangerous troublemaker. He rebelled against you, declaring, "Zeus and all the other gods have no power."

I'm satisfied that the group meeting shortly before the trial made the correct decision: to begin the expropriation of Antipas's village immediately. This means that our victory over the atheists will soon be complete. I was not happy, though, to see the expression on the lawyer's face. Marcos showed hesitation to initiate the confiscation of the Ben Shelah estate. However, when that village belongs to Pergamum, as it rightfully should, then Zeus will have triumphed! Imagine that little man claiming to be an overcomer!

Antipas would no longer bring foreign ways into the city. Zeus had triumphed over one more enemy, and tonight Lydia-Naq would sleep well.

Chapter 45
The Traitor

ANTIPAS'S VILLAGE

Marcos left his house early on Monday morning, still in shock over the vicious punishment inflicted on his friend and mentor. The scenes of flames, of Antipas being lowered toward the boiling oil, and the great flash of fire at the end were sickening. The speed with which the religious establishment had demanded that the court initiate the expropriation of Antipas's estate kept him from sleeping that night. Marcella awakened and asked what he was thinking about.

"Domitian's new regulations demand it, they insisted, but they don't yet know the detailed information of Eliab's will. It will complicate their confiscation process and will offer a valid excuse for me to go slowly on any of the village property. The legal complications give me a long time to unravel things.

"The will must take precedence in court over any confiscation. And since Antipas had paid all his taxes before his death sentence was declared, I'm not sure what legal grounds the city could use to confiscate. Miriam will still be wanted for whatever legal claims the city council thinks it can make against her as Antipas's heir.

"I must be very cautious, or the authorities may believe that my loyalties are divided between them and my faith in the Jewish Messiah."

Great caution was required. He could be accused of partiality to Antipas's family. Some might even question his position of serving the city as lead counsel. Miriam's safety could be jeopardized if her being Antipas's heir became public knowledge. With his death, she could be pursued outside of the city, and that meant she should not go to Thyatira as they had planned. They would very likely be watching for her at their city gate.

Marcos knocked at Onias's door. He was also up early due to the events of the prior evening. They greeted each other with words of consolation on the loss of their friend.

"A new concern has come up," Marcos told him. "You must send another message by pigeon to Uncle Jonathan right away. Use two separate pigeons. Write, 'Antipas was killed last night. Miriam may be in danger. She is in one of our four wagons coming to Thyatira on the Postal Road. Have a messenger tell her to stay at the Forty Trees farm instead.'"

Onias wrote the message down, and Marcos added, "Don't write this, but Jonathan's farm at Forty Trees will be a safer place until we find out what's going to happen."

Together they went to the cages and took two pigeons from the cage marked Thyatira. They attached the small strips of parchment to a leg of each pigeon. Onias had written the same message in tiny letters, and by using two pigeons, the chances of the message getting through were increased.

LYDIA-NAQ'S HOME

Lydia-Naq awoke much later than usual. The Festival of Zeus was in full celebration, and her understudy was taking her turn this morning at the altar. Her slave woke her. "Hail, mistress! Your son is here!"

She got up and looked into the great room, where she could see Diotrephes. He seemed to be disturbed and very upset. She told her slave to go and buy fresh, hot flatbread from the bakery while she prepared to meet him. She called another slave to do up her hair in braids so she would be more presentable. She was ready for a celebration, but when she went from her room to meet him, she found her brother had just arrived and was talking with Diotrephes.

"Hail," she said, greeting Diotrephes and Zoticos. "Why the sour face, my son?" she asked. "We should be rejoicing. The authorities will start to expropriate Antipas's property this week," she stated as if it were already happening. She stretched, saying, "What an end to a man who loved beauty and truth. No! A man who, in the end, confused error with truth. And Diotrephes, I have received some great news from Sardis about something we discussed previously."

Diotrephes ignored her words and took a deep breath.

410

Tension lined his face. "Thank you, Mother, for breakfast, but you don't yet know the whole truth about last night. These atheists are far more dangerous than you think. Do you not understand what has happened?"

She kept silent, wanting him to carry on. "The plan to make Antipas's trial a public event was a mistake. How many people heard him speak? How many households were represented? In the marketplace, people are already asking questions about the things Antipas said."

He got up from his chair and paced in front of the window. "Antipas manipulated you! He never spoke once against Domitian. He could have complained about how the Jews were expelled from Rome twenty-one years ago. Or how his people were killed in Jerusalem by Vespasian and Titus, who destroyed the city and then became emperors. But he accepted the emperor's full authority.

"One man in the Lower Agora this morning said, 'For a hundred years we only had to say, 'Caesar is lord.' Now, under Domitian, we have to call him god, even though the Roman Senate has never permitted anyone to proclaim himself a god.'"

Lydia-Naq wanted to jump in to answer him point by point. However, she knew if she listened long enough, she would learn where Diotrephes was going with his concerns.

Diotrephes's face was strained. "We wanted to stamp out the teaching, get rid of Antipas, and extinguish the influence of the atheists, but I don't think we have been successful. We have failed! The news spread quickly this morning. Some people are saying an injustice has been done. 'He was a kind old man. He showed love to everyone, especially to widows and their children. The torture of an old man is unjust.' *That* is the sort of thing many are saying.

"Do you remember you thought that you would get rid of them by killing their leader? But Antipas has several people who could take over. He prepared others for leadership by meeting with them quietly and in a small group. I was there! I realize now exactly what he was doing. Who do you think their new leader is? The city counselor who quietly came to this city from Nicomedia!"

Lydia-Naq gasped. "Not Marcos! That's not possible! I explained everything about the Altar of Zeus to him. He even brought a sacrifice, a lamb."

411

"Yes, Marcos! Remember when he bought that home overlooking the lower city, in the Villa Nova area? Well, he bought two more villas, right beside his house. Why did he do that? Families in Antipas's village told my informant, and he told me this morning: 'Marcos is their new leader, and he bought them for their Household of Faith!'"

He was talking so fast that he was almost out of breath. "He has been planning this for months. He has a sealed certificate of the city by the authority of Pergamum and the governor. Marcos has not only paid his taxes for this year but for many more years as well. Now, why would he do something like that? This lawyer Marcos is going to be another dangerous enemy."

She leaned forward, very close to him. "My son, how did you learn all this?"

"I told you before about my friend Yorick at Antipas's village. Yorick is my paid informer and a willing traitor against Antipas. What a good name for him! His name means 'tiller of the soil.' He has tilled successfully and dug up all kinds of information. He was a slave, but Antipas bought him from the slave market about five years ago; he gave the poor man a home and a job mixing perfumes. But not enough money...or so Yorick says. He wanted more pay, but Antipas would not give him more. He spends his money at the tavern; he is not very reliable in many ways.

"Well, I started paying him some money each month to keep me informed on what was happening there. Yorick told me a lot of things this morning. He believes that one must be taught secret knowledge, which is what I've been teaching him. Also, Yorick does not like the teaching about forbidding sex outside marriage. He says about a quarter of the people at the cave think like he does, but I don't think it's that many. He calls himself a Nicolaitan.

"I had Yorick snoop around Antipas's house early this morning to see if Miriam was hiding there. The whole house was empty, and all of her belongings were missing, so I think she may have left the city. He did find this scrap of parchment on the floor where her bedroom was. Since it's a summary of the curriculum you teach, Uncle Zoticos, I know it belonged to you, but I don't know why she would have it."

He handed the scrap to Zoticos, who questioningly looked at both sides. At first, he puzzled over the writing on the scrap, but as Diotrephes continued to talk to his mother, Zoticos's mouth slowly opened in realization.

"Yorick told me that Marcos went to Kisthene last summer and sold his properties there. Those transactions gave him enough cash in his pocket to buy the two empty villas next to his own house. As I said, the gossip in Antipas's village this morning is that Marcos is going to use one as a meeting place for the Household of Faith...and maybe the other one too. Do you realize what this means?"

He paced the floor. Diotrephes was almost yelling now. "You got rid of a Jewish leader yesterday, and today they have a new leader, a Roman citizen! Marcos was attending meetings there and became a follower of the Way after his daughter was healed. Surely you remember, Mother."

Lydia-Naq's face was red at this long outburst, but she still said nothing. *My son almost had his head turned in the direction of the atheists! That was not why I sent him there. I sent him to be a spy, but I think he has become infected with some of their teachings.*

Diotrephes grew louder and bolder. "When you are with the crowds at the Altar of Zeus, you think the whole world follows Zeus. But go into that cave with those poor people, and they sing from the heart. It is different."

Up to this moment, Lydia-Naq had listened quietly, but now, as Diotrephes skirted heresy against Zeus, she exploded. "Enough," she commanded.

"No, there is more that you don't know," retorted Diotrephes. "Listen, Mother! Miriam married a Roman soldier, Anthony Suros, in a secret wedding just a few days ago. Yorick is a fountain of information. Who married them? Yes, the same lawyer: Marcos! Not only that but they now have a baby. Yorick told me that Miriam found a baby at the city dump a couple months ago and was raising it at the village. The day after they were married, Marcos had an adoption formally carried out in his home."

Lydia-Naq could see that something dramatic had happened in her brother's mind. At the mention of the baby, Zoticos's eyes opened wide. He looked back at the scrap of parchment. Lydia-Naq saw the expression on Zoticos's face as he lowered his head into his hands. "My brother, what do you think of all this? You have been completely silent."

Zoticos's answer stunned his older sister. "My thoughts have been elsewhere. I told you last August that I had an affair with a student named Trifane during the Festival of Zeus. She is the most beautiful creature I've ever known. I fell in love with her, as I never was in love with anyone before. She was my best scholar, quiet, witty, and deep in her spirit. Before I could tell her that I would marry her, she left the city. I think I know why she left. I am absolutely certain she was expecting my child.

"She came to my office and stole a piece of parchment when I was not there. This piece of parchment in my hand came from the sheet that was taken. I had used it to start planning a curriculum, and this is her writing. She even made a suggestion on how to improve the curriculum for the next group of students. Look, right here! These are her ideas, the changes in the curriculum I was planning for October. It all fits together now. My clerk told me she had come to my office and taken the parchment."

He passed the parchment around for his sister and his nephew to see Trifane's writing and to read, on the other side, "Her name is Chrysa, born on February 8."

"The handwriting on the front is that of Trifane. I think she is the mother of the baby girl. However, someone else wrote 'Chrysa' on the back, see? It's a different handwriting. Who wrote the name of the baby? I believe this scrap may have been an attempt by someone else to get in touch with me and tell me what has happened. So it looks like Miriam has my baby, and her name is Chrysa, the Golden One. I want Trifane! I want us to be a family!"

For her part, Lydia-Naq could hardly believe the news. Her brother was a father, and she had her first niece! It was good news, yet the implication was terrible! Her niece was in the hands of the atheists! How had all this happened? Lydia-Naq looked out of the window at Antipas's property far below, stretching up to the other side of the valley. She couldn't collect her thoughts quickly enough.

Miriam and Anthony have taken our baby. They are enemies of the Naq Milon family. Zeus will help us find Miriam, and Chrysa must be returned to my brother. Zoticos will take Trifane as his wife, and the city has to expropriate Antipas's property.

Diotrephes put some more pieces of the puzzle together after hearing his uncle's guess at what had happened. "Miriam and Anthony disappeared yesterday around noon, and today Yorick says several wagons and some wagon drivers are missing. That confirms my thought that they have left the city. Antipas baptized Anthony about a year ago. After that, Commander Cassius would not let him be an instructor of scouts anymore. That's why Anthony was relieved of duty at the garrison and sent to teach sports to boys at the gymnasium.

"Mother, speculation has spread around their village that Antipas's will leaves his entire estate to Miriam. Yorick believes this includes the land in the village, all the houses, the workshops, two shops on the acropolis, and two shops up the coast. Marcos will probably work as Miriam's counsel to defend any legal case regarding the expropriation of the property. Miriam will be one of the richest women in Pergamum." The tension of being the bearer of bad news accentuated the lines in Diotrephes's face.

Lydia-Naq paced from one side of the room to the other. *How could all this have happened without my knowing? What will the consequences be if they escape? Not only has Miriam taken Zoticos's baby but she is now the heir to Antipas's property. The village must come back to the city through expropriation. Anthony will try to take Miriam away from the city. It will take soldiers on horseback to find them. So many things to consider... Which to attack first?*

"Marcos is dangerous to our cause," she announced. "He pretends to serve the city council. However, the authorities in our city will know how to bring him to heel. He has planned mischief in the dark; we must find ways to undo it, bringing it to light."

Over the years, she had learned to understand what her son was really thinking by listening. For half an hour, she had heard his words. As always, she found the thread of his thoughts, his central concern. He needed encouragement and praise.

"Son," she said, "I see that you are concerned that we did not completely conquer the atheists last night, and I agree with you. Yes, they will attempt to spread their message. But you know and I know that their stories are simply myths. Their Jewish leader didn't rise from the dead. A deeper wisdom is required to open up those truths. It takes special knowledge to become a leader, and you are a leader. Zeus, the father of the gods, chose you. Think about your name—Nurtured by Zeus! It means you now have, and will obtain, more specialized knowledge, the kind that can only come from Zeus, the father of all the gods."

She would bring Diotrephes around to completely support

her goals, as she had done so many times before. "Now listen! I have received word from Sardis that you may be accepted as the director of the Department of History. Go to Sardis for two purposes. First, I want you to interview as a candidate for the position in the gymnasium. I can influence your acceptance. As I told you before, I intend that you will find ways to teach the Lydian language and history.

"You will also join whatever group the Household of Faith in Sardis calls itself. From what you learned during your time with Antipas's group, you will fit in without question. You must destroy the Household of Faith in Sardis and prevent what happened here from happening there. You were destined by Zeus to perform a great task."

Zoticos's mind was still in turmoil, and he had not been paying attention to the discussion. "I don't know what to think," he interrupted. "The person who wrote Chrysa's name is not Trifane. Her writing is neat and strong; see how she wrote the curriculum? This writing, on the other side, looks like that of a person who hardly studied. We really don't know anything about the baby's birth or the people who were there. Did someone kidnap the baby without Trifane knowing it?"

Zoticos's relationship with Trifane was anything but certain. "Lydia, I agree with you about starting a search, but I don't want the whole city knowing about my affair. I would be ashamed if the details of our relationship got out. I really want her to love me, and if too much were revealed, she would be so embarrassed that she might decide not to marry me."

Lydia-Naq again faced her brother's indecision. It made her angry to continually have to make things happen. "We must send the soldiers to bring Miriam and the baby back. We can't wait! Call my steward right away!"

The steward rushed in from the kitchen when he heard his name and was immediately sent to fetch the guards of the acropolis.

Diotrephes added, "I remembered something. Miriam often spoke of an uncle in Smyrna; he takes care of their shipping. And she spoke of another uncle in Thyatira, a man involved in producing clothing and metal objects."

Lydia-Naq took control. "In a short while, the soldiers will be arriving. We must have them search the coastal road south to

Smyrna and the postal road eastward to Thyatira. We need to find a couple fitting their description. They have kidnapped your baby, Zoticos. Diotrephes, write a description of Miriam and one of Anthony too."

Diotrephes added his opinion. "We might learn more from the mayor as well; he was required to be at the adoption. Perhaps he can tell us something we don't know yet. If the soldiers can find Miriam, then she will have to come back with the baby. Maybe the mayor will declare Uncle Zoticos to be the father of the child, and that will give him permission to try to bring Trifane, the baby, and himself together as a family."

He wrote Miriam's description to give to the soldiers.

A few minutes later, the soldiers arrived, and Lydia-Naq gave them instructions. "Antipas was killed yesterday. We believe his granddaughter has left the city, and she is the only one likely to inherit the estate. She must be found and returned here since the court case for the city to expropriate the village and Antipas's shops will begin soon. We also believe that she has kidnapped a baby. Search the roads leaving Pergamum. She will have the baby with her; it is a few months old. Here is Miriam's description. She is twenty-six years old, has long black hair, and will be wearing a blue and white headscarf. Look for a man with her. He is taller than her. On the right side of his face, he has a long scar from his eye to his chin. One of them will be holding the baby. They will probably be in a wagon and trying to get away as quickly as possible. I want all three of them brought back here!"

Chapter 46
Olive Grove Farm

ON THE ROAD TO THYATIRA

The trip from Pergamum to Thyatira in horse-pulled wagons would take almost three days. The first night's stop had been at the new home of the widow who had lost her house in a fire the previous year.

At noon on the second day, Anthony looked from Miriam to Arpoxa and saw that both women were tired. "Only four more hours on the road, and we'll reach Uncle Jonathan's farm just this side of Forty Trees, the military outpost that controls the postal road. We can rest for the night at Olive Grove Farm. Your grandfather told me Jonathan employs five farmers and their families. They harvest olives and crush them for oil, take care of the trees, and make olive soap. He also said they grow plants used in making red dye."

"Yes," said Miriam, "and by tomorrow night, we will be in Thyatira."

The postal road swarmed with people: merchants, farmers, and holiday travelers with their animals. Most were going westward. Groups of young people came by, singing loudly on their way toward the Festival of Zeus.

The wagons stopped for a meal break and a rest for the horses beside a stream flowing from the west flank of Hunt Mountain. Other travelers were also there for a noon break as they headed for Pergamum.

As they ate, two soldiers on horseback passed, headed toward Thyatira. Anthony spotted them coming on the road, so he and Miriam stayed close to the young girls and the four wagon drivers. The soldiers stopped on the road and looked at them and then at another group nearby, as if searching for something. The two talked together for a moment and headed off again toward the east. From his scouting experience, Anthony suspected these soldiers were looking for them.

After they had eaten and the horses had rested, they continued on toward Olive Grove. A short while later, a horseman from Thyatira galloped by in the direction of Pergamum, but the man turned around and came up to them on their side of the wide road. He was a messenger from Uncle Jonathan, who was reacting to the warning letter by carrier pigeon. First, he had stopped at Olive Grove to inform them that the group might be staying there longer than previously planned. He had been fearful that they had somehow taken a different road because he had checked dozens of wagons without finding their group.

"This is only for you," he said in a low voice to Miriam. "I have bad news. A pigeon was sent by Onias in Pergamum with a message to Jonathan. It read, 'Antipas was killed last night. There is danger in Thyatira for Miriam.' As a result, your uncle wants you to stay at Olive Grove for a couple days. You can neither go to Thyatira nor return to Pergamum. I am so sorry about the death of your grandfather, Miriam. When I pass the farm on the way back, I will tell them you were found and will be there tonight, unless you want to make other plans."

Miriam bit her lip and looked away, tracing the long line of the road at the foot of the mountain. Tears poured out, and she used both hands to wipe them away. Anthony immediately guessed what had happened. "I can see that the news was not good, Miriam. Please tell me."

In short sentences between sobs, Miriam told Anthony the news from the messenger. Since Ateas and Arpoxa were in the wagon with them, they also heard what Miriam had to say. They looked at each other wide-eyed and quietly spoke to each other in their Scythian language.

The four of them quickly discussed the change of plans and agreed that continuing on to Olive Grove farm was their only option. Anthony started immediately thinking of what to do from there. Bit by bit, he explained his thoughts to Miriam.

"The message from Onias—it must have been written by Marcos. It's helpful and confusing. 'Danger for Miriam in Thyatira.' Is there danger also for you in other towns and cities? Could you stay at Olive Grove for several days or weeks when I'm not there? I don't know anyone there, and I've no idea if the farm is secure. No, I must take you somewhere safer with family members."

He looked fondly at his wife. "Your Uncle Simon lives in Sardis. Taking you to your Uncle Amos in Philadelphia is out— that would take two more days. And staying with your Uncle Daniel in Laodicea is impossible. It's so much farther. I must be back in Pergamum for the Games, so I don't have much time." He shook his head. "Sardis is our best choice."

Anthony had to make instant decisions on many days while scouting, and already a plan was forming in his mind. His decision reminded him of having to walk through thick, dark forests with dangers on every side, deathtraps that he could not see.

"Well," he said, including Miriam, Arpoxa, and Ateas, "I think the two wagons with the young ones should go on to Thyatira tomorrow. The four of us will rest a day at Olive Grove. If we cannot go to Thyatira because of some kind of danger, then perhaps we should go to Sardis instead. We can stay there with Miriam's Uncle Simon until we understand the dangers. But we will have to be cautious about entering the city in case the authorities are watching for us there too."

Ateas and Arpoxa quickly agreed to be part of the adventure. Almost everything they owned was in the wagon anyway, and they felt safe with Anthony and Miriam.

Anthony gathered the others of the group together. He explained that the four adults had decided to stay at the farm with the babies without mentioning the possible trip to Sardis. That should remain secret for now. The messenger was told of the decision; his horse would take him to Olive Grove, where he would tell the farmworkers of their arrival in the early evening. He would return to Thyatira to inform Uncle Jonathan to prepare for the arrival of the remainder of the group.

As the wagons continued on toward Forty Trees, Anthony and Miriam passed Chrysa Grace back and forth between them. Ateas sat in front beside the wagon driver, where they talked of horses, races, and travel. Ateas had a good grasp of Greek now and was learning a little Latin as well.

Arpoxa took turns feeding the two infants. Now she was exhausted and needed to sleep, so Anthony held Grace and Miriam held Arpoxa's little boy, Saulius.

Miriam occasionally fell into a deep sadness and wailed in a quiet voice. She was bent over in grief, unable to speak at times, and her face was covered with tears. She sobbed, "How could they do this? What did Grandfather ever do against anyone? I feel so lost without him!"

The magnitude of the realization overwhelmed her, and Anthony began to understand how little he knew about talking with women. He had no idea of the words of comfort she needed or how to share the sorrow of the woman he loved.

Miriam had wrapped her arms around her body and was swaying back and forth in the Jewish way of expressing sorrow. "He never did a thing to deserve to die! He loved people," she sobbed. Her stomach was churning. "He did good things, and everybody in Pergamum knew him as a teacher, a businessman, and a producer of fine glassware and good products. They loved to buy things made in our little village. It is not right that he was put to death!"

Anthony tried to comfort her. "I don't have the right words to tell you the pain I feel for your grandfather having died," he said softly. "I love you, and I will always be with you. You can count on my love forever."

She gave a half-smile through her tears. "We are a family now, and I always want to be with you too, Anthony."

The big wheels of the wagon made their thud-thudding sound against the pavement stones of the Roman road, but one of their wagon's four wheels was developing an annoying squeak. The squeaky wheel started to repeat his thoughts. "Not right! Not right! Not right!" It seemed to echo Miriam's sentiments.

Anthony recalled something Antipas used to say repeatedly. "Whoever tries to keep his life will lose it, and whoever loses his life will preserve it."

Antipas had not preserved his life. He had walked a road that had only one destination. The Messiah had preached selfless love, and Antipas had applied that love to shape his life decisions. Anthony still found it difficult to understand that Antipas had become wealthy in the process. The more he gave away to other people, the more he seemed to have. However, in the end, his convictions had cost him his life.

Anthony laid Grace in a little cradle on the floor of the wagon. The sun was hot in the afternoon sky, yet to their right, close to Soma, the next city, the very top of the mighty Hunt Mountain still sparkled with the remains of winter snows. Ateas and Arpoxa continued to try to comfort Miriam. In the wagons ahead, the girls had stopped singing, not knowing how to comfort their friend.

Miriam was angry, sad, afraid, and regretful all at the same time. She had not given her grandfather the farewell she wanted before leaving Pergamum because they were forced to leave in a rush.

Further, Marcos made her afraid by saying they had to leave as they did, like criminals running away. Considering the fate of her grandfather, he was probably right in his concern.

She wept for the loss of her community and Antipas, the only person who had known her since birth. Where would she find a love like that of her grandfather again? She had so many questions and was grateful that God had given her Anthony at this time.

How had her grandfather died? Had something he said in his second trial been taken as speaking against the empire? Why did he have to die the same night as he was put on trial? However, the words of love and comfort from Anthony gave her a sense of hope in this moment of anguish. *I am not abandoned.*

Remembering her last breakfast with Antipas, when he prayed by quoting a psalm asking for mercy from the Lord,[89] the words of the ancient writer came to mind. She sang to herself the last song she had composed the night before her wedding. It expressed the feelings she had now. She turned the last part of Antipas's prayer into a song, sung silently within her heart, which was comforted by having Anthony so close by.

I call out to you, High God of my salvation;
Hear our groans, count our scars, deliver us from fears.
How long must we suffer confrontation?
'Where is your God?'
These never-ending taunts and jeers!

But even if we find no safety in this place,
'You are our God!' So this truth forever we'll raise.
Proclaim your majesty, the grandeur of your grace.
Coming generations will shout unending praise.

---

[89] Psalm 79

You take my hand, holding me. Prayer has set me free.
Hardships have become a transforming hallelujah.

Anthony, too, was going over scenes from the last few days. Antipas had been teaching several young men how to memorize the psalms, and one in particular came to mind. Anthony repeated the words that had brought tears of joy to the old man's eyes.

I love the LORD, for he heard my voice;
    he heard my cry for mercy.
Because he turned his ear to me,
    I will call on him as long as I live.
The cords of death entangled me,
    the anguish of the grave came upon me.
    I was overwhelmed by trouble and sorrow.
Then I called on the name of the Lord;
'O LORD, save me.'[90]

Shortly afterward, the road reached Soma, turning north around the skirt of the mountain. From there, it turned sharply southeast around the peak that had been ahead of them all day. It occasionally blocked the afternoon sun, revealing dark, black cliffs; the shadow cooled the air. They stopped for a rest beside the little river flowing from the mountain.

Once past the pine trees, olive trees spread in every direction, even up the sides of the mountain. Travelers on foot stopped to stare at the strange little group: two wagons full of happy young girls singing songs followed by two wagons with people who looked like they were going to a funeral.

"We will make it," Anthony whispered in Miriam's ear. "We escaped the soldiers at lunchtime because they only saw all the young people and their chaperones having a picnic at the base of the mountain. I'm certain that we are safe for today. Your uncle's olive farm will be a secure place to rest for today."

"Why would soldiers want us?" she asked, looking up at his face. Her hand felt his scar, and she still did not understand the magnitude of the events.

---

[90] Psalm 116:1–4

He wanted to tell her his suspicions, but he struggled between being a realist and an alarmist. Then he realized he had promised to be open with her, to tell her the truth, to never lie to her. As he remembered this decision, he sensed another degree of healing in his own spirit. Honesty was part of love, part of overcoming the trauma of the hurts he had carried since he had left Upper Germanica.

"Miriam, I am guessing that the authorities in Pergamum will want to claim ownership of your grandfather's village, the workshops, the cave, and the shops on the acropolis. You are the only one who can legally inherit his estate.

"We know that Marcos was very concerned that you were in danger, and I think the inheritance issue is why he wanted you out of the city. Don't worry; I will stay with you, my precious one." His eyes strayed to the baby in his arms. "Or I should say, my precious ones. We are not alone." He still was not used to saying things like the Jews did. He could have added, "God is with us," but he knew she understood his meaning.

Miriam now understood that the future was going to be very difficult and asked, "You aren't hiding anything from me, are you?"

He was quiet for a moment. "Those events of Upper Germanica when I was in that province... I must tell you about that soon. When this is all over, I will tell you what I know of my father, the trumpeter going over the wall in Jerusalem when our troops invaded under General Titus. I will tell you of Jewish defenders that outnumbered our soldiers in the narrow space on the top of the wall. I promise to tell you everything, but I can't tell you right now. So much about my life, my parents, and my wound... We have years to fully understand each other.

"I don't know what's happening in Pergamum, but there are secrets...about my family...about me. When the time is right, I'll tell you. You can be assured that there is no dark evil that I am hiding. I want you to know it all, but there are too many details to tell you everything right now."

She hugged him, feeling her breasts close to his warm body. His embrace was comforting and reassuring.

It was time for Anthony to think things through step by step. The security of Miriam and his daughter, Chrysa Grace, depended on what he did next. Even his own life might depend on the right course of action.

His senses, so keen as a scout in Upper Germanica, were once again engaged in a fight for survival. Anthony's wits had been alerted as soon as he learned that he had to leave their home in a secretive way. This time he would not have the benefit of highly skilled fellow soldiers beside him.

The Games would start on Tuesday, May 1. If he didn't show up for his assignment at the gymnasium, Cassius could charge him with leaving his post. He enjoyed being a reservist, training scouts. He had even learned to enjoy coaching young athletes for the Games, encouraging each one of the young men in their own individual gift.

Like all instructors at the gymnasium, he had to be back in Pergamum before the Games began. He would ensure that he returned on time. Most of the other teachers stayed in the city, but some had gone to Ephesus.

Anthony's skills in making decisions in the forests of Upper Germanica were back. His mind now going at full speed, he quickly made several decisions. He would continue to be loyal to his legion. If Domitian launched his attack on Dacia soon, then his legion would need all the good scouts to be found. He was committed to training; maybe Cassius would allow him to do so again.

He spoke again. "If Marcos says there is danger for you in Thyatira, then we will slip into Sardis secretly as an alternative. You and the two Scythians can probably stay with Uncle Simon in Sardis for a long time if necessary. I'll go to the Sardis garrison and request to be transferred there. As a legionary, the only safe place for me is in a garrison.

"If the commander of the Sardis garrison tells me to return to Pergamum, I shall do so, leaving you and Grace with your Uncle Simon Ben Shelah in Sardis. I shall go back to the gymnasium and work out your future with Marcos."

Anthony calculated the time he had left to be away. "We have seven days to accomplish several tasks. We will need a day of rest in Olive Grove. Then it will take two more days to drive a wagon to Sardis. It might take two days in that city to settle in with Uncle Simon and work things out with the garrison. All this will leave me with only two days if I need to return quickly on horseback to the gymnasium in Pergamum to attend the games on Tuesday, May 1.

"My position will be precarious if Commander Cassius chooses to act harshly. My worst fear is being court martialed because then I might be demoted...or worse."

The thought brought a frown. Questions about the future were so real and so urgent. The bumps of the wagon were so endless and the squeaking wheel so irritating!

Suddenly he sat bolt upright. He realized he had never told Antipas the story behind the scar on his face.

Spiritually, he felt a new power, a new identity. From now on, his security and refuge would have to come from the God of Abraham, Isaac, Jacob, and Moses. How could he bring his family, his position in the army, his present responsibility to the gymnasium in Pergamum, and the kingdom of God into balance?

He continued sharing his thoughts with her. "Before...in the legion, I fought alongside thousands of soldiers. Is the legion still my army? Yes. As a reservist, that is where my loyalty must lie. But now I belong to another community, not an army but a community composed of old people and little children, of people whose lives might be in danger even if they have high positions.

"This isn't an army; it's a disorganized community, lacking a recognized leader and unable to fight. Their training and fields of battle are different from those of my legion. The widow in Gambreion won a battle over fear. She rewarded us last night with hospitality. Skilled and unskilled men and women working for Antipas come together, singing songs and praying. Slaves rejoice because they are freed. Antipas taught about an army under a different commander. 'Our identity is a chosen people, a called-out nation, a new priesthood in which all of us are priests of God, through Yeshua His Son.' This is a community bound by a different oath of loyalty."

The community he had joined seemed so helpless. Their help came from God above, who could not be seen. Their strength lay in character, love, and a sound mind.

The plan to get Miriam and Anthony out of Pergamum was on schedule. They were beyond Soma, hugging the mountain and heading south toward Forty Trees. In the late afternoon, the red, yellow, and white wildflowers spread as far as they could see.

Some fields were covered with so many tiny white spring flowers that they looked like snow covering the green grass. Orchards were sprouting new leaves, and small wheat stalks were already pushing out of the ground; the scene was one of complete serenity. Only the horse's hooves, the repeating thump, and the squeaky wheel interrupted their thoughts.

In less than an hour, they would arrive at Uncle Jonathan's olive farm. Chrysa Grace slept on. It was Miriam's favorite time of the day, when she loved to take a walk. If she were home, she would bathe before her evening meal, feel refreshed, and be ready for times of fellowship with friends. She squeezed Anthony's hand and wiped tears from her eyes.

The sun burst through another small cloud in the west for the last time that day. Just before it slipped behind the distant edge of the mountain, long shafts of sunshine darted between the olive trees, sprinkling fresh green leaves with a yellow glow.

The tired horses pulled on steadily. A mile before the military checkpoint, the road to Olive Grove Farm left the postal road. They would avoid going past the road guards entirely for now.

Anthony and Miriam went through their change of plans for the trip to see if some unseen problem could be determined. The message had said some kind of danger for Miriam was in Thyatira. Consequently, only the girls would go there the next day before returning to Pergamum before May 1.

The third cart would be unloaded at Olive Grove. All Antipas's scrolls and personal things would remain there until they determined what kind of danger was afoot.

Arpoxa was exhausted from the ride and from feeding both the infants, who sometimes would not stop crying. She was almost in tears because her feet ached so much. She could hardly walk, and the effort of moving about during the noon picnic meal stop was too much. She would spend tomorrow in bed.

Far down the road, on a small rise, they saw the roofs of the houses where the farm laborers stayed. Anthony realized how long it had been since he had a sense of being at home. Evening was coming on, and all were looking forward to being out of the wagons.

In the twilight, the full extent of the olive trees was lost, but they extended as far as the eye could see. The land sloped down to a valley where a river flowed, and olive trees continued up the other side. The shadow from Hunt Mountain completely enveloped the travelers as they approached the farmhouses.

"If you could summarize your grandfather's life in a few words, what would you say?" Anthony asked as the wagon continued bumping down the road toward the farm,

Miriam snuggled against Anthony. The wheel was making its annoying noise again. She looked up at him but couldn't answer.

Anthony suggested, "Maybe his gravestone would say, 'a man full of faith,' 'a kind man,' 'a generous man,' or 'a man full of love for God and for others.' He was amazing!" Anthony said. "Your grandfather accomplished so much!"

She drew a deep breath. "Yes, for almost nineteen years, he worshiped, taught, baptized, prepared new leaders, and helped the poor. He made new copies of scrolls, training scribes and leaders for other Households of Faith in other cities. All that time he supported the synagogue in the city and a growing village. I grew up in that atmosphere, and it all seemed so natural. It happened every day, and I never thought it was anything but normal."

She wiped tears away as the shock of recent events rolled over her once again. "The most incredible thing is that he was able to bless his enemies. I want to find out how he died. Once he said to me, 'If I am attacked by people who hate me, I will respond with love and forgiveness.' That is how I want to live. And I want Grace to grow up that way too."

"I want that for me too," he whispered.

The songs and the noise of the girls in the first two wagons rose to a high pitch. Everyone was excited to be within sight of Olive Grove. The wheels seemed to agree as they went around, squeaking repeatedly. They were close to the farm now. The olive trees silently touched the evening sky.

She told him the one simple phrase that said it all. "Anthony, I would write on his gravestone, 'A Faithful Witness.'"

He fell silent. It was the end of the day, and the squeaking wheels would only make that unwelcome noise a few more times before their journey ended.

Ateas and Arpoxa were chatting in their Scythian language. They were excited about staying at a farm where olive trees spread out in all directions. They held each other close as they held Grace and Saulius.

Anthony repeated Miriam's words in his mind with every turn of the wheel—"A Faithful Witness." When the wagon stopped, he jumped down to help Arpoxa and the babies into the farmhouse. Still, the phrase kept going around in his mind. Anthony knew that Antipas's few remains would not be buried in the Jewish cemetery because he was no longer accepted as a Jew.

Yellow candles could be seen in the doorways of the houses on the farm. Excited to have ended their second long day of travel, the girls jumped off the wagons, shouting and chattering like swarms of blackbirds finding their place for the night. Nikias and Penelope and their four children and the other families on the little farm greeted them warmly. Young children danced around them as each family welcomed the guests.

They were invited into the farmhouse where a warm dinner was ready to be served. It was good to be with new friends, but nothing could erase the sense of shock of the news about Miriam's grandfather.

For tonight they were safe, and in a few minutes, the horses would be brushed down and fed.

Before Anthony had helped Miriam down from the wagon, he whispered, "You are right. We will write those words someday on a white stone in the cemetery in Pergamum. You've captured Antipas's life in a single phrase."

"Yes," Miriam said. "A Faithful Witness."

MAKING SENSE OF THE NOVEL AND THINKING ABOUT *THROUGH THE FIRE*

The following questions are intended to encourage the reader to consider how each character in the novel fits into the overall story. These characters will continue throughout the seven books, and it is helpful to consider the motives and past experiences that drive them.

1. What kind of suffering or grief did each person experience in the past?
Marcos, Marcella, Florbella, Arpoxa, Antipas, Miriam, Anthony, and Lydia-Naq

2. As the novel opens, what is the core motivation or life purpose of each person?
Marcos, Antipas, Miriam, Anthony, Lydia-Naq, and Diotrephes

3. As the novel ends, what changes have taken place in each of these five groups?
Antipas and Miriam; Marcos, Marcella, and Florbella; Anthony, Ateas, and Arpoxa; Trifane, Zoticos, Lydia-Naq, and Diotrephes; Mithrida, Sexta, and Craga

4. Significant harassment and persecution takes place in the story. What motivates the persecutor? How does each person respond?
Marcos, Ateas and Arpoxa, Trifane, Antipas, and Anthony

5. Who in the story is giving or receiving training? How are skills and knowledge passed on in these three groups?
Commander Cassius, Anthony, and Diodorus Pasparos; Lydia-Naq, Zoticos, and Diotrephes; Antipas

6. In first-century Asia Minor, gathering at Antipas's cave for worship of Yeshua Messiah would have been a relatively dangerous activity. Why do you think people were drawn there?

Give examples.

7. What were the understandings of life and religion for each of these four groups?

People supporting the Roman Empire; those supporting religious traditions; those caring for family members; those profiting from slavery

8. How was the gospel made clear to each person, and how did it affect their lives?

Marcos and Marcella; Anthony; Ateas and Arpoxa

If you enjoyed this book, please consider ranking it on Amazon or another book site and posting a brief review. You can also mention it on social media.

Please contact the author if you would like a Zoom visit to your book club or an interview for your blog.
centuryonechronicles@gmail.com

Website:

https://sites.google.com/thechroniclesofcourage.com/chroniclesofcourage/home

Revelation 2:12–17

To the angel of the church in Pergamum write:

These are the words of him who has the sharp, double-edged sword. I know where you live—where Satan has his throne. Yet you remain true to my name. You did not renounce your faith in me, even in the days of *Antipas, my faithful witness* who was put to death in your city—where Satan lives.

Nevertheless, I have a few things against you. You have people there who hold to the teaching of Balaam, who taught Balak to entice the Israelites to sin by eating food sacrificed to idols and by committing sexual immorality. Likewise, you also have those who hold to the teaching of the Nicolaitans. Repent therefore! Otherwise, I will soon come to you and will fight against them with the sword of my mouth.

He who has an ear, let him hear what the Spirit says to the churches. To him who overcomes, I will give some of the hidden manna. I will also give him a white stone with a new name written on it, known only to him who receives it.

3 John 9–13 [91]

I wrote to the church, but *Diotrephes*, who loves to be first, will have nothing to do with us. So if I come, I will call attention to what he is doing, gossiping maliciously about us. Not satisfied with that, he refuses to welcome the brothers. He also stops those who want to do so, and puts them out of the church.

Dear friend, do not imitate what is evil but what is good. Anyone who does what is good is from God. Anyone who does what is evil has not seen God.

Demetrius is well spoken of by everyone—and even by the truth itself. We also speak well of him, and you know that our testimony is true.

I have much to write to you, but I do not want to do so with pen and ink. I hope to see you soon, and we will talk face to face.

Peace to you. The friends here send their greetings. Greet the friends there by name.

---

[91] For the purposes of this novel, I am assuming that 3 John was written after Diotrephes had started causing trouble in a congregation and before John was banished to Patmos. In reality, a clear chronology of the last books of the Bible is difficult, if not impossible, to determine.

CHRONICLES OF COURAGE

Book Two

Never Enough Gold
A Chronicle of Sardis

Part 1

Strangers in Sardis

April AD 91

Chapter 1
Commander Felicior

THE GARRISON OF SARDIS, THE ACROPOLIS, SARDIS

Anthony wiped the sweat that was pouring down his face as he dismounted from his horse at the gate leading into the acropolis garrison. Although he had rehearsed a dozen times what he would say in the next few moments, he was still fearful of the possible results. His heart was beating wildly. He didn't know if a soldier in the Roman army was permitted to do what he had planned. He knew he was risking his life.

Below him, in the early morning light, lay the city of Sardis spread out across a level plain. He hoped the guard would not notice the nervous movements of his hands as he passed the reins.

"I need to speak to the commanding officer," he said, attempting to control the panic rising in his throat.

"Why are you here?" demanded the guard. "Are you a courier?"

Anthony looked intently at the guard. "No, I am a reservist requesting a transfer from Pergamum. I have been training scouts for the impending battle in Dacia."

The garrison, located close to the acropolis gate, protected four prestigious institutions of Sardis: the Temple of Athena, the City Treasury, the *Odeon*, or City Hall, and the army's garrison. Anthony was led into a sparsely furnished office. The commander, sitting at a table, looked up from a large map.

Keeping his voice well controlled, he said, "Anthony Suros, Legion XXI, the Predators, instructor of scouts in Pergamum." He paused and quickly added, "Reporting for duty, sir!"

Commander Felicior Priscus raised his thick black eyebrows and examined the soldier standing in front of him. A scar marked the right side of the man's face. He had thick, curly black hair and strong shoulders.

"I was not expecting and did not ask for another instructor," stated Felicior bluntly. His expression indicated interest because no soldier had ever reported for duty like this, merely arriving at his office and saying he was offering himself for service. "Where did you come from?"

"I have been serving in Pergamum."

"And last night? Were you in our barracks?"

"No, sir, I stayed at Green Valley Inn. I came alone. My wife and daughter are arriving later today or tomorrow."

Felicior wore a puzzled look. "Were you sent to Sardis by your former commander?"

"The transfer from Pergamum is by my own request, sir."

"Under whose authority?" Felicior's low, insistent voice had risen sharply. Irritation showed in his words. "Who transfers without orders from their commander?"

"This is a special circumstance, sir."

"Nothing in the Roman army warrants the expression, 'a special circumstance.'"

Commander Felicior Priscus was clean shaven with a long face, a straight nose, and penetrating eyes. Anthony wondered if the man's deep frown and bushy eyebrows combined with a strong, commanding presence left new recruits asking if he was a friend or a foe.

Maps on a table showed that the commander had been studying the coming invasion against Dacia. The garrison's eagle standard stood in one corner. The standard of Sardis, a scarlet flag with a black eagle over a cluster of grapes, stood in another corner.

Anthony felt sweat trickle down his back. He knew that if he didn't present something in his favor quickly, the commander would arrest him as some kind of rebel. Glancing at the maps held open on the table with weights on the four corners, he began talking about Emperor Domitian's coming attack against the barbarians.

"My arrival here is directly involved with the success of the invasion against Dacia, sir."

"What do you know about Dacia?" A dark frown crossed Felicior's face.

"Sir, I served with Legion XXI, the Predators. We fought and subdued great sections of Upper Germanica. I fought in terrain similar to that which the XXI is about to invade."

Lines appeared on the commander's forehead. "And you were so successful that you are now a soldier without a garrison?"

"Sir, these are unusual, highly irregular circumstances. I am requesting to serve in this garrison. I am on holiday leave from Pergamum during the Festival of Zeus. I am not absent without leave. If you refuse to accept me, I will return to Pergamum to serve under Commander Cassius Flamininus Maro. You will know what decision to make after you hear me speak."

"All right, soldier, your story. Make it brief."

"Thank you, sir. I enlisted at the age of seventeen. My father was Aurelius Suros, a renowned legion trumpeter in Legion X. He was killed in action twenty-one years ago when leading the charge under General Titus against Jerusalem. He died with honor.

"I wanted to avenge the defeat of our legions in the Battle of Teutoburg Forest. Barbarians had wiped out Legions XVII, XVIII, and XIX. Therefore, when I turned seventeen, I took the Solemn Oath of Loyalty to become a soldier.

"For the past twenty years, Legion XXI has been securing the high ground west of the Neckar River bit by bit. Tribal villages were given the choice of loyalty, to be part of a province. Towns have emerged with taxes being paid; laws are being learned. The region is now a province."

The commander nodded, narrowing his eyes.

"I was good at archery and was trained to be a scout, sir, a dangerous job. Every village has to be brought into submission."

Weighing Anthony's words, Felicior turned to look out the window. He stood tall and squared his shoulders, a sign that he appreciated loyalty being shown to the empire. Turning back to interrogate Anthony, he asked, "How did you get the wound on your face?"

"I was recently wounded in an ambush and almost died, yet I survived and became a reservist. I was assigned to the Pergamum garrison to train scouts for Dacia. Here is the assignment authorization issued by our superiors." Anthony pulled a scroll from a small leather bag. He presented the military orders that had been written in Philippi two years previously.

Outside the office, there was a sound of running feet and two loud knocks on the door. Before Felicior could speak, an exhausted soldier rushed in with news. "Two more robberies have been reported, sir."

"Where?"

"In the same area, sir. The mayor doesn't want his home to be the next one to suffer loss.

Felicior swore and asked the messenger, "What is happening? Who's behind these robberies?"

Turning to Anthony, he barked, "Soldier, I'm going to be busy for the next few days. We are facing a serious situation, having suffered several robberies. As for you, remain in the garrison barracks. I will discuss this with you further on Saturday, two days from now."

THE HOT BATHS OF LAODICEA

In Laodicea, three days' travel east of Sardis, a young man named Little Lion arrived with a small pull-cart at the city bathhouse with another cumbersome load of firewood.

The oldest man in the room, the manager, shouted, "Titus, drop the wood over there."

Little Lion tipped the cart, dumping the load near the roaring furnace, and cursed as a splinter dug into the little finger of his right hand. He hated his name. Titus Memmius was eighteen years old. The manager of the hot baths would never call him by the name his friends had given him, the name he preferred.

He frowned, avoiding coming too close to two city counselors who had just arrived for their daily bath. However, he became curious when he overheard their conversation, and he edged closer. One of the well-dressed men was disrobing and said, "I just heard that Domitian is planning to invade Dacia again."[92]

The second one was already naked, and he responded, "Domitian needs brave men for the fight against King Decebalus. He's the wiliest barbarian Rome has faced in decades. Our armies trapped him once, but every effort so far has ended without a victory."

---

[92] Four invasions were made by the Roman military against King Decebalus. The ruler of the Kingdom of Dacia governed the area today known as Romania and Moldova and smaller portions of Ukraine, Slovakia, Poland, Hungary, Serbia, and Bulgaria.

"Rome will need the best soldiers we can send," said the first man. The two men walked over to benches around the edge of the steaming room, and Little Lion couldn't hear the rest of their conversation.

A slave covered with sweat poured more water on the heated floor. Men came in, filling the spacious bathhouse. They had spent the previous two hours watching young naked athletes preparing for their races.

Wiping the steam from his eyes, Little Lion tucked his daily payment into a small leather pouch. As he left the bathhouse, Little Lion's imagination took wing. He imagined himself as a soldier going against King Decebalus, the smartest opponent Rome was facing. The Laodicean authorities described the barbarian king of Dacia as intelligent and cunning, able to outsmart the best army general.

Little Lion had attended the Laodicea Gymnasium before his father died. That fever took many lives and left families more destitute. After the death of his father and his three sisters, he and his mother survived by what he earned, bringing firewood to the bathhouse. Now he had barely enough to keep himself and his mother alive.

His father always had more than enough to pay for classes at the Laodicea Gymnasium. At age fourteen, his last year he studied there, Little Lion won some unofficial contests against some fellow classmates who ganged up on him. Although he was smaller than most, he wrestled skillfully, and that was when his best friend gave him his nickname. Since that day, people said Little Lion never gave up when facing difficulties. Then came that dreadful week when four of the six people in his family were taken away. Their bodies were piled on a loaded cart that inched its way along wide city streets.

He stepped out into the bright sunlight and stretched as high as his short stature permitted. There was a new spring to his step. He eagerly pushed his cart to the southern gate of the city. Bringing in the last load of firewood for the day, he imagined what he would say at home. That was where he lived in a tiny two-room apartment on the second floor of a dilapidated, dirty building.

Every conversation he created ran up against the same problem. His mother, Charmaine, would never let him go to war.

AFTERWORD

How did a tiny group of followers of Yeshua Messiah not only survive persecution in the Roman Empire but continue to grow in number in spite of pain and suffering? How did their faith in a Jewish Messiah spread, reaching both rich and poor, men and women, Jews and non-Jews, slaves and free?

Such thoughts intrigued me while living in Turkey, with its 5,600 archaeological sites. My teenage interest in the Roman Empire as a boy in Kenya returned. Later I was blessed with other teachers who made history come alive.

Turkey's unique geographical features are enhanced with the unending beauty of changing seasons. The visual attractiveness of the land is deeply satisfying. The country is famously known for its millions of tourists that arrive each year.

Seeing this opportunity, I joined others in promoting faith tourism, which is important to the country. Tourist groups I hosted wanted to spend time at the sites of seven ancient cities. At the end of each day, we relaxed and often engaged in questions and discussions.

Having explored Troy with a tour group, we sat down for a fish dinner. We searched our imaginations to describe people who might have lived there three thousand years ago. What were their professions? What happened at the port every day? Who built the buildings? Out of that conversation came a strong impulse to go beyond the stones strewn over the ground to imagine an ancient city throbbing with all sorts of people.

From this came the idea of Antipas being the central character of a novel. I wanted readers to travel in their imaginations, to walk up and down steep streets, to learn to shop in markets, and to receive invitations to come for a meal in ancient homes. It was important to meet living, breathing people. What were their hopes and fears, their politics and religious beliefs? I wanted to understand their conflicts and difficulties, their victories and defeats.

At first, I thought a single book would do. It would include seven sections, one for each ancient city. But as I thought further about each city, it became clear that a single novel would not do justice to the geography, history, civic functions, Roman government, and Greek culture in each case.

Three years passed before the story spanning seven novels had jelled in my mind. The seven novels would weave elements of the seven letters of the Revelation into the cultural background.

Unlike the order of the seven churches as they appear in the first chapters of the book of Revelation, the narrative in this saga begins in Pergamum and ends in Ephesus. At the conclusion of the story, many characters from the earlier novels are brought face to face for a climactic ending.

ACKNOWLEDGEMENTS

For years my wife Cathie and I were privileged to live in Turkey, where we learned to appreciate the commitment of present-day believers in Jesus Christ. We have friends who live in the same region as these seven novels. Our Turkish friends encouraged me in ways they will never know.

During those years in Turkey, many Turkish citizens offered us friendship and hospitality. They not only helped me to enjoy their country but they made us feel safe. My thanks to them for helping us to learn about their way of life and the history of their land.

Archaeologists continue to uncover numerous ancient cities in Turkey. Findings by these researchers supplied dates, names, and details for cities and towns mentioned in these seven novels.

Museum staff were delighted for interested visitors to examine their displays. They passed on much helpful information. I am grateful to the countless scores of people who enriched my life in all the locations mentioned in these novels. Without their help, none of this would have been written.

During my high school years, I was blessed by capable history teachers at Rift Valley Academy, Kenya. Dr. Ian Rennie at Regent College, University of British Columbia, guided me in historical research at an important time in my life. He demanded accuracy, which was character forming.

Several friends provided the impetus for the effort needed to create the story line and bring it to a conclusion. Blair Clark worked with me for several years, especially in coordinating faith tourism. Raye Han, a Turkish tour guide of boundless enthusiasm, taught us about her country, giving endless details and sharing a spiritual passion. Visitors to Turkey were amazed at her professionalism, as well as that of other tour guides.

Friends at the City of David Messianic Synagogue in Toronto, Canada, contributed much to the Jewish aspect of the novels. I am thankful to each one in this Messianic congregation. Through them, I became aware of various aspects of Jewish life and thought, and they helped to build me up in my faith.

Without the help of Jerry Whittaker as an editor, these volumes would not have made it to the press. No one could wish for a more capable and discerning friend. His creative suggestions and analyses improved the story line and character development at each stage.

Friends and family members enriched the story through their comments. Robert, Elizabeth, Samuel, and Aimee Lumkes offered unique intergenerational feedback. Pearl Thomas, Anne Clark, Magdalena Smith, John Forrester, Susan and Max Debeeson, George Bristow, Noreen Wilson, Frank Martin, Ken Wakefield, Lou Mulligan, George Jakeway, and Michael Thoss provided helpful opinions as early readers. Other support came from friends and churches; their names are found in the Book of Life, and my appreciation extends to each one.

LeAnne Hardy graciously became my final editor, and I am grateful for her careful reading and her willing spirit in going through the final steps before sending this manuscript to the printers. She helped me immensely.

My wife Cathie has been patient with me through the many ups and downs while working on these manuscripts. No words can express my appreciation for her unending encouragement.

Appendix: History of Pergamum

(All dates BC unless otherwise mentioned)

2000 – Hittite trade provided links to the interior of Anatolia.

1100 – The arrival of the Sea Peoples from the west provided links with other regions, such as Troy to the north and Greece and the islands to the west.

750 – Kings of Sardis established a wealthy, powerful kingdom based in Sardis with the introduction of coins coming shortly afterward.

550 – Persian rule began in Sardis and spread westward.

333 – Arrival of Alexander the Great and the beginning of Hellenistic influence

320 – Division of Alexander's kingdom between four generals. Lysimachus inherited South and West Anatolia.

315–301 – Lysimachus: war with Seleukos, the Syrian king, and Ptolemaios of Egypt against Antigonos, a general who was capturing Alexander's previous kingdom

301–283 – Lysimachus: married Amastrias, daughter of Persian King Oscartes, and then married Arsinoe, daughter of Ptolemaios I; killed in Sardis in a battle against King Seleukos of Antioch. Lysimachus is noted for having chosen Pergamum as his capital; he ordered Ephesus to be rebuilt.

283–263 – Philetaerus was the commander of the castle in

Pergamum. He turned against Seleukos, and believing the acropolis to be the safest place in the world, he deposited his state treasure of nine thousand talents of gold. Then he used his wealth to secure peace with his rivals by sending expensive treasures as gifts. Gods and goddesses Athena, Artemis (known as Kybele, or Cybele), Apollo, and Demeter were honored with temples. Games began as annual events. Philetaerus adopted his nephew Eumenes.

263–241 – Eumenes I fought the Syrian king, Antiochus, who wanted the return of the nine thousand talents of gold taken by Philetaerus. Antiochus was killed in battle at Sardis (262 BC). Eumenes I expanded his fortifications after this war and reinforced the wall on the acropolis. He governed with the *Stategoses,* a council of five attorneys elected annually by the *Bouleuterion,* the People's Council. His love of horse racing was noted for a famous win in the two-wheeled chariot. Raising racing horses became a passion. Apparently, he died from alcohol addiction.

241–197 – Attalos I fought and won battles against three Galatian tribes. The war equipment of his enemies was placed in the Temple of Athena. Following his death, these words were added to his name: "Soter – Our Savior" to commemorate his victories in war. Additional triumphs extended his reign into the Kaikos domain (219 BC), the southwestern portion of modern Turkey. Relations with Greece developed after 221 BC and with Rome after 203 BC. Important buildings were initiated under his rule, including the Altar of Zeus. The brothers Attalos I and Eumenes II loved each other and worked together so well a city was founded based on their relationship: Philadelphia, which means City of Brotherly Love.

197–159 – Eumenes II was the oldest son of Attalos. He fought with Rome against Philippos V in Macedonia and against Antiochus III of Syria with a great victory on the Manisa plain, near Thyatira. This victory enabled the Kingdom of

Pergamum to expand to include Bithynia and Cappadocia, or most of present-day Turkey. His long reign of thirty-eight years is known as the Golden Age of Pergamum and was marked by intelligent governance. Military success and state affairs initiated the development of the arts, sciences, philosophy, mathematics, literature, astronomy, mechanics, shipbuilding, architecture, and leather manufacturing. The library was enlarged and enriched and became a museum with artifacts from around the kingdom.

159–138 – Attalos II was twelve years old when Eumenes II died. Wars took place to the west in Macedonia (Greece) and to the north with King Prusias of the Kingdom of Bithynia. Prusias invaded Pergamum and burned the lower portion of the city, but with the help of Rome, Prusias was overcome. Prusias withdrew to Bithynia, and Rome began the conquest of Bithynia, today's region of Istanbul and also along the Black Sea. Prusa, the ancient capital of King Prusias, is today Bursa in Turkey. Attalos is known for developing diplomatic relations with Rome, public projects, and generosity in remitting taxes and sending skilled artisans. The most famous of these projects was the dredging of the harbor of Ephesus, permitting large ships to anchor close to the city. (Ephesus overtook Pergamum as a result and then became the capital city of the province of Asia.)

138–133 – Attalos III was more of a diplomat than a king and had become enamored with Rome due to his visits there. He experimented with poisonous roots and tried them on criminals and sick people. His wars included a further conquest of Bithynia. He became cruel toward his subjects following the death of his mother, Stratonike, and his wife, Berenike (both named for Nike, the goddess of victory), and in his will, he wrote, "Populus Romenus bonorum Meorum heres esto," with the result that the kingdom was willed to Rome. Apparently, he feared a civil war following his death. Importation of papyrus from Egypt was halted, and Pergamum invented a new writing material, parchment, made from calfskin.

133–129 – Many in the kingdom were extremely upset that Attalos III had bequeathed his kingdom, and riots developed. After four years, Rome took complete control and organized the Province of Asia. Many artists left Pergamum during the uprising and went to a small city, Aphrodisias, where they founded the School of Sculpture, which eventually made that city famous.

129–63 – Rome faced King Mithradates VI of Bithynia and Pontus, who soon became Rome's greatest foe. Mithradates claimed roots in both the Persian and Greek worlds, and he eventually captured almost all the regions now known as modern Turkey as well as large areas around the Black Sea. In 88 BC he led a slaughter of Romans in Asia, with about eighty thousand Romans, Italians, and other foreigners being killed. Three wars followed. After Mithradates was killed in 63 BC, Rome designated Ephesus the capital city.

63 BC–AD 114 – Pergamum developed under Roman rule, gradually losing its former glory to Ephesus and Smyrna. Under Caesar Augustus, a small Imperial Temple was built on the acropolis, and many important public buildings were erected. Pergamum was rebuffed in about AD 87 when Domitian decided to build a second Imperial Temple in Ephesus. Under Trajan, AD 98–117, and Hadrian, AD 117–138, an Imperial Temple was built on the acropolis on a much larger site than the one Caesar Augustus had commissioned. Ruins of this temple are part of the open-air museum.

AD 320–900 – Pergamum became the seat of ecclesiastical power, and the majority of the population was Christian, belonging to the Eastern Orthodox Church.

AD 1200–2000 – The arrival of Turkish tribes in Anatolia coincided with the general decline of Pergamum. Its name was changed to Bergama under Ottoman rule, and two large alabaster urns were taken to the Hagia Sophia (a church and then a mosque) in Istanbul. Today the population of Bergama is about fifty thousand. Annually, around four hundred thousand visitors take in the Pergamum ruins.

Made in United States
Orlando, FL
20 July 2023

35311424R00275